For My Brothers

MARK ABRAMSON

For My Brothers

MARK ABRAMSON

WILDE CITY PRESS

WILDE CITY PRESS

www.wildecity.com

For My Brothers © 2014 Mark Abramson
Published in the US and Australia by Wilde City Press 2014

Published by Wilde City Press

ISBN: 978-1-925031-85-0

Cover Art © 2014 Wilde City Press
Courtesy of the Gay, Lesbian, Bisexual, Transgender Historical Society.

ACKNOWLEDGEMENTS

This memoir got its start in the spring of 2012 when Kirk Read invited me to take part in a series of workshops called: "THE BIGGEST QUAKE - New thinking on the San Francisco AIDS epidemic," culminating in three amazing nights of free public readings at the Metropolitan Community Church in San Francisco's Castro district. In addition to Kirk, my fellow "Quakers" Brontez Purnell, Dr. Carol Queen, Ed Wolf, Julia Serrano, Justin Chin and K.M. Soehnlein inspired me to continue telling my part of the story. Everything I read at the church on those three nights is included in this book.

I owe a great debt of thanks to Owen Keehnen in Chicago. Although we have yet to meet in person, his encouragement, keen eye and love of history convinced me that these stories were worth telling and kept me on track while writing their first drafts. Others who lived through the AIDS years were helpful in jogging my memory, providing names and details, particularly performers Gail Wilson (who also remembered the lyrics to her "Fireman's Song"), Sharon McNight, Wayne Fleisher, Michael John Frangella, Bradley Connlain, and my dear friend and birthday-mate Rita Rockett. I also want to thank Roddy Williams at the AIDS quilt, former *Bay Area Reporter* columnist Wayne Friday, *San Francisco Chronicle* columnist Leah Garchik, and authors Armistead Maupin and Anne Rice for their memories of specifics. Thanks to the San Francisco LGBT Historical Society and especially their managing archivist, Marjorie Bryer, who arranged for us to use some of the wonderful photographs of the late Robert Pruzan. I am grateful to everyone who brought this book to fruition, especially Ethan Day and Geoff Knight at *Wilde City Press*, and my editor Jerry Wheeler. I am indebted most of all to those who are no longer here to tell their own stories, my gay brothers who nurtured me, inspired me, and taught me how to laugh death in the face.

FOREWORD

When Mark Abramson first contacted me, I had just published *Leatherman: The Legend of Chuck Renslow*. Mark emailed that he was working on a story about a trip to Chicago with John Preston and was looking for the address of Renslow's popular leather bar The Gold Coast in the early 1970s. I reread the email and shook my head at how small the world can be. Early in my writing career, John Preston had been kind enough to take me under his wing. He mentored me with advice and introductions, but he was even more helpful by just being there and giving me the confidence I needed at that point in my life.

I told Mark about my connection with Preston, and he wrote back saying that he and John had been roommates in Minneapolis and again in San Francisco while Preston was the editor of *The Advocate*. John eventually moved back to the East Coast, but Mark stayed in San Francisco. Mark asked if I'd be interested in reading the piece he was writing about my mentor. Of course I was. It seemed fated. After reading the story, I made some suggestions about rearranging and expanding it. He then sent me another section he had written about Preston. This tale was just as engrossing, and I knew Mark had the pacing and clarity of a great storyteller.

Although I was in the middle of finishing the biography of another gay Chicago legend, *Jim Flint: The Boy From Peoria*, I asked to see what else Mark was working on. Mostly these were assorted stories from his years as a bartender, events producer, and activist in San Francisco. He said he was thinking about writing a memoir about living through the epidemic. I told him I thought it was a terrific idea. As someone who had spent the previous year or so piecing together history from the AIDS era and before, I knew how crucial the preservation of first hand accounts from the period could be.

Before I knew it, I was involved and then engrossed—energized by the pieces I was reading. The sections came in two and three page installments at a pace of a couple a week. My primary function in the evolution of the memoir was that of informal editor, advisor, and mostly cheerleader. It was easy to encourage something so worthwhile and compelling. I was just thrilled to be a part of the process. Most stories needed a bit of work, some expansion or cutting or added explanation, but I never doubted their relevance and power. This was great stuff. Mark was at ground zero of the epidemic as a bartender in various San Francisco gay taverns since the late 1970s, through the darkest days of the epidemic, and into the new millennium. He had a lot of history to share.

Overwhelmed by the fear and devastation all around him, Mark responded by stepping out from behind the bar and doing more. The AIDS era required action. With his musical skills as well as his experience in staging and booking bar talent, Mark co-produced several early AIDS fundraisers including the *Men Behind Bars* shows, *Pier Pressure*, the Bare Chest Calendar contests, and many other creative ways to raise money. Oftentimes tinged with drugs and alcohol, the resulting tales are raunchy, hilarious, sweet, gritty, and poignant in a way that makes history pop from the page. Mark has created a brilliant snapshot of San Francisco during that turbulent time, and watching it come together was thrilling. By the time *For My Brothers* was completed, Mark's personal story had expanded to include the larger story of love and loss in that pivotal time in our community's history. The AIDS epidemic is the mere backdrop for the rendering of a larger picture and a bigger story as well.

The disease is a catalyst for capturing the heart and soul of a city, an era, and the resourcefulness of a community. But mostly, it is the story of people.

Mark has an amazing gift for bringing these mad and wonderful characters to life and infusing them with a vibrancy that never falters. He remembers the men and women he has known in his roles as a bartender, friend, activist, and lover. He captures so many colorful and dynamic people, gone before their time, leaving so many dreams and such potential unfulfilled, and he does it without being maudlin. *For My Brothers* even has celebrity tales with Sylvester, Edith Massey, Al Parker, Connie Francis, Randy Shilts, Eartha Kitt, Johnnie Ray, and more.

Many of the people in these pages have been forgotten, but thanks to Mr. Abramson and his brave, funny, and sometimes audacious memoir, they have not been lost. They are ready to be discovered (or rediscovered) and enjoyed. *For My Brothers* is an account of personal loss and survival, the chronicle of a man reviewing his past and trying to make sense of that turbulent era. The people and lives contained in these pages deserve to be remembered and thanks to Mark's skilled storytelling they will be. Just pull up a barstool and get ready for a great story.

Owen Keehnen

For My Brothers

... A Memoir

MARK ABRAMSON

Chapter One

When a young man believes that he only has a short time left to live, his most logical response might be to spend his remaining days living as hard and as fast as he can. At least that was my gut reaction to the AIDS pandemic. It was also my excuse for every excess during those years. I had spent three seasons tending bar at The Woods, a big gay resort north of Guerneville, California, when the long, wet winters started taking their toll on my summertime enthusiasm for living in paradise. By the winter of 1983-84 when I started packing up my belongings and moving back to San Francisco, one rusty old pickup truckload at a time, we had heard about AIDS up north, but it hadn't taken over our lives. In my conversations with other bartenders at the Russian River, it had only affected friends of friends or maybe an ex-boyfriend's former roommate or...

"You remember that hot bodybuilder couple from Tiberon? They come up every year for a couple of weeks in July and drag guys out of the hot tub for three-ways in their cabin. The redhead's a flight attendant for Delta. They both drink Dewar's and soda...you know them."

"Yeah, what about 'em?"

"One of them died."

"The red-head?"

"No, the other one. He got some kind of pneumonia and went into the hospital and died the next day."

"How old was he, anyway?"

"Twenty-six."

My ex-boyfriend, Jonathan Berdell, was one of the first people I knew with AIDS. He had bought the house on Orchard Avenue that lured me up to Guerneville in the first place. We'd discovered back when we first met that we'd both moved to San Francisco the same month—July of 1975—with less than two hundred bucks in our pockets. We were about the same age too, although I don't remember his astrological sign, much less his birth date. Like a few other industrious gay men I knew, he created his own business. In Jon's case, he bought, restored, and resold cheap real estate in the Haight, the Castro, the run-down Western Addition, and now the Russian River, all the while holding down a high-paying job as a hospital administrator. Jon had his whole life planned out. He was going to retire young and travel and live comfortably off his investments. I heard him vow more than once, "I will never work a day after forty!"

I met Jon on the dance floor at the Music Hall, a disco on Larkin Street. I spotted him a few feet away, and I thought he was cute, the thick, dark hair on his bare chest glistening with sweat in the flickering lights of the mirror ball. Gay gyms were just starting to catch on in the late 70s and he obviously worked out. He invited me home that night to a Victorian house he owned on Fell Street. I could hardly wait to get him out of his blue jeans, and I was happy to discover that his legs, thighs, and ass were just as well-muscled as his chest and arms.

The next morning, I met his roommates Bob and Bobby over coffee. Bob was a few years older than us, with a gray beard and a deep voice to match his butch demeanor. Bobby might have still been in his twenties, as Jon and I were, and he reminded me of myself—friendly, funny and horny all the time. All four of us soon became good friends. We danced a lot in those days, rarely missing a Sunday T-Dance at the I Beam on Haight Street. We divided our nights between the Music Hall, Trocadero Transfer, and Dreamland, the latter two located south of Market.

When Jonathan bought the house on the Russian River, we all became like family. Jonathan and I had long ago stopped having sex with each other, but as is so often the case with gay men after the fireworks cool down, we developed a comfortable and caring friendship. I rented the main part of the river house, which was on two levels and led directly out to the pool. Bobby rented the second floor apartment above the driveway for the first year. All of us worked to convert the garage into a fancy little studio apartment with a big deck facing south toward the flower and vegetable garden. It was very high-tech with track lighting everywhere, and we painted the walls gray with white woodwork. Gray was the "in" color that year. That apartment was supposed to be Jon's, but sometimes Bob stayed there or else Bob pitched a tent on the lawn if all of us had guests.

When Jon was diagnosed with AIDS, he traveled to the same clinic in Mexico where the actor Steve McQueen had gone to cure his cancer, and we all know how that turned out. When Jon returned from Juarez to his gingerbread Victorian on Fell Street, he hired a live-in nurse whose duties included operating a new stainless steel gadget that squeezed the juice from the calves' livers that he had delivered fresh every morning. He drank it raw.

I was drinking upstairs at Chaps bar on 11th and Harrison on a Sunday afternoon, standing at the railing checking out the guys at the main bar below me when I heard of his death. My Australian buddy, Kym Whittington, was tending the balcony bar off to my left with the sun shining through the windows, silhouetting him. I was probably still stoned from the night before. Bob and Bobby came up the stairs, walked over to me and said, "Jonathan died this morning."

He was one of the first people I knew who got AIDS, but not the first person I knew who died from the disease. Maybe the raw liver had bought him some time. Who knows? I just remember standing there with a drink in one hand, holding onto the rail with the other, while the music pumped and the laughter of strangers echoed through the cavernous room. I was already numbed to the news of death by that time. I remembered what Jonathan had always said about never working a day over forty. He was right. When he died that morning, he was still in his early thirties.

Jonathan's roommate Bobby had his own business laying linoleum floors. He drove a white van, the back of it filled with so many rolls of new linoleum he didn't have much room for anyone or anything else. One rainy winter night when Bobby and I both lived at the Russian River, we each went home with someone we met at one of the bars in Guerneville. My trick lived high above the flood plain off Old Cazadero Road. In the morning the rain had stopped and the sun, so rare that time of year, shone through the gaps in the giant redwood trees.

I drove down through the winding canyon toward River Road until I came around a corner and saw that the road ahead was underwater. I couldn't tell how deep it was through the murk, so I stopped and debated whether I should try to drive through it. I didn't like to drive that beat up truck through water unless it was pretty shallow because I could see the ground through a hole in the floor. I noticed something white in the giant puddle up ahead. It was flat, like a huge, white tabletop submerged under a couple of inches of water. Then I heard someone calling my name. It was Bobby, stepping out from behind a tree on the opposite side of the water and zipping up his pants. He was soaking wet. "Have you got a light?" he yelled at me. "At least I saved the joints that were on the dashboard!"

The white thing in the water was the roof of Bobby's van. That was how deep the puddle was. He told me he had climbed out the window as it started to sink, but he'd managed to grab two joints he'd rolled that morning and held them above his head as he swam to dry ground.

I yelled across, "Wait right there. I'll come and get you." I backed up my pickup, turned around and found another road a little higher that led me back to where Bobby was waiting on the other side of that flooded low spot. He jumped in and we smoked one of the joints on our way back to Orchard Avenue where Bobby called AAA and his insurance company.

We used to listen to the local radio station for weather forecasts, road closures, and predicted flood levels. I didn't mind being flooded in for a day or two if I had enough warning time to stock up on groceries, batteries and reading material. Sometimes I drove into town to the Rainbow Cattle Company, the gay bar on Guerneville's main street, to find someone who wanted to come back and share my food and have sex for a couple of days. When the power went out, I couldn't read once the sun went down, so sex was always a good way to pass the time. One day we heard on the radio that anyone who was flooded in and needed help should spread a white sheet on their roof or on their driveway or lawn so that it could be seen from a helicopter. Bobby said, "A lot of good that does us. Don't they realize this is a gay neighborhood? Nobody has white sheets!"

Bobby left us long before he died. He fell in love with a guy named Ray whom I never even met. He went from being a big party-boy to being the foreman of Ray's rose ranch outside of Petaluma. They got rich—or Ray already was—and famous for their flowers and beautiful pictorial coffee-table books about gardening. One of their books even had a foreword by Martha Stewart. I don't remember how I found out Bobby died a few years later. His name wasn't listed in the obituaries in the *Bay Area Reporter*. I bought one of their books on growing fragrant plants, mainly for the picture on the cover of Bobby dressed in bib overalls and holding a rake, surrounded by flowers and grinning from ear to ear. Most of the pictures I have of him, he's either dressed in Halloween drag or he looks very stoned. I prefer to remember him healthy and happy, smiling and in love.

I first got to know Roger as a weekend customer at the Woods. He never lived at the Russian River, but he was good friends with one of my bosses and we all partied together. When I came down to the city on my days off, I often stayed at Roger's apartment on Seward, a little two-block street that curves around the hill above the Castro. My old boss called me there one day from the Woods Resort, asking me to produce the Mr. Northern California Drummer contest again. I had started it and the Mr. Russian River Contest a year or two before. I had also started the yearly bartenders' bash and any other gimmick I could think of that would bring people and money up from San Francisco outside of the peak tourist months. Those of us who spent winters on the river were always broke and horny. Fresh meat is rare in the off-season, and resort towns become tragically inbred.

I agreed to produce the Mr. Drummer weekend for a thousand dollars plus expenses. This time was easier because I was already in the city. I could line up contestants and sponsors, judges and entertainers without having to drive back and forth all the time. I spent hours at Drummer Magazine's office south of Market planning events ranging from a Thursday night welcoming party through Sunday afternoon's T-Dance when the winner would be announced. I found vendors to set up booths to sell their wares all weekend—lubricants, poppers, leather goods, sex toys, and the like. On Friday and Saturday we held pre-judging rounds both inside the old Hexagon House and outdoors beside the "clothing optional" pool on the west side of the main building, which was away from the road that led to Armstrong Redwoods State Park.

For judges, I lined up Alan Selby, founder of Mr S Leather, photographer Robert Pruzan and Jim Cvitanich, who had been Mr. San Francisco Leather the previous year. I knew Jim as a bartender at the Pilsner Inn on Church Street. Jim followed me around that weekend of the contest like a lost puppy, watching everything I did and helping me out when he could have been socializing. Most of San Francisco's leather community was there.

Years later, when Jim and I had become friends and business partners, I realized that he really didn't like many people. That must have made it hard to be a bartender, but with his bouncy pecs and beautiful gym-toned body, he might have made even more tips being rude. Lots of people are into that sort of thing. The dance floor headliner Saturday night was Eartha Kitt, who had a disco hit at the time, "Where Is My Man?" That afternoon I rehearsed the eight contestants to carry Miss Kitt on a velvet-covered platform above the heads of the crowd across the middle of the dance floor at midnight and then carefully lower her to the stage.

I found out later that Eartha Kitt was also booked at an earlier gig that same night at Davies Symphony Hall in San Francisco. One of the major jewelers near Union Square had decked her out in a million dollars worth of diamonds for her number. When she finished singing, guards took the diamonds back to the store and someone led Miss Kitt to her limousine. They told her that now she was going to perform her disco hit for a much younger crowd at a gay club "across town."

I can only imagine the look on her face when they took the diamonds from around her neck and hustled her into the back of a limousine where she was trapped for an hour and a half after being told it was only a short ride. The limo pulled up to the side door of the Woods Resort at a few minutes past 11 p.m. I got word that she had arrived, so I ran outside to show her to her dressing room and tell her about the eight half-naked muscle boys who were getting ready to carry her to the stage at midnight. Right now they were busy pumping up, oiling their bodies and slipping into their matching black Speedos.

When I explained the situation, Eartha Kitt said, "I'm going on *now* or I'm not going on at all!"

I couldn't get those eight contestants ready in time. She gave me a couple of minutes to go in and alert the DJ, Paul Dougan, the lighting man, Steve Mart, and the sound engineer, Bruce Trondson. I also grabbed a few of the beefiest guys on that side of the dance floor to form a human wall to create a path from the edge of the stage to the eastern door of the building where she was waiting.

The next thing I knew, she was on stage doing her number and the crowd went wild. This was one of those songs that everyone was dancing to everywhere you went that season, and here she was—LIVE—in our presence. But before long, she was taking my hand to steady herself as she came back down the stairs from the stage. She hadn't even performed for five minutes. I couldn't believe it! The crowd was still cheering behind us, and she said to me, "You guys are too much!"

Five minutes and she was back in the limo on her way to catch a flight out of SFO. Most people we'd booked at the Woods stayed on stage for as long as the crowd kept cheering. I said, "Yeah, Miss Kitt, so are you. Way too much, that's for sure." She took my remark as a compliment, but I really meant that she cost way too much for such a short performance. I've always considered Eartha Kitt, with her trademark growl and sex-kitten attitude, as more of an icon than an artist, anyway.

Morgana King was the only other singer I could remember who'd left without doing an encore. When I told her in the dressing room that the audience was going nuts out there, she said, "Oh, they always do that." She didn't even sing "A Taste of Honey" or talk about what it was like being in *The Godfather* movies. Her car must have been halfway to Santa Rosa before the crowd stopped stomping and cheering. Etta James played there twice a year. Her shows never started on time, but she would sing all night. Most entertainers loved the sound of applause and would take all they could get, but not Eartha.

The next day beside the swimming pools at the Woods I heard everyone talking about what a great time they had the night before. They got to see Eartha Kitt live on stage in person. Maybe they were all too stoned to notice that her show only lasted a few minutes.

Chapter Two

There was a lot going on in San Francisco in the 1980s besides AIDS. The Castro had changed in subtle ways since I'd lived there in my twenties. I had come back from the Russian River dozens of times to visit the old neighborhood, as well as South of Market, but when I moved back, the changes became more apparent. Hardly any of the guys wore long hair past their shoulders anymore. Butchness had always been "in" among the South of Market crowd, and now it was spreading to gay men elsewhere, even those who weren't into leather. The Castro Clone look was starting to catch on – boots and Levis, plaid Pendletons, tight t-shirts and tank tops – as more and more of my friends joined the gym. Hooded sweatshirts could be zipped up when the fog rolled in and fleece-lined denim jackets were perfect for San Francisco's chilly summer nights. The clone look of gay San Francisco would never become anything like the Calvin Klein 'heroin chic' look that came along in the early 1990s. If you were gay in SF in the mid-1980s, being overly thin didn't mean chic. It meant you were sick.

When our friends began to die, we tried hard to hold on to our shared sense of humor. As the plague wore on, it became vital. Drag queens played a big part in keeping us laughing. The Sisters of Perpetual Indulgence had just been established in 1979 before I moved up north. They were even more visible by the time I moved back in 1984, taking on the role of both educators and fund-raisers to combat this mysterious new health threat. Sister Boom-Boom had even run for the San Francisco Board of Supervisors in 1982. Her campaign poster depicted her on a broomstick flying over City Hall. It trailed purple smoke that spelled out Surrender Diane, an intentional misspelling of Mayor Feinstein's first name. Boom-Boom didn't win a seat on the board, but she got 23,124 votes. The next year, she set her sights even higher and ran for Mayor against Dianne Feinstein. If nothing else, she would go down in history for forcing the city to pass the

"Boom-Boom Law" which required candidates for public office to register under their legal names.

The Sisters seemed to me to have captured the energy that began with previous drag troupes, the Angels of Light and the Cockettes. The Sisters' type of drag blended in-your-face street theatre with "gender-fuck" political activism. They were not to be confused with the drag queens who ran for titles like Miss Gay and Empress and Grand Duchess. The titled queens raised money for charity too, but most of them tried to look as pretty as possible doing it. And some of the same men who donned dresses and high heels to compete for drag titles and crowns might also have closets full of leather which they wore to vie for the sashes of Mr. SF Leather, Mr. CMC Carnival, Mr. Drummer, or Emperor or Grand Duke, although maybe not in the same season.

One fun event each year was called "The Closet Ball." Gay bars sponsored contestants who spent weeks gearing up for the big night. They had gowns created for them, learned to walk in high heels and, most importantly, made sure their friends bought tickets to cheer them on. One of the rules for this contest was that these guys could never have "officially" been in drag before, although my understanding was that "officially" came with a good deal of leeway. At the start of the Closet Ball, each contestant came out in male attire, looking as butch as possible. Then they had one hour to go back stage, shave, get fully made-up and dressed and come back out to be judged in elegant gowns and ladies' wear.

Although these events provided a way for gay men to express themselves as well as to entertain and have fun, in those days they were also crucial in raising money to combat this rapidly spreading disease. The Federal government under the Reagan administration was far too slow to react, so new service organizations sprang up to fulfill a variety of needs. Older ones like the Shanti Project, which began in the Bay Area in 1974 to provide support to people with life-threatening illnesses, shifted its emphasis to people with HIV/AIDS. In the early years of the epidemic, at least, this was primarily gay men.

In the winter of 1983-84, Jim Cvitanich had an idea to put on an AIDS benefit variety show featuring area bartenders, since so many of them were frustrated performers. Divine had been in town with a play called "Wo*men Behind Bars*" at the Alcazar Theatre, so Jim decided we should call our show "*Men Behind Bars.*" He told me that ever since we had worked together on the Mr. Drummer contests at the Russian River, he thought I'd be the perfect person to help him put together this one-night show, and we decided to make it a benefit for Shanti. Somehow that one night turned into ten years of my life.

Jim first wanted to do the show at Chaps, since the landing at one end of the room was visible to everyone in the bar and would make a good stage. They already had a sound system, and we could bring in a piano. I convinced Jim that we should go bigger by holding the event in a real theatre and assembling a live band in the pit. I had played the saxophone and clarinet for musicals in high school, college, and at the Minneapolis Children's Theatre. I missed doing that.

Jim told me he'd always dreamed of doing something at the old Victoria Theatre on 16th Street in the Mission, so we talked to the owners, Bob and Anita Correa. They were wonderfully supportive of the idea. We scheduled our first "*Men Behind Bars*" show on a Monday night in January. All seats were ten dollars, and we were allowed to set up our own bars in the lobby and on the balcony and keep all the profits. Bartenders who claimed that they had no talent besides tending bar eagerly volunteered to do just that.

With Jim Cvitanich outside the Victoria Theatre
Photo courtesy of Michael John Frangella.

"But to have no talent is not enough!" is a line from *Gypsy*, Jim's favorite musical. He decided to use that as part of the show, so we rewrote the lyrics to "You Gotta Get a Gimmick" and put together a take-off on the song with himself and two other sexy bartenders demonstrating what made their bartending skills special. Our original plan was to use only bartenders in the show, but we soon added others—friends of bartenders, bar owners, cocktail waiters, bar backs, bouncers, and basically anyone who had ever set foot inside a bar. Then we invited the San Francisco Tap Troupe to give the show some class.

The B.A.R. leather columnist, Mister Marcus, agreed to emcee the production , a virtual guarantee that he would promote the hell out of it in his column, and I suggested getting a guest star for the finale. Val Diamond was one of my favorite cabaret acts when I worked at the Woods Resort. I got to know her when she sang at the Russian River several times with her back-up trio, Crosswinds. They'd all been performing together since their high school days in Hayward, California. By 1984, Val was the star of the world's longest running musical revue, Steve Silver's *Beach Blanket Babylon* at Fugazi Hall in North Beach, but they were dark on Mondays. When I called her, she told me that she'd thought about doing an AIDS benefit ever since her friend, the original Mr. Peanut, the tap dancing Planter's Peanut Man in *Beach Blanket Babylon*, died of AIDS. We got Scumbly Koldewyn of Cockettes fame to play the piano. I played tenor sax. Though I don't recall all the other musicians, I do remember that we sounded pretty good.

A group of bartenders from the Ambush did a hilarious belly dancing act years before big hairy men were called "bears." These guys showed off their bellies dressed in beads and lace with lots of jewelry and finger cymbals. At least one of the bartenders at the Pilsner—Ron Brewer—was a member of the Barbary Coast Cloggers, so he got them to perform in our show. The touring company of Dreamgirls was in town and someone called to offer us its star, Linda Leilani Brown, as long as she didn't perform anything from the Broadway show.

Ed Stark put together a Swan Lake number he dubbed "Le Grande Ballet de Nothing Special" with some of his bartenders from his bar on Castro Street. Edwin Stark, aka Edwina Ballerina, was one of the cleverest people I ever met and eventually became one of my best friends. The story goes that he and his lover Jack South rode their motorcycles from Kansas to San Francisco in the late 1960s and discovered a hippie/biker bar on Castro Street called the Club Unique. It had beaded curtains, fake Tiffany lamps above the bar with mismatched mirrors framed and scattered across the walls and the ubiquitous smells of stale beer and cigarette smoke. The Castro was just over the hill from the Haight, and the old-timers said that Janis Joplin used to hang out there drinking Southern Comfort. They even pointed out which stool she liked best. When Ed saw the bar for the first time, he took one look around and said, "Club Unique? There's nothing special about this place." He and Jack bought the bar and renamed it The Nothing Special.

Ed had taken ballet classes since childhood. He told me he'd auditioned for and been accepted by the drag troupe called Les Ballets Trockadero de Monte Carlo when they were formed in 1974, but decided that he couldn't be out on tour dancing while trying to run a busy gay bar in the heart of the booming Castro district.

In the first *Men Behind Bars* show, we set some precedents that we followed in the years to come. Although most of the show was live, we ended the first act with a medley of lip-sync hits of the 1960s. Three black drag queens did the Supremes. One of them was Empress Connie and maybe the other two were contestants for royal titles that year. So many title contests went on that I couldn't keep track of them. All the years we produced *Men Behind Bars* shows, we tried to include as much royalty as we could find. Drag queens, like bartenders, had friends who would buy tickets to come and see them. Some of the title holders were bartenders too.

Pat Montclaire wouldn't become Empress of San Francisco for a few more years, but she was a bartender, and we used her in the first *Men Behind Bars*. Her lip-sync to Lesley Gore in the first act finale was lousy, but she was well-loved, and her transformation was amazing. Pat had silicone breasts surgically implanted long ago, which made her change from a rather frumpy balding man into a ravishing female beauty even more astonishing. She was also one of the sweetest people in the world, at least to me.

Another part of that first act finale was a group of four bartenders from Castro Station and the Brig. They called themselves "The Foreskins" and did a medley of boy-group songs from the 1960s that included "Rama Lama Ding Dong" and "Blue Moon," at the end of which they mooned the audience to thunderous applause.

Each year's second act finale featured "The Follies Men." The major prerequisite for being a Follies Man was a gym membership, the ability to learn a few basic dance steps, and the willingness to appear on stage in little-to-no clothing. Val Diamond's big closing number in that finale was "Ain't There Anyone Here for Love?" from *Gentlemen Prefer Blondes* with the Follies Men supporting her. Our one rehearsal with Val was on the Saturday afternoon prior to the show in a warehouse space down an alley South of Market. I knew Val would never find the rehearsal space on her own, so I gave her directions to the Ramrod and told her to meet me there.

Since we only had that one rehearsal with Val, the band, and the dancers, we ran the number two or three times and decided we were good to go. That first year's show was only a one-night performance on a Monday in January. We had no idea it would be a sell-out, much less the beginning of a tradition. In the finale, Val flubbed a couple of the lyrics and some of the bare-chested back-up boys might have missed a few dance steps, but nobody cared. By that point, the audience was so wound up, not to mention drunk, they were willing to forgive anything. We were ecstatic!

Looking back at the videotape—we didn't have DVDs in those days—I remember the wild reaction from the audience. They were so excited to see their bartender friends on stage that it wouldn't have mattered if the acts were horrible. In truth, some weren't too good, but some were great. The sold-out crowd at the Victoria Theatre screamed and cheered and hooted and hollered and rose to their feet time and again, from the front row orchestra seats to the top of the balcony.

Val Diamond and the Follies Men finale of Men Behind Bars I
Photo by Robert Pruzan, courtesy of the Gay, Lesbian, Bisexual, Transgender Historical Society

I called Val a week or so after the show to thank her again and tell her how much money we raised with her help. We rehashed the evening over the phone, and she relayed to me a scene I had completely missed. There were rest rooms in the lobby, of course, but they were always crowded with audience members. Val told me that in their tiny dressing room, the only room on the basement level that had plumbing, she and Miss Brown had a steady stream of muscle boys and drag queens squeezing behind their make-up chairs to pull down their dance belts or lift up their skirts in order to pee in the sink in the corner. Val said she'd seen a lot worse conditions and chalked it up to show business, but Linda Leilani Brown appeared to be rather shocked. Val and I had a good laugh over that.

The Victoria Theatre only seated five hundred, but people talked about the show for weeks afterward. Word spread quickly, especially through the gay bar community. The people who missed it didn't dare admit they hadn't been there, and those who saw it insisted that you had to have seen it to believe it. That was true enough. There had been gay shows before in San Francisco, of course. The Cockettes had caused a sensation in the late 60s with their midnight shows at the Palace Theatre on Broadway, but they were a troupe.

Our show was a collective of people coming together to raise money for a good cause. It was unique at the time. There was nothing but love in that theatre that night, and that warmth was a welcome feeling in a time when more and more of our friends were getting sick.

When all was said and done, our one-night stand at the Victoria Theatre, *Men Behind Bars* was able to donate a little more than ten thousand dollars to the Shanti Project. The local gay papers wrote glowingly about the event, and Jim and I were full of ideas for another show next year—bigger, better, brasher and with even more performance dates. It was just as easy to rehearse for two or three nights of shows as for one, and the possibilities for even greater fundraising and exposure were obvious. There was no stopping us.

M&M Technical Productions ran our sound and lights and videotaped the first show, which eventually found its way into video stores. When we got the very first copy, we guarded it carefully. Every couple of weeks we showed the *Men Behind Bars* tape in a different bar, usually one in which several of the employees had performed in the show. We asked for a two dollar donation. People who had missed the show but heard about it and those eager to see it a second time were happy to spend a couple of bucks to see the tape. Cast members dragged their friends to the showings, especially since the people in the cast had never had the chance to see themselves, much less the rest of the show in sequence.

As I remember, we had the first showing at Chaps bar and made a couple of hundred bucks for Project Open Hand. I remember another showing at Deluxe on Haight Street when it was one of several gay bars in the Haight/Ashbury neighborhood. We did one in the gay bar in the Casa Loma Hotel off Alamo Square, near where the landmark row of Victorian houses, the

Painted Ladies, stand. Rita Rockett was bringing Sunday brunch to the AIDS ward at San Francisco General Hospital, and we donated one night of the VCR showing proceeds to her brunch fund. Each showing had a different beneficiary.

When Shanti learned that the funds we'd made from the bar showings of the MBB video were going to other worthy causes, someone at their organization notified us by mail that all donations from the MBB production, as well as its reproduction on video, should go to them. We thought otherwise. It was a difference of opinion, but because of their insistence on receiving all the money raised from the show, Jim and I decided that Shanti would not be our beneficiary the following year. We were just happy that our little show was still spreading the money around for weeks afterward.

Chapter Three

Patrick Toner was one of the Follies Men in *Men Behind Bars* for the first few years of the show, but I already knew him from my time at the Russian River. Everyone adored Patrick. Lots of people also lusted after him. He was classically handsome and sexy enough to have his face and body plastered across the covers of glossy gay magazines. He was muscular, but in a natural way, as if he'd been born with a sculpted body. He didn't have any attitude about it. Or about anything else for that matter. Patrick was just plain nice, the kind of guy who would help an old lady across the street, carry her groceries up the stairs and put them away for her too.

The first time I met Patrick Toner was on a Saturday night when I was tending bar at the Woods Resort. John Embry, the owner of *Drummer Magazine*, brought him up from the city and introduced us. I was producing the annual Mr. Northern California Drummer contest in those days, and Embry wanted Patrick to be the next Mr. Drummer, but first he had to win the regional contest. I told him that before he could win he had to have sex with me. I was only teasing, but he waited for me to get off work at two a.m. and spent the night at my place on Orchard Avenue.

Patrick came from Alabama, and he oozed Southern charm. He could have been a very popular gigolo if he was straight or could have made one hell of a gay hustler. He could also have been a highly successful con man, but he was too honest, too good. However, Patrick was just kinky enough to avoid being overly wholesome. He came back up to the river by himself a few more times that year, and he was always welcome in my bed as summer drew to a close and the nights grew colder. We got to talking one time after sex, and he told me that his birthday was coming up on September 20 and he was going to be twenty-one years old! The legal drinking age in California was twenty-one. I wasn't concerned about the fact that I'd been having sex with someone so young—although my preference was usually for guys that were older than me—but I could be in big trouble for serving drinks to him at work. I told him we had to stop this! At least we had to stop having him drink at the bar for a few weeks.

September came soon enough and with it Patrick's birthday. Labor Day weekend is the official end of the resort season, even though some of Northern California's best weather is yet to come. We tried to prolong business as long as we could with holiday parties and events, but by January we were only open on weekends and then only to sparse crowds.

I remember one stormy night with Patrick that winter. The Woods was closed, and the owners were away in Hawaii or Florida or someplace warm. One of them had asked me to stay in his cabin and Patrick stayed there with me. The bedroom was up a short flight of stairs, so it was high and dry, but the first floor carpets were still damp from the most recent floodwaters. It rained again all day, but we ran to the hot tub and back a few times to soak. We cooked a nice dinner and started to watch some porn that night until the lights flickered off and on…and off again.

Patrick and I were stoned on something. It could have been pot or hash or acid. We figured we would be fine in the upstairs bedroom, no matter how much it rained outside, but we didn't have any heat when the power went out. We needed to build a fire in the Franklin stove in the bedroom, and we couldn't find a stick of dry wood.

It was pouring by now, and we didn't want to get our clothes wet, so we pulled on our socks and boots and ran outside naked. The redwood trees broke some of the rain from above, but they also made the night so dark we could hardly see each other. I went first, since I knew my way around, and Patrick took my hand. We checked some of the other cabins, but the only logs we found were soaking wet. Then I remembered the dry firewood was under an awning behind the old kitchen. We were stoned enough that our search for firewood became an obsession, almost a religious pilgrimage, but with laughter.

The main structure of the resort had been built as an art school in the 1940s by the heir of the Toni Home Permanent fortune. In the 1960s and 1970s, it housed an elegant restaurant called the Hexagon House. Each year the Bohemian Grove encampment was held some distance down the river, so many of the wealthiest and most powerful men in the world spent their evenings dining there. They chose the Hexagon House not just for the food, but because some of the most beautiful and expensive hookers in the world rented all the rooms and cabins during the same week. Now that it was gay-owned, the central hexagonal dining room had been turned into a big disco, complete with state of the art sound and a laser light show—when there was electricity.

Off one side of the dance floor, sliding glass doors led to a patio with a beautiful wooden footbridge over Fife's Creek. Patrick and I stood on the bridge for a while and held each other, naked and laughing, listening to the water roar beneath our feet and overflow the banks on its way to the Russian River and out to sea. Then we came around the building from the back and found the stash of dry firewood. We used newspapers to shield our bare skin from the rough logs and carried all we could manage back to the cabin. Once we got a good fire going, we found a bottle of champagne in the fridge and celebrated with a toast and another joint. Then it was time to get back to sex.

When spring came, Patrick was one of the men who was supposed to carry Eartha Kitt across the dance floor to the stage, but that plan didn't work out. Neither did John Embry's plan for Patrick to win the title. Sonny Cline won the Mr. Northern California Drummer contest that year and went on to win the National title too. I think Patrick came in third, but he would go on to win an even bigger contest a year later in 1985.

During that spring of 1984, Chicago played host to the International Mr. Leather contest, as it does every Memorial Day weekend, and I decided to go. I had no job and no steady income besides my meager unemployment checks which barely covered the cost of my cocktails. I had no home but on my friend Roger's couch on Seward Street. My belongings were all in boxes in his garage. I did have a new credit card, however, so when I discovered that a lot of my friends were going to Chicago, I decided to go too. Jim Cvitanich had been a contestant the year before when he was Mr. SF Leather, but he didn't win, so he wasn't going back.

A couple of bartenders I knew were going. Mister Marcus always went because he was one of the judges. Some of the Follies Men, the half-naked dancers from the finale of *Men Behind Bars*, were going. Some of them were even contestants. Even my favorite cocaine dealer was going. I'll call him Jim Bayer. Some of my friends hardly went anywhere without knowing that Jim would be there too.

I reserved a plane ticket and a single hotel room. I didn't want to deal with any roommates barging in on me in the midst of my sex-capades, and I was sure I'd have many. I wasn't particularly interested in the "contest" element of the weekend, to be honest. I just wanted to have fun.

Most of my San Francisco friends and I were on the same red-eye flight from SFO to O'Hare. You could still smoke in the last three rows of domestic flights in those days, so I'm sure we took up all of the seats in the back of the plane. That was also conveniently close to the liquor cart and the toilets, should anyone need to powder his nose with cocaine.

I'd been to Chicago lots of times during my college days in Minneapolis. John Preston and I used to take the Amtrak "Empire Builder" down for weekends, especially in the wintertime. I loved the snowy scenery from the frosty train windows all along the St. Croix River, and I loved Chicago—the architecture, the food, the men. John had also, of course, introduced me to the leather scene, back when the Gold Coast was still on the 500 block of North Clark, and I still needed a fake ID to get into the bars.

My friends and I wanted to arrive a day or two early to get our bearings and a head start on having fun. We landed in Chicago on Thursday morning, found the Allerton Hotel, and dropped off our bags. I dragged my friend Butch Freeman along to see the view from the top of the Sears Tower. I do remember that much.

Butch and I bought our tickets in the lobby for the elevator rides to the top, and we were suddenly met with long lines of school children on a field trip. I had been up all night on the plane, totally fucked up on cocaine and vodka and pot and now, in my stoned state, I was surrounded by all these miniature people. They were identical in size, and their lines snaked around and around that huge lobby full of big shiny doors that slid open and closed with tall rows of round numbered buttons that lit up when you touched them. I don't even remember the view from up there. The sky might have been just as dull as my brain. Years later, I am impressed with what a good sport Butch was, going along with me to the top and back in my twisted condition.

Then we must have gone back to our hotel and slept for a while because the next thing I remember was a cocktail party where Marcus introduced me to a lot of people, including Chuck Renslow, owner of the Gold Coast Bar and founder of the IML Contest. I had probably already met Chuck through John Preston when I was a mere twinkie, but he wouldn't have remembered me. The contest judges were at the party, too. I don't remember all of them, but I know they included Mister Marcus, the artist Etienne/Dom Orejudos, Colt Thomas from Texas, who was the previous year's winner and currently a medical student and now, somehow… Mark Abramson!

I don't know how it happened. One of the celebrity judges had to cancel at the last minute, and Marcus suggested that they ask me, since I had been the producer of so many contests and parties at the Russian River. I could hardly say no. "When your country needs you…" and all that. But this was the International Mr. Leather Contest, so maybe I should have said, "When your planet needs you."

Now I had a schedule. I had to be certain places at certain times, something I'd never considered when I agreed to be a judge. I was busy with rounds of pre-judging events leading up to the big show on Sunday afternoon, plus various meetings and contestant interviews, appearances at bars, restaurants and house parties all weekend. Having fun and getting laid took a back seat to this judging business, and I soon realized that my time was no longer my own.

On the other hand, I got to wear a badge that said JUDGE, which meant that my drinks were free in all the leather bars all weekend. I probably tipped more than the drinks would have cost me, not wanting to jeopardize my bartender's karma. My JUDGE button also meant that all those hot, sexy contestants were my new best friends. I did manage to get laid a few times, but not with any of the contestants—at least not before the contest. The one real new friend I made that weekend was Kenny Sacha.

Kenny was the emcee at IML that year. He was a female impersonator best known for doing Barbra Streisand. I had first seen him in the movie *The Rose* in the scene where Bette Midler's character and her chauffeur go into a gay bar and happen upon a drag show starring Michael Greer and Sylvester, already friends of mine from their performances at the Russian River, along with Kenny and a couple of other drag performers I never met.

I'm not sure how I first met Kenny in Chicago. We were probably on the same floor in the hotel. The day of the contest, the judges and performers all shared a dressing "area," but Kenny and I spent a lot of time together before Sunday. The other performers, aside from the contestants, included Judy Tenuta. She was fun backstage and everyone seemed to love her accordion and tattered prom dress and snarky humor. Also performing was a guy who juggled running chain saws. I couldn't look. I'm not squeamish about watching almost anything if it's sexy, but I went out for a couple of lines of coke during his act. I only have one word to say about juggling chainsaws: Why?

If I had been attracted to a type at the time, Kenny Sacha wasn't it. But he was sort of adorable, like a lost child who needed protection. He'd spent months in drag as part of Cher's "Take Me Home" tour in Vegas, Australia, and Europe and now here he was in Chicago, surrounded by all these big leather men from all over the world. He and I often walked down to the coffee shop on the corner near our hotel to eat and talk. On Saturday night, I was supposed to go to a couple of big parties where all the leather "royalty" would be and then out to the bars, so I invited Kenny to come along with me.

I was getting into my leather chaps, boots, vest, and jacket when Kenny showed up at my room early. Here we were all set to go out into the most dazzlingly decadent night of Chicago's biggest leather weekend of the year, and he was dressed in tan slacks and sneakers, an ecru polo shirt and a baby blue sweater draped around his shoulders. It was like a scene out of *Preppy Goes to the Folsom Fair,* but I didn't say anything. I just thought I'd better keep an eye on him. Regardless of how inappropriately he was dressed, Kenny was always fun to hang out with.

I remember one house party where at least thirty guys were lined up on a stairway to get into the second floor bathroom, and the line wasn't moving. I had to piss and Kenny was about to wet his pants, and I noticed a pair of sinks right outside the locked toilet door. I said, "This is ridiculous! These sinks drain into the same sewer as the toilet. I'm not shy! Let's just piss in the sinks." Kenny was mortified at first, but he stood on his tiptoes in his little sneakers and pissed in the sink beside me. And all the guys in that line who really had to go, rather than just needing a private place to do their drugs, were grateful that we'd started something so sensible. Their long wait was suddenly cut in half.

Sunday afternoon at the Park West Hotel, Kenny Sacha emceed the first half of the contest as his little vanilla West Hollywood/Vegas drag-queen-out-of-drag self. It had nothing whatsoever to do with leather, but I suppose anyone could read a list of names as the contestants walked onto the stage. For the second act, he came out as Bette Midler and no doubt behaved as he imagined Bette would in that situation. Kenny was famous for his visual impersonations, his lip-sync, and maybe his dancing—not his ad-lib stand-up comedy. He seemed so out of place there. I just hope he got paid well.

My original intention for going to Chicago that weekend was to meet a lot of hot guys and have as much sex as possible. Several of the contestants would have traded their bodies for my vote, but I didn't want to be accused of that. I suspected that once the contest was over, very few of the also-rans would still be coming onto me.

I supposed I wanted Michael Marriot, one of the contestants from San Francisco, to win. He was definitely a beautiful man, but I didn't think I was in his league at all, and he ended up coming in second. Marcus was pulling for a different contestant from San Francisco, but I thought that kid was an obnoxious punk, so I gave him my worst scores without letting on to Marcus. The winner, Ron Moore from Denver, was my second choice. I was happy enough to see him win, mostly because he was the first black International Mr. Leather.

The only time I remember getting laid in Chicago was with the first hot guy I saw when we registered for the weekend's events. We'd checked each other out while standing in line that first day, but we didn't speak and we never saw each other again until the night the contest was over. He must have seen me on stage when the judges were introduced, but that was the last thing on our minds when we finally got around to having sex.

He told me he was the conductor of a major symphony orchestra in Boston or Baltimore. Or was it Pittsburgh or Philadelphia or some other big city back East? I didn't care. He was hot! If he was famous, I'd never heard of him before and haven't since. Maybe he was the assistant conductor. Maybe it was a high school orchestra. Maybe he lied. Who cares?

Later that afternoon, Kenny and I shared a cab to the airport. He flew back to L.A., and I went on to Minneapolis to visit family and friends back home. I'm sure that Kenny was glad to get back to Hollywood, and I realized that I wasn't really a hard-core leather man, although I wasn't nearly as out of place in Chicago that weekend as Kenny Sacha was.

Chapter Four

When I returned to San Francisco, I realized that my friend Roger's apartment on Seward Street was too small for me to stay there for long. It wasn't as if I was there every night. I could spend a few bucks for a locker at one of the half-dozen or so gay bathhouses or a few more to rent a room with a bed, if any were available. Or I could put my name on the waiting list and at some point, if I was listening, I might hear an announcement over the intercom: "Locker numbers 86 and 37, your rooms are ready now. Please bring your keys and clothes to the front desk."

There were plenty of after-hours sex clubs, too. They didn't have private rooms, but who could sleep on the drugs we took in those days? Or with that music blasting? Even though we heard more and more about AIDS or GRID or "the gay cancer" in the newspapers and on the television news, I wasn't yet convinced that sexual transmission was the sole cause of the disease

Roger was nice enough to let me store my scant furniture and a few boxes of clothes, books, and dishes in his garage. When I stayed overnight, I slept on the fold-out couch in the living room and woke on weekday mornings to the drone of the alarm clock in his bedroom. I was never sure exactly what Roger did for a living. I think he said he was in accounting, but he put on a suit and tie each morning and drove his late-model sports car down to the financial district. While he got ready to leave for work, he downed two or three stiff drinks of gin with orange or grapefruit juice, usually—sometimes cranberry, but always Bombay gin.

Roger complained constantly about every aspect of his life in such a way that it made me laugh out loud. Compared to me, he had it made. He had a great car, a nice apartment, a high-paying job, and plenty of money for clothes and travel and drugs and booze. He was known to have an enormous dick too. I would point these things out to him, then he would laugh at himself and pop a couple of valiums on his way downstairs to his car, still muttering about how difficult his life was. In those days of three-martini lunches, I'm sure Roger had four. After work he would stop at Sutter's Mill, a downtown gay bar, in order to take the edge off before his drive home to the Castro. Then he'd change out of his work clothes, snort a couple of lines of coke and head out to the local neighborhood bars for Happy Hour.

I came home one morning after a night at the 21st Street Baths to find Roger's mattress on the sidewalk. He confessed to me later that he'd fallen asleep with a burning cigarette in his hand, but he managed to wake up in time to wrestle the mattress out through the sliding glass doors and toss it over the balcony before it burned through the box spring and set the whole apartment on fire. When I arrived that morning, the place stank of smoke and he was passed out on the couch, so I gathered a few of my things and went to stay with another friend for a couple of nights.

Then Laura moved in. Laura had once been a guy named Larry and had gone to Denmark for "the snip," as Roger called it. Laura had had the procedure done years before by the same doctors who had operated on Christine Jorgensen.

I'd gotten to know Christine Jorgensen at the Russian River, where she did her cabaret act at the Woods the previous summer. She called me at Roger's one day to invite me to lunch at the Cliff House restaurant while she was in town, but I had a doctor's appointment. I really liked Christine. I found her history fascinating and enjoyed her company, so I was interested in knowing more about Laura, but Laura had apparently drawn a veil over her past and refused to discuss it.

Roger told me that Laura wasn't really moving in. She just needed a place to stay now and then when she didn't feel like going all the way home. The two of them proved it to me by taking me to Laura's house once. I couldn't find that house again if my life depended on it, but I remember that it was on a corner lot in Bernal Heights. She rented out the upper floors and was having tenant problems, so she wanted two men to act as bodyguards. Her tenants weren't around that day, so Roger and I weren't required to butch it up. We entered the bottom flat because one of us needed to use the toilet, probably me, or maybe I was just curious and wanted to see the place.

Laura turned out to be a collector of priceless antiques. Her hobby bordered on hoarding, but this place looked as if an expensive antique store had gone out of business and moved all its merchandise here for temporary storage. The main room had high ceilings, and in order to get to the bathroom, I had to follow a narrow pathway between dusty statuary, huge gold-gilded picture frames, ornate tables, marble lamps and heavy tapestries.

Laura and her business partner, George, had just bought The Eureka Valley Club, the last straight bar in the Castro, and were turning it gay. Seward Street was much closer to the bar than Bernal Heights, so she needed to crash with Roger in his bed some nights. George seemed kind of scary to me. Roger told me that George was in the Mafia and a while later, when we read in the *Chronicle* about human bodies found sealed in oil drums in Golden Gate Park, Roger told me that was some of George's handiwork. Roger also insisted that their bar on the corner of 18th and Collingwood was merely a front to launder money from their much more lucrative drug business.

Roger told me about Laura driving a truck across the Golden Gate Bridge to meet the delivery from Colombia. He said they would strip a small plane of everything but the engine, the gas tanks and pilot's seat to make room for all the cocaine it could carry. The pilot would fly up the coast below the range of radar and land in a desolate field somewhere in Marin County. The pilot and Laura would load up the truck and abandon the airplane, since its worth was minimal compared to its cargo. I saw enough with my own eyes to think the stories I heard from Roger weren't far from the truth.

Before George and Laura bought the place, my friend Gretchen used to fill in behind the bar when it served the old Irishmen who had lived in this neighborhood for generations. Gretchen was born in the old St. Joseph's Hospital across the street from Buena Vista Park where condominiums now stand. Gretchen told me that in the early 70s, when the neighborhood started changing, "The gay guys would come in the bar too. Everyone knew who they were and what was what and it was no problem. They were nice guys. They had money. Everybody got along."

When George and Laura bought the bar, they changed the name to the Pipeline, an appropriate name since it was, according to Roger, a pipeline for delivering drugs into the Castro. It has officially remained a gay bar ever since, changing names with successive owners. After the Pipeline it was called Festus, then Francine's and now, for many years, the Edge.

I don't remember who owned Festus, only that it had a country/western theme. The building's next incarnation was as Francine's, a lesbian bar. Men were not welcome. I only went inside once, in the company of two women, a couple who were friends of mine. We sat down at the bar with me in the middle and ordered drinks. The woman bartender brought the drinks for my companions, and they asked her where my drink was. She looked straight at me and said, "I don't see anyone else here." So we all got up and left the two drinks on the bar, unpaid for and untouched.

Francine was a transsexual who never had "the snip," and rumor has it that it would have been major surgery. As a man, Francine had been an army officer and fathered a few now-grown sons. She had breasts and wore make-up, but not wigs. She pulled her thinning strands of hair back into a tight ponytail that only emphasized her beak-like nose. She wore very short skirts and hobbled around on bowlegs in high heels, but the most striking thing about Francine was her voice. To call it gravelly would be an insult to gravel. She made Jimmy Durante sound like Julie Andrews. And she never left a tip in her life.

Francine owned other bars in the Tenderloin and tried to open one at the Russian River, but was denied a liquor license in Sonoma County due to an arrest record for indecent exposure when she lifted her skirt to take a leak in the alley behind the Rainbow Cattle Company. I heard that Francine went to Detroit every year to buy a brand new Corvette from the factory because driving it back to San Francisco herself was cheaper than going through a dealer.

Speaking of dealers, Laura and George's bar business at the Pipeline was nothing compared to their drug business. The bar was so poorly run that whenever the bartender on duty ran out of something, he would pull a ten or twenty out of the till and ask one of the regulars to go buy a bottle across the street. Dino's Liquors was located where Magnet, the Gay Men's Health Center, is now.

At the Pipeline, two pool tables were crowded into the back end of the room and beyond them were the toilets and a door leading to the office upstairs. Laura invited Roger and me up there often. We brought our drinks with us and sat on an old ratty sofa beside a glass-topped coffee table. A crystal chandelier hung down from the low ceiling, almost touching the table where huge piles of white powder glistened like snow. Laura would chop a few fat lines with a single-edged razor and roll up a hundred dollar bill to use as a straw.

We could look down at the bar from a couple of carefully placed peepholes. Laura kept an eye on what was going on and when it wasn't busy, which was most of the time, we took turns running downstairs for another round of drinks.

Chapter Five

I first met Jack McCarty in the late 1970s over morning coffee in the kitchen of a guy named Ron Thill, who'd picked me up the night before under a full moon at the top of Buena Vista Park. Jack had spent the night with Ron's roommate, whom I'll call Darin. Ron and Darin lived in a nice two bedroom apartment at 4636 18th Street, about five blocks west of Castro. I lived around the corner on Douglass and 19th, just a short walk uphill past the Caselli Mansion. This was a year or two before my time at the Russian River.

I got to know Jack over the course of the next few weeks because we both spent many nights in that apartment and drank lots of coffee while our bed partners, Ron and Darin, were getting ready for work. Jack and I were bar and restaurant people, so we never had to be up that early in the morning.

Ron worked at the clothing store All American Boy on Castro Street. He only had one testicle, but everything else about him more than made up for that missing ball. After he told me what happened, we never mentioned it again. It was too frightening to contemplate testicular cancer at such a young age—we were only in our twenties—in a time long before AIDS forced us all to consider our mortality.

Darin was a dark, stocky little guy, bulging with muscles. I don't know what he did for a living. I didn't like him much because he complained about everything. He resented getting up in the morning, hated his job and was annoyed by any expectations anyone made of him. He lived for his hours at the gym, but often complained about those too. The temperature was either too hot or too cold. It was too crowded. His favorite piece of equipment was broken. I don't know what Jack saw in him, except that he had a great body.

Jack McCarty reminded me of my older "brother" John Preston, who had moved from San Francisco by that time. Both of them were tall and lean with long straight spines and an erect posture that suggested to me their very proper New England breeding. That was definitely the case with John. I found out later that Jack was born and raised in Boston.

Ron was from Detroit, blond and boyish, cute and friendly, warm and very sexy. We were buddies from the beginning and remained friends until he died. Our friendship was a natural progression from sex partners to running-mates. I could call him when I felt like a day trip to the nude beach near Wohler Bridge at the Russian River. He could call me when he felt like going to the Sunday T-Dance at the I Beam. We often grabbed a bite to eat at the Norse Cove or Castro Café on his lunch break and spent many nights tripping on acid under the mirror balls at the Trocadero or the Music Hall on Larkin or at Dreamland, bare-chested, dripping with sweat, passing the poppers back and forth.

Jack and I remained friends too, long after Darin became a part of his past. Our friendship never had a sexual aspect to build upon, but it was familial. I looked up to him, I suppose, in much the same way as I did to John Preston. I saw him as a wise older brother who might be able to teach me a few things. Jack and I also worked together in a gay restaurant in the Castro. The job was fun, with fast, easy money from tips but, as was all too common in those days, the owners liked cocaine more than they liked the restaurant business. The profits went up their noses, paychecks stopped coming or bounced, and the vendors who supplied everything from meat to wine to napkins and tablecloths simply stopped delivering. The last few weeks we worked for tips only.

When I moved up to the Russian River in 1981, Jack came up on weekends with another boyfriend I'll call Dan, a big bearish redhead. They slept on a foldout bed in my living room on Orchard Avenue. It was on the lower level of a split-level house where they could open the sliding glass doors in the morning, roll out of bed and take about five steps to dive into the pool. Jack offered me rent for their weekend visits to Guerneville, but I refused. I was at work most of the time they were there, tending bar at the old Woods Resort at the north end of Armstrong Woods Road. I made plenty of money during the summer season and Jack and Dan were always welcome. Besides, they never came empty-handed. Jack never failed to bring up gifts from the city: frozen bottles of Absolut or Stoli and a cooler full of chilled wine and at least a couple of grams of coke. House guests like those were never in the way.

During my first year back in the city, I did whatever jobs came my way in order to make some money. Jack had become the chef/manager of the Elephant Walk by then. He called me up one day with an offer. The Elephant Walk, on the corner of 18th and Castro, was famous for having been the site of the climax of the White Night Riots. On May 21, 1979, Dan White, who had assassinated gay rights leader Harvey Milk, was given a verdict of manslaughter. The people who knew Harvey and worked hard for him to be elected to the board of supervisors were so enraged by this slap on the wrist that they descended on City Hall, smashing windows and upending and torching several police cars. Later that night, the police got even by storming the Castro in riot gear, smashing the windows of the Elephant Walk, bashing heads and sending several people to the hospital. In later years, the place was sold and renamed Harvey's, after Harvey Milk.

When Jack called me in 1984, I was hoping for a bartending job, but all their bartenders had been there for years and no one was leaving. Jack's idea was to introduce a new menu of evening "suppers" and bring in live entertainment, which he wanted me to book. I'd had lots of experience with entertainers when I worked at the Woods, but I didn't think the Elephant Walk was a place for one-hit disco wonders on weekday evenings. I remember being there on acid to hear Sylvester sing with his back-up singers, Two Tons of Fun: Martha Wash and Izora Rhodes-Armstead, before Wash and Rhodes recorded "It's Raining Men" and renamed themselves The Weather Girls. I'd gotten to know all three of them and had fond memories of passing a joint with Martha and Izora while we waited backstage at the Woods for Sylvester to bring them out.

Sometimes Sylvester added Jeanie Tracy to make it Two and a Half Tons of Fun, but those concerts at the Elephant Walk were on Sunday afternoons with all the windows wide open and the crowds spilling out into the intersection and blocking traffic on 18th Street and Castro. I told Jack I thought a piano would be better; someone tickling the ivories with light jazz, semi-classical or even show tunes, but not disco. Jack agreed that what he had in mind was cocktail lounge music, an alternative to what people could already hear in all the dance clubs.

I didn't know a lot of piano players other than the ones who played for the cabaret singers performing in the many gay clubs in San Francisco in those years. I must have put an ad in one of the gay papers advertising for pianists because I got dozens of calls, and I kept careful track of all the applicants. Night after night I sat in that bar with Jack and listened to them, a different one each night, while I drank and made a few notes and tried out all the dishes on Jack's new supper menu. I don't remember if I got paid or how much. Maybe I got my food and drinks covered. I do know that we ended up with a handful of piano players on a rotating schedule. They were happy, Jack was satisfied, and I was no longer needed.

I didn't see Jack nearly as often after that. Frankly, I was burned out on the Elephant Walk. It was the sort of place I would take a visitor from out of town to have a weak drink and sit in the window to watch the ever-changing view of the intersection at 18th and Castro Street, catch up on each other's lives in relatively quiet surroundings, and eat unsensational gay overpriced food. I remember a Sunday brunch when my date and I both ordered Eggs Benedict, and the English muffins were still frozen. Even so, Jack's creations were certainly an improvement over some of the meals I'd had there before.

Still, the Castro is like any small town, so Jack and I ran into each other in the bars, on the streets, and at memorial services for mutual friends. At one of them, Jack told me that he'd been training to become a Shanti volunteer in order to counsel people with AIDS during their dying days. He felt that was his way of giving back, and we agreed that each of us had to do what he could.

Jack seemed to fall in love harder than most of the guys I knew, and he finally found his soul mate in a guy named Victor Amburgy. He was a postman, ten years younger than Jack, even a little younger than me. I liked Vic. He was unassuming and sophisticated, smart and sexy, but in a quiet way. Vic and Jack stayed together until the end, which almost came sooner than either of their illnesses.

Jack invited me to a party that Christmas at his apartment on 17th and Ord. When I found out that my old boyfriend Ron was going too, we decided to go together. Both Darin and Dan were ancient history by then, but Jack's new lover Vic was central to his life. Jack and Vic seemed very happy together and announced that they were planning a major trip for the following summer. It was to be the European tour of a lifetime, to include all the famous sights and cities and end with a long cross-country drive back from the East Coast to California. Whenever I heard people talk about making plans like these, I assumed that they planned to die soon. I fantasized about a fabulous trip, but I never had the nerve. I knew several guys who spent their life savings or ran up their credit cards to take a trip around the world and then came back to San Francisco broke under a mountain of debt and lived on for much longer than they expected, having to suffer the indignity of aggressive bill collectors hounding them during their final days.

Jack and Vic's grand adventure the next summer was tragically memorable for a different reason. One hundred and four Americans were among the one hundred and fifty-three passengers on TWA flight 847 from Athens to Rome on June 14, 1985 when it was hijacked to the Beirut airport by Shiite Muslim militiamen. One of the passengers, a U.S. Navy diver in uniform, was tortured and murdered on the plane and his body dumped onto the tarmac. For two days, the plane flew back and forth between Algeria and Lebanon. According to Randy Shilts book *And the Band Played On*, passengers with Jewish sounding names were taken off the airplane, but the forty remaining Americans, including Jack and Vic, were held hostage for seventeen days.

Amazingly, the world press never mentioned the fact that Jack and Vic were lovers. Their homosexuality would have been a sure death sentence in that part of the world. When they were finally released and returned to the United States, they held each other and walked arm in arm as they left the airplane in front of all the network news cameras and President and Mrs. Reagan, although neither of them had come out to their parents. That Sunday also happened to be Gay Freedom Day in San Francisco. They dropped their plans for the long drive back across the country and flew home instead.

After Jack and Vic returned, Armistead Maupin emceed a big hometown reception for them at the corner of 18th and Castro Streets with the Gay Marching Band and the Gay Men's Chorus. Armistead included it in *Significant Others*, the fifth book in his *Tales of the City* series. Michael Tolliver witnesses the event, complete with the gay marching band and a chorus, on his way to a JO party at 21st and Noe Streets, four blocks away.

Jack later wrote an article in the Shanti newsletter about how his training with the organization had helped him stay calm while he became an unofficial counselor for the other passengers. During the next few years, I saw less and less of Jack and Vic. When I did run into them, they never talked about the hijacking. I would never press them to remember something that I'm sure they wanted to forget. Jack died of AIDS on May 18th, 1989. My old boyfriend Ron died eighteen months later on November 3rd, 1990.

I finally got a bartending job in the city. It was only one shift a week, Sunday mornings from six a.m. to one p.m., but I could always clear about three hundred dollars in tips. The End Up is on 6th and Harrison, which is south of Market, but it was by no means a hard-core leather bar. The very young twinkie crowd it usually drew made it an unlikely place for me, but the money was good. I used to go there in the 1970s for the Jockey Shorts dance contest, made famous in Armistead Maupin's *Tales of the City*. The contests were still going on, but they were at night and I rarely went to the End Up to dance anymore. There were too many much nicer places.

I usually just stayed up all night on Saturday, rather than worry about oversleeping for work. Who needed sleep when we had cocaine? On Sunday mornings I would usually shower at the baths or at Roger's apartment on Seward and be on my way by five a.m.. By the time I found parking, people were lined up down the block, waiting for The End Up to open at six a.m. Most of them had been up all night too, out dancing at the bigger clubs like the I Beam, Dreamland, the Music Hall, or Trocadero Transfer or they'd been at the baths since two a.m. when the bars closed.

Now they were tweaked up and sexed out and needed to dance it off with a stiff drink in them and maybe meet someone in a similar condition. Every Sunday morning when I walked up to the front door of the End Up, someone would yell, "Hey, buddy! The line starts back there!" I would show them my key, open the door with it and politely ask them to step out of my way if they wanted a drink when they got inside.

I was thirty-two years old, the old man among the staff. Most of the bartenders were boys and girls in their early twenties or younger, with fake IDs. Al, the owner, seemed to hire a new "manager" every week and most of them weren't old enough to legally set foot inside the bar. People warned me that Al was a little crazy, and he was rumored to have a severe drug problem. One day he told me I should be the manager. He said it only made sense because I had the most bar experience, I was always on time, was dependable, and my cash drawers balanced. Al said, "Come and see me in the office when you pick up your paycheck on Thursday."

I had my doubts by Thursday. Did I want more responsibility in this crazy place? Did I want to spend more than my seven hours a week here for three hundred bucks in tips plus minimum wage? Did I want to work for Crazy Al? I needn't have worried. On Thursday after I picked up my check out in front, I screwed up my courage to go back to the office and stick my head around the corner. Al looked up from his desk and asked, "What's going on?"

"You wanted to see me?"

"I did?"

"You said to stop by the office today."

"Oh yeah? What about?"

"I don't know...sorry...see ya." I left that day with my paycheck and a sigh of relief.

I was just getting used to this schedule of wasted weekends— or being wasted on weekends, when they switched me from Sunday mornings to Saturday nights. I could relate much better to the Sunday morning crowds of leather men and druggies than I could to the "bridge and tunnel" patrons on Saturday nights. They were lousy tippers and most of them didn't look old enough to be there. The doorman was responsible for checking their Ids, so I didn't have to worry about that, but I missed the money I was making on my old schedule.

One Saturday night I was working the station nearest the entrance on 6th and Harrison. The crowds were three deep all around, mostly ordering soft drinks or asking for hot tea, which we didn't carry. Al pushed his way to the bar and yelled, "Mark, call the police! We have aliens in the bar! Call 9-1-1 right away!"

I said to him, "Al, we have customers from all over the place, but whether they're illegal aliens or not isn't really our concern, is it? As long as they have money and an ID, we can't throw them out."

"No, I mean we have aliens! The spaceship landed on the

freeway out back. They put ladders over the side and climbed down onto the patio. They didn't pay the cover! Call the cops right now!"

So I called the cops. When they arrived, I pointed to Al and said, "Talk to that man. He's the one causing the disturbance. He's kinda crazy...must be on something. He'll probably tell you he owns the place. Can you just get him out of here?"

They did. And Al never mentioned that night to me again, but I didn't work there very much longer, so I didn't give him much of a chance.

Chapter Six

When I was growing up, we didn't have any openly gay or lesbian newscasters or talk show hosts or financial gurus. Television only used gay characters as comic stereotypes and even then, they were never called homosexual. They were just the spinster secretary or the goofy uncle or maybe the nellie neighbor. When I first heard about people who were actually "queer," they were either flower arrangers or interior decorators or hairdressers. Male ballet dancers were always heterosexual, weren't they? Not Nureyev. I used to see him at the Ritch Street Baths, but most of them—no matter how stunningly they danced, no matter how beautiful they appeared in black and white photographs in magazines, no matter how much we may have wanted them to be gay—were straight. All these years later, I am not out to disparage florists or designers or hair stylists, but when I got to San Francisco all of my preconceptions changed.

We were rebelling against the stereotypes by being masculine. We were also proving to ourselves that we could do anything straight men could do and accomplish anything we put our minds to. I grew up on a farm, after all. I was no stranger to physical labor. In San Francisco, I discovered gay men who were plumbers and carpenters, house painters and construction workers...as well as drag queens and hair-benders and everything else. Lots of guys started their own small businesses, but other than writing and selling a magazine article now and then, which certainly didn't pay the rent, I always worked for someone else. Waiter jobs, catering and bartending gigs meant quick cash tips and a lot more chances to meet sexy guys than sitting behind a desk all day.

My old boyfriend Jonathan's roommates each had his own floor business. Bobby laid linoleum, and Bob did hardwood. Bob was one of the butchest gay guys I had ever known, so masculine I never would have believed he was gay if he didn't live with Jonathan and Bobby. Well, there was also his collection of Yma

Sumac records. When I only had one bartending shift a week at the End-Up, Bob asked me if I wanted to make some extra money working with him.

It was hard work hauling heavy sanders and buckets of stains and finishes up the hills and flights of stairs, but I got to see some amazing San Francisco residences—palatial homes in Sea Cliff, Victorians in the Western Addition, luxurious condos in Pacific Heights. We did a flat at the end of Alta Street on the very edge of Telegraph Hill. Bob said it belonged to one of the columnists for the *San Francisco Chronicle*, but I don't remember which one. It took us weeks, during which time all the furniture had been moved out. I remember stripping and sanding and staining and finishing an enormous expanse of old oak laths in a huge room surrounded by windows with such breathtaking views that I could hardly concentrate on the work. After days of heavy rain that winter, I watched the local news capture that entire building as it slid down from the eroded cliff and broke into pieces.

I was one of Bob's steady workers, but he also hired lots of other guys for short terms when he had large jobs. I don't remember where he found them and didn't usually see them again after the jobs were done. One house we did on Potrero Hill was two stories, four bedrooms, three baths, and a grand open staircase—all of it hardwood that had been neglected for decades until we brought it back to life. In spite of the hard work, it was satisfying to unearth such beauty and to witness the careful craftsmanship of other men who had been here in San Francisco and installed those floors long before I was born.

One morning Bob dropped me off there, and I spent the next few hours with a hammer and the nail set, which looks like an awl with a flat dull point. Once the old finish is removed, all the old nails show, so you have to tap each one to sink it below what will be the finished surface of the floor. Setting nails wasn't a bad job. It was time-consuming and mindless, so I could let my thoughts go anywhere. I turned thirty-two that year, and my mind was usually on my crotch.

Later that day, Bob dropped off another guy to help me set nails. What a beautiful young man! The work should have gone twice as fast, except that now I had another distraction besides the view. My new co-worker was distracted by me too. It was a warm day, not really hot, but warm. We didn't talk much, but we did agree that it was hot enough that we needed to take our shirts off. Wow!

We took a smoke break shortly after that—everyone smoked cigarettes in those days—and we finally touched, accidentally at first. I was probably offering him a light when my hand somehow brushed his hard, bare chest. We had each other's belts and pants undone in seconds. Conveniently, we both had knee pads on already.

We wiped up the floor with paper towels afterward. It would get another sanding after the nail holes were filled anyway. We went back to work and still didn't talk much, but we smiled a lot more. I asked Bob the next day where the guy was. I don't even think I knew his name. Bob told me the two of them had finished a big job on Potrero Hill that morning and that Bob had dropped him off at the Greyhound station. He didn't really have any more work for him, but the guy needed a few more hours of pay to earn enough money for a bus ticket back to wherever he came from.

I remember another time in the fall we were doing a spectacular pre-1906 earthquake (these were still pre-1989 earthquake days) house overlooking Alcatraz and Fisherman's Wharf. It must have been on Russian Hill. Bob left me alone one afternoon to set nails in the dining room. An hour or so later, I heard someone else arrive. It was the plumber, coming to work on the kitchen, right next to the dining room. He had red hair—everywhere— and he was as cute as a Boy Scout merit badge. He must have worked for a good hour before anything happened between us. By that point, I was on the verge of going crazy wanting him. I kept staring at his ass while he was bent over or crouched in the corner, hooking up two sinks, a disposal, a dishwasher, and a line to the ice maker in the refrigerator door. This was one case where I didn't mind seeing the plumber's ass crack at all. I finally went into the kitchen and said something innocuous like, "Excuse me. I don't mean to bother you, but I wanted to get a drink of water. Is this sink hooked up yet?" That sounds about like something I would have said.

Then he looked up to notice how hard my dick was in my dusty Ben Davis work pants. Damn, he was sexy! And self-employed. Why didn't I ever hook up with one of those kind of guys for the long haul at that age, before I got HIV? I always went for waiters and bartenders and nurses and barbers and other people with odd hours.

I never saw the redheaded plumber again either, but what I remember best about that afternoon, beside the sex, was that it was a Thursday in October. It was Fleet Week, and the Blue Angels were practicing for their weekend show over the bay. The jets were so loud over that old house that all the windows shook and so close that we could almost see the color of the pilots' eyes through their windshields. The plumber and I made a lot of noise too before we cleaned up the kitchen floor. It was easier this time. It was tile.

Bob often had more than one job going on at the same time somewhere in the city. He and I spent many hours working together that summer and fall, and some days he would drop me off to get started on one project while he went to finish up on another one. Sometimes I didn't see him again for hours. He was the boss, and I didn't question his methods, but I discovered that I wasn't the only one getting in some recreational sex during working hours.

One day Bob pulled up to the house where I was working, a two-story faux-Victorian on Roosevelt Way with spectacular views of the city. He usually drove because he kept so many tools we needed in a lockbox in the back of his Jeep. It was quitting time and on his way to take me home, he told me he'd stopped off at the Badlands for a beer that afternoon. He said he met someone there who invited Bob home for sex.

Before AIDS decimated the gay population, all the Castro

bars opened at six a.m. and stayed relatively steady all day, so it wasn't unusual to stop at a busy bar to look for sex on a weekday afternoon. Even the sidewalks in the Castro were crowded twenty-four hours a day, something we only see now on Pride weekend or at the height of the tourist season. These days the crowds are also much more mixed. In the 70s and 80s, the people walking those blocks of the neighborhood were mostly horny, sexy, gay men cruising one another. I asked Bob how his trick was, and he started to laugh. "It was great!" he said.

"Then what's so funny?"

"When I was getting dressed to leave, I noticed a table in the corner of his bedroom. It was covered with little jars and tubes of make-up. He saw me looking at it so he told me who he was."

"Who?" I was getting impatient now.

"I just fucked Sister Boom-Boom!" Bob began laughing so hard that I joined him, even though I wasn't sure why it was so funny. Maybe he felt embarrassed, as butch as he was, to have picked up someone for sex who also did nun drag. Or maybe he was simply proud of having had sex with such a well-known celebrity.

Chapter Seven

One morning I was coming out of Cliff's Variety, the hardware store on Castro Street, when I saw a silver Toyota pull into the parking lot behind the Castro Theatre. There were lots of silver Toyotas around town, but I had a funny feeling that this one belonged to my old boyfriend Kap, so I waited on the sidewalk. I hadn't seen him in a long time, and I'd heard he was sick.

As he locked his car door and walked the few yards to where I was standing, I replayed our time together, starting from the first moment I saw him and fell crazy in love. It was about five years earlier at the old Midnight Sun. Seeing him again that day, I still loved him as skinny as he was and knowing he had AIDS. There was nothing I could do about it. Nothing I could do for him and nothing I could do for me.

When I met Kap, the Midnight Sun was smaller than it is now. Its original location was on Castro Street a few doors south of the Elephant Walk. I remember it was always crowded. It was the first video bar in the Castro and one of my favorite hangouts for a time in the late 70s. I always ran into people I knew there, guys I liked to laugh with and catch up on the latest news. That was where I got to know Randy Shilts. We always had great long talks about being writers, though I didn't know his last name until I saw his picture on the jacket of his first book, *The Mayor of Castro Street: The Life and Times of Harvey Milk* a couple of years later. John Preston and I sometimes had drinks there after dinner in one of the nearby restaurants. I often ran into artist friends at the Midnight Sun, people like Wayne Quinn or James Moore, who was one of the very first of the Sisters of Perpetual Indulgence.

When I met Kap, I was standing against the wall watching the videos on the big screen. He was sitting on a barstool and he turned around, leaning back against the bar facing me. We smiled at each other and kept smiling until I could take the couple of steps through the constantly moving crowd and get up close enough to ask, "Who are you?"

"Kap, with a 'K.' What's your name?"

"Mark, with a 'K'," I said. "Let's go someplace and I'll buy you a drink. How about the Badlands around the corner?"

"But we're already in a bar and I still have a drink. Look, so do you."

"Then let's chug 'em and go someplace else. I know too many people here. C'mon, it'll be fun!"

And it was fun. It was always fun with Kap, for the next few weeks or months or however long it lasted. He was so beautiful, so dark and lean and muscular and handsome. His smooth olive skin was always a deep tan in contrast to the marble flesh on his perfect melon ass-cheeks, so white that tiny blue veins showed through. I've always thought of myself as versatile, but when I think of Kap, I picture that ass as much as I remember his face.

We didn't even stop at the Badlands. We went directly to my place at 19th and Douglass, a few doors south of the old Caselli Mansion. Once inside my bedroom door, we leapt out of our clothes and tore at each other. Sex with Kap was always wild and wonderful. I was twenty-seven and by no means naïve. I'd probably done everything sexual that I'd ever heard of aside from scat, but when Kap and I were together, it all felt new, like we were inventing it on the spot, and Kap was just about the kinkiest guy I've ever fallen in love with. He was a little older than me, too, maybe thirty, so he knew some things he liked that I hadn't even tried before, but I was definitely willing.

Kap lived in the upper Haight on Ashbury and Frederick, in a studio apartment across the hall from his best friend Fred. They talked every day. Kap was often on the phone with Fred first thing in the morning when I woke up there. When he saw that my eyes were open, he'd say, "Hey, Mark, how long did we have sex last night?"

And I would answer, "I don't know… an hour and a half, maybe two. We both came twice."

"Did you hear that, Fred? We both came twice. Mark said it was close to two hours!" Then Kap would put his hand over the mouthpiece and whisper to me, "Fred's never lasted more than five minutes in his life, I'll bet."

Kap's other best friend was Divine, the drag star of all of John Waters' early films. Kap called him "Divvy," and they talked on the phone a lot too. Kap had a framed photograph on his desk of Divvy, not in drag, but wearing sort of a muumuu, on water skis with forests in the background. Kap told me he took the picture while steering the boat. His family had a cabin on Fallen Leaf Lake, a branch of Lake Tahoe. That was where he'd spent most of his summers growing up.

Kap's brother Peter was gay, too. I never thought he was as handsome as Kap, but he was incredibly sexy. Peter was an electrician, and they were that rarest of breeds here called "native San Franciscans." The family home was on Lake Street out in the Richmond District. I never met their parents, but from the way Kap talked about his mother, Ava Jean, she seemed to be very much a "high society" lady. I saw her on a local TV commercial that ran for a while to encourage support for the arts. Kap told me she was on the board of practically everything.

After a few weeks of "dating," we decided that we needed a "honeymoon" out of town, so we drove up to the Russian River for a couple of days that turned into nearly a week. I was working as a waiter in the Transamerica Pyramid building, and I called my boss to tell him I was having the time of my life with the man of my dreams. I must have sounded deliriously happy, and he was a very cool straight guy. He said, "Have fun. I got you covered. Come back smiling!"

Kap and I stayed at Fife's Resort, which had just been remodeled and was in the process of becoming a gay getaway. He told me that he'd helped his brother Peter rewire all the cabins, so he'd spent a lot of time there already. All the staff seemed to know him, and they treated us like royalty. We spent hours beside the pool or floating on thick air mattresses, maneuvering them side-by-side for a kiss and then getting so turned on we were popping out of our Speedos, so we would roll off and meet underwater in a tangle of arms and legs until we had to breathe. Then we grabbed our belongings and raced back to our cabin dripping wet, holding our towels over our crotches.

Once inside, we tore our swimsuits off as we kissed, tongues reaching for tonsils, licking each other's teeth, hands on flesh everywhere, teeth on nipples while I fingered his sweet hole until I could get him down on the bed, knees up with his legs over his head, and my tongue buried deep inside his ass until he begged for my cock and more. It was always fun with Kap.

Every night we went out to a different restaurant for dinner. The Russian River area has dozens of wonderful places all the way from Highway 101 out to Jenner-by-the-Sea and on back roads branching out in every direction from there. It was asparagus season, so everywhere we ate that week, they served asparagus with dinner. Having grown up in Minnesota, I knew it was one of those things like spinach that tasted terrible out of a can. I'd recently discovered that I loved fresh asparagus, but Kap didn't want me to eat it because it makes urine and cum taste bitter, and he knew we would want to play after dinner.

One night I snuck a spear of asparagus into my mouth when I thought he wasn't looking, and it was delicious. Kap didn't say anything, but he took the rest of it off my plate and put it onto his, even though he wasn't going to eat it all. He was a California boy, so fresh asparagus was nothing special to him. When the waiter came to ask if we wanted dessert, Kap ordered for both of us. It was also raspberry season, so he asked for two bowls of fresh raspberries in a little cream. When the waiter brought them, Kap put his bowl next to mine. "Don't you want any?" I asked. "Then why did you order them?"

"They're for you," he said. "Eat them all. They'll counteract that asparagus I saw you eat earlier."

We spent several nights a week together in the city, alternating between his place and mine. When I had days off from work, we often made love in the afternoon at his place. Those long, lazy hours of naked foreplay were easy-going, comfortable, and romantic. Eventually we would get around to having orgasms, even though it didn't really matter. At night we fucked!

Kap was sort of a health nut. He hated my cigarettes. I can still hear him saying, "You would be absolutely perfect if you didn't smoke." He was one of the only people I knew who didn't smoke in those days. After sex in the afternoon, Kap would slip into a pair of shorts and his running shoes and jog up to the top of Twin Peaks and back like it was nothing while I would kick back in his bed and smoke cigarettes. Days when I was at work at my lunchtime waiter job, he would go windsurfing on the bay or take long bike rides far north into Marin County and back across the Golden Gate Bridge.

One day he took me to the top of Mt. Tamalpais. I'd seen it in the distance ever since I arrived in San Francisco but never considered actually going there. I didn't know it was possible or that there was a road. I also had no idea how long that road was or how winding or how many hours driving up to the parking lot would take, plus the climb all the way to the top. It was a crystal clear day. The Farallon Islands looked to be just offshore, and the view of the entirety of San Francisco Bay was like nothing I had ever seen except from an airplane window. It felt surreal to be out in the open and up so high. Kap told me he wanted to see it again through my eyes, with my sense of wonder and awe, and I was glad he had dragged me all the way up there.

We looked down at eagles' wings spread wide in flight. We looked down at airplanes flying below us. We looked down at Angel Island and Alcatraz and the city of San Francisco in the sparkling sunlight, and it took my breath away and made me even happier to realize that our magical city was real and that it was home. The only trouble with Mt. Tamalpais was that it didn't provide us with a place to get naked. We tried to kiss a couple of times, but people were always around somewhere on the paths and trails above or below us. We were so out in the open.

We had to drive all the way back down the mountain, through the rainbow tunnel, over the Golden Gate Bridge and across the city to find a bed with a door to close behind us. That might have been the best day we ever spent together, not only for the beauty of it but for our eagerness to get back to the city and get naked again.

Seeing him again brought it all back. But all of that had been five years ago, and now I was standing on Castro Street next to All American Boy, the clothing store, waiting for Kap to come and give me a hug.

In the five years since Kap and I broke up, I had moved to the Russian River and back. I had gotten to know Divine pretty well myself because he performed at the resort where I worked. We even talked about Kap, and I suspected that Divine had a crush on him too. Now I was standing with my arms outstretched to greet him, but he said, "No, I'm diseased, you know. Don't touch me. I've got the gay plague."

I said, "Kap, I heard you were sick, but I can't catch anything from you just by giving you a hug."

"They don't know that…" he protested, eyeing me like a frightened stray dog looks at a stranger offering food.

"I don't care, Kap. I'm not afraid. Hear from Divvy lately?"

"Yeah, just last night we talked on the phone for an hour. We mostly talked about *it*, you know."

"Where you headed?"

"Cliff's. I need a light bulb."

"I was just in there myself. Now give me a hug."

"Okay." I suppose we held each other for a couple of minutes. Time meant nothing anymore. I felt bones through his clothes where there used to be muscle, and he slowly relaxed into my arms. I kissed his cheek and told him how good it was to see him again and then we parted for the last time.

Kap's brother Peter died of AIDS a while later. When I heard about Peter, my first thought was that I felt sorry for Ava Jean, whom I had never met. An amazingly beautiful ex-boyfriend was dead, but I'd already lost him years ago. She lost two beautiful sons.

Chapter Eight

Growing up on a farm in rural Southwest Minnesota with my mom and dad and three older sisters, I also had fifteen aunts and most of my cousins were girls. I sometimes longed for an older brother. Whenever I hear the absurd claim that all gay men are child molesters, I can honestly say that the only time I was ever interested in sixteen-year-olds was when I was twelve! I left the farm on my eighteenth birthday to tour Europe playing my saxophone with the Band of America. Then I moved to Minneapolis to go to college at the University of Minnesota. While living in Minneapolis, John Preston became my first adopted big brother.

Ours was never a sexual relationship, but we were roommates or neighbors during most of my years in Minneapolis and again when I moved to San Francisco after college. By the time the AIDS pandemic started, John Preston had become famous for writing *Mr. Benson*, among other scandalous books. He eventually left California and settled back in Portland, Maine, having returned to his New England roots at last. He always encouraged my writing, and we kept in touch with letters, phone calls, and his frequent visits to San Francisco.

Terry Thompson became my next adopted older brother. He and I had both grown up in Minnesota, but our backgrounds were very different. Estranged from most of his family, he'd left home in his teens to make his own way in the world. Terry and I met when I was still working at the Russian River. At the time, he was the manager of the Arena, a popular SOMA leather bar on the corner of 9th and Harrison. The Arena was always well represented at the Woods when I produced an event there. Terry would rent a large cabin, sponsor a contestant, host a cocktail party, and offer prizes of free drink tickets and Arena t-shirts and sweatshirts. These were standard goodwill gestures from one bar to another, good advertising and probably a tax write-off too.

The first time I remember meeting Terry was at the Woods. He and his lover Blair arrived on a Friday evening, and I went out to their cabin to welcome them. It was hot, the summertime air scented with the smell of the redwoods. Stars sparked overhead through the towering branches. It was still too early for the disc jockey to have cranked up the music for the dance floor crowds, so we probably heard the swimming pool motors running the filters and water pumps.

I was always tan at the river, usually dressed in nothing more than sandals or sneakers and my favorite red gym shorts with an elastic waist, easy to slip off and on again. Even at night it was usually hot, and I never knew when I might want to get undressed quickly, if for no other reason than to take a dip in the clothing optional pool. Blair was setting up a full bar on the dresser, complete with all the basic liquors and mixes, cocktail napkins in neatly twirled stacks, bar fruit already cut, a case of plastic glasses for guests, and a huge tub of ice. Blair made me a drink and we talked for a while. The next thing I knew, Terry's hand was on the back of my thigh. He slid it up higher, under my red shorts and then he pushed something deep inside my ass with his finger—MDA. It was already starting out to be one of those weekends.

I don't remember much about the rest of that leather event, but everyone seemed to have a good time. According to what people told me later and from what I read in Mister Marcus' column in the next week's *Bay Area Reporter*, I had a good time too. That was the weekend I first got to know Terry and we never even had sex, at least not with each other. He was already too much like a big brother to me, and I rarely give in to incest. Never say never.

Terry Thompson started the Bare Chest Calendar contests when he was the manager of the Arena. They still continue to this day, raising thousands of dollars annually for the AIDS Emergency Fund. I remember the first one because I was one of the judges.

When Terry left the Arena to manage The SF Eagle, three blocks down the street to the south, at 12th and Harrison, he took the Bare Chest Calendar contests with him and asked me to take charge of them. I still didn't have a real job, but running the contests was easy enough. I lined up some celebrity judges, signed in the contestants each night and oversaw the vote counting at the end. In general, I tried to make everyone happy. Nearly all of the Follies Men from our MBB shows, many of whom had become friends of mine by that time, were contestants. Some of them more than once. If the turnout looked like it was going to be small, I would make some calls and tell them to come down to the Eagle and try again. Everybody wanted to be in the calendar.

Mister Marcus was always the emcee in those days. He was funny but could be caustic and almost rude. He also had his weekly column in the *Bay Area Reporter*, the biggest gay newspaper, so some people were afraid of him. For the first contests at the Arena, Terry and Marcus had lined up judges from the gay/leather/bar community – people like me – but I thought we should use people who were more interesting than me. I knew a lot of performers from my years at the Russian River, so I got singers like Gail Wilson and Sylvester, "Daddy" Alan Selby, the founder of Mr. S Leather, photographer Robert Pruzan, and comic Danny Williams.

Terry also thought I might make a good assistant manager and decided to "groom" me for the job, so I finally got two bartending shifts – Monday and Tuesday nights from nine p.m. to two a.m. I followed the afternoon bartender who was also known as Empress Jane Doe. While at the Eagle, though, he was a man. He opened the place at four p.m. for Happy Hour.

One of my regular late-night customers at the Eagle was the well-known clothier Wilkes Bashford, who would come to the South of Market after a more genteel function in a much classier part of town and stop in with his driver for a nightcap. I always enjoyed visiting with him and asked him if he would consider being a judge. I was thrilled when he agreed, and I called on him to judge the contest more than once. Wilkes' upscale store off Union Square sells to the very rich and features some of the top men and women's clothing designers in the world. Ironically, he was just as happy to be one of the judges in a contest where more working-class men took their shirts *off*. He was always cheerful and fun, and I really liked having him there.

I thought my two weeknight bartending shifts would be terrible, but I never left the place with less than a hundred dollars in tips, and I always had a good time. I had a lot of regulars who liked to come in and keep me company on slow nights. One was John Gilkerson. John was involved with a Gilbert & Sullivan group called the Lamplighters. They rehearsed in a space south of Market, and he would stop by for a beer or two afterward. At one point they loaned us some props and set pieces for one of our Man Behind Bars shows. We didn't talk much about our early backgrounds, but we had a common interest in theatre. Years later, after he died, I was amazed to hear Tom Hanks thank my old friend John Gilkerson when he gave his acceptance speech for winning the Oscar for Philadelphia.

The other Eagle parties tend to get jumbled and run together in my memory. I know we had bar anniversaries that went on for two or three nights in a row. One night was "pin night," when patrons had to be present to get that year's Eagle pin to attach to their leather jacket or vest. Another night we'd have food and speeches. Local politicians are always happy to present certificates to honor gay bars, especially the ones that raise a lot of money for charity. The final night was the one I was most concerned about, the night of entertainment. Planning a party in a bar has some great advantages over some other venues I've done. The stage on the Eagle patio was already wired for sound. The liquor and ice and bartenders were already a given. My major concern was lining up the performers and coordinating the timing to keep everybody happy.

One of my favorite memories of my time at the Eagle was the night I hired Val Diamond, star of *Beach Blanket Babylon*, and her trio, Crosswinds. Other acts were on the bill, but hers was the main attraction, and they did two full one-hour sets. I'd heard that Sylvester was a big fan of Val's, so I told him she was going to perform that night and suggested that he come down. Booking him to sing would have cost us a fortune. When I worked mornings on Castro Street, Sylvester used to park his scooter in front of Cliff's Variety, when he was shopping on Castro Street. He would stick his head in to say hello and sometimes sit down for a cup of coffee, but I never saw him when I was bartending nights South of Market. Still, Terry Thompson assured me that Sylvester always bought his poppers at the little leather/gift shop inside the Eagle.

Sylvester arrived after Val's first set had started. We stood and listened together and at the break, I took him to the back-stage area, which was really just a little storage room beside the patio bar. It turned out that Val was a fan of Sylvester's too, but they'd never met. I introduced them and hinted that it would be fun to hear them sing together. Then I left them alone to attend to something else for a few minutes. When I came back to make sure that Val was ready for her second set, they told me that the two of them wanted to do "Steamroller Blues."

Terry and I had already made sure there was an extra live microphone ready for Sylvester in hopes that this would happen. We were thrilled that it did and so was the audience. It was a magical night all around. Hearing those two powerful voices together was something I will never forget. If only we had recorded it! They wailed, they crooned, and they passed the lyrics back and forth to each other and dared one another to press on, higher and higher with their amazing energy. People talked about it for weeks afterward. Val and her band got paid in cash that night and Sylvester got a couple of free bottles of poppers and whatever he was drinking on the house.

Chapter Nine

Even though I still didn't have a regular job or a real home, I wasn't worried about it. If I was, I've blocked it from my memory. I'm sure that worry never stood in the way of partying and getting laid as often as possible. There were still about a dozen gay bathhouses open twenty-four hours a day. All the bars still opened at six a.m., and I still had my old green beat-up Datsun pickup. I went so far as going to the junk yards around San Francisco to look for a cheap camper shell. If things got bad enough, I could throw a mattress in the back and sleep there. If things got good, I could fuck there.

One day I noticed a FOR RENT sign on an apartment building on McCoppin, a little two-block long street south of Market, about half way between the Castro bars and the SOMA bars, and it was cheap. French doors divided the front parlor from the bedroom. Landlords often seal the French doors shut in this layout and advertise the places as two-bedroom apartments, but this one was still intact. Down the hall were two doors to the water closet and the bathroom. The windowless living room came next and, finally, a big kitchen with a roomy pantry. Beyond the kitchen was a tacked-on back porch or sun room that had screen stapled over the holes in the outer walls. One wall was the outside of the building next door and one wall was the outside wall of the kitchen.

Even though the place was tacky and cheap, it cost nearly a thousand dollars to move in, counting first and last months' rent and security deposit. Before I returned the keys to the realty office in Noe Valley, I parked in the Castro and stopped for a beer at the Badlands, where I ran into Armando. He'd been my first boyfriend and live-together lover in San Francisco and was now a very successful caterer. He bought me a beer, and I told him about the place I'd found.

I offered to show it to him since I still had the keys, and

the next thing I knew he was writing me a check for a thousand bucks. We called it a "loan," but he knew as well as I did that he would never see that grand again. I thought of it as well-deserved, albeit delayed, alimony after our breakup of several years ago.

I've always had women friends. I am able to spend long periods of time in strictly male environments, but growing up with so much female energy in my family, I eventually begin to miss women. Jane Dornacker was becoming one of my closest women friends. I'd gotten to know her when she performed at the Woods. When I moved back to San Francisco, I booked a few paying gigs for her and asked her to do some benefits too.

Part of my reason for wanting women in my life might also have been because they weren't dying of AIDS like so many of the men around me were. When I made friends with a woman I assumed—no—I *expected* our friendship would last forever. My first day on McCoppin Street, I moved the few boxes and small pieces of furniture out of Roger's garage on Seward. Jane came by that night with champagne and sushi from our favorite Japanese restaurant near Union Square, just south of the Stockton tunnel. We sat cross-legged on the floor, eating and laughing, drinking and smoking pot and cigarettes. Jane smoked unfiltered Camels, the smoke wafting up through her huge mane of burgundy hair. We did a few lines of coke and laughed some more, listening to an old transistor radio for music.

Jane was a local radio star in those days. She was a stand-up comedienne by night, but in the daytime she was the "trafficologist" on KFRC. She made traffic reporting funny. "We have a vehicular flambé in the northbound lanes of the Golden Gate Bridge, so there'll be some delays if you're headed out of the city that way. It looks like yet another driver has failed to maintain the master/subordinate relationship with his automobile…"

One of the characters Jane did in her comedy act was Marge Battaglia, renowned "snackologist" in an apron with her hair pulled up on top of her head and a pair of goofy glasses with black and white op-art swirls for lenses. She made her voice sound an awful lot like Julia Child as she tore apart Hostess Sno-Balls to show how they could be used for condoms and spoke about the shelf-life of Twinkies, while making sly put-downs of President Reagan.

On one of her visits to my new apartment, I suggested that Jane make a recording on my answering machine as Marge Battaglia. She needed no coaxing.

"Hi, this is Marge—not Mark—Marge! Mark just stepped out for a little snack, so leave a message at the tone. That reminds me… I'm getting kinda hungry myself. I suppose it's about time I had head back up to Snackramento and rustle up something for Bill and the kids to eat, too. Now, don't forget to wait for the beep. If you want either one of us to get back to you, you'd better leave a message!"

My parents back in Minnesota wouldn't deal with my answering machine. They treated the very idea of leaving a recorded message of their voices in the same way that some tribes fear that having their photographs taken steals a part of their soul. The next time I spoke to my dad, he asked, "Who is that strange woman answering your phone? Madge something?"

"No, Dad. That's Jane Dornacker. She's a comedienne, and that's a character she does named Marge Battaglia. Jane was in that movie *The Right Stuff*, you know the one about the astronauts?"

"Last time we went to the movies was to see *Dances with Wolves*," Mom said. "They shot a lot of that around here, well… over in the Dakotas, you know."

"Well, Jane Dornacker isn't really here answering my phone, you see. It's just her voice on my answering machine. If you listened to the end, you'd hear her say to leave a message and then I could call you right back when I get home. If you don't leave a message, it just shows a number of how many calls I got, but I don't have any way to know who to call back." This was a lie, of course, since my parents were the only people I knew who wouldn't leave a message.

"We never listen to the end," my Mother piped up on the extension in their bedroom. "If a woman answers, we hang up right away. There's no sense running up a long distance phone call when you're not even home."

"But if you leave a message, I'll call you right back."

"Naw, that's okay. We can always try again later."

Sometimes I would come home and discover that I'd had ten calls, but no messages and I'd only been out grocery shopping.

My new apartment on McCoppin Street was really a dump, but it was my dump. It was cheap and well located. If I didn't want to drive, I could walk to the Safeway on Church Street for groceries and to the South of Market bars and bath houses. I'm sure that my friend Roger was glad to have his apartment and his garage on Seward Street all to himself again. I don't know how I intended to pay the rent, but I figured that my life was headed in the right direction now that I had a home of my own.

My good friend Kym Whittington was a bartender at Chaps at 375 11th Street at Harrison. Kym was Australian, the son of some important government figure and from a very wealthy family. Whenever he spoke about the cost of something extravagant that I could never afford, Kym would joke about calling home and telling his family to shear some more sheep. I guessed that he meant they would sell the wool and send him the money. Maybe it was only funny when he said it. He never lost his thick Aussie accent in all the years he lived in San Francisco. I often suspected that with his family's support, he didn't need to bartend, but he did it because it gave him something to do here and a way to fit in and meet a lot of people.

I hung out at Chaps mostly on the weekends. It was a huge place with balconies around three sides overlooking the main bar in the center of the room. The layout was perfect for cruising. You could stand in one position and pose like fish bait or you could work the room. Either way provided a changing kaleidoscope of hot guys on display. It was a great place to be stoned, to lose yourself and maybe meet someone.

In the summer of 1984, the owners of Chaps asked me to meet with them about producing some special events. Kym picked me up on his motorcycle that morning, and we met his bosses at a restaurant called Dish on the corner of Haight and Masonic. Their first idea was a leather title contest, something extravagant to rival Mr. Drummer or maybe International Mr. Leather.

Over the next few weeks, the contest idea was dropped for some reason, but I thought Chaps would make an ideal place for live entertainment. At one end of the bar, the stairs from the balconies met in a wide landing, creating an almost perfect stage. I thought I could use that design as well as the bar's motif and clientele to create a leather bar/cabaret. I began booking a roster of performers to appear there on what we ended up calling "A Blue-Collar Bash for Labor Day Weekend." The first performer I wanted was Tina Turner. Her agent had tried to book her at the Woods when I was working at the Russian River the previous year, but my boss at the time said he wasn't having that "tired old washed up hag" trying to make a comeback in his club. I called her agent to see about getting her for Chaps, and he told me that her new album *Private Dancer* was climbing the charts. He would love to book her in San Francisco, but the rate had gone up about ten-fold from last year, so she was now out of my price range. I told him I wished her well, and I hoped my old boss had realized his mistake.

I booked gay comics Marga Gomez, Danny Williams, Tom Ammiano, and the not gay, but far from "straight" Jane Dornacker, plus Val Diamond and Crosswinds. I've forgotten some of the other musical acts, but for the grand finale on the Monday night of Labor Day, I booked Edith Massey, "Edie the Egg Lady" from John Waters' classic cult film *Pink Flamingos*. Her other roles included my personal favorite, as "Aunt Ida" Nelson from 1974's Female Trouble in which her character says to her nephew Gator, "Queers are just better…the world of heterosexuals is a sick and boring life!"

My love for Edie, aside from her movies, went back to when she performed at the Woods Resort. I'd produced "Leather Weekend at the Russian River" with Edie as the final act on a Monday night. After her performance, I ended up spending the rest of the evening in the room adjacent to hers in a threesome with Edie's manager and his boyfriend who was acting as her "tour photographer." I wish he'd taken some pictures of that!

In the morning, I took the two of them and Edie to breakfast at the little café that was perched over Fife's Creek. I ordered an omelet and Edie had pancakes. She said, "You know, Mark…I don't even like eggs. That egg-lady thing was just for the movies. That was John's idea."

I will never forget that amazing voice of hers, a nasal high-pitched shriek. That morning at breakfast, she also told me, "You know, Mark… I could afford to get teeth now, but John said it might ruin my image."

Edie's trip to the Woods had been a year or two earlier, but I'd held onto her phone number and address. By this time she had left behind her twenty-four hour thrift store in Baltimore and opened a "new" thrift store on the West Coast in Venice, California. Edie was thrilled to come and perform for me for yet another Monday gig. She didn't get many offers for Monday nights. She told me she would be in Phoenix that weekend, so I arranged a flight for her which was due to arrive at SFO on Labor Day Monday shortly after noon.

To get ready for the weekend, Kym and I ran all over town on his bike or in my old Datsun ordering advertising posters, printing tickets and taking them to the ticket outlets, booking hotel rooms and making airline reservations. This was years before the Internet and cell phones. We typed up contracts on paper with carbon copies, and we sent them through the U.S. Mail. Everything was falling into place for a terrific weekend.

Then only a couple of weeks before Labor Day someone called me at home and said we had to cancel everything. We needed to call it all off, get hold of all of the entertainers and let them know the event wouldn't be happening. Evidently, someone had seen our advertising for a "Blue Collar Bash" and reported to the authorities that Chaps was planning to have live entertainment without the proper licenses and permits.

When I first heard this, I thought they were joking, but they were dead serious. This was a disaster. I was ruined. I didn't know anything about licenses and permits. I'd seen performers at Chaps before with no problem. I called Harry Britt in a panic to see if he could help us. Harry had taken over Harvey Milk's "gay seat" on the Board of Supervisors after Harvey was murdered. Harry was our only hope, but he couldn't help either. Someone had filed a formal complaint against us, so the police were obligated to act on it.

We were never told directly who had done this to us, but we figured out that it was a competitor. I would never have suspected a cutthroat action like that from another gay businessman. I always thought gay people were supposed to look out for one another and try to improve things for the community. I was so naïve not to realize there were already "Gay Republicans" among us in 1984.

If Harry Britt could do anything, it would be to help us get the proper permits in time for me to reschedule the entertainers for an event over Thanksgiving weekend. I called them all and they understood that the situation wasn't my fault. I rebooked all of them except Edith Massey. I didn't know how to reach her in Phoenix, and I couldn't get hold of her at home in Venice either because she was already "on tour."

Then I got an idea. If we couldn't cancel Edie, we would just have to make the best of it. If she didn't sing, we wouldn't get in any trouble with the authorities. Edie couldn't really sing, anyway. People would come to see Edie just because they wanted to see her in person and hear her speak in that strange childlike voice they knew from the John Waters' movies. In those days, Sunday afternoons south of Market meant hundreds of people at the Eagle beer bust and good crowds at all the other leather bars too, especially when that Sunday was part of a three-day weekend. It also meant hundreds of motorcycles. Kym and I got cards printed up that said:

If you would like to be part of a motorcycle escort from SFO for

"Edie, the Egg Lady"

Wear your leather and show up with your bike tomorrow morning at 11am

at Chaps   375 – 11th Street   FREE Bloody Marys!

We tucked one of those cards on every motorcycle outside every bar in the SOMA neighborhood that afternoon. With our work finished, all we could do now was wait and see. I had no idea what to expect on Monday morning. I was worried that people might be too fried after partying the last two nights to come out that morning, or that nobody would want to get up when they could sleep in on their holiday Monday.

I needn't have worried. Things turned out perfectly. At least two dozen men in full leather regalia showed up on their hogs and Hondas. Many of them were strangers to me, but all of them were die-hard Edie fans. For being part of the motorcycle escort, they each got a free drink or two before we took off for the airport. Someone we knew had a big old chrome-encrusted pink Pontiac convertible with giant tail fins. Edie would ride in that. We decorated the bikes with rainbow flags and American flags, maybe flags with the Chaps logo.

The motorcycles rode two abreast, half in front of the car and half behind it. We roared into the airport, pulled up to the American Airlines terminal. No one said a word to us or bothered us or said we had to keep moving. I ran inside and found Edie, gave her a quick hug, grabbed her bags and told her I had a big surprise waiting for her outside. She couldn't believe her eyes.

Mark greeting Edith Massey at SFO

"All this for me?" she screamed. I perched her on the backseat for our drive through the airport. The motorcycles roared their engines, and we started to slowly move. Edie sat above it all wearing a big floppy hat, sunglasses, and a faded print housedress. Other passengers stopped and stared. Cab drivers hooted and whistled. Edie waved at the throngs of strangers and yelled out, "Yes, it's really me! I'm a movie star! It's me! I'm Bette Davis! (Which she pronounced "Bet" as one syllable, a la Midler) I'm a movie star!"

I pulled her down into the back seat with me just before we got onto the freeway to head back into the city. We pulled up to Chaps for more drinks and for all the guys in her cavalcade to get their pictures taken with Edie and visit with her for a little while. Then I had another idea. Since everyone was having so much fun, I thought we might as well continue. The leather men got back on their bikes, and we returned Edie to her backseat perch. Kym slapped together some pasteboard signs we taped to both sides that said:

Edie the "Egg Lady"

Join us tonight - 9pm

CHAPS Bar – 375 - 11th

We took Edie up and down all the major gay streets of the city. This time, unlike at the airport, the people on the sidewalks really were her fans. This time she yelled out, "Yes, it's me! It's Edie! Come and see me tonight at the leather bar!"

On Polk Street, hairdressers flung open their second floor windows, waved their combs and scissors and yelled out to Edie. People in restaurants came outside to cheer and whistle. On Haight Street, people emptied out of head shops to see what was going on. When they realized it was Edie, they came into the streets and crowded around the car to shake her hand. On Castro Street, people poured out of the bars and climbed between all the motorcycles to get close to her. When people asked for autographs, she told them, "Come and see me tonight at the leather bar, and I'll sign anything you want!" I smiled. Edie was far more clever then she looked.

We finally made it back to Chaps. The motorcyclists dispersed, but all of them promised to come back that night even though we weren't promising that Edie would do anything but take pictures and sign autographs. For Edie fans, that was enough. This was a soul who had witnessed incredible highs and lows in her time on earth. We needed symbols of that spirit of survival more than ever. By Labor Day weekend of 1984, the deaths from AIDS were increasing every week. The names rang out like the toll of funeral bells, and their faces stared back at us weekly in black and white newsprint in the back of the *Bay Area Reporter*. We needed to laugh, and we loved Edie. She was a survivor of her own hard times, and her spirit and sense of fun were still intact.

That evening the owner of the pink Pontiac took me to pick up Edie at the Atherton Hotel where she introduced me to her old friend Ruth, who would be coming along to keep her company. Edie had called her as soon as she got settled in her room, and they had been reminiscing all afternoon. Edie left me alone with Ruth for a minute while she yelled from the bathroom, "I'll be right out. I just have to put on my glamour wig."

I looked at Ruth and smiled. She was kind of scary-looking. She reminded me of a retired athlete or maybe a jockey, a lean, tough little old man. In the car on the way to Chaps, I listened to Ruth and Edie in the back seat talk about all the Tenderloin bars they recognized from back in World War II. In those days, Edie and Ruth had been B-girls together. They would sit in bars and entertain gentlemen, flirt with them and get them to buy drinks. The house would charge the men top-shelf prices, serve the B-girls juice or soda water and split the profits later.

"Oh Edie… look! We got out through the back door of that place more than once or twice!"

Then Edie would laugh and point to a bar in the next block. "Remember the sailors we met in there?"

When we got back to Chaps, I propped up Edie on a bar stool near the stage so that she was visible to everyone in the room. Soon the line was out the door and down the block. It should have been a huge night for the bar's cash registers, and I'm sure they did all right, but most of the people didn't come to drink. The bulk of the crowd had just come to see Edie.

She had a huge stack of postcards from various John Waters' films, each of them showing Edie in one of her most outrageous costumes. Anyone who wanted her autograph had to buy one of those first for a dollar. Once they did, she'd sign anything else the person wanted signed as well, from a VHS tape to a plaster cast to a bare butt. Ruth sat beside her, making change and keeping track of the money so that Edie could keep her fans happy and keep the line moving.

It must have been past midnight when Edie called me over. "Mark, do you still think the cops will come tonight?"

I said, "No, I don't think so, Edie. Why do you ask?"

"Because I could still do the songs on my tape." She pulled a cassette from her purse. "You got me all this way to sing, so I could at least give them a couple of numbers, can't I?"

"Okay, Edie." We had the sound man cue up her tape, propped Edie up on the stage in a spotlight, and she did "Big Girls Don't Cry" and "Punks! Get Off the Grass!"

Since she was the only one of the entertainers I couldn't cancel and reschedule for Thanksgiving weekend, we decided to wait a while and have her back in the spring instead. She and I talked that night all the way back to the Atherton about doing a big Sunday afternoon event called "Easter with Edie, the Egg Lady."

Labor Day was on September 3rd that year. Only a few weeks later, I was riding the #8 Market bus home from the Castro one afternoon when my truck was in the shop. Reading the afternoon *San Francisco Examiner,* I saw Edith Massey's obituary. She had died of cancer on October 24, 1984. I stuck the paper in my backpack and trudged the rest of the way home that afternoon with thoughts and fond memories of dear Edie.

When I got there, I opened my mailbox and found a letter addressed to me in crayon that looked like it was written by a drunken child. I was amazed that the U.S. Post Office had even been able to get it to the right address. Inside was a one-page note from Edie, thanking me again for such a swell time in San Francisco. She wrote that she wanted me to send her "love to all those nice boys down at the leather bar and tell them I'll see you all at Easter."

I brought her letter to Chaps that weekend to show it to Kym. We decided to put it up on the bulletin board in the office for all of the bar staff to see.

Someone stole it.

Chapter Ten

While Jim Cvitanich and I were planning the second, now annual, *Men Behind Bars* show for Presidents' Day weekend of 1985, I was still putting the word out that I was looking for more work. When I got a call from Ed "Edwina Ballerina" Stark, I hoped that he was going to offer me a full-time bartending job at the Nothing Special. Instead, Ed had called to tell me he was planning to buy Febe's, and he asked me to manage it for him.

Febe's opened in 1966 and was considered the premier gay biker bar for many years. Febe's was well known for a statue of Michelangelo's *David* in a leather cap and jacket. It became the emblem of the bar on all their matchbooks and advertising. Febe's was located at 1501 Folsom Street, a block north of the original Hamburger Mary's and just up the street from the original Stud, where Etta James sometimes used to pop up and sing on crowded Sunday afternoons.

I had been to Febe's, but not often, even in the days when John Preston and I ended up at the SOMA bars nearly every night. I don't think we even called it SOMA back then. It was "the Folsom" or "Folsom Gulch" or "South of the Slot" or most commonly "South of Market" unabbreviated. In 1977 the Village People recorded a song called "San Francisco," but it was really about the Folsom district.

Ed told me that his offer to buy Febe's was contingent on his being able to also buy the building next door. He wanted to expand from the one narrow room with a staircase at the end of the bar leading up to what was the original location of A Taste of Leather, a leather and sex toy shop. A pool table was also upstairs, but in my memory of earlier trips to Febe's, a lot more was being played upstairs besides pool. Most of the bars had darkened back rooms upstairs or downstairs or in the alley out back which were well-suited for oral sex and foreplay, but if you wanted to do more than stand and/or kneel, the several nearby baths were more practical.

So ironically at the same time I was being "groomed" for a management job at the Eagle, I was tentatively offered another management position at Febe's when all I really wanted was a couple more bartending shifts somewhere so I could make decent tips and not have to worry about much more than having fun on my days off. Besides, *Men Behind Bars* took up a lot of my time.

While I waited for Ed's offer to materialize, Jim and I started auditions and rehearsals. In rounding up people to be in the second year's show, we discovered how many of the first year's cast had died. Realizing this made me all the more determined to live in the moment. I tried to block out any bad news with the help of sex, drugs, alcohol, and dancing until dawn as often as possible, whether on an actual dance floor, in a cubicle at the baths, at a sex club, in the backroom of a bar, in a stranger's bed, or prowling the streets and alleys and the paths in Buena Vista Park.

Dianne Feinstein had been appointed mayor after the assassinations of Harvey Milk and George Moscone in 1978, but she'd been elected on her own by this time. Her reaction to AIDS was to shut down all the baths. The opposing viewpoint was that the baths, unlike the parks and adult bookstores, at least had showers where people could get cleaned up between partners. The baths could also be used as places to promote safer sex. In our opinion, the mayor's position seemed downright schoolmarm-ish, so Jim and I wanted to make fun of her. We had both gone to see *Best Little Whorehouse in Texas* starring Alexis Smith when it had come to San Francisco, so we got the idea to do a spoof from the musical with Feinstein singing "Frisco Has a Bathhouse In It."

The San Francisco Gay Men's Chorus had an offshoot group called "Men About Town" who agreed to portray the Board of Supervisors, but we needed one strong singer who was willing to get in drag to play Dianne Feinstein. The only one who didn't have any facial hair was a guy named Tim Garner, so he got the part. We couldn't have made a better choice. He was perfect.

The entire Gay Men's Chorus recorded the introduction to the number, which was played to a dark house with the show curtain closed:

"Feinstein will get you, if you don't watch out.

Dianne sees and Dianne knows... Feinstein keeps us on our toes.

Dianne assures you that the law's the law...

No exceptions to the rule, Dianne ain't no fool!"

The show curtain remained closed, but now it began to be lit from the rear with flashlights as the Chorus continued to sing:

"Dianne will get you, she's out on the prowl.

Guards and checks the best she can...

Dianne is a tough woman.

If some folks don't toe the line, Dianne's light will shine.

Feinstein's here! Feinstein's here! Feinstein's here..."

And the curtain rose to reveal the Men About Town dressed as the motliest crew of business people imaginable, wearing ill-fitting jackets with neckties, a few of them in women's suits with wigs and padded breasts, still with their mustaches, singing live now, "Feinstein's here..."

Then Tim Garner made his entrance in a skirt and blouse with the trademark Feinstein bow at the neck, only this one was severely oversized. "Thank you, my fellow San Franciscans! You know lately, my spotlight has shined on a situation that has been allowed to exist right in the shadows of City Hall..."

I was responsible for most of the adaptations (some would say bastardizations) of lyrics that we did, and this number was lots of fun to rewrite in reference to the gay men's bathhouse issue. I remember one night at rehearsal in the Metropolitan Community Church in the Castro, the Board of Supervisors were singing, "Dianne hates those poppers...." and I thought Feinstein should raise her finger and interrupt them with, "and so does Quentin Kopp!" He was one of the more conservative members of the real Board in those days, and it rhymed with the next line that ended, "...and it must stop!"

The first act finale that year was another lip-sync medley, starting with Wayne Wenger as Ethel Merman doing "There's No Business Like Show Business." Wayne worked at the Nothing Special on Castro Street as a swamper, the person who comes in to clean the bar when it closes at two a.m. Every bar has one. They stack the stools on top of the bar in order to sweep and mop the floors, clean the bathrooms, round up any leftover bottles and glasses, and maybe help the bartenders stock warm beer into the coolers. Wayne would stay around until five a.m. or so when the morning bartender arrived in order to set up and open at six. It was my understanding that the insurance policy was cheaper if there was someone on the premises twenty-four hours a day. I've known some swampers who work seven nights a week on that strange schedule and manage to survive.

Everyone knew Wayne better as "Wanda June" in those days. I still see him around the Castro, sometimes walking with a cane, but in MBBII he danced across the stage in a long, pinkish evening gown with a back up line of male dancers in tap shoes with canes and top hats.

Ethel Merman segued into Carmen Miranda, played by a tiny drag queen known as Desiree, whose day job was hairdressing. He styled all the wigs for the show that year. His number was "The Lady in the Tutti-Frutti Hat" from *The Gang's All Here*. She was backed up by some of the Follies Men wearing nothing but swatches of tropical print fabrics around their waists while twirling six foot tall plywood bananas on loan from the Gay Men's Chorus. Or maybe we borrowed them from the Lamplighters, the Gilbert and Sullivan group.

Next came three drag queens dressed as the Andrews Sisters with a couple of USO boys doing the jitterbug. They were three former Empresses: Miss Remy Martin and Jonni and Sissy Spaceout. Jim and I were not directly involved with the Court system, but we always tried to include them in the shows. Some years their coronation fell on the same weekend as our shows, so timing was tough, but the contestants for Empress each year were always glad for the exposure they got in our shows, not to mention that it was always a lot of fun.

The first act finale ended with our emcee, Mister Marcus, coming out in dowdy drag and lip-syncing to Kate Smith's "God Bless America." The stars and stripes descended behind him while members of the Gay Marching Band's Flag and Twirling Corps joined him on stage, followed by the rest of the first act finale cast for a grand curtain call. Jim and I had gotten hold of Alan Greenspan, the man who made the huge mechanical hats for North Beach's decades-in-the-running show *Steve Silver's Beach Blanket Babylon.* Alan created a Statue of Liberty hat for Marcus as Kate Smith, complete with floodlights at the base that shined up at the statue. On the final "home sweet home" of the song, Lady Liberty's robes snapped open on the hat to reveal a foot tall replica of a muscleman in a jock strap underneath. The audience loved it.

I still didn't have enough work to support myself, but I was high on the success of that show for the next several weeks. If nothing else, I had the satisfaction that Jim and I had done a good job, made a lot of people happy and raised some needed funds to fight AIDS.

Chapter Eleven

Shortly after the second edition of *Men Behind Bars*, Jim and I decided to go on a weekend bus trip together. It was called Ski-Dazzle, although skiing was the farthest thing from our minds. The California Motorcycle Club produced the CMC Carnival every year. During the summer, most of the clubs had weekend camping trips called "bike runs" during which lots of drinking, drugs, and sex transpired and usually a big drag show on Saturday night. Ski Dazzle was a similar event. It was put on by the Coits Motorcycle Club, named after Coit Tower on Telegraph Hill. It might have been a fundraiser, but more likely it was just something fun to do.

With people dying at a greater pace, we had to do things just for fun now and then. More and more pictures of the dead appeared in the B.A.R. Every week they took up more space, and every week they looked more familiar. They became the faces of people I'd served drinks to then they grew to be the faces of guys I'd seen around on the streets or in the bars, to faces with names that I'd met at a party last Christmas, to people I'd worked with, partied with, men I had cruised on the dance floor, slept with and eventually the faces of people I'd even lived with.

This ski trip was different for me. The bars were mostly where I had fun working or drinking. When I arrived here in 1975, San Francisco had over two hundred gay bars according Lou Greene's Bar Guide, a big poster you could find in most bars thumb-tacked to the wall outside the door to the toilet. Those two hundred listings included drag show bars, dance bars, piano bars, gay restaurants, and coffee shops. Most of them were in the Polk Street/Tenderloin area or South of Market, several in the Haight with more and more spilling into the Castro, but almost every neighborhood in the city had at least one or two little gay bars. By the mid-80s, the Castro and Upper Market had at least a couple of dozen listings and nearly all of them were open every day from six a.m. until two a.m., and they were usually crowded.

Ski Dazzle simply took the bar experience one step further. The cost was ridiculously cheap—seventy-five dollars for the bus trip, two night's hotel accommodations in South Lake Tahoe plus food and all you could drink all the way up there and all the way back.

I think there were four busloads that year. We all met at the Mint on Market Street on Friday afternoon after work. The Mint is still there, but it used to be twice as big with a restaurant attached. Everyone was pretty well tanked by the time we boarded the buses. Just as soon as we got across the Bay Bridge, a crew of drag queen/stewardesses appeared from the back of the bus to entertain us all the way to Tahoe. They were hilarious and kept us laughing, not to mention serving some kind of bag lunch suppers and all the vodka we could drink, mixed with orange or cranberry juice. We also played some silly games they had planned, something you didn't have to think about too hard, like bingo. They made sure that everyone won some kind of goofy gag gift or drink tickets to various bars in San Francisco that had donated them for the sake of advertising.

We also smoked tons of pot and ate pot brownies on the ride. I found out later that Jim had asked for the pot bus. I don't remember that he even smoked pot, but the other options were the LSD bus, the Quaaludes bus, or the speed bus.

The snowstorm started halfway to Tahoe. As we got higher and higher into the Sierras, we could see miles of taillights on the highway in front of us and miles of headlights behind us as traffic crawled to a snail's pace and finally stopped. This was the place where we could go no further without chains. I hadn't seen snow falling this thick and wet and fast since I was a kid in Minnesota. All of the stoners on our bus just looked out the windows and said, "Isn't that pretty?!" It really was beautiful. The guys on the LSD bus must have thought they were on the moon. The ones on the speed bus were clawing at the windows, and the people on Quaaludes hardly noticed that their bus had stopped.

I will never forget looking out the window at all the colorful drag queens wading through ankle-deep snow, stoned out of their minds and trying to help the bus drivers put chains on the tires. My favorite of the drag queens was one I'd never met before that trip. She went by the name of "Connie Cadaver," and I found out later that he was a mortician in real life. I thought she was the cleverest and most fun-loving of all of them.

I had never been on skis in my life, and I don't think Jim had either. And this drunken weekend was no time to start anything at which we might hurt ourselves. We finally made it to our hotel late that night and checked in. For the next couple of days we slept some, gambled some, ate some, and drank some more. On Saturday night, one of the local Tahoe gay bars hosted a party for us with food and cheap drinks and entertainment, the highlight of which was the crowning of one of our group as the "Queen of South Shore and Protector of the State Line." I must have been in the men's room when that happened.

When I came out Jim told me they had crowned this drag queen named Erica, self-named after Erica Kane, the vixen on the daytime soap opera *All My Children*. I knew him as a guy named Dennis who did a lot of sewing for us for *Men Behind Bars*. He was a sweet, chubby, affectionate, effeminate man/boy who lived in an apartment in the building above the Village, where The Mix is today. His living room windows overlooked the back patio bar, and I'd always suspected that he had a crush on me.

The next think I knew the emcee was asking Erica to name her king. She had been elected by some sort of balloting process that I was too stoned to notice, but she apparently got to choose her own king. Then I heard my name called, and I had to go on stage and get crowned and pose for a bunch of pictures with Erica at my side, looking up at me admiringly. So even though I've never run for anything in my life, I cannot say that I've never had a title. The crown was heavy. It looked like someone had made it in his garage out of old bottle openers, sequins and bits of broken colored glass. I wonder what ever happened to that ugly old thing.

On Sunday morning after breakfast, we all gathered at the bar in our hotel where the drag queens from all the buses handed out prizes in various categories having to do with things that went on that weekend, like "first prize for the couple who had the loudest sex" or for "the guy that got fucked the most times" or for the person who "lost the most money in the casinos." I think they made sure that everyone won something again. They gave Jim and me a prize that had something to do with producing the MBB show. It wasn't a campy award like the others. The prize made me realize that people appreciated something we had done. It was nice to be recognized.

Then we all got back on the buses. Our bus actually had one passenger who skied. He had been up on the slopes all morning, so we all drove up to Heavenly or Kirkwood or Alpine Meadows or whichever one it was to pick him up before we could head back to the city. He climbed up the front steps onto the bus with snow still on him. He had his skis and poles and scarves and everything! He took off his gloves and stuck one index finger under the front of his stocking cap to pull it off. Snowflakes fell to the floor of the bus and a thick, soft, blond head of hair fell around the face of an angel. He was hot. He was sweet. And to top it all off, he had an accent. He was from Switzerland, and his name was Roland. Blue-eyed, blond-haired, beautiful, uncut, and hung-like-a-horse Roland.

We had play-dates and dinner together once or twice a week for the next few months until he moved to L.A. It was great sex, full of fun and passion and lots of laughter. But we never fell in love with each other. Sometimes great sex is all a person should ask for.

Chapter Twelve

I don't remember what I did on Memorial Day weekend of 1985, but I do know that San Francisco sent three contestants to Chicago for the International Mr. Leather contest. We had no Mr. San Francisco Leather contest that year, so each of the contestants were sponsored by bars. James Hamrick represented the Detour, a leather bar on Market Street in the Castro neighborhood. The Eagle sent Pete Pettine, and my old fuck-buddy and now good friend Patrick Toner represented Chaps bar on 11th Street.

I was home on McCoppin Street when I got a call from Kym Whittington, whose Aussie accent was hard to understand, especially when he was excited. He blurted out, "Patrick Toner took the International Mr. Leather title winner!"

"Took? Took him where?"

"No, Patrick took the title. He won! Patrick is the new International Mr. Leather!"

"Woo-hoo, that's great! Party at Chaps! See you there in about fifteen minutes!" Even though Patrick wouldn't be back in San Francisco for another day or two, I knew that all of his friends who didn't go to Chicago would gather at his sponsor bar anyway. When Patrick got home, we would all just celebrate with him all over again.

Patrick Toner was only twenty-two years old, the youngest winner of IML in history, and it couldn't have happened to a nicer guy. In some cases winning a title allows people the confidence to step outside their comfort zones and use their newfound fame for a worthwhile cause. Jim Cvitanich was Mister San Francisco Leather when we started *Men Behind Bars*. After winning the title of International Mr. Leather, Patrick decided to start a new street fair called "Up Your Alley."

The Folsom Street Fair had started in 1984 and was already notorious as being similar to the CMC Carnival, only several blocks long and held outdoors. Patrick wanted to create a smaller version of Folsom, but geared more to the locals. Instead of a street, he just wanted an alley. Ringold Alley was known in those days for heavy late night cruising, so that's the one Patrick chose for a daylight event. Patrick convinced all his friends to help him get it off the ground, and the "Up Your Alley" Fair has continued as an AIDS benefit and annual tradition every since.

Rita Rockett was also one of Patrick's closest friends. She volunteered to work with Jim Cvitanich and me to run the dunk-a-hunk attraction at "Up Your Alley." We lined up all the guys who had been Follies Men in our first two *Men Behind Bars* shows, plus that year's Bare Chest Calendar winners, other friends of ours and basically anyone with a good body and a streak of exhibitionism. At least thirty guys must have signed up. They looked great and drew a lot of attention, hanging out in the sun in nothing but their Speedos, but most of them didn't stick around very long after their dunking. The tank had been filled with water from a nearby garden hose, so that water was cold even though it was a sunny day. As sexy as those boys looked glistening in the sun, some of them didn't like getting their hair wet, and then there was the shrinkage factor. After one plunge into that icy tank, they didn't fill out their Speedos nearly as well.

Rita, Jim and I spent all day picking up the balls that rolled back down between the legs of all the onlookers in the crowd and our aching backs were killing us. At three balls for a dollar, we figured there had to be a better way to raise money for a good cause. Jim lost interest after the first couple of fairs, but for the next decade or more I continued to organize the booth to sell "Rita's Margaritas" at both "Up Your Alley" and the Folsom Street fairs. We made enough money to cover the grocery bills for the Rita's Brunch Fund for most of the year.

Chapter Thirteen

In the late spring of 1985, I got another call from Ed Stark. I was sure he must have finally bought Febe's and wanted to hire me as the manager. I remember the gist of what he said all these years later: "Mark, I've watched you produce those big weekend-long parties at the Russian River when you lived up there, and now I've been through two of these *Men Behind Bars* shows with you, and I've just gotta say I've never seen anyone who could get so fucked up, drink and party and do drugs to the extent that you can and still keep it together and always know exactly what's going on and what needs to be done. You have *got* to come and work for me. The Febe's deal fell through, but I can give you some bartending shifts on Castro Street."

Ed was a funny guy. Months later when we were out to dinner one night, he told me the story about when he hired Danny Marsh, another bartender. Danny was fondly known in the Castro as Mitzi Marsh. I guess it was an old-school practice that gay guys would give each other campy drag nicknames, even if they never went in drag. They could be used interchangeably with their real names and everyone understood who you meant.

Danny Marsh was bartending at the Pendulum one night when Ed was there for a fundraiser of some kind. Even before AIDS, the gay bars were always having fundraisers for one cause or another: Toys for Tots, Guide Dogs for the Blind, Thanksgiving Dinner for the Homeless. The list goes on and on. The Pendulum was located on 18th Street near Collingwood, across the street from the Edge, where the second incarnation of Toad Hall now stands. The Pendulum was known as the Castro's predominantly black bar for many years, even though most of the bartenders were white.

One night the bar was packed and one of the customers—Ed described him as "a big fat loud drunken queen" in white Levis—climbed up and sat on the bar in order to get a better view of the stage. In doing so, he knocked over someone else's fresh drink and didn't even notice or chose to ignore the fact. It was a tall Bloody Mary.

Ed told me he watched Mitzi grab a bar towel, but instead of wiping up the mess, he gathered it all together with the towel—the gooey red drink along with the melting ice, wedge of lime, pickled green bean and olive on a toothpick—and carefully pushed the entire puddle up and around the drunk's "big fat ass," staining the white Lev's bright red. The guy still didn't notice. Ed said he decided right then and there that someday Mitzi would have to come and work for him.

I was still working two nights a week, Mondays and Tuesdays, at the Eagle, nine p.m. to close, and all that Ed could offer me to start was Friday, Saturday, and Sunday mornings, six a.m. to noon, with a promise that I would move into a better shift as soon as one opened. I said, "Sure, I'll take it!"

My first day of work at The Special, I arrived at five a.m., Ed met me there along with Wanda June, the swamper, and the general manager, a tiny old man that everyone called Mother. I think his real name was Robert, but he preferred Mother. He also expected a card every year on Mother's Day, if not gifts and flowers. If anyone who worked there didn't buy him at least a Mother's Day card, he never heard the end of it.

Ed and Mother showed me the set-up system, the till and the backup bank, how to work the register, including the much-used "comp" key, the prices, various glasses for different kinds of drinks, the liquor room, the office, and all the things I'd need to know. There is really no way to learn a new bar better than just jumping back there and going to work. Any questions soon become apparent. Eventually, just about every possible situation arises and you learn how to deal with them all. I was never robbed at gunpoint, as friends of mine have been, but I've experienced a lot of crazy things over the years.

At six a.m., we opened the front door and the crowd piled in. Ed told me there were a lot of loyal regulars. He also told me, as part of my starting instructions, "Pour heavy and comp heavy—every third drink to regular customers. That's how I got rich in this business." I had worked in other bars where the management expected to get twenty drinks out of a bottle. There is a process of measuring "pour count" by dividing the number of drinks sold per shift by the number of bottles emptied per category of well, call, premium and top shelf. Ed said, "I'd like fifteen, but I'm happy with twelve and usually have to settle for ten." Most of the regulars drank well drinks or domestic beer and lots of shots of schnapps in any of a dozen different flavors, starting with peppermint, then spearmint, apple, cinnamon, peach and melon until there wasn't room in the cooler to keep any more of the sweet, sticky stuff cold.

The doors opened, and I soon met Greg and Jimmy, Bill (better known as Juanita), Woody, Lopez, Bob (a still-married-to-a-woman guy who drank scotch), Braxton Hancock (better known as Judy), and Kenny (the coke dealer for the morning shift). Kenny also made sure the ice machine was always working and fixed it if it wasn't. Dorthy Duster, with one O, whom nobody ever called Gene, came in every day. Another regular was Big Alice whose real name was Richard, I think. There was Tom and George, little Tom and Squirrel, Tom and Vince. There must have been lots of gay baby boys named Thomas who were born in the 1930s and 40s.

My first day at The Special was a little nerve-wracking, but everyone was really nice to me, and I had no problem pouring with a heavy hand, so the customers liked me. I was also fairly buff and thirty-two years old. Tips were good. Ed sat at the end of the bar to keep an eye on me, answer any questions that came up and make sure I was doing all right. At one point I held down a key on the cash register for a second too long and instead of the total coming up three-fifty, I had rung up three hundred and fifty dollars. When Ed saw the look on my face, he jumped up and came behind the bar.

"What do I do now?" I asked.

"Whenever something like this happens, first try to collect." He looked around the room and saw the regular who was waiting for his change of a ten and said, "Oh, *her*? She never carries around that kind of money, even after a good night on her favorite corner. Here, we'll just have to void that out, then."

It came time to wash some glasses, so I turned on the water to fill the three narrow sinks—one soap, one rinse water and one disinfectant. At The Eagle, the soap dispenser was built in, but not at the Special. Ed came back to show me where they kept the soap and how much to add. "I'm not worried about germs," he said. "That disinfectant will kill anything. But if you don't use soap, you'll never get the lipstick off."

Everyone cracked up. On that particular day, of course, there wasn't one tube of lipstick among them. I looked around at the room of early morning drinkers. Each of them would eventually reveal some of his history to me. They had all lived in San Francisco before my time, some of them knowing gay life in an era before I was even born.

Within a few days, I realized that I could almost make a dozen drinks at five forty-five every morning and set them up on the bar in the exact places I knew those regulars would soon be sitting. They owned those barstools for as long as they could last, many of them through my entire shift and well into the afternoon.

We had dozens of other regulars too. Some arrived at seven or eight or nine. Night shift workers from nearby hospitals flooded the Castro bars. The Special was also a popular place for other bartenders and bar owners to hang out when they weren't in their own bars, plus bar managers and cocktail waiters from all over the city, but especially from South of Market and the Castro.

After I got off work at noon, I counted out my till in the office and often joined my customers at the bar. I drank just as much as some of them did in those days. They liked to roll dice for drinks, sometimes for a round for the house. The bartender was expected to play and sometimes lose, but it kept a good crowd and added up in the till overall.

Tourists flooded in too. People found us just because we were in the middle of the first block of Castro Street, only doors from the Castro Theatre. We weren't a famous bar, not nearly as well-advertised as the Badlands or the Midnight Sun. Down on the corner was the Elephant Walk, immortalized when the police smashed windows and heads the night of the White Night Riots.

When I lived and played in the Castro in my twenties, The Special was still called The Nothing Special and I never went there—maybe once, on a dare, on a bar crawl with friends, determined to have a drink in every single bar in the neighborhood in one Sunday afternoon. There were only about twenty bars, so that was doable.

Looking back, I realize why so many bar people hung out there. Aside from the strong drinks, you could always score some cocaine. And right across the street was the Castro Station, where you could always buy some speed. They even had a live DJ, and Rita Rockett was the cocktail waitress. I always hated crystal meth, but I loved cocaine. It wasn't as long-lasting, which simply meant you had to keep doing more of it. I especially loved cocaine for sex, but it also made me crave cigarettes. The vast majority of the people I knew smoked cigarettes in those days, so we'd take lots of breaks during sex to have a smoke. As long as you were sitting up and you'd already wiped the lube off your hands to use the lighter, you might as well chop a couple more fat lines on the mirror.

Bars that opened at six a.m. had three shifts a day. At The Special, when the bartenders changed, so did the coke dealers. They just weren't quite as obvious about it. They overlapped a bit sometimes, or they'd get someone to fill in if they were out of town. Or they'd fill in for each other or even work doubles if someone needed time off. Their schedules were never written down anywhere, but their patterns were so predictable they might as well have been. I never dealt drugs, but I know lots of bartenders who "took care of" their customers.

During one of my first morning shifts at the Special, a customer everyone else recognized as one of the regulars came in. He had just gotten back from vacation and had apparently been missed people started buying him drinks right away. He sat down, opened a Walgreens bag and pulled out an envelope. "Look, everybody! You won't believe what I got. I went to pick up the pictures from my trip, but they must have got them mixed up with someone else's. Look at these guys!" The photographs were of several bodybuilders, maybe porn stars, most of them nude and posing or having sex. I didn't get a good look because everyone else was crowded around him.

I asked, "What about your vacation pictures? Don't you want them? These guys will be surprised to see shots of your trip when they're expecting these."

"Oh, you're right." He jumped up and put them back in the bag. "I've gotta take these to another Walgreens and have them make me a set of prints from the negatives, and then I'll go back and trade these in for the ones of my trip. They're nowhere near as exciting."

I never had sex with any of the "old-timers" who arrived at six a.m. every day, as much as I grew to love some of them. I thought about what it must have been like in their day, when they were my age. These guys were about the same age as my parents. When I was a kid, being gay just wasn't talked about. It was only hinted at if you were lucky enough to get to see certain "artistic" movies or maybe a Tennessee Williams play. When they were kids, being gay was not only considered sinful but in many places, people were jailed or put in mental hospitals. It's no wonder that so many gay men fled to cities like San Francisco and found bars where they belonged. The bars became their sanctuaries, an extension of their living rooms, a place to make friends in a hostile world, and a place to have fun, to really let go and laugh. That's why so many of that generation became alcoholics. The amazing thing about them was that most really knew "how" to drink. They knew how to drink and laugh and last all day.

And I learned a few things about drinking from them, even as AIDS was descending upon us. Drinking that hard and that regularly was serious business. You could start early in the morning, but you had to pace yourself, know just how much you could take. You had to learn how to time your food intake to have the energy to keep going, but not kill your buzz. The ability to drink and laugh in the face of what they had endured was vital to their survival. As AIDS began to take over the lives of my generation, vodka and cocaine became vital to my survival as well. We had to keep going. We had to drink, and we had to remember how to laugh. I also needed to get laid as often as possible.

Soon after I started working on Castro Street, Jane Dornacker told me she was moving to New York for the sake of her career, which was ready to take off in a big way. She and Whoopi Goldberg had done a two-woman show at the Victoria Theatre back when Whoopi was getting started. Jane was always generous in helping other comics. Whenever I booked her in San Francisco, she would ask me to call Marga Gomez, who was well on her way to becoming a beloved lesbian comedienne, and ask Marga to attend the show so that Jane could bring her on stage at some point. Jane also knew Robin Williams from the local comedy scene. She told me Robin and Whoopi convinced her to move to New York.

Jane's fame grew with her appearance as Nurse Murch in Philip Kaufman's 1983 blockbuster film *The Right Stuff* in which she instructed astronauts in how to provide a sperm sample: "The best results seem to be obtained by fantasization accompanied by masturbation followed by ejaculation."

Jane was one of many well-known comics to work in San Francisco's legendary comedy clubs like The Other Café and Valencia Rose. I'd seen pictures of her performing at the first Haight Street Fair back in the late 1970s and heard about her hosting the Grateful Dead's New Year's Eve shows with Father Guido Sarducci, but those events were before I knew her. Jane had also written songs for and toured with The Tubes and been the lead singer in a rock group called Leila and the Snakes.

She did everything from the dog show at 18th and Castro with Sharon McNight to emceeing the Miss Haight-Ashbury beauty Pageant.* In addition to performing her comedy act, Jane was doing the daily traffic report on KFRC Radio, making drive-time entertaining for commuters stuck in their cars.

The thought of her leaving San Francisco was hard for me. I knew I would miss her, but I was also happy for her. She already had a job lined up in Manhattan doing the helicopter radio traffic report. She had friends in New York with connections. I could easily imagine her as a regular on *Saturday Night Live* within a few months with more movie offers to come.

Jane's daughter, Naomi, was just finishing her senior year in high school, so she would stay with her dad, Jane's ex-husband Bob Knickerbocker, so that Naomi could graduate with the rest of her class. Now I was more determined than ever to get Jane more bookings on the West Coast. That way she could come out and stay with me and visit her daughter while she was in town.

I loved tending bar on Castro Street. It was fun, I was good at it and I made a lot of money doing it. It also seemed like something I wanted to do than something I had to do. The regulars genuinely loved and cared for each other, which is why gay men of that era often referred to their time at the local bar as "going to church." Like church, the bar was especially popular on Sundays, since it was crowded with Saturday night hangovers and all the people who had to work regular jobs during the week.

One Sunday morning my friend and fellow-Minnesotan David Sarathain came in during my first hour of business to tell me about his night at the Slot, one of the last of the sleazy bath houses on Folsom Street. His story was so funny that he soon had the full attention of all my other six a.m. customers.

The Miss Haight-Ashbury Pageant winner that year was Cobalt Blue, one of the Balloon Girls drag troupe, whose talent was mixing martinis for the judges. She did this by holding a three-foot-tall cocktail shaker while four musclemen picked her up and shook her.

The Balloon Girls were each named for the color they wore. There were at least six of them but I only remember the names of Tawny Gold and Cobalt Blue. They made a party out of their booth at the Folsom Street Fair and always had a contingent in the Gay Pride Parade. I loved when they hung out at (and in front of) the Special each year during the Castro Street Fair. That was where I first met Cobalt Blue. I eventually got to know a hot guy who hung out at the Eagle always dressed in full leather and discovered that he and Cobalt Blue were the same person.

David told me he'd passed out in someone's room. When he came to, the other guy had checked out. David was naked with nothing but his locker key on an elastic band around his ankle. He found his locker and inside it were his boots, leather jacket, car keys and wallet, but no pants. He pulled on his boots and zipped up his jacket, then turned in his locker key at the little window over the front desk. Then he ran bare-assed down Folsom Street to his car. It was still dark outside so nobody saw him, but daylight was just breaking. By the time he got back to his place in the Duboce Triangle, the sun was up and according to David, "everyone on my block was out walking their dog!" I'd been to David's house a couple of times. The front door was up a tall flight of outdoor stairs and to top it off, another car was blocking his driveway. By this time, everyone in the bar was howling at his predicament.

Every day at the Special, people told stories and I loved to hear them. Some, like David's, were current while others had been dredged up from years past. Some of the customers had been out and gay since before I was born and had stories they told again and again.

Chapter Fourteen

Most people know about the big annual gay events in San Francisco like Pride and Halloween, but before AIDS hit, there were lots of others. I had been aware of the Great Tricycle Race since I moved to San Francisco in 1975, but I'd never actually seen it. My first Memorial Day at the Special, I witnessed it firsthand because I was working. Each year, every gay bar in town was eligible to enter a team, which consisted of two people; one to steer and one to push. They could switch off whenever they wanted to and since only child-sized trikes were allowed, the one who steered usually had his legs up over the handlebars. Both contestants on each team were required to check in at every participating bar on that year's route, which meant signing their names to prove they had been there and also having a drink. The race started and ended at an old gay bar on Market Street called the Mint, which is located practically in the shadows of the San Francisco Mint where United States coins are made. The bar is still there, but in those days it was twice as big and had a full-service restaurant attached.

The gas station next door allowed the use of their grounds and parking lot for the crowds who would gather before and after the race, when the winners received prizes, not only for who came in first, second, and third, but for categories like "Best Decorated Tricycle," "Best Theme," and "Best Costume."

My friend and boss, Ed "Edwina Ballerina" Stark, the owner of the Special, usually won at least one of the prizes for creativity. He was always willing to throw on a wig and some make-up and have fun. One year he decorated the Special's trike to look like the Transamerica Pyramid. His racing partner was someone in an ape costume as King Kong, and Ed went in drag. I'm not sure whether he was aiming to be Fay Wray's Ann Darrow from 1933 or Jessica Lange's Dwan from the 1976 remake, but they had a great time and brought back the "Best Theme" trophy to display in the bar afterward.

The day I worked the tricycle race, we set out plastic cups at the front corner of the bar beside the sign-in sheet. I filled some with orange juice, some with cranberry and some with water. The runners who were serious could just scribble their names and toss down some juice and be on their way. Some merely grabbed a plastic cup of water and dumped it over their heads to cool off.

The ones who wanted to win were dressed in spandex and expensive athletic shoes. The less serious ones who were just out for fun, often in some kind of drag, came along later. They might even sit down and pant for a while, ask for a Coke on ice and take their time sipping it. Some ordered a shot of schnapps, maybe hoping that the sugar rush would help propel them to the next bar. The runners and tricycle riders who were vying for the costume prizes came in last. They were in no hurry, as long as they got back to the Mint by whatever time the prizes were awarded. They sat down and ordered real drinks, took their time enjoying them and if they smoked, had a cigarette too. I often had to remind those guys to sign in, or they would have forgotten.

The route varied each year. One year it would cover the Polk Street and Tenderloin gay bars. The next year it might include the bars around Church and Market Streets, the Pilsner, the Transfer, the Balcony, and a handful of the many bars near 18th and Castro. One of the last years the race began and ended on the Eagle patio and the route covered all the South of Market bars.

Ed liked to have the bar represented in everything from the tricycle race to *Men Behind Bars* to the Gay Parade, where one year he appeared in full ballerina drag *en pointe* on the top of his van while Roz drove him all the way down Market Street. Ed was always eager to sponsor a softball or bowling team or a contestant in the Closet Ball, no matter what the cost. These things were not only fun for everyone involved, but good advertising for the bar and probably tax-deductible as well.

The Special's anniversary party was always a big project. Each year had a theme, and Ed worked for weeks planning every detail of the food, décor, and entertainment. The one I remember best had an aquatic/underwater motif. The invitations announced that costumes were encouraged and promised food, an open bar, and an Esther Williams look-alike contest. I don't recall all the items on the main buffet, but the office doorway was turned into a seafood stand, and Ed hired someone to stand behind a table and shuck cases of raw oysters and clams all evening long.

He decorated by suspending a rowboat from the ceiling with artificial mosses and seaweed hanging down. Two hunky men on pedestals posed as underwater statuary wearing nothing but tiny flesh-colored G-strings with their bodies painted like *trompe l'oeil* marble. I believe one of them was Ray Perea, the winner of the first Mr. Drummer contest in 1981. We had worked together at the Woods Resort north of Guerneville when I lived at the Russian River, and Ray also worked at the Special at least part of the time I was there.

Of course, the highlight of the evening was the Esther Williams look-alike contest. Half a dozen drag queens paraded across the stage in wigs and one-piece women's bathing suits, but none of them stuck out as being especially original or exciting. Just then, my friend Jim Bayer —everyone's favorite cocaine dealer, including Ed's—arrived fashionably late, or as he called it "on CPT," which stood for "Colored People's Time," which was even a little later than "gay time." Jim was dressed, as usual, in jeans and a long-sleeved shirt under a down vest. Pulling him into the back room, Ed lit a handful of Fourth of July sparklers and stuck them in Jim's medium-length Afro and shoved him out onto the stage in a recreation of Esther Williams' scene from *Million Dollar Mermaid* where she emerged from underwater with a crown of lit sparklers on her head. Everyone recognized that moment from the movie. The crowd went wild, and Jim won the contest hands down. I'm sure he did a huge amount of business that night too.

Whenever a bar had an anniversary, the other bars sent flowers. There were so many bars, we couldn't find a place to put them all. The year of the underwater theme, Terry Thompson sent the biggest arrangement of all from the Eagle. I'm sure it was his lover Blair's idea. It was so huge, it had to go in the center of the back bar where it was the focal point of the room. The flowers were tall and tropical, and the vase was a clear glass fishbowl with live goldfish swimming between the stems.

Later that year, Ed loved my suggestion for an arrangement from the Special when the Eagle's anniversary came around. The flowers we sent were in a vase that was mounted on a platform covered in jars and tin cans full of pickled herring, tuna, sardines, and smoked clams and oysters. The gang at the Eagle loved it too.

One of my favorite customers at The Special was an older guy everyone called Juanita and we became great friends over those six a.m. bar conversations. I can still see his face when I opened the front door onto the darkness of Castro Street to start the day's bar business. He was at least six-four and his eyes were bleary, sagging—and only one of them worked. He held a cigarette in one corner of his mouth, which had nearly a full set of upper teeth but very few lowers. I'd say, "Good morning, Juanita!" as cheerily as I could, knowing he was in dire need of alcohol.

He would glower down at me and grumble in his deep Texas voice, "Fuck you in the ass! Get me a damned drink!"

Bill "Juanita" Wallace had moved out to San Francisco with a group of gay Texas boys back in the late 50s or early 60s. Most of them were tall and lanky, and I imagined that they all could have been cowboys if they'd wanted to remain in Texas and stay in the closet. Charlie "Fanny" Fulbright always dressed like one anyway. When H. Ross Perot ran for President in 1992, Fanny told us about spending childhood Saturday afternoons with him in the back row of the Princess Theater in Texarkana, Texas and we teased Fanny about how he might have become first lady.

Sam Houston was another regular, but he didn't have a campy girl's name, maybe because he just wasn't like any gay guy I knew from his generation. They were all in their 50s by the time

I met them, but Sam Houston was still really handsome and a total gentleman. He looked like a hero from the movies, a cross between Paul Newman and Sean Connery. Sam was "married" to a guy named Danny, so Sam wasn't available and hadn't been on the market for years. Danny was a likable guy, but I could never figure out how he snagged Sam. Danny reminded me of a movie star too, but someone more like Shirley Booth or Shelley Winters. He must have had qualities I couldn't see.

When I worked Sunday mornings from six a.m. to noon, I usually went out to brunch afterward at one of the dozens of gay restaurants with full bars and sometimes live entertainment. One trick I'd learned from the old-timers was that you needed to put some solid food in your stomach on top of all the morning drinks of screwdrivers and Bloody Marys. Sometimes I would meet up with friends at the Elephant Walk or the Galleon off Church Street. Sometimes I would say to Juanita, "Let's go eat something." I had my little old green Datsun pickup truck parked outside.

Juanita and I would usually head South of Market to eat at Lenny Mollet's Chez Mollet or Hamburger Mary's or a place farther north on Folsom Street with a country/western motif. I can't remember the name of it, but it had a nice patio where we could eat outside on sunny days. One morning Mother, the manager, overheard Juanita and me talking about going to brunch after I got off work. Mother looked at me in my tight Levi 501s and even tighter T-shirt and said, "You're going to brunch dressed like that?"

It was still only 11:15 or so. Mother flew out the door and came back a half hour later with shopping bags from Cliff's and Walgreens and the little antique store that was across the street next to Rossi's Deli. She said, "You can't go to a decent ladies' luncheon without being properly dressed!" Mother handed me a strand of fake pearls from one bag and a silver cigarette holder from another. I've forgotten what all else—white gloves, no doubt, and maybe a brooch. Even though Mother was just a tiny little old man, I was always intimidated enough by her that I put everything on for inspection before Juanita and I left the bar and got in my truck.

One evening I went out with Juanita. We had heard that a Sizzler restaurant had opened in the Tenderloin, and we were determined to find the place and have a big steak dinner. Juanita insisted that we stop at some of the bars he knew in that part of town on our way to eat. He knew the bars all right, and everyone in the bars knew him. It turned out Juanita had been a bartender and waiter in some notorious gay places that were long gone before my time in San Francisco. I heard stories about On the Levee and Off the Levee, and I think I even made it to Jackson's once. Juanita and I only made it to one bar that night, but I'm glad we did because I got to see the original Ginger's before it closed.

The owner was a guy named Don Rogers who was a big fan of Ginger Rogers or maybe she was his sister or maybe that was his drag name. At any rate, the bar had pictures of her all over the place. Later on there was a Ginger's Too on the sleaziest block of 6th Street just off Market. And Ginger's Trois was actually a nice little bar in the financial district. The last remaining gay bar in that part of town, it remained long after the legendary Sutter's Mill and Trinity Place had closed.

Juanita and I sat down at the long dark bar at Ginger's and ordered our vodka drinks. When the other customers discovered that Juanita was in the house, they started coming by to pay a visit, one or two at a time. Old fashioned gay bars are like that. If you're a regular customer, you get to know everyone. You could move away and come back on vacation a year later and everyone would flock around you and treat you like visiting royalty. Juanita wanted everyone to meet me, of course.

This was the bar I had heard about, where Rock Hudson used to hold court on Sunday mornings when he was in town, but I never knew quite where it was before. It had a long open staircase at one end with a beautiful, wide wooden banister that continued around a balcony at the top. I'd heard that there were racks of women's dresses and evening gowns in extra large sizes at the top of the stairs, along with a selection of high heels, mirrors, make-up, and jewelry. "Do you want to go up and look around?" Juanita asked me.

I declined. I believed him. As drunk as we were, I didn't want to climb any stairs, and I didn't want anyone getting ideas about dressing me up in drag. I'd had to do it for work a couple of times on Halloween, and I looked about as feminine as Bea Arthur. Juanita told me some men would have a few drinks at the bar to get up the nerve to climb the stairs and transform themselves into ravishing beauties, exotic creatures of the night. When their metamorphosis was complete, they would appear at the top of the stairs to riotous applause and then slide down the banister where a fresh drink would be waiting for them on the bar.

We stayed as long as we could, but we didn't see any transformations that night. An hour or so later, we each had seven or eight upside-down shot glasses lined up behind our drinks. Everyone who knew Juanita told the bartender to buy us another round. I told Juanita that we'd better go or the Sizzler might be closed by the time we staggered in. We couldn't finish all those drinks, but we tried.

I wish I had gone upstairs that night to have a look around at all those dresses hanging on their racks. Someone should have taken a picture of it. I only have a mental image of what I was told. The entire block where Ginger's once stood was torn down to make room for another luxury hotel or multi-storied parking lot in the dirty Tenderloin.

I don't remember our dinner at the Sizzler at all.

Chapter Fifteen

Even though the *Men Behind Bars* performances only ran over the course of one long weekend, Jim and I realized that each time one show closed, we had to start working on the next one. Jim worked at the Pilsner Inn on Church Street, "a little south of Market." That phrase was part of their logo for years since their location, between the Castro and Folsom Street, meant that they drew customers from both areas. When Jim was at work, the bar surface at the Pilsner was often covered with sheet music, costume sketches, set designs, contracts, and all sorts of paperwork. We did a lot of the plotting and planning and bounced ideas off of each other at that bar.

Somewhere along the line, we hit upon the idea that since we had produced a successful variety show in a theatre, we should try throwing a party where people could dance while we also gave them a show. The earliest gay dance parties I remembered were back in the 1970s when someone threw an evening called "Night Flight" at the Gay Community Center on Oak Street. One called "Stars" had everyone send in their pictures beforehand, so that all through the party the faces of the guests were projected on the walls around the dance floor.

I remember dancing with Sylvester at one called "Snow-Blind" in an old building on Mission Street where the heat from the dance floor condensed on huge windows and ran down the glass in rivulets like the sweat rolling down our half-naked bodies. Since then there had been Halloween and New Year's Eve dances at the Gift Center and the Galleria, plus a big gay dance party with Patti Labelle when the Moscone Convention Center opened. Jim and I were inspired by all of this history and wanted to build on tradition to create something new.

We also wanted to find a fresh location where a gay party had never been held before. The first two events we did outside the Victoria Theatre under the name *Men Behind Bars* Productions were on Pier 45, which was in the middle of Fisherman's Wharf. We called them *Pier Pressure*, and they were both in November, a year apart in 1984 and 1985. Our third dance party was the following June, and we called it "High Tea" because it was a Sunday afternoon tea dance. That one was at Fort Mason, the pier that looks out on the Golden Gate Bridge.

We did *Pier Pressure* on Saturday night in conjunction with the CMC Carnival that lasted all day Sunday. The California Motor Club had been holding its annual day of debauchery since long before I moved to San Francisco in 1975. There were several bike clubs in those years before AIDS: the Coits, the Warlocks, the GDIs (which stood for God Damned Independents), the Constantines, the Recons, the Centaurians, the Barbary Coasters, the Aquilas in the South Bay, and the Valley Knights in Sacramento.

One or two of them actually required their members to own motorcycles. Most of them went on annual bike runs, held holiday toy drives for children or sponsored turkey dinners on Thanksgiving or Christmas for the down-and-out, but the CMC also held a carnival, which was a huge money-maker. People flew in from all across the country to experience it. The CMC Carnival had the same raunchy spirit as the Folsom Street Fair, which came later, but it was indoors and ten times more outrageous.

The first time I ever went to a CMC Carnival was with John Preston at Seaman's Hall. I was twenty-three years old, and he would have been in his early thirties, still the editor of the *Advocate*, but not yet having written the tomes of S&M for which he would become famous. I lived with him on top of Potrero Hill, and he did his best to introduce me to the seedy side of gay San Francisco.

John and I were stoned, of course, mostly from smoking pot and drinking beer all afternoon as we wandered among the booths and cruised the other horny men at the carnival. When it was finally time to announce that year's winner of the title "Mr. CMC Carnival," John and I were crowded up against one side of the stage. The contestants entered by way of a catwalk over the crowd and lined up in front of us. John and I both had to piss like crazy and one of us—probably John—pointed to the big plastic garbage can beside us. We unbuttoned our Levi 501s and pissed in the trash, though we could have just gone on the concrete floor and nobody would have cared.

A few minutes later, we discovered that someone did care. A guy who was pressed up against the stage on the other side worked his way over to us as soon as the contest had ended. He started yelling at us that we should be ashamed of ourselves. I was a little frightened at first, but John just laughed at me and at him. The guy wasn't angry that we'd pissed in full view of everyone; he was angry that we'd wasted all that good clear beer piss. He'd wanted to drink it.

An entire floor was dedicated to sex, plus a glory hole stand with bed sheets stretched on frames with holes at crotch height and one-dollar blow jobs for charity. I heard about one of the guys working that booth who got so sick he was rushed to the hospital to have his stomach pumped. As soon as he was released, he jumped in a cab and raced back to the Carnival to reclaim his spot behind the sheet for one last hour.

The carnival was held in the old Seamen's Hall for several years, in the center of what was then a warehouse district south of Market in the shadow of the towering concrete and steel roadways leading onto the Bay Bridge. One year it moved to a taxicab parking garage across the street from the Bulldog Baths in the Tenderloin. No matter the venue, one level of the carnival was always a dark room for sex. They even hung sheets of black plastic over any windows to block out the light on a sunny day. The taxicab garage was made up of several stories connected by ramps. Upon arrival in my stoned state, it reminded me of the layout of the Guggenheim museum. Later on after the acid kicked in, I imagined that all the liquids that were spilled at that year's carnival—beer and urine, sweat and semen—were flowing down the ramps and out onto the street.

Another year it was held in California Hall on Polk Street, the site of a historic 1964 costume party fundraiser for the Council on Religion and the Homosexual. Despite its less than pithy name, the evening turned into one of the most famous pre-Stonewall confrontations between the police and the gay community. I have often wondered if the aspiring young chefs taking classes at the California Culinary Academy have any idea of some of the things that happened in the building where they are now standing. By the mid-80s when we were throwing these parties, the AIDS epidemic was in full swing, so the CMC Carnival was toned down considerably.

Cvitanich and Abramson inspect the piers

Thousands of people came to the *Pier Pressure* parties, and we made more money than I had ever seen in my life, most of it in cash. We ran free shuttle buses all night to pick up and drop off people at gay bars in the Castro, Polk Street, and South of Market. Asking me to remember all the details of those two nights would be like asking someone who has dropped acid a thousand times to explain the nuanced differences between their third trip and their sixty-fourth, but I do remember a few things.

I recall three black drag queens who had appeared in the first *Men Behind Bars* show as the Supremes. One of them was also San Francisco's first black Empress Connie, but the tall one, whose name I can't remember, looked an awful lot like Diana Ross. She had the shoulder movements down perfectly in her long red satin gloves. At some point in the evening of the first *Pier Pressure*, the three of them got onto a scissor lift in one corner of the huge dance floor. A fog machine kicked in beneath them, and a spotlight caught them as they rose from the crowd in a billowing cloud. We'd built them a little stage at the top that looked like it was hanging in the open air. These three brave drag queens in red shuffled out onto it, lip-synced to "Stop, In the Name of Love," and the crowd went wild!

I also remember dancing with Jim. We agreed before the party started that no matter where we were or what we were doing, when Kelly Marie's song "Feels Like I'm in Love" came on we would drop everything, find each other in the middle of the dance floor of our fabulous party and celebrate the success of what we had created.

At some point in the midst of *Pier Pressure*, about three a.m., the mirror balls stopped spinning, and the lights went out on the dance floor. A set of headlights switched on from a car parked behind the fence at the end of the pier. The gate opened, and the crowd parted to let the car drive slowly down the middle of the dance floor. It was my friend Jim Merron's 1947 Dodge convertible, pale blue with white interior and dripping in chrome.

He and his lover Ron—with whom I'd had a few wonderful three-ways at the river—were both in full leather in the front seat. Rita Rockett was perched up on the back seat in a prom dress and tiara with a dozen long-stemmed red roses in her lap. The DJ played Julie Brown's song "The Homecoming Queen's Got a Gun."

Rita pulled a big black toy machine gun out from under the roses and sprayed everyone with water. I wanted to fill it with poppers, but Jim thought that would be too dangerous. I had heard in the 1960s when everyone went from bar to bar in buses on Halloween, a group of drag queens called Zelda and the Pink Palace Girls won all the costume contests by spraying the judges with poppers from one of those old-fashioned sprayers that farmers use to keep the flies off of cattle. Zelda was still alive in those days and, as a man named Dick, he was a regular customer of Jim's at the Pilsner. Luckily, we didn't use poppers in that gun since it sprayed more in a stream than a mist.

Having Rita Rockett as part of our show for that first *Pier Pressure* was wonderful. Many in San Francisco's gay community knew Rita since the 1970s when she used to dance on the pool table at the Balcony on Market Street every Sunday morning at six a.m. Others knew her as a cocktail waitress at the Castro Station or from earlier, at the Palms on Polk Street where Sylvester used to perform and they became great friends.

Most remember Rita for the wonderful tradition she started. When one of her best friends was in the hospital with AIDS, Rita told him that instead of having him miss brunch on Easter Sunday, she would bring Easter Sunday brunch to him. Rita's friend died before Easter, but she still made enough food to feed all the other gay guys with AIDS on Ward 5-A at San Francisco General Hospital. She came back the next Sunday with brunch for the boys and then the Sunday after that as well. Rita not only brought food, but she cheered people up. She wore crazy outfits, and she tap-danced from room to room, cracking jokes and visiting with the patients, trying to get them to eat something, to keep up what little strength they had, getting to know their visiting families and comforting them as well. Rita's brunches became legendary.

For the *Pier Pressure* parties, someone loaned us a camper that we parked inside the pier but beyond the fence that marked the area that wasn't open to the public. It was fancy inside with a kitchen, a bathroom and a bed, if anyone needed to lie down. It was our on-site office and a good place to get away for a moment of sanity. Plus I made sure the bar was well-stocked. It also had a good-sized mirror on the table with short straws and straight-edged razors that saw plenty of cocaine that night. This was also a good place for people who needed to change clothes and served as a VIP lounge where we could invite our friends.

Pat Montclaire, one of San Francisco's drag legends for decades, arrived at *Pier Pressure* in a full length chinchilla coat that must have been worth thousands of dollars. I didn't want to hang that up on a wire hanger in the coat check in exchange for a numbered paper claim ticket, so I escorted Pat and her entourage to the camper where we had drinks and did a few lines. I don't remember what happened to that coat, and I can't imagine that anyone would have asked me to watch it, considering how much was going on and the shape I was in. Maybe Jim locked it up in a cupboard for her before she hit the dance floor. She had to be seen by everyone at the party, like visiting royalty, even though she wouldn't be crowned Empress for a few more years.

Just before sunrise, we stationed friends along the eastern wall of the pier to pull the big chains that rolled up the massive doors. The disco music stopped, and the disc jockey segued into a recording of a giant pipe organ playing classical music at top volume. As the doors reached the top, everyone turned and walked outside toward the early morning light and watched the sunrise under the tall silver towers of the Bay Bridge. They breathed the fresh air for a few minutes until the dance music came back on. Then they came back inside, and the doors closed so that the place was soon filled again with the smells of cigarette smoke and pot and amyl nitrate and sweat and beer. The organ concerto at sunrise was Jim's brilliant idea. I am just happy we were able to make that memorable moment happen.

At six a.m., we reopened the bars because we could legally start selling liquor again. I hired thirty-two bartenders for sixteen stations in three shifts. From two a.m. to six a.m., we could only sell juices, sodas, bottled water and coffee, so we didn't need as many bartenders during those hours. Surprisingly, it wasn't hard to line up guys—and a couple of women too—who would work those shifts. Jim and I knew all the hottest gay bartenders in town, and they knew they would all have fun working together at one event. I know of a few bartenders that hooked up with each other when they were done. Several of the evening workers volunteered to stay and party from two a.m. to six a.m., then work another shift in the morning. They knew exactly how much and what kind of drugs to take to pull that off professionally because many of them had been doing it for years.

Pier Pressure was on Saturday night both years, so we just kept the music going into Sunday morning, and the CMC took over from there. We didn't see any sense in chasing people out only to have them come back again. I don't remember exactly how we arranged the changeover of the staff or dividing the take from the gate, but I would have remembered if there had been a problem. It must have gone smoothly.

I do remember Sunday morning, having been there all night, standing in the midst of what was now the CMC Carnival in the same clothes I'd put on when I left home the day before. I was drinking coffee with cream from a Styrofoam cup and someone introduced me, as one of the producers of the event, to State Senator Milton Marks. "Uncle Miltie," as we affectionately called him, and his wife had always been great supporters of gay rights. They appeared together in the Gay Pride Parade every year, but instead of riding on the back of a fancy car, they walked the entire parade route down Market Street, smiling and waving to the crowds. Senator Marks reached to shake my hand and accidentally hit my Styrofoam coffee cup. He apologized profusely, but I was so stoned that the coffee felt really good running down my chest and soaking through my sweaty t-shirt. I didn't admit to that, of course. I was shocked that he was even there.

The second year of *Pier Pressure*, Jim and I wanted to give our party more of a carnival atmosphere than ever. We thought it would be fun to bring in a carnival ride to run all night and let people go on it for free, so we rented a Tilt-A-Whirl and had it installed on one end of the dance floor. We rented a bunch of carnival games, too. People could test their skill or strength or aim or luck and win stuffed bears or silly prizes. We also wanted to have blackjack tables for illegal gambling, but we knew that was pushing our luck.

The permit process just to get the Tilt-A-Whirl approved was hard enough. We'd already had several meetings with the Port Authority about renting the space, paying for electricity, security, insurance, sewage, and water. Every item on their list seemed to need a separate permit, and each permit had to be signed by three different people whose offices were on opposite sides of the city. When we told them we wanted a Tilt-A-Whirl, they went nuts! We had to bring them a blueprint of the ride with every detail of its dimension, weight, horsepower, and capacity. Then a fastidious little lady in a gray suit wasn't sure if the port was strong enough to withstand the vibration of the ride in conjunction with its weight. She thought that major seismic testing might be necessary. Jim and I couldn't believe it. I said to the panel, "What does a ship weigh? Weren't these piers built to withstand several tons of ships loaded with tons of cargo banging up against them year in and year out for decades? Do you really think a Tilt-A-Whirl is going to bring them down?" One of the men on the panel saw my point and went on to the next item on their agenda.

Our meeting with the police department didn't go nearly as well. Four of us went to Police Chief Frank Jordan's office at two p.m. on a Thursday afternoon. Jim and I represented MBB Productions and two guys from the CMC were there.

I know that one of them was David Sarathain, a friend and fellow Minnesotan. He'd told me that his mother managed the Laundromat at Chicago and Lake Streets in Minneapolis. I'd spent many Saturday afternoons doing my laundry there when I lived with John Preston in the gay commune nearby.

What we hadn't known at the police chief's meeting was that a regulation required there to be one fully armed policeman for each of us. Four big guys in SFPD uniforms escorted the four of us in to ask Frank Jordan how we could go about setting up illegal gambling tables at our parties without getting busted. We'd heard that they did it all the time for the Junior League or the Opera Guild or whatever. If society ladies in gloves and pearls could play cards for money, why couldn't a couple of thousand gay men in leather and Levis?

Chief Jordan was not moved. He told us that the ladies who played cards for cash at charity events were attending private parties. If not private, they were only playing for tokens or for tickets to win door prizes or something. The answer was no.

My other memories of that party weekend are sketchy. Susan Fahey, one of the lesbian bartenders from the singing group The Pussies, took me to her apartment at some point in the middle of the night or early morning and drew me a hot bath where I could soak and come down from whatever drugs I was doing. She also let me use her phone to call Jane Dornacker in New York. I was used to talking to Jane in the middle of the night when I was stoned out of my mind, so that must have been comforting.

I also remember the cash. It must have been Monday morning after the party weekend when I went down to the Special to sort out the money. We'd stashed several zippered bags from the door and bags of money from the sixteen bar stations in the safe at some point. Neither of us wanted to be responsible for taking it to our homes, and someone was at the bar twenty-four hours a day.

After Mother had finished her office work, I went in and sat down at the desk with tens of thousands of dollars, mostly in twenties and ones, fives and tens, but with loose change as well. I started adding up the money from each cash register separately—minus the opening banks—and comparing them with the totals on the register tapes. I rolled all the quarters and faced all the bills the same direction, bundled them with paper clips and rubber bands. I did two or three bags of money like this before I stopped to think about what I was doing. I had no reason to do all this work. Jim would have tried to match the money with the registers, but he had either gone home to crash for a few days or continued partying at one of the bath houses.

Even if the tapes didn't match the totals, what would we do about it? The bartenders we'd hired to work the party were all friends of ours. Even if they were wildly off, the party was over. We couldn't fire them. I couldn't picture either Jim or me confronting any of them about it. Besides, the bags weren't marked. We didn't know who had worked which of these banks. I just dumped everything out of the desk and kept counting, wrapping coins, and bundling bills. It was nearly noon by the time I totaled everything, filled out a deposit slip, chopped and snorted a couple of lines of cocaine from the office desk, and got ready to head for the bank.

I stumbled out the front door of the Special into daylight, bleary-eyed and wasted, with fat zipped fake-leather bags of money under each arm. Officer Ray Benson, one of San Francisco's gay policemen, just happened to be on the beat and saw me coming. He started to tell me that he'd heard how great the party was, but he'd had to work. Then he looked at me again and realized what was going on. He said, "That's all the cash from the party, right? I think I'd better give you a police escort to the bank."

Bank of America was just across the street on the corner of Market and Castro. Ray made sure I got all the way inside and safely up to a merchant teller's window. Sometimes the cops *are* around right when you need them.

Chapter Sixteen

When Jim Cvitanich and I were in sync, it was almost all about the work, the creativity, the next show, the next party, the next fundraiser. Even when we were doing something just for fun, we were making plans. In the winter of 1985, after the first *Pier Pressure* party and our second successful *Men Behind Bars* show, an old friend of Jim's died of AIDS and left him some money. He had always wanted an old convertible. In those days before the Internet, he had to search hard, but he finally found his dream car, a '62 Thunderbird, in Michigan. Jim offered to pay my one-way airfare and all expenses if I would help him drive it back to San Francisco. I flew on ahead to visit old friends in Minneapolis and met Jim a couple of days later at the airport, where we boarded a much smaller plane to a much smaller city where we rented a car. We were on the road for at least another hour because we got lost a couple of times trying to find the farmhouse of the middle-aged couple who were selling the car.

I had forgotten how early the sun sets in the winter time, especially in the northern states. And it was snowing. We had already decided that Jim would pick up the car and follow me back to return the rental, then we would continue in the Thunderbird as far as Chicago where we would spend our first night on the road.

By the time we arrived, the couple was about to sit down to dinner, and they insisted that we join them. I just wanted to get the car and get going, but first we were subjected to a meal without wine or cocktails, during which I felt like we were being interviewed to see if we qualified to take their daughter to the movies. It might have been interesting if they'd had a hot son, but I didn't see any family pictures on the walls, only President Ronald Reagan and Jesus.

We finally got on our way and reached Chicago before midnight. I'd been there the previous Memorial Day weekend when I was a judge at the International Mr. Leather Contest and stayed in a nice hotel full of sexy men. Jim found us a fleabag on the north side with drunks howling outside the windows and narrow twin beds with lumpy mattresses and threadbare sheets. I slept in my clothes out of fear of bedbugs or any other vermin. The next morning we stopped at McDonald's for breakfast. Some said that Jim's biggest flaw was his ego, but he was also pretty cheap. He thought nothing of spending a couple of grand on a gown for a show, but his favorite place to eat was McDonald's. To this day, the rare times I find myself in any McDonald's the smell still reminds me of Jim Cvitanich.

We stopped for gas before we left Chicago, and I bought a red spiral notebook to write in. We had already started talking on the plane the day before about our next project. We had the seeds of some kind of show in mind in addition to *Men Behind Bars*. We took turns driving, so whoever was in the passenger seat was responsible for taking notes as we bounced ideas off of each other. It was a fun way to pass the hours and the miles.

We decided we wanted to do a long-running show, like Steve Silver's *Beach Blanket Babylon* in North Beach, but ours would be much more gay and subversive. We wanted it to be scandalous and underground. When we got home, we even looked at a space that was literally underground, on the corner of 9th and Howard Streets, south of Market, which would later become Asia SF, the restaurant where the waitresses are Asian drag queens who also perform. We wanted a smaller cast than *Men Behind Bars*, maybe eight or ten people playing different roles. We wanted live music—not a full pit orchestra, but at least a trio. We agreed right away that we would use Gail Wilson in our show, and that we would call it Fiasco.

The next day we drove as far as Kansas City, where we spent the night in a huge motel at the side of a parking lot. The motel had a restaurant attached where we discovered that all the other guests were in town for a big farm machinery convention. Jim and I seemed to be the only two people at the motel without bib overalls and a cap with the John Deere logo on the visor. I somehow knew I wasn't getting laid that night. We ate dinner at a Denny's, which was a step up, and that night something went wrong with the electrical system on Jim's new used car. It was too cold to put the top down, but we could no longer open the trunk. That meant we couldn't lock up our belongings when we got out of the car. We had to take everything inside with us. We couldn't leave anything on the seats and lock the doors for fear of someone cutting the rag-top roof, but Jim was happiest with drive-through restaurants anyway.

The next day we thought about Tim Garner, who had played Mayor Dianne Feinstein in our last MBB show. We could use Dianne again, and Tim could also play the part of Steve Perkins. He was a "sex-worker" with a long-running notice in the back of the *B.A.R.* advertising that he gave enemas. His picture was posted in the ad, so we recognized him when he was out and about in the Castro. I never saw him hanging out in a bar, but he shopped in the neighborhood, and I noticed him sometimes on the sidewalk. He was very thin, not someone I would expect to be a hustler, but I imagine having a specialty helped.

Jim wrote as I drove and thought of how to rewrite the lyrics to well-known show tunes. One of the first big production numbers we conceived had Tim Garner as Steve Perkins singing a song called "High Colonics" backed by a chorus line of dancing douche bags or maybe all the other cast members dressed as nurses carrying hoses.

We spent the night in Denver at a big gay bathhouse. While most people checking into the baths might carry a backpack, at most, we had to carry all our luggage inside since we couldn't lock anything up in the car. I felt awkward, but at least Jim paid for a private room for each of us. I'm sure that night cost him a lot more than the rat hole in Chicago or the Kansas City Motel. The place had a waterfall and a grotto of pools where everyone swam around naked. At least I finally got my rocks off that night, but it was hard to sleep on the hard pad of a mattress and no top sheet combined with the pulsating bass of the loud house music pounding all night long.

Leaving Denver in the morning, we were hit with a huge snowstorm. I was glad I was driving at the time. Having grown up in Minnesota, I trusted my ability to navigate the icy roads more than that of a California boy. He was still busy writing down ideas for *Fiasco* in our notebook. We decided that we'd ask for help with writing our show from Tom Ammiano, a former teacher turned comic who later became a politician. We would get Wayne Love as our musical director. He did all the musical arrangements for the big band City Swing, which became our pit orchestra for MBB. We wanted to make it topical and keep it fresh, the way *Beach Blanket Babylon* has characters from the news pop into their show. Instead of Hollywood celebrities, we would use gay ones, or at least gay icons.

As we neared Salt Lake City, Jim was furiously writing everything down, and we were both laughing. I was driving just above the speed limit in the far left lane in heavy traffic when I noticed that the lights on the dash suddenly lit up, and the speedometer needle fell. I didn't mention it to Jim for fear of him freaking out, which would only make me more nervous about getting the car off the road. The engine was dead, but I was going fast enough that I managed to get all the way across four lanes of traffic and onto the shoulder. Jim was still writing until I tapped on the brakes, and he looked up to see what was going on.

The first thing that came to my mind to say was, "Isn't Utah a dry state? I refuse to spend the night here if I can't get a drink after this!" We were just out of gas. We walked along the shoulder half a mile to the next exit, found a gas station and were on our way again before dark.

We spent that night in Reno at the MGM Grand. Jim had gotten us a discount room because it was a weeknight. This was the home of the legendary show called "Hello Hollywood, Hello!" with its one-acre stage, three-story waterfall, a recreation of the San Francisco earthquake of 1906 and a 737 jet that lands on stage with scantily clad girls dancing on the wings. There was no performance that night, but Jim and I were excited just to be in the presence of such showmanship. We managed to find an open door so that we could at least peek in at the darkened house filled with endless rows of empty seats.

I was driving again when we reached the California border the next day. Two handsome men in uniform at the Truckee agricultural checkpoint wanted to know if we were carrying any plant life, raw fruits or vegetables. I said no, and he asked me to open the trunk, so I said, "There's nothing back there but a case of overripe peaches, and they're probably rotten by now because something went wrong with the electrical system in this car my friend bought in Michigan. We haven't been able to open the trunk since about Chicago." They didn't laugh. One of the inspectors forced a smile as he looked back at the line of cars and trucks and campers behind us and told me to move along.

Fiasco never happened. We did meet with Tom Ammiano at his home in Bernal Heights. I don't remember his thoughts about the show at all. What I remember about that day is that his lover Tim, an early casualty of the AIDS epidemic, was still alive and we got to meet him. Tim was a teacher and Tom was still involved in the politics surrounding gay teachers, even though the Briggs Initiative, which attempted to ban gay teachers from working in public schools, had been defeated several years earlier, in large part due to the efforts of Harvey Milk.

Jim and I went to Wayne Love's apartment one evening to make our pitch about wanting him to be our musical director. I remember both of us laughing on our way to sit down in Wayne's living room. We must have been giddy with excitement about our show. Or it could have been cocktails. Or both. Wayne wasn't interested. He shot down every single suggestion we made. We brought out our notebook filled with brilliant ideas for skits, dance numbers, special effects, and rewritten lyrics to songs that would become anthems when sung by the characters of the gay celebrities our actors portrayed. We thought we were so clever and funny, and Wayne could say nothing but no. He was already gearing up for the next *Men Behind Bars*.

Jim and I left our meeting with Wayne so deflated that we

didn't mention *Fiasco* again for a long time. By the time one of us brought it up again, *Fiasco* had moved down a long list of other projects that we wanted to pursue.

Chapter Seventeen

I've been trying to remember the first time I ever put on a condom. Back in the 1970s, I met one of my neighbors in the Castro, and it was lust at first sight. Even though one of us had the clap, sex would not be delayed. We drove over to 20th and Valencia because the only place we knew to find a condom was the vending machine in the men's room at the Mexican restaurant, La Rondalla.

A few years later, my friend James Moore, a wonderful artist, became one of the original Sisters of Perpetual Indulgence. The Sisters printed up a safe-sex flyer called "Fair Play" that they handed out at the Gay Parade in 1982. Free condoms seem to have been readily available in all the gay bars ever since.

The first time I remember using a condom post-AIDS was during Fleet Week in 1985. I am not sure why they call it that, since it's more like a long weekend. Weather permitting, The Blue Angels practice on Thursday and Friday for their air shows on Saturday and Sunday, so we get four afternoons of window-rattling noise to set everyone's nerves on edge. When Dianne Feinstein was mayor, she was a huge supporter of Fleet Week and even went for a topsy-turvy upside down ride in one of those supersonic jets.

For me, the best part of Fleet Week is on Saturday morning when naval ships from all over the world sail under the Golden Gate Bridge and into the bay in one long procession with crews of sailors in uniform standing outside on the decks. During the event, fireboats shoot huge streams of water while low-flying antique airplanes fill the skies. I've only actually made it down to the waterfront twice in my life to see this spectacle. The crowds are horrific. Parking is even worse than normal at Fisherman's Wharf. Public transit is overburdened and a nightmare. Most of the locals know better and watch from distant hilltops.

Throughout the weekend, we had fun watching sailors from

various countries wandering throughout the city in their matching uniforms, up and down Market Street, Haight Street, Union Square and North Beach. I've worked in gay bars where we've put signs in the windows that say "SAILORS WELCOME!," but I don't think they did much good.

The Eagle never put any kind of sign in the window, but its address must have been listed in all the gay guides. I was tending bar on the Monday night after Fleet Week weekend when a group of five American sailors came in, dressed in their crisp white uniforms like something from an old movie musical or maybe a porn film. They stood in the corner for a moment to get their bearings, then one of them walked up to the bar, set his hat down and very politely asked for five bottles of Budweiser. I lifted his hat off the bar and plopped it onto my head. I looked deep into his big blue eyes and said, "Cute! Where'd you guys rent the sailor suits for Fleet Week? Yours looks really good on you."

He said, "No, they're real. They're ours. We're all from the same ship." He gave me the name of it, but I don't remember. He pulled out his military photo ID to prove it. I beckoned the rest of them over so that I could check theirs too. They were all old enough to be in the bar, but just barely, so I popped the tops off of five beers, rang up the money and the sailors moved back toward the dark corner where they started. The one who'd ordered the beers returned. His name was Donny. He told me he needed his hat in order to be in full uniform to get back on the ship.

I told him, "Don't worry. You'll get your hat back in the morning." I don't know what made me so brazen, but we held eye contact this time until he grinned. Donny and the rest of the sailors had a couple more beers and loosened up enough to play pinball and shoot some pool, but they didn't interact much with the rest of the late-night SoMa crowd. When I called "last call," everyone gradually left except Donny. He sat down on a stool at the end of the bar and kept me company while I counted out my tips and register and stocked the liquor and beer. He told me it was his first time in San Francisco. He grew up on a farm in Indiana and had never really been anywhere. He'd joined the

Navy to see the rest of the world. I told him I grew up on a farm in Minnesota, so I knew what it was like to feel landlocked, especially during my horny teenage years.

Donny hopped in my truck, and we were back in my bedroom on McCoppin Street in no time. I took his hat off my head, twirled it on my fingertip and told him, "Get undressed. Take off your uniform…shoes and socks…everything. When you're naked, you can put your hat back on. I want to fuck you in it." Once we were both naked, except for his hat, I lifted his long, lean legs over his head and bent his knees. Then I knelt down and buried my face in the sweet boyish scent of his flesh. I could almost smell the rich Midwestern farmland where we were both raised. My tongue licked the moist, salty taste that my sailor had brought from the sea. Though I wasn't diagnosed as HIV positive until three years later in 1988, I always figured I might be, so I put on a condom that night just before I slid inside him. He was too pure, too precious to take any chances, his skin smooth and soft as a peach, as pale as the color of fresh cream.

In the morning, he told me what a thrill it had been to stand on the deck of the ship with his buddies as they sailed in under the Golden Gate Bridge and followed the coastline of the Bay while thousands of people cheered from the shore. This happened years before "Don't Ask, Don't Tell," but Donny said he and his friends who'd been at the Eagle the night before were fairly open about being gay, and they knew lots of others. He said it was really no big deal in the Navy at the time. I wondered if all was as hunky-dory as he claimed, but I had no reason to doubt him.

I had an idea. "How would you like to drive over the Golden Gate Bridge before you leave?"

"Sure!" he said. We got back in my truck, and I took him across the bridge to Sausalito. We drove up to the Alta Mira Hotel for brunch overlooking the Bay with the city of San Francisco sparkling above the water in the distance. Donny looked stunning in his white sailor suit while I was in my usual boots and blue jeans and a scruffy leather jacket. After brunch, I drove him back to the pier where his ship was docked. We had a long kiss good-bye, and he walked away, waving to me with his white sailor hat. I went home for a nap before I got ready to go back to work at the Eagle that night.

Chapter Eighteen

In December of 1985, Jim Cvitanich and I got tickets to the *Dance-Along Nutcracker* at the Gift Center Pavilion. The LGBT Freedom Day Band does this show as an annual Christmas-time fundraiser with a different theme each year, and it's always a big hit with kids of all ages. City Swing, an eighteen-piece offshoot of the marching band, was also performing that night with their new lead singer Gail Wilson.

We were looking for a guest star for our next *Men Behind Bars* show, and we wanted to hear her with the band. I knew Gail from her performances as a solo cabaret singer. We had booked her at the Woods, but she didn't remember me and Jim had only heard of her. One of the songs she sang that night was the Eartha Kitt classic "Santa Baby," and she performed it perfectly. She had just the right combination of voluptuousness, good humor, and sex appeal with an apparent willingness to get down and dirty. Jim went home after the concert that night, but I went backstage.

Jose Sarria had been part of the show that night too. Jose is also known as the Widow Norton, one of San Francisco's earliest gay heroes in the ranks of Harvey Milk and going back even further. He became the first openly gay candidate for public office in the United States when he ran for the San Francisco Board of Supervisors in 1961. He also performed in drag at the Black Cat night club in North Beach until it closed in 1964 and was the first Empress of San Francisco. He founded the Royal Court system in 1965, which has since grown to more than seventy chapters in the United States, Canada and Mexico.

When I stuck my head in to say hello to Jose, I discovered that he and Gail were sharing a dressing room. I told Gail that we loved her performance and wanted her for our bartenders' variety show on Presidents' Day weekend. I don't know what her first thoughts might have been, but we exchanged phone numbers and addresses and discovered that we only lived a block apart.

That night I offered her a ride home in my old beat-up green Datsun pickup truck. On the way there, I took her to the drive-thru Burger King on Van Ness Avenue. It might have been the Whopper and jumbo fries that sealed the deal.

Soon after, Jim, Gail, and I got together and decided that she would do a novelty number in the first act, a big production number in the second act, and that she would have a featured role in the finale. Her first appearance was with four bare-chested muscle boys in red fire hats and suspenders who danced and sang back-up to a sort of rap-song she wrote about firemen. The lyrics had a lot of double entendres about firemen's poles and hoses and partway through the song, a gorgeous muscleman came out carrying a fire hose and nozzle while she sang, "I'm a hot tomato for your information and I wanna be the queen of the fire station!"

That was also the first time we had an all-female act in the show. We included the singing group of lesbian bartenders from Amelia's and Maude's who called themselves "The Pussies." We put together a medley of songs from *West Side Story*, and rewrote the words for their number we called "West Side Pussies." Any lack of talent or professionalism was easily made up by their enthusiasm, and the audiences loved them every time they hit the stage.

During Patrick Toner's year as International Mr. Leather, he not only performed in *Men Behind Bars* and started the "Up Your Alley" Street Fair but he also threw a party on January 31, 1986, near the end of his IML reign, called the *Military Ball*. It was a fundraiser for Rita Rockett's brunches at the AIDS ward at San Francisco General. He held the *Military Ball* in a warehouse south of Market, and I still have the dog tag on a chain that was my admission ticket. I remember little about that night aside from getting very loaded and running into Sharon McNight at the party. She told me she was up from Los Angeles especially to do our show that she'd heard so much about, *Men Behind Bars*. This was news to Jim and me.

I'd known Sharon since my time at the Russian River. I

don't know anyone who has performed in more benefits or been more willing to donate her talent for good causes than Sharon McKnight. That night at Patrick's party, however, she pissed me off. I told her that Gail was our guest star this year, and she'd been working her ass off rehearsing with the boys for weeks. "And besides," I told Sharon, "I asked you to be in the show last year. Remember when I saw you at the memorial gathering at Harvey Milk Plaza when Rock Hudson died? I told you all about the show and invited you then, but you never got back to me."

She said, "Well, I'm here now to do whatever I can to help. I'll just sweep the stage every time the curtain goes down if that's all you can find for me to do."

As I remember, I thought about making some choice and regrettable remarks about brooms and broomsticks. The next day when I sobered up and remembered our conversation, I felt foolish. Sharon McNight has long been a very big name in San Francisco entertainment. She's released several albums and done one-woman stage shows. Three years later she would receive a Tony nomination for best actress in a musical on Broadway for the leading role in *Starmites*.

The day after our conversation at Patrick's party, I called Sharon and told her that I thought we could use her in the show after all. "You can do some stand-up comedy shtick in the first half and then introduce the country/western dance group called, 'Winchester.' We'll work you into the end of the second act, give you one verse of 'Anything Goes,' and then you'll be onstage for the final bows." She was game, but I wasn't finished. "BUT you have to enter tap dancing in a gorilla suit, and you will NOT upstage Gail Wilson! I know how you are."

We held most of our rehearsals that year on the second floor of Amelia's, a lesbian bar on Valencia Street. The gay-run Community Thrift store across the alley loaned us a ladder that the boys used to carry Gail off the stage at the end of her "Fireman" song. The first night we worked with the gorilla suit was also the first night that Sharon McNight came to rehearsal. She arrived at the top of the stairs at Amelia's, and the ape costume was spread out over a couple of chairs with the head perched on top. Ed Stark, my boss at the Special on Castro Street, saw her first and he piped up, "Sharon McNight! I hear you get to wear the fur this year!"

She was, of course, only one of three performers to wear "the fur" that year and, as the shortest of the three, Sharon must have been drowning in that costume. I was surprised that she didn't turn around and go right back downstairs to the bar or flee into the night.

One of the things I loved most about *Men Behind Bars* was that each time we did it, the experience brought together so many diverse people from every part of the community who otherwise might not have met. Friendships were made, and some long-term relationships grew from the seeds of those meetings. Singers and ballet dancers, drag queens and gym queens, comics and tap dancers, the Barbary Coast Cloggers and muscled male strippers were all crammed together back stage. Most years, the cast numbered well over a hundred, not counting the crew. The weeks of rehearsals felt almost like summer camp in wintertime. People rehearsed their numbers in various groupings, but the long weekend of the show was really the first time the entire cast was finally all together.

That was the year that Alan Greenspan, the man who makes the gigantic mechanical hats for *Beach Blanket Babylon*, created a hat for Mister Marcus to wear in the first act finale lip-syncing "Downtown" in drag as Mrs. Miller. The hat was a collection of buildings with the names of all the remaining bath houses and after-hours sex clubs. At one point in the song, the hat lit up and at another cue, the roofs of the buildings popped open and live doves flew out of them. I found a local magician who used trained doves in his act. We rented his doves for the long weekend and hired him to train them to fly from Marcus's hat to the top of the balcony at the end of the first act. That way we had all of intermission to find and retrieve them. It never worked. The doves hopped out and flew around the stage. Some of them flew out over the audience a bit, but none of them made it anyway near the balcony. The funniest shows were when a couple of them hopped down onto Marcus' shoulders and pecked at him.

Charles Batte is a brilliant designer who created several props and set pieces for our shows. He worked for the San Francisco Opera at the time, so he must have had something to do with their donation to us of over two hundred yards of gold lamé fabric. That year's show also featured what Jim and I called the big girls—bears in drag—most of whom really were bartenders. Jim took one look at all that fabric and came up with the idea to do an opera parody called "The Revenge of the Valkyries," starring the big girls doing lip-sync as "The Greater Ukiah Opera Company."

Jim was a total opera freak, so he took the reins on creating that number. My only responsibility in that part of the production came at the end when the curtain was lowered. Monte Reddick was the biggest of the big girls. He must have weighed at least three hundred pounds, so we decided to fly him up out of sight in a harness at the end of the production. We planned it so I would stand in the stage right wings and be ready for the song to end. When the curtain fell, the work lights came up and the guys in the fly loft lowered Monte to the stage where I ran out and released him from the harness. It was a fairly quick set change, and then we were on to the next number.

Everything went fine in dress rehearsal, but whoever fastened Monte into the contraption on opening night turned the nuts and bolts so tight that I couldn't get them loose with my bare fingers. I needed a wrench and everyone else on the stage crew was busy moving set pieces around. When the curtain went up again, the only solution was to pull Monte as far upstage and to the right as possible. The only way to get enough slack was for Monte and me to climb up on a ladder. Then I grabbed the right rear teaser curtain and pulled it in front of us. It was such an awkward position that Monte and I had a tough time not laughing out loud through the next number until someone finally handed me a pair of pliers.

In the second act, Gail Wilson performed "Hot Voodoo," Marlene Dietrich's big number in the 1932 film *Blonde Venus*. This time, Gail entered from the back of the audience dressed in the gorilla suit, surrounded by the Follies Men wearing loincloths and carrying spears. While they worked their way up the aisles of the theatre, a kid named Joey came out on stage dressed in nothing but billowing, almost transparent harem pants and did a belly dance.

A couple of days before the show opened, Joey showed up at the theatre. He told us he was a bar back at a gay bar in San Jose, and he wanted to be in the show. We asked him what he could do, and he said he could sing. He could dance. He could do anything we wanted. I told him we'd already set and rehearsed all the song and dance numbers and asked if he had any specialties. He told us he could roller skate, and he could belly dance. He could not only belly dance, but he did so with an enormous tray of lit candles balanced on top of his head. We also used him in another number where he came out in a poodle skirt and a cotton candy pink wig on roller skates. He was awesome!

Working with Gail Wilson was wonderful, because she came with her own costume designer, Kirk Ramsey. He and Gail had been close friends for years. Kirk worked for Bob Mackie in L.A. at the time, so some of Gail's most glamorous gowns were made in Mackie's costume shop. Bob Mackie was responsible for designing some of the most fabulous clothing worn by superstars like Cher, Whitney Houston, and Diana Ross. The outfit Gail had on under the gorilla suit was unfortunately not one of them.

When Gail finally reached center stage, she removed the ape hands first to reveal her own long red fingernails before taking off the furry head with a flourish. Gail has always worn her hair very short and dyed a color never seen in nature, somewhere between red and purple and orange. She let the oversized gorilla suit drop to the floor and stepped out of it wearing a white dress with long silver tassels all the way around it from the neck to the hem of the short-short skirt. I teased her and called it her "mirror ball dress," but Gail was nothing if not a good sport.

Gail Wilson in the gorilla suit with the Follies Men ready to enter from the rear of the house

In that year's show, cast member Tim Garner returned as Mayor Dianne Feinstein in drag and sang a number to the tune of "Hernando's Hideaway," referring to her new mansion in Pacific Heights as "The Mayor's Hideaway." We kept the jungle theme going through to the end of the show by having Tim wear a giant bone like a bow tie instead of the traditional Feinstein bow. We then had a big muscled fireman from Gail's first act appearance put on the gorilla suit and carry Tim out in his arms while singing the opening chorus of "Anything Goes."

The show curtain rose, and the cast began coming out for bows. Each solo act or pair or group came to the front of the stage for applause and then stood along the stage aprons until the enormous cast was gathered in one place. When the music and applause died down, Gail introduced Jim and me. We came out to make curtain speeches thanking everyone in the world from our first grade teachers to the governor. We were overwhelmed and ridiculous.

But I still had one more treat in store for the audience—Jose, the Widow Norton, who had been suspended in the fly loft for at least a half hour. I ended my curtain speech by something like, "…but it wouldn't be gay or San Francisco without…Jose," at which time City Swing in the orchestra pit started playing, and Jose was lowered into view on a swing while singing the opening verse of that old Jeanette MacDonald classic about a tiny corner of this great big world and then the entire cast and audience joined in on the chorus of "San Francisco."

The Victoria Theatre is an old vaudeville house and was never meant to house the size of extravaganzas we produced. In the far corner upstage left is a steep stairway that is really little more than a ladder leading down to the low-ceilinged hallway and four small dressing rooms. Downstage left is a door that leads to a tiny alley between the theatre and the building next door. The rusty fire escapes in that alley are coated in pigeon shit, but they are the only ways to get to the street from backstage without having to go through the house. People went out there to smoke or, paradoxically, to get some fresh air, but it seemed like it was always raining during *Men Behind Bars*, so pigeon shit alley wasn't good for much more than a quick nicotine fix under an umbrella.

Whenever I went down the ladder/stairs during the show, I was amazed at how crowded it was, but everyone seemed to be having a ball. Jim and I would go down there before each performance to give last minute notes, and we would find the cast in any and every stage of undress. Boys in g-strings were drawing dark shadows with make-up on each other's chests to make them look more defined. Bald men in pantyhose and jockey shorts, full face and false eyelashes were donning their wigs and slipping into their heels and dresses awaiting their cues.

One of the times I went backstage, I found Jose in a chair at the end of the narrow hallway surrounded by a number of young people, mostly muscle boys and lesbians. There he was, knitting and telling stories to a rapt audience, as if they were sitting at the feet of one of the most revered elders of the tribe.

Another time between the matinee and evening performances, although most of us went down the street to El Rio, the nearest gay bar, I found Jose sitting out in the auditorium. He was surrounded by at least a dozen young cast members and was telling them all about what it was like to be gay in San Francisco in the olden days, before some of them were even born. When he saw me coming, Jose finished his story and said hello. I asked him how things were going and whether or not he was comfortable being up on that swing for so long, during all those choruses of "Anything Goes" and everyone's bows and our curtain speeches. I had unintentionally set him up to start turning his experience into another hilarious story right on the spot.

He explained how the first night they'd raised him up just high enough so that the hem of his dress cleared the top of the show curtain. That would have been fine except that his head was at the same level as the mirror ball we had used in another number, and it was still spinning. Jose said he stared at it so long that he started getting dizzy, so he looked away, but it was too late. His head was spinning, and he was afraid he was going to fall off the swing and kill someone below. He decided that next time he would be careful not to look at the mirror ball at all, but he needn't have worried.

The next time they raised him up so high he couldn't even see the mirror ball. It was blocked by the skirts of his dress and he was way up in the fly loft near the top of the building. He said the people on the stage looked like ants, so he just closed his eyes and held on tight.

I talked to the guys who did the rigging, and we marked that rope at a sensible place for them to stop hoisting him. It wasn't really the stagehands' fault. We always had so much stuff flying in and out of our shows that they probably couldn't even see Jose. Alan Greenspan had also loaned us an enormous three-dimensional, fully-lit detailed model of the San Francisco skyline, complete with the bridges and cable cars and the pagoda in the Japanese Tea Garden in Golden Gate Park. It was almost the width of the stage, so I'm sure the fly-guys couldn't see Jose with that blocking their view. We mounted the cityscape on white cotton to look like clouds and lowered it in over the heads of the cast at the very end of the show. It must have weighed even more than Monte.

Chapter Nineteen

Most of the gay men I have known possess a higher than average sex drive. When AIDS first hit, I heard guys say things about a potential trick like, "He's hot and he's supposed to be good in bed, but he's not worth dying for." Some guys vowed to use condoms every time from now on. But what about oral sex? Could you spread it by kissing? I heard that some guys stopped having sex altogether, but I didn't know any of them personally.

Some people thought you might catch it from a drinking glass, so they switched to drinking bottled beer when they went to the bars. Or they started using straws in their drinks. Who knew if those disinfectant chemicals the bars used to clean the glasses really killed everything?

Phone sex was an option for some. What could be safer than having sex with someone who was on the other side of town? It didn't really work for me. The whole listening/talking thing was not how I was hard wired. Dirty talk usually comes off sounding silly to me, like the dialog from a cheesy porn movie. Besides, I like using all my senses at the same time. Sight and smell and touch and taste are just as important as sound.

The entire idea was so foreign that the first time I heard the term "phone sex," I thought it meant people were using their telephone handsets as dildos. That would make more sense to me. Before personal computers and smartphones, before websites for every category of desire from vanilla to heavy fetish, the gay magazines all had phone sex ads in the back pages. Sometimes they even outnumbered the ads for escorts and hustlers and masseurs. Gay plumbers, carpenters, gardeners and other trades were advertised in the back of the news section of the B.A.R. so that no one with a tool belt fetish would get confused.

I'm not sure how all of those phone sex outfits worked. They're still around, but I don't know why anyone would use them instead of the Internet. I suppose some took credit cards if you were foolish enough to give out your number over the phone. Others put the charges on your phone bill and charged by the minute, so you wouldn't know how much time you had spent until the end of the month. These were the kind where you talked dirty with a real person who was paid by the hour and wanted to keep you on the line as long as possible.

Another kind was more computerized. You called the number and maybe entered a few details about what you were looking for, and it matched you up with another caller. This service was considerably cheaper because it didn't use those sexy-voiced operators. People often used this kind of site to make dates and hook up in person rather than to get off while talking to someone over the phone.

I tried that type of computerized site once. One weekday during the summer, I was desperately horny and my pickup truck was in the shop again. If I'd had wheels, looking for sex would have been easy. I could have driven to the top of Buena Vista Park or out to Land's End or the north end of Baker Beach just beyond the Pacific Ocean side of the Golden Gate Bridge. There were Devil's Slide and San Gregorio, the nude beaches to the south, so many beautiful places for gay men to hook up outdoors, but not without a car. I could have taken the bus over to the bars in the Castro to look for a trick, but I didn't feel like drinking all afternoon. Sometimes on my days off from tending bar, I didn't feel like drinking at all.

I probably smoked a joint before I called one of the numbers in the back of the *B.A.R.* or the *Sentinel*. It rang and a recorded voice came on and explained how it worked. I don't remember all the details, but after a few clicks and several seconds of static, I heard a soft male voice say "Hello?"

"Hello?"

"What's going on?"

"Not much...you?"

"Nothing...just hanging out."

Gay men might be some of the most creative people in the world in terms of the arts and culture and fashion, but sometimes we're absolutely terrible at making sexy small talk with strangers on the phone. That's the way it was with Rob.

In the end, we decided that I should take the bus over to his place in the lower Haight. We agreed on half an hour. Rob. Scott Street. Age thirty-four. Lower Haight. Hung and horny. That was about all I knew about him, but it was all I needed to know. I pulled on my Levis and boots, grabbed my keys, wallet, and leather jacket and stuck a couple of joints inside the cellophane wrapper of my cigarette pack. I got on the bus.

I found the address. His building was a cute little two-story, two-flat in the middle of the block. He told me he was in the lower one. I looked at my watch. I was three minutes early. What the hell? I rang the doorbell. Nobody answered.

I waited a minute and tried again. Then I saw a white Buick convertible with its top down pull up and park in front of the building. The very sexy guy behind the wheel jumped out. He smiled and looked me up and down as he came closer. "Hi, are you Rob?" we both said at exactly the same time.

"No."

"Oh."

It took only a moment for us to realize that we were both there for the same reason. We were both there to have sex with Rob. Did that make us rivals? Just as I was wondering that, another guy came up the sidewalk and asked which one of us was Rob. We both shook our heads. The three of us had little to say to one another, but we were allies now, joined by our awkward situation. We could at least complain a little bit to each other about the unknown Rob.

"He must have called a few backups, just in case one didn't show."

"He must get stood up a lot."

"He deserves to, the asshole!"

We even considered holding down the doorbell or raising a racket to disturb any sex Rob might be having with whoever had gotten there first. We decided against it. What good would it do?

Then the guy with the convertible said to me, "I guess I'll head back to South of Market. Do you need a lift somewhere?" I think his name was Hank. He had a terrific loft on Natoma Street. He also had a fully-equipped playroom and lots of cocaine. Who needed Rob?

Chapter Twenty

I was working at the Special one morning and picked up a copy of that day's *Chronicle* to read Herb Caen's column in which he had a lighthearted report about Jane Dornacker's helicopter going down in the Hackensack River while she was on WNBC radio in New York, doing a traffic report. The column was full of laughs, but I was shocked that I knew nothing about this! With my strange work schedule and the time difference between California and New York, Jane and I had gotten into the habit of talking on the phone about once a week around three a.m. On the nights I worked at the Eagle, I'd be just home from work and since it was six a.m., Jane would be getting ready for her morning. I called her that night. I was stoned, but we spent so much of our time together stoned that it didn't matter. I used to write a gram of cocaine into some of her contracts. I told her that night I was really worried about her when I heard about the accident, but Herb Caen made it sound funny.

Jane said, "Yeah, I told him I swam from Alcatraz to Aquatic Park twice, but it's different with a two-ton helicopter strapped to your waist."

"I know. He used that line in his column and your joke about nobody noticing if you were brain damaged. I'm glad you could joke about it, but still..."

Then Jane turned so serious on the phone that it scared me a little. "Mark, it was terrifying! By the time I talked to Herb Caen, I'd had some time to recover from the shock and find some levity in the situation. But you know how they say your whole gosh-darn life flashes before you in the last few seconds when you think you're going to die? It really does! The first thing I thought of was Naomi, of course, and how I would never see her again and that was devastating. And then I thought about you and I thought I'm gonna miss that danged old Mark...yep, I sure will miss that guy. And then when I realized I was gonna live I thought the next time

I talk to you I'd better tell you that."

As I said, I was taken aback by her seriousness, but I was also stoned. I just wanted to laugh with her again. I told her to cheer up and not to let the accident change her, not to let anything frighten her. I told her she was about the bravest woman I knew, and that was one of the qualities I loved most about her. I said she had to get right back up in that helicopter because "lightning never strikes twice, you know..." and "It's just like falling off a horse. You have to get right back on or you'll be too scared to do it again."

We talked some more that night and got out our calendars. Something was coming up at the Eagle in a month or two where I could book her to perform. I could work her airfare into the price, and I would be able to see her again in a few weeks.

Chapter Twenty-One

Rikki Streicher was one of the most successful business people in the gay community and a true angel. She owned the popular lesbian bars Maud's Study—immortalized in the historical 1993 documentary film *Last Call at Maud's*—in the Haight. She also owned Amelia's, named for Amelia Earhart, in the Mission district, as well as a restaurant called Pier 50 and a convenience store called Rikker's Liquors on Market Street. Jim Cvitanich and I got to know Rikki as one of the members of the Pussies, the singing group that appeared twice in our *Men Behind Bars* shows. She was also a big sports fan and a major financial backer of the gay sports leagues and the Gay Games. When she died in 1994, the softball field on 19th and Diamond Streets in the Castro was named Rikki Streicher Field in her honor.

After the success of *Pier Pressure*, Jim and I wanted to do another pier party, but we wanted to be more creative. We decided that a tea dance would be fun on a Sunday afternoon with lots of live entertainment. Our only trouble was that we didn't have much money. After our last event, we had paid ourselves each five percent of the net profits, paid the charity seventy-five percent and the other twenty percent went into the MBB account to use as seed money for our next show. We had about eight thousand dollars, but we figured we'd need about forty-five grand.

One Sunday we were having brunch at the Galleon, a gay bar and restaurant off Church Street, only a few blocks from Castro. The host seated Rikki Streicher and another woman at the deuce right next to us. We all greeted each other and then Jim and I went back to eating while the waiter took the women's order. As soon as he left I said, "Excuse me, Rikki. I just had an idea. Could you loan us forty thousand dollars?"

Rikki didn't bat an eye. She just smiled and said, "Sure. What are you boys planning now? Never mind, you can tell me about it later. Come by my office about four this afternoon, and I'll write you a check."

When we finished eating, Jim and I went back to his apartment on Noe Street off Market, right behind the Muscle System gym, more popularly known as "Muscle Sisters," and spent the next few hours making concrete plans until it was time to go meet Rikki. We agreed on a loan of forty thousand with ten percent interest to be paid back after the party. Rikki wrote us a check to Men Behind Bars Productions and we were on our way.

Rather than going back to Pier 45 at Fisherman's Wharf, we found out that we could rent a pier at Fort Mason, the pier farthest west and nearest the Golden Gate Bridge. It had windows and access to a wide walkway outside, plus a terrace inside with a huge built-in bar and terrific views of the bridge. The major work we needed to do inside was to install a temporary parquet dance floor over the cement and to erect a stage and sound system and lighting for when it got dark.

Another wonderful surprise was that this pier was owned by the Federal government and they rented it out all the time. We didn't have to jump through all the Port Authority's hoops or deal with the obstacles and bureaucracy of the San Francisco city and county government. We didn't have to run all over town trying to catch someone in his or her office to get a signature on a permit for Port-A-Potties or anything else. At Fort Mason, one person handled everything, and she couldn't have been nicer. We still had to fill out forms and cross off checklists, but everything was spelled out so that it made perfect sense. We even told the woman that she should give classes to train people in charge of government- owned public properties how it could be done efficiently, starting with the San Francisco Port Authority. She just laughed.

We had the stage built on one side of the pier, opposite the upstairs bar. We rented round tables and chairs to place around the perimeter of the parquet dance floor, enough to seat at least a couple hundred people. Between the groups of tables, we placed enormous rented palm trees surrounded by low white chain fences. We put colored spotlights at the base of each tree to extend the shadows of their fronds across the ceiling above the dance floor.

We contacted the Freewheelers, the classic car club. They're a group of mostly gay guys who have invested their time and money into buying, fixing up, maintaining, and showing off some gorgeous old leather and chrome-covered pieces of machinery. We ended up with six or eight guys willing to drive their cars down to the pier that day. Each performer was driven to the stage in a different car, and then the cars were each parked next to one of the palm trees inside the chain fences.

Everyone said it was a sensational party. Most of our friends came. Friends of the entertainers came. Most of the people from the MBB mailing list probably came, but it wasn't enough. It was too civilized. It was a sunny Sunday afternoon in June when people had better things to do outside. Even with our track record of two successful *Pier Pressure* parties, we hadn't tapped into that hard-core dance crowd this time. High Tea drew more of the white gloves and pearls kind of crowd…jewelry, sunglasses and Tiparillos.

We got good press about the party. Friends told us that they loved it. I hoped they really did. I wasn't sure if our friends would have told us the truth if they hadn't loved it. In the end, we lost about eight thousand dollars, and we still owed Rikki ten percent of her forty thousand dollar loan, so we were twelve grand in the hole. The cost and expenses completely wiped out our joint MBB bank account, which was going to be the seed money for our next show. Even worse, the charity benefactors received nothing. The dedicated volunteers who had helped by taking tickets or tending bar or sweeping up afterward had given all their time in hopes of helping their cause. I felt terrible when they came up empty-handed, but we couldn't do anything.

When we had to pay Rikki Streicher back, she suggested that we meet for lunch at her restaurant on Pier 50, south of the Bay Bridge. We ordered our food and drinks and visited with her about lots of other things besides the party. When we tore out the check from our check book, Rikki shook her head and said, "I was at your party. It was wonderful, but I know business and I know you didn't make any money that day. I'll bet you might have even lost some. Tear up that check and forget about paying me interest. I was glad I was able to help out. Just write me a check for the forty grand. I'm sorry it didn't work out better for you."

Chapter Twenty-Two

When I was a poor college student in Minneapolis, friends regularly went to San Francisco on weekends and told me how magical it was. My best friend Carl even encouraged me to move out there after graduation. He told me about going to a bar called the Stud on Folsom Street one Sunday afternoon. Everyone was stoned, smoking pot and drinking heavily on that hot day and, suddenly, Etta James appeared on a little stage in the middle of that crowded bar. Carl told me she poured out her heart and soul, and that it was a performance and an experience he would never forget. I always thought of that story when I planned an event. I wanted to give some of that magic to people who might just have stumbled into the bar. I wanted them to experience something unforgettable, something they would take with them and talk about.

When Jane Dornacker came back from New York to perform at the Eagle for the gig I'd booked, she took a cab directly from the airport to the Special. I didn't get off work until seven, and the bar was packed for Friday Happy Hour. I looked up when I heard some commotion at the front door and saw my Amazonian friend come in through the swinging Dutch doors. Jane was well over six feet tall, always wore very high heels, and often piled her thick mane of red hair on top of her head. That day on Castro Street, she pulled at the strap of her huge rolling suitcase and yelled, "Poochie! Get in here! Bad dog!" The men in the front end of the bar stepped back to make room for her. Jane shoved the suitcase under the pinball machine in the front corner and said, "Stay, Poochie, stay!" Needless to say, the rest of my shift was a lot of fun with Jane in the bar, and my regulars buying her drinks and shots of tequila.

We worked out a system when Jane stayed with me on McCoppin Street. I loaned her a spare set of keys to my apartment and whoever got home first with a trick got the bed. Jane had a "thing" for black guys, and I remember more than once waking up on my couch to see a gorgeous naked black Adonis emerge from my bedroom door and walk down the hallway to the bathroom.

Mark with Jane Dornacker at the Eagle

Photo by Robert Pruzan, courtesy of the Gay, Lesbian, Bisexual, Transgender Historical Society

The rest of the weekend is a bit of a blur to me. The show at the Eagle was on Sunday afternoon, and I'm sure she spent time with her daughter Naomi. Shortly after Jane moved to New York, her ex-husband Bob had died suddenly of a massive heart attack and Naomi had moved in with the family of one of her high school friends to finish out her senior year. After graduation, she planned to join her mother in New York.

I don't remember much about the details of Jane's Dornacker's appearance at the Eagle, but I'm sure she did the character of Madge Battaglia for all she was worth, along with the rest of her best material. When she played to a gay crowd, especially, she always included the song she wrote about walking down Polk Street thinking she was "a picture of femininity" but having someone shout at her—and this was where she encouraged the audience to join in—"Drag queen! Drag queen! Drag queen!"

What I remember best from that visit is Monday, the day after the Eagle. Jane and I had a late breakfast at Orphan Andy's on 17th and Castro. Her flight was later on in the afternoon. With some time to kill before she left town, we walked around the Castro a while, window shopping and greeting the fans who recognized her on the street. We ended up at the Village on 18th Street, the place that would later become Uncle Bert's and the Mix.

Jane and I got stools about halfway down the bar and ordered a couple of beers. The Village was empty at that hour except for a couple of guys playing pool. Maybe a liquor delivery came while we were there. Maybe the mailman came along. Maybe someone was playing a video game in the corner. I just remember drinking Heinekens out of the bottle with Jane, smoking cigarettes—she always smoked unfiltered Camels and I smoked something mild and low-tar like Merit—bothering the bored bartender now and then for a chilled shot of Stoli and a couple more beers.

When the time came, I helped pull her suitcase, "Poochie," down to 18th and Castro. She hugged me goodbye and got into a taxi at the corner while the driver wrestled her monstrous piece of luggage into the trunk. I watched her pull away and wave to me out the Yellow Cab's rear window. It would turn out to be the last time I saw her alive.

A couple of weeks after Jane's performance at the Eagle, I was at a party where I didn't know anyone. I don't remember who had invited me to tag along, but I'd already lost him, and I felt like I didn't belong there at all. It was at an old warehouse or some kind of factory South of Market that had been converted into a fabulous living space with high ceilings and skylights, with all of the latest in modern appliances and high-tech gadgetry, expensive modern furniture, lots of wood and glass and steel, orchids in bloom everywhere and huge potted palm trees.

Not only was the place awfully fancy for my taste, I thought that the people were too. They all looked like the ultimate A-Gays, the *crème-de-la-crème* with designer muscles and fabulous clothes. I was intimidated by all of them and just wanted to go back to the bars. I was about to slink into a corner near the front door and give the "friend" who had brought me here one final chance to reappear when I overheard someone mention the Eagle.

I listened closely as he told his friends that he didn't go to the Eagle as a rule, but he had just happened to stop in there on a recent Sunday afternoon and something special was going on besides the usual beer-bust and raffles. He described it as a magical afternoon and said he couldn't believe they had gotten Jane Dornacker to appear there. He talked about how she'd played the piano and sang some of the songs she wrote when she was with the Tubes. He had remembered Jane since she performed as Leila with the Snakes back at the Palms on Polk Street, and that he was thrilled to see her again. He used the word magical a couple of times, and I was glad that I'd stuck around long enough to eavesdrop. It was nice to know that I had given someone a magical experience by arranging for my friend perform.

Chapter Twenty-Three

That fall the Special got together a team to join the gay bowling league. Edwina Ballerina was just Ed when he butched it up and traded his ballet slippers for bowling shoes. He was the boss, after all, so if he wanted a bowling team, he would have one. Ed was an excellent bowler. I wasn't. I sucked at bowling, but we had fun. Gay bowling was so popular in those days that the gay leagues took over all the lanes at both Japantown Bowl and Park Bowl, on the far end of Haight Street, a couple of nights each week.

Bowling was something different to do on a weeknight besides go home to watch TV or sit in a bar or take advantage of the early-bird discount cover charge at one of the few remaining sex clubs. Maybe it was a sign of the times. Some of us were consciously curbing our sexual carousing a bit, even though our libidos were still raging. Our friends were dying, but we still needed to be social and blow off some steam. You could meet and be surrounded by as many gay men at the bowling alley as you might find on the dance floor or in a busy bar on a Saturday night, but on a Thursday in a well-lit place.

Our team was made up of some serious drinkers, so serious that we checked out both locations before we joined the league. First we went to Japantown Bowl, which was closer to the Castro. It had two levels of bowling lanes with the bar on the mezzanine between. That meant having to run up and down half a flight of stairs every time we wanted drinks. Park Bowl was further away, and also a little older and more run down, but it was all on one level. There the bar was only steps from the ball return. Their drinks were stronger too. The vote was unanimous. Park Bowl won hands down.

On October 22, 1986 I was home on McCoppin Street, getting ready to go bowling when my phone rang. It was Gabriel Starr, one of my best bartender friends. He said, "Mark, you better turn on the news. Your buddy Jane in New York went down in the helicopter again, and it doesn't look good this time."

I hung up the phone and turned on the TV set in my living room. The national news from New York had already started. They flashed a picture of Jane, and her name was spelled out across the bottom of the screen. A man in a suit came on next, a Brokaw or Cronkite or someone of that ilk, to say that Jane Dornacker had gone down in the helicopter while she was on the air—again—only this time in the Hudson River. It had only been six months since her helicopter crashed in the Hackensack and she swam to shore.

A few weeks ago, she'd been sitting right there on the couch beside me, her suitcase having erupted all over my bed, and we were laughing together and drinking champagne to toast her arrival.

The news cut to a commercial, and I called Ed Stark at the Special. I told him I couldn't bowl that night. They'd have to line up an alternate for the league. I needed to stay at home by the phone in case it rang. I was sure that Jane would call me as soon as she could.

Then the news came back on, and I turned up the volume again. The man behind a desk in New York announced in a somber voice that Jane Dornacker was dead. Paramedics had tried to resuscitate her but failed. I sat back down on the couch, and a stream of pictures played across the screen. Or were they only in my head? Jane on stage with the Tubes…Jane as Leila with her trio, Leila and the Snakes…Jane as Madge Battaglia with that huge mop of red hair piled atop her head and tied up in a wide ribbon…those goofy glasses she wore. Jane was dead? No! All of my male friends were dying from AIDS that season. Three or four of the pictures of the mounting death toll in the back of the *B.A.R.* each week were guys I had slept with. I counted on my women friends to live forever, to cheer us on, to take care of us as we slid from our deathbeds into our graves.

That Sunday I got a call from our mutual friend Robert Pruzan, the photographer. Jane and I had been to his apartment on Ashbury Street during her last visit to look at contact sheets from a recent photo shoot and a couple of black and white prints he'd made and hand-colored. One was of Jane sitting in front of a huge stack of firewood, a glass of wine and an avocado on a stump beside her. Robert had colored the wine and her lips red and the avocado green. I would love to have that print now.

Robert said he was coming by to take me to a small private memorial for Jane's closest friends. He drove up in his old black Thunderbird with the bad muffler, and we went to a place on Divisadero, just up the hill to the south of where it splits off from Castro Street. The house was filled with people I had only seen on TV or on stage and voices I had only heard on the radio, Jane's co-workers when she was the trafficologist on KFRC. Framed photographs of Jane were everywhere and upstairs one room had a TV monitor showing videos of Jane performing. Robert and I stuck together at first, got something to drink and went out to the backyard to sit and smoke.

We went back inside and wandered into a large bedroom where a tall young blonde had her arms around an older lady who was bawling her eyes out. I told Robert that we should probably leave, and then I heard the young woman say, "There, there, now...Mother wouldn't want us to carry on so."

Mother? I realized this had to be Jane's daughter Naomi, whom I hadn't actually seen in person in years. She was all grown up now, a senior in high school with all the maturity of someone much older, wiser, and stronger. I said, "Naomi?" and she turned to me next, put her arms around me and gave me a hug.

"Mark, I recognized your voice. We've talked on the phone so many times when you've called for mom." I could hardly believe how composed she was. Her father, whom she had been living with, had died a few weeks earlier of a sudden massive heart attack in his early forties. Maybe Naomi was still in shock. She told me she was staying with a family friend until graduation, then she wanted to study to become a veterinarian. She was already volunteering at the San Francisco Zoo.

I lost track of Robert for a while and found my way to the kitchen. There was an ice chest full of Heineken, the kind of beer Jane always drank. I popped one open and took a long swallow. People had formed an impromptu circle there and were going around the room in turn, telling the rest of us about their last conversations with Jane. They all said that they had told her— begged her, even—not to go back up in that helicopter again.

It wasn't my last conversation with Jane, but when my turn came, I said, "I told her to go back to work. I told her it was like being bucked from a horse, that she had to get right back on again or she would be afraid and Jane wasn't the type to live in fear of anything. I told her lightening doesn't strike twice, you know, and…" One by one, the other people left the kitchen very quickly and left me standing there alone as if it was all my fault that Jane was dead.

Robert found me there and asked if I was ready to leave. I was, but now everyone was gathering in the living room, and we were on the opposite side of the crowd from the front door. People were making speeches. Michael Pritchard, another well-known local comic, talked about going with Jane to perform inside San Quentin Prison. She'd been wonderful in front of that crowd, but was traumatized in the car on the way home afterward. The helplessness and sadness of those men's lives devastated her.

Jane's sister from Albuquerque was there. She looked exactly like Jane but with dark hair. It was hard to look at her and impossible not to. I had a moment's fantasy that Jane was playing a colossal joke on us all, that she had faked her death and come here today in a dark wig to fool us all. If only it could have been true.

A woman spoke last. I think she was Jane's friend who owned this house we were in. She said that several months ago, just before Jane moved to New York, a bunch of her best girlfriends had gotten together for lunch to say goodbye and see her off. At the end of their time together that day, they all gathered around the piano. Jane played and they sang the old song by Roy Rogers and Dale Evans called "Happy trails."

To end this memorial gathering, someone sat down at the baby grand in this large living room on Divisadero Street and all of these friends of Jane's sang that song again. I looked around at all the pictures of Jane and the tears fell freely. Robert drove me home afterward, and I wanted to listen to the recording of Jane's voice doing Marge on my answering machine one more time and then figure out what to do with it. I couldn't erase it, but it seemed kind of weird to have people call me and hear the voice of a dead woman. I couldn't simply change the tape. It was built in, and I would have to get a new one. I pressed the button to "play outgoing message" and heard, "Hi, this is Marge--not Mark…" Then the tape broke. I had to go out and buy a new answering machine anyway.

I heard that at some later date they were going to hold a public memorial for Jane Dornacker at the Warfield Theatre on Market Street. That venue is home to rock concerts, mostly, although I have gone there to see such diverse acts as Joan Rivers and the Smothers Brothers and live interviews with Sophia Loren and Mae West. That place has been there forever.

I thought about going to Jane's public memorial, but decided against it. There would be tons of people I didn't know, but most of them would be fans, not necessarily friends of Jane. When that day came, it made more sense to me to stay home and sit on the couch, drink a toast to Jane and remember our good times there together.

Chapter Twenty-Four

Ed Stark always told me that as soon as a better shift opened up at the Special, it would be mine. He said I would make more money tending bar nights, but I told him I would rather work afternoons. The money might not be as good in the afternoons, but I wanted to slow down a little. I had paid my "disco dues" working nights at the Woods and early mornings and nights at the End-Up before the Eagle. It finally happened. I had four afternoons a week on Castro Street, and I told Terry Thompson I would have to give up my two night shifts South of Market.

My apartment on McCoppin Street was a dump, but at least it was dirt cheap. I didn't really need two bedrooms, a living room, an eat-in kitchen with pantry, an enclosed back porch and a split water closet/shower all to myself, but I hadn't formally lived with anyone full-time in a long while. The last time had been about 1980, when I lived on 19th and Douglass in the Castro with my old platonic roommate Emilio before I moved up north to the Russian River. Before Emilio, I lived with my first San Francisco "husband" Armando.

I could easily afford the rent by myself and didn't even consider getting a roommate until one day when Marcus called and said, "You need a roommate, and I need a place to live. When can I pick up a set of keys?"

My life was so busy around the time that Marcus called that I never stopped to think about whether I really wanted a roommate. He just moved in. Marcus was also known as "Emperor I Marcus" meaning that he was the first Emperor (after Norton) of San Francisco in the Royal Court system. Jose Sarria had named himself the Widow Norton and first Empress of San Francisco many years earlier. Marcus also wrote a weekly column, "Southern Scandals," in the *Bay Area Reporter* that ran for years and which primarily covered the South of Market leather scene. Jim Cvitanich was thrilled when he heard that Marcus was moving in with me because Marcus covered everything that Jim and I did as *Men Behind Bars* Productions. Jim assumed that having Marcus under my roof would assure that our free publicity would continue.

Marcus was about twenty years older than me. I had always had friends who were older than me, and I considered him a friend, though not one of my closest. I had known him since he came up to Guerneville to emcee some of the contests I produced when I worked at the Woods Resort at the Russian River. We had also worked together when I organized the Bare Chest Calendar Contests that he emceed at the SF Eagle.

Shortly after moving in, Marcus started causing problems. He was always dragging home stray boys. One day I came home after spending the night elsewhere, and I noticed that five rolls of quarters had vanished from the top of my dresser. I went straight to Marcus and asked, "Did you have someone over last night?"

"Yeah, Jake (or it could have been Joe or Pete or Sam or Tom, Dick or Harry) was here, why?"

"Did he go in my room?"

"I don't think so."

"But he could have, right? I had five rolls of quarters on my dresser. I was going to take them to the bank when I deposited my paycheck today."

"Well, if they don't turn up, you be sure to let me know."

"Turn up? They didn't roll off all by themselves and go hide under my bed. They're gone, damn it! Your trick must have taken them. You owe me fifty bucks!"

"I'm running late…gotta go, but you let me know if you don't find them." That was strike one. Neither of us ever brought up the subject of the missing quarters again. I chalked it up to my learning a fifty dollar lesson about never leaving anything of value lying around.

Marcus didn't cook, so at least the kitchen always stayed the way I left it. He wasn't a slob or an idiot, but some of the guys he brought home were. Marcus could use his name and popular column to talk his way into a lot of guys' pants. I sometimes met them on my way to the bathroom or saw them stumble out of his bedroom the next morning. Marcus seemed to be partial to rough-looking guys with homemade tattoos and greasy hair.

One Sunday shortly after Marcus moved in, my parents called from Minnesota to tell me they were planning a trip out West. They asked if I had room for them to stay with me. Some of my favorite childhood memories were of our family camping trips "out West." Every year just before school started, we would pack a tent, sleeping bags, and air mattresses and set out on a family vacation. Some years we travelled in a caravan of cars and campers along with aunts and uncles and cousins my age. We would drive to South Dakota's Black Hills the first night, maybe spend a day in the Badlands and then on to Yellowstone and the Grand Tetons. We'd drive up to Tacoma to see my dad's sister, Ann. Her husband Dick would take us out salmon fishing in the Pacific. Then we would go down to Eugene to dad's younger brother Alfred's place for a visit.

I told my parents on the phone that I would love to see them, but I had a roommate now and didn't want him to feel put out. I offered to get them a room at the Travelodge Motel around the corner and promised that we would spend lots of time together. I considered giving them my bed. I could have easily slept on the couch for a couple of nights. I knew they would never stay more than three days, even if I wanted them to. "Guests and fish," my mother always says. "The Chinese were right about them. More than three days and they start to stink." But the thought of my parents staying there and Marcus possibly dragging home thieves and street punks worried me.

My mother reminded me of how nice my roommate Emilio had been when they came to visit a few years earlier. He had offered them his bedroom for a couple of nights while he was out of town. I said, "Yes, Mom, I remember. Emilio was such a thoughtful and generous person." I wanted to add, "Emilio was a Tai Chi instructor, after all. My new roommate Marcus is totally different. He writes a leather column and emcees slave auctions," but I didn't.

If only I had been living alone, it would have been great to have them stay with me, but I didn't want to risk Marcus dragging home some seedy, drugged-out character to spend the night under the same roof as my parents. My parents made their trip "out West" that fall, but they only came as far south as Medford, Oregon.

Chapter Twenty-Five

I was no stranger to drugs by any means, but I could always take them or leave them. I was hooked on nicotine for many years, but I did recreational drugs out of habit rather than addiction.

My first experience with "uppers" was with white cross-tops in my college days. They were supposedly good for staying up late when you had to cram for a test, but I only used them to party. When I had an important test in the morning, I usually smoked a big fat joint right before it and I did just fine in college.

In San Francisco in the 70s, Black Beauties—Biphetamines— were around. Housewives took them to lose weight while they went on marathon cleaning binges. We gay kids used them to go dancing non-stop for hours, but I hated coming down. Most people used valium for that part of the trip, but I never planned that far in advance. Quaaludes were popular too, but the only time I took one I just walked into walls. If I wanted to feel drunk, I preferred alcohol. By the time I moved back to the city from the Russian River, two big changes had occurred. One was AIDS, and the other was crystal methamphetamine. I still wonder which of them did more damage in the long run. My drug of choice—besides alcohol, nicotine and marijuana, which were as commonplace in my diet as Jello and cornflakes were while I was growing up—was always cocaine.

The handful of times I remember doing crystal, it was always by mistake. I might be standing at the urinal at the I-Beam or Trocadero and spot someone I knew heading into a stall. He would gesture with his finger to his nose and beckon me to join him and shut the door. "Want a line?"

"Sure!" Cocaine was so expensive that I never turned it down for free, no matter what the circumstances. But in this case, before I could even thank my benefactor and hand him back the straw, the powder hit the back of my throat like a blowtorch. Then I knew I would be up all night and out on the dance floor until dawn. The next day would be a total waste.

The comedown from crystal meth was worse than any drug I had ever known. It felt like ground glass was pumping through my veins. I craved the peace of sleep, but couldn't reach it. I have always tried to avoid meth and those who used it, but then one of them moved into my apartment on McCoppin Street.

I was tending bar on Castro Street one afternoon when my roommate Marcus called me at work. I told him I was fairly busy and didn't have time to chat. He said that was okay because he just called to ask a question. He said that he'd told his friend James he could stay at our place for a couple of days because he was having trouble with his roommates. The question was, "Where should James put his plants?"

"Plants?" I asked Marcus over the phone, just as six more tourists walked in the door and a couple of regulars started waving their empty glasses at me. "I don't know. The only sunny windows are in your room in the front and in the living room in the back. I've gotta go!"

When I got home I discovered that his belongings took up the entire living room. Even more disturbing, James was high all the time. He was completely lacking in charm and was arrogant and rude. Maybe he was more polite to Marcus than he was to me, but I doubt it. Marcus seemed to like young guys who lived on the edge. He regarded their egotism as "personality" and would be smitten with their "boyishness."

Like I already said, the apartment was a dump. I didn't spend much time there, but the next time I wanted to sleep late, James was in the next room talking on the phone. No, he was yelling into the phone, over the sound of the television at top volume. I was ready to scream, but I got dressed and left before I could kill him.

I put up with it for a couple of weeks until I couldn't take it anymore. I don't even remember what strike three was, but one morning on my way out the door, I told Marcus, "You brought that asshole into this apartment. He's your responsibility. You deal with him. I want you both out of here by the end of the month!"

"Me? What did I do?"

"You subjected me to him! This is the last straw. I don't need a roommate, much less two roommates. I need some peace and quiet around here. And to think I told my parents they would have to stay in a motel because I wouldn't want to inconvenience you! You thought nothing about inconveniencing me! Get out! Both of you!"

I don't know how we managed to continue working with Marcus in *Men Behind Bars* after he moved out. Jim must have handled all dealings with him. Marcus was no longer the emcee after the first couple of years, anyway. We just put him in drag as part of the first act finale each year, and he continued to give our shows lots of good coverage in his column. He probably had a crush on Jim Cvitanich. Lots of people did.

I encountered James again on opening night of the next *Men Behind Bars*. After the orchestra played the overture and the singers and dancers finished the big splashy opening number, the audience finally stopped applauding and sat back in their seats to watch the rest of the show. All but one person, that is. Someone was still hooting and hollering, "Woo-hoo! Yeah! Do it! Come on! Yeah! Woo-hoo!"

I peeked out from the curtain and saw James in the front row of the balcony, standing up, clapping, leaning over the rail so far I thought he might fall and then standing back upright and never shutting up. I raced out the stage door and was through the front door to the lobby in seconds.

For each show, two off-duty members of the SFPD were in the theatre out of uniform. Jim and I had several gay friends who were cops, so they were happy to volunteer and got to see the shows for free. We rarely needed them, but that opening night I knew they were sitting in the back row of the orchestra section. They were already out of their seats when I gave them the go-ahead to remove the loudmouthed troublemaker from the balcony. I figured if I could throw James out of my apartment, I had no qualms about throwing him out of the theater. The policemen dragged him kicking and screaming all the way out to the street. The audience applauded and the show went on. I hate meth!

Chapter Twenty-Six

When Gail Wilson and I were both young and single, we not only did "show-biz" stuff together, but we liked to hang out sometimes, too. I would invite her to events or ask her to be a judge at some of the Bare Chest Calendar contests at the Eagle when I ran them. She was always fun to be with, and her celebrity was growing quickly during those years. I couldn't walk with Gail one block down Castro Street without people stopping her to say hello every few steps. She and her eighteen-piece big band, City Swing, were part of the San Francisco Band Foundation, which included the Gay Freedom Day Marching Band and Twirling Corps and the San Francisco Tap Troupe. Gail was the guest star of most of our *Men Behind Bars* shows with City Swing in the orchestra pit, but she and her band also headlined the Castro Street Fair, the Folsom Street Fair, and numerous other gay functions and fundraisers, between working their paying gigs at large private parties and business conventions.

Gail and City Swing used to perform on the Eagle patio at least once a year for one of their notorious Sunday beer busts. Whether it was with the band blasting "Opus One" or Gail belting out "Tangerine," she always wore her sexiest outfits to tease the boys. On the microphone, Gail could outdo any drag queen with her charm, humor and class—though not too much class for the Eagle crowd.

A week after one of Gail's triumphant performances at the Eagle, she and I decided to spend the day together. We started with brunch at the Galleon and then walked back to my apartment by way of a video store where we rented a couple of movies on VHS tape. Neither of us had seen *No Way Out* or *Who Framed Roger Rabbit?* so we settled on those two. We'd been drinking Bloody Marys at the Galleon, but all I had to drink in abundance at home was gin. I found a liter of Sapphire and a bigger bottle of regular Bombay in the freezer, where I also kept a couple of martini glasses, just in case. I had some olives were in the fridge, along with a couple of kinds of cheese. I'd also picked up a box of fancy crackers earlier at Safeway and some tins of smoked shellfish and maybe some salmon mousse.

We started with *No Way Out* and the regular Bombay Gin. Even though it had been in the freezer, I poured it over ice with a whisper of dry vermouth. I know I had to get up a few times to refill the shaker so we must have been pretty drunk by the time *Roger Rabbit* came on the screen. When we finished the first bottle, I went out to the kitchen and got the Sapphire. As drunk as we already were, the gin went down as smooth as water. We finished that bottle by the time the cartoon movie was over, so I said, "Well, we're out of gin. We'd better walk over to the Eagle. They'll have some."

We both put our shoes on and tromped over to 12th and Harrison Streets. Maybe the fresh air was invigorating. I felt fine. When we got to the Eagle, nearly everyone we knew was there. Two stools magically appeared at the bar, so we sat down in David "Stella" Stoll's section. He was one of the most popular bartenders in town and had also appeared in *Men Behind Bars* a couple of times in drag as Jane Russell. Gail and I couldn't pay for anything. She was surrounded by fans flashing money at Stella to buy our drinks, Cuervo Gold tequila and orange juice for Gail and vodka tonics for me. We forgot all about getting more gin. Between cocktails, we downed shots of whatever flavors of schnapps were most popular that month.

The next thing I remember I looked around and noticed that Gail was gone. I figured that if she was half as smashed as I was, she could be in trouble. After all, I was a professional. She was an amateur by comparison. I was so used to drinking, I could handle amazing amounts of alcohol, especially if no other drugs were involved…and sometimes even when drugs were necessary to keep drinking. The only times I ever blacked out had been from mixing things, sometimes just two simple things like pot or hashish and beer, especially if I threw in some poppers.

I stood up from my bar stool and headed toward the corner

entrance where the doors were standing wide open. The sun was setting, and I could see Gail sitting on the sidewalk, her back up against a street sign, legs splayed apart, shoes off, smiling. I got her up slowly. "Gail? I think we should head home, don't you? Let's get your shoes on and walk back to my place. You left your big purse and your keys and everything in my living room. Come on."

Gail tried to be cooperative, but she wasn't very functional. Once we got going, I wanted us to move a little faster, so I started to sing "Seventy-six trombones" from *The Music Man*, and got her to march, march, march. "Come on, Gail… cornets… sing it with me. Step, step, step." By the time we got to McCoppin Street, we had moved on to belting out "One" from *A Chorus Line* complete with high kicks and Gail didn't even lose her shoes. I told her the couch was hers, and I was going to bed. Goodnight!

The next day Gail called me in the afternoon to see how I was doing and to say thanks. I told her I had expected to find her asleep in the living room when I woke up. She said she'd thought about crashing on the couch, but knew she had to be at work on Monday morning, and it would be easier to get it together if she woke up at home. She only lived around the corner from me on Duboce Street.

"Work!? You went to work today?" I often forgot that she had some kind of fancy-schmancy day job in the financial district.

"Yeah, I'm at work now. Boy, was I hung over this morning!"

"Well, we did put away a lot of gin. You were so funny, singing show tunes with me and marching all the way back to my house from the Eagle."

"What? Wait a minute! We went to the Eagle? You're kidding me!"

"Yes, don't you remember? You were chatting with everyone and charming the pants off of all your fans, and they kept buying us drinks and shots. You were so nice to Mister Marcus, you were almost kissing his ass."

"Oh, God, now I'll be in his column again, I suppose. He wouldn't write something nasty about me just because you kicked him out of your apartment, would he?"

"I don't think so. He's not like that and besides, he can't afford to offend you. The next thing you know he'll want you to sing at another AIDS benefit."

"I guess so. Hey, honey…I've got to get back to work. I still can't believe we went to the Eagle and I don't remember a minute of it."

"I still can't believe you went to work!"

Chapter Twenty-Seven

My apartment on McCoppin Street was within walking distance of both my jobs. When I first lived there, I tended bar at the Special on Castro Street and the Eagle on 12th and Harrison, not that I walked to work much while I had my truck. I usually walked in that neighborhood late at night after the bars had closed, but for other reasons. When the baths were shut down by the city because of the AIDS epidemic, gay men had to be creative and find other places to cruise. Old secret places that might have been busy periodically were getting crowded once again. I discovered that the little alleyways near my apartment, especially Pink and Pearl and Elgin Park, were as busy after two a.m. as Castro Street on a sunny afternoon.

My neighborhood had its own gay bars, too. The Eagle Creek Saloon was nearby, and The Mint Bar was a little farther up Market Street toward the Castro. The Rainbow Cattle Company on Duboce and Valencia, which later became Zeitgeist, was probably the largest and the best known of them. Upstairs, people lived in rented rooms with hot plates and shared a bathroom at the end of the hall. I heard that most of the tenants were gay men or drug dealers or both.

I met a guy in the bar one night who invited me upstairs where we had sex and then passed out. I woke up before dawn and walked the one block home. I only have a vague recollection of the dark, cramped room, and none at all about the man, but what I remember most about the experience was telling my friends the next day that I'd spent the night "over the Rainbow" and everyone knew what I meant. Many of them had their own stories to tell about the place.

A big black friend I'll call Jim Bayer, my favorite coke dealer, lived on Hayes Street, the other side of Market. He had a name for those darkened blocks where men cruised after hours. He called them *Green Acres* like the old television show. I don't know why he made that association, but it stuck. I could go to work on Castro Street the following day and mention to my customers at the Special, "I ran into Jim Bayer on Green Acres last night," and they understood. "Running into Jim Bayer" also meant that I had probably pulled some cash out of the pocket of my tight Levi 501s in exchange for a little paper packet of magic white powder that would help keep me up much of the night.

A little farther west at Church and Market Streets was the twenty-four hour Safeway where it still stands today. Someone once told me that it was the largest supermarket in San Francisco or maybe all of California. They could have said it was the largest one in the world and I would have believed it. I never saw Patrick Toner out on Green Acres, but he told me once that if he didn't pick up a trick by the time the bars closed, he went to Safeway after hours. He would put a can of Crisco in his shopping cart and push it up and down the aisles until he met another horny guy. According to Patrick, the vegetable aisle was always busy with guys examining the English cucumbers, which came pre-wrapped in their own condoms, and looking for the largest zucchini. I loved this idea so much that I used it in the first of my books in the *Beach Reading* series. I could picture Patrick going up and down the aisles with a smile and a can of Crisco, and I could definitely see my character of Jake doing it too.

On Elgin Park, someone rigged up closed circuit cameras so that he could see everyone coming and going outside his tiny Victorian cottage without having to get out of his wingback chair. Across from the windows, in full view of the sidewalk, he played gay porn on a big screen TV in order to lure in passersby. The door was always open. One night I went inside and found three or four other guys already standing in the shadowy living room. The resident of the house sat back and watched, masturbating in the dark, I assumed. I started messing around with one of the other guys, but the situation was too weird for me. I am neither an exhibitionist nor a prude, but I felt like we were putting on a show for someone's grandmother. I couldn't tell if all the furniture had hand-crocheted doilies and antimacassars, but as stoned as I was, I thought the ceramic sheep and angels on the knick-knack shelves were staring down at us. I got out of there and never went back.

A couple of the houses on Pearl Street had a space between them. In this gap, a few concrete steps led down to a covered walkway and into a little back yard. That was a hot spot for a while. It was a good place to beckon someone in from the alley for a modicum of privacy, but it became too popular. I went down those steps one night and found a big crowd of men back there in the shadows, standing, kneeling, bending, a jungle of arms and legs and tongues and cocks in the dark. Bringing someone down there after I'd caught at least a glimpse of his face from the street lamps was okay, but you couldn't see any faces in the dark. The place must have gotten too hot for the unfortunate people who lived there. Several weeks later when I went by, they'd installed a heavy locked gate.

One autumn I noticed a new building going up on the corner of Pearl and Market Streets. By the time winter came, the building had a roof but was lacking walls. It had staircases without railings. It was a skeleton of a building that would one day house retail shops and rented offices.

When the rainy season started, the workmen wrapped the building at Pearl and Market in pale blue plastic. One Saturday night I was out after the bars closed, and it was pouring! I'd had too much to drink and had probably bought some cocaine from Jim Bayer as well. I was in no mood to go home and stay there, so I put on a raincoat and rubber boots and went out for a walk. I didn't expect to see many people out in this weather, but at least there was some life on the street. I saw someone coming toward me on the sidewalk in the downpour. I guessed I was in luck if he and I were the only two guys out here tonight. I had no competition, and I couldn't afford to be choosy either. Besides, from what little I could see of him in his rain gear, he looked hot. He half-walked and half-ran with a sexy swagger while holding his hat down and his collar up.

I watched him turn down Pearl Street. When I got to the corner, I saw him lift up a loose flap of blue plastic and slip inside. Seconds later, I followed him. The rain had not deterred everyone from coming out that night. This place was crawling with men. I looked around at silhouettes of the brims of black leather biker caps on guys in full-leather Folsom gear. Some were in raincoats and jeans like me. Others were already bare-chested. I could see the glow of cigarettes in the darkness. I lit one too while I got my bearings. I thought I saw the guy I'd followed into the building heading for an open flight of stairs, so I followed him up and then up again, but he disappeared. The roar of traffic on the central freeway outside was even louder at the top of the building. Suddenly my fear of heights kicked in. I avoided the hands reaching out for me as I brushed past other men in the dark and retraced my steps down the center of each flight of steps until I was safely back on the ground floor.

Zippo lighters snapped shut and the moans of orgasms rose and fell, but mostly I heard the cars on Market Street, tires on the wet pavement and the squeals of brakes when the light turned red. When cars turned off Octavia Street, their headlights spread beams across the blue plastic and illuminated the skeleton of our shelter. In that eerie glow, I imagined I was with all those horny men aboard a spaceship somewhere in the cosmos.

The back of the building was quieter and much darker, so I decided to head in that direction. A few steps later, I fell into what was going to become the elevator shaft for this new building. It happened too fast for me to be afraid. I landed with a thud on a pile of dust or sand. I stood up and brushed myself off. Then I reached up and realized that the shaft was deeper than I'd thought. I couldn't quite reach the rim on my tiptoes, not even if I jumped as high as I could.

All I could see was the outline of the elevator shaft that appeared like a square of dim light above me. Suddenly the empty space filled with heads popping out from each side: two here, three there, all the way around me. Someone whispered, "Are you alright?" And I whispered back, "Yeah, I think so…" No other words were spoken. Arms reached down to me. Strangers' hands opened up to clasp my hands. Arms pulled me higher as more hands reached under my shoulders and other hands grasped my belt loop in the back. Once I was safe on the plywood floor beside the open hole, everyone silently faded back into the dark corners and returned to the business at hand.

I sat there for a minute and realized I was sober now, no doubt due to the shock of the fall and the adrenaline rush that followed. My habitual horniness had passed, and I decided it was time to go home to bed. I carefully made my way back to the flap where I had come in. I pulled up my hood and ran home through the driving rain. I didn't need sex with another man that night. I had just been lifted up by the loving arms of nameless, faceless angels in the form of my horny gay brothers.

Chapter Twenty-Eight

Patrick Toner was twenty-two when he won the International Mr. Leather title, so it must have been his twenty-fourth birthday on September 20, 1986 when I took him to the baths. A decade earlier there had been almost thirty gay bathhouses in San Francisco, but the Health Department closed them down one by one in their attempt to combat the spread of AIDS. The last one—the 21st Street Baths—closed in May of 1987. It drew a more local, blue-collar crowd than some of the larger and fancier ones like Ritch Street or the Club Baths on 8th and Howard. For the kinkier places like the Slot or the Hot House or the Folsom Street Barracks, you had to be in the right kind of mood. Going to them required more of a commitment to the evening. If I was going on a Saturday night, I would plan accordingly, starting midweek to adjust my sleep and meals and planning which drugs to take. The 21st Street Baths were much more casual. I could go on a whim, sit in the hot tub or laugh with a bunch of guys dressed in towels watching TV comedy shows in the lounge. If the other baths had video, it was usually showing porn.

Unlike Rita and me (and Al Parker/Drew Okun, after he joined us), Patrick Toner kept his birthdays quiet. I was hanging out after work at the Special one night when Patrick came in, so I joined him for a drink at the bar. At some point, he let slip that it was his birthday. I asked him, "What are you doing? Isn't anyone taking you to dinner? Aren't you going to celebrate?"

"No, no, no…" He didn't want any fuss. We talked about other things for a while, which in those days meant discussing who had died that week and if there was a "send-off" party planned for them. Any conversation in the Castro during the late 1980s was sure to cover deaths and illnesses and someone's latest lab results. Discussion also included recent stories in the news about what the city, state or federal government was doing to address the AIDS crisis, which didn't seem to be much. Patrick and I probably discussed the fact that all the baths were closed now except for 21st Street. I told him I would always have fond memories of some great times there. That's when he told me he'd never been.

"You've never been to the 21st Street Baths?"

"No, I've never been to any of them."

"You're kidding! Come on. It's your birthday. This might be your last chance. It's my treat. I'm taking you." So on the night of Patrick Toner's twenty-fourth birthday, we drove over to the Mission, parked my pickup truck in the lot across the street and checked into the baths. We got one room with two keys and agreed that if either of us brought someone back, the other was welcome to join in, even though Patrick and I hadn't had sex with each other since he was twenty-one. We got undressed, locked the room behind us and set out on our adventure wearing only our little white towels. I hadn't been there in a while, but I'd never seen the place so deserted. No one else was around. No one was sitting in his room with the door open, legs spread, waiting to lure in a passerby. Nobody was wandering the hallways. Patrick and I went downstairs and had the hot tub all to ourselves. We soaked for a while, and then I showed him the empty orgy room and the upstairs cubicles. Afterwards we went back down to the steam room and then the TV lounge. Shag carpet on hard steps was considered lounge accommodations at most of the baths. And I suspect you wouldn't want to see that shag carpet in anything resembling daylight.

Patrick and I soon realized that we were the only two customers there, so went back to our room. We curled up naked on the flat sheet on our hard bed, and I put my arms around him and we fell asleep for a little while. A short time later, the roar of a vacuum cleaner woke us, so we got up and showered again, got dressed and turned in our keys and left. I told Patrick I was sorry that he didn't get to enjoy the whole bathhouse experience, but he said he didn't mind. We drove back to the Castro, and I took him to Orphan Andy's for a day-after birthday breakfast instead. It was probably just what we both needed.

Chapter Twenty-Nine

Eventually, I got a new roommate on McCoppin Street. Derek was a bartender at the Eagle, a tall redheaded Canadian who always looked like he was smuggling one enormous hunk of salami in the crotch of his pants. I soon discovered that it was a "shower" and not a "grower," but that was fine. Even though it stayed about the same size when it got hard, it was still much bigger than most. Derek and I became friends and occasional fuck-buddies, but only when we were both too horny, too loaded and too lazy to go looking for someone else. Some rainy, wintry nights having sex with each other was more convenient than venturing out into the storm.

What was even better about Derek was the men he brought home. Derek attracted men that I might be interested in. I don't know how many times I ended up carrying on with one of his hot tricks in my bed—or in the bathroom, living room or kitchen. They would come out of his room to use the toilet and "accidentally" enter the wrong bedroom when they returned. If I protested that I didn't want to get into any trouble with my roommate, they would invariably say, "Don't worry; he's already passed out."

It was true. Derek never objected, if he even remembered in the morning that he'd brought someone home the night before. They often turned out to be from out of town, anyway. Sometimes I even made them coffee and toast in the morning before I called them a cab. Derek slept in.

Chapter Thirty

Dorthy Duster was a very tall and, from my perspective at the time, very old drag queen. She insisted that her first name be spelled with one "O". She adopted the last name "Duster" because she cleaned people's apartments for a living. His real name was Gene, but nobody ever called him that. She was always Dorthy and referred to with the feminine pronouns "she" and "her," whether in or out of female clothing.

Dorthy Duster lived in a little apartment above one of the retail stores across Castro Street from the Special, so she was in the bar nearly every day, either before or after her cleaning jobs. She cleaned my apartment on McCoppin Street for a while when Derek and I were roommates after Mister Marcus moved out, but Derek always complained that she wasn't thorough enough in her housekeeping to be worth the money, so he fired her.

Dorthy didn't seem to mind being fired. She could always get another job. Dorthy was in demand. People constantly hired her to clean or do whatever odd jobs they needed done, and it wasn't because of her charming personality. Dorthy Duster could be a nasty and cantankerous old bitch, but we all put up with her foul temper. Maybe the fact that so many people we knew were dying every week made us more tolerant of each other's foibles. Despite her crusty exterior, Dorthy could be highly entertaining, a quality which was sorely needed in the darkest days of AIDS. Even after Derek fired her, I hired her back to help me paint my bedroom, and I remember that as a day full of laughs. I always dreaded painting by myself.

Dorthy, as Gene, once had a high-powered career in the cosmetics industry and before that had worked as a model, but she rarely talked about those days. I only found out about that side of her life because of the old framed pictures of a handsome young man in her living room. The resemblance was clear. I asked her if he might be a relative since so many gay men of that generation had once been married and fathered children. I thought he might be a long-lost son, but Dorthy told me those were his own pictures from an earlier life, long before landing on Castro Street.

In 1985, a retired grandmother named Ruth Brinker heard about a neighbor who died and was shocked to discover that malnutrition was as much the cause of death as AIDS. She began preparing meals in her kitchen and delivering them to seven people. In the days before protease inhibitors, when the only approved AIDS drug was AZT, many thought that food might make the difference between life and death. Ruth Brinker went to her kitchen, cooked for her ailing friends and began organizing volunteers to deliver hot meals to other AIDS patients throughout the city. In 1985, this led to the establishment of the nonprofit Project Open Hand, one of the first HIV/AIDS service organizations in the country.

Dorthy Duster and I were talking about Ruth Brinker's project at the Special one afternoon. In the beginning, most such organizations functioned on a shoestring budget with someone passing a hat in a bar to raise enough money to buy a sack of potatoes or a few loaves of bread. Having been in several bars where such impromptu pleas for funds had occurred, we thought it might be a good idea to organize an actual fundraiser. Dorthy thought she could come up with her own perfume. In 1981, Sophia Loren had become one of the first to launch a "celebrity scent," as we know them today. Dorthy was ahead of her time, since this was before Cher released "Uninhibited" and well before Elizabeth Taylor's many perfume varieties. To hear Dorthy tell it, all those celebrity scents were inspired by her. Dorthy Duster followed in no one's footsteps.

Launching Dorthy Duster's "Le Pew," named after the cartoon skunk Pepe le Pew, became a team effort among several friends in order to raise funds for Ruth Brinker's Project Open

Hand. Terry Thompson's lover, Stephen Blair, in addition to being a bartender at the Eagle, was a talented graphic artist. He volunteered to create a label for the perfume. It had the name and a caricatured portrait of Dorthy Duster which resembled cartoon character Cruella De Vil from Disney's *101 Dalmations*, who did look a great deal like Dorthy in drag.

Chris Osborne knew someone in town who manufactured amyl nitrate poppers, so he was able to rustle up a gross of plain brown bottles to hold the secret scent. We thought that whatever we used had to be ingestible, just in case anyone was foolish enough to drink it, so we decided to use what we all knew best— liquor. Dorthy wanted a subtle scent, despite the fact that there was never anything subtle about her. One afternoon when I was bartending, we held a little meeting—Terry, Blair, Chris, Dorthy, Fluffy, Fanny and whoever else happened to be in the bar at the time—to do a taste test of several kinds of liquor. We finally settled on straight Tanqueray gin.

I don't know why we ended up doing the fundraiser at the Village bar (around the corner at 4086 18th Street where the Mix stands today) instead of at the Special, but various neighborhood bar owners including my boss Ed "Edwina Ballerina" Stark each donated a bottle of Tanqueray so that we had enough gin to fill one hundred and forty-four little bottles. We completed that chore in Dorthy's kitchen across the street one evening after I got off work with enough gin left over to drink martinis while we filled the bottles and tied the cardboard labels onto them with ribbon.

The night of Dorthy's debut of "Le Pew" at the Village turned into an all-you-can-eat spaghetti feed as well. The Arab families who owned Rossi's Deli next to the barber shop and Valley Pride, the grocery store and butcher in the middle of the block, donated most of the meat, tomato sauce, French bread, and the ingredients for a simple salad to feed several dozen people.

Ruth Brinker arrived at the Village and sat between Dorthy and me while I collected the money and made change. Ruth charmed everyone with her sweet grandmotherly demeanor. We had planned to charge a nominal amount to those who wanted to eat and sell the "perfume" for a couple of bucks per bottle. Then Ed Stark came up with the idea that since the bottles were numbered, we should auction off specific ones. I think he ended up buying number one for seventy-five dollars and Terry or Blair bought number fifty for fifty bucks. The more people drank, the more they got involved with the silliness of this whole event and the more generous they became.

Afterward, I invited Ruth Brinker to the Special to show her where I worked. We sat at the bar and continued our visit while Ed took the small bills into the office and counted them out for us. The entire donation to Project Open Hand from Dorthy Duster's "Le Pew" couldn't have come to more than about five hundred dollars, but Ruth Brinker appeared to be thrilled with that amount. It was much better than passing the hat.

What started with her caring for one sick friend grew into feeding a few more and then a few more and then dozens and hundreds. Ruth Brinker died in August of 2011 at age eighty-nine. By that time, Project Open Hand was feeding thousands of people per day on a budget of over five million a year in public and private donations. Her vision of providing "meals with love" has inspired over a hundred similar organizations throughout the U.S. and worldwide, bringing people together to provide nutrition with compassion to their neighbors in need.

Dorthy Duster ran for Empress at least once and for Grand Duchess too, I believe. I wasn't interested enough to keep track of all the royal titles that people were vying for in those days, but it was jokingly said that Dorthy Duster had run for "everything but the border!" Since the Emperor and Empress Coronations were around the same time of year as *Men Behind Bars*, Jim Cvitanich and I always tried to incorporate those contestants into our shows. For part of the Act I finale medley of *Men Behind Bars III* in 1986, we used the three drag queens vying for Empress that year—Dorthy, Deidre, and Sable Clown—doing lip-sync as a 1960's girl group.

Jim and I assumed there was a bitter rivalry between them, so we thought it would be funny to put them as close together as possible. I remembered a scene in the Broadway musical *Hair* in which three girl singers stood very close together as they performed until a point in their number when they stepped apart to reveal that all three of them were wearing one dress with three holes for their heads and six sleeves. Since our costume budget was limited, we resolved the sleeve issue by putting six arm holes in the dress and putting the three drag queens in long gloves. It was a funny moment in the show, and the three of them managed to get through it without killing each other. I imagined one of them might have a knife under that dress one night—most likely Dorthy—but they made it through each performance with big smiles.

Sable Clown became Empress XXI of San Francisco that year and died two years later in November of 1988 at the age of thirty-three. Deidre died a few months earlier that year on the Fourth of July. Dorthy escaped the ravages of AIDS somehow and survived many of our mutual friends, but she was plagued with other health problems a few years later.

So many people were dying of AIDS in such rapid succession that to hear of someone dying of something else was a shock. I came into work one morning and sat down at the bar about eleven-thirty, as usual, to have a drink and get my bearings before my shift started at noon. Braxton "Judy" Hancock came and sat at the barstool next to me and Ed stood nearby. Right away, I sensed that something was wrong, but I couldn't imagine what it was. The bar was fairly busy, but unusually quiet.

"I guess you haven't heard about Juanita," Judy said.

"No, what about Juanita?"

"He died this morning. Heart attack. About six a.m. His roommate heard him thrashing around and went in to check on him. Juanita asked him to bring a glass of water so he went to the kitchen to get it, but by the time he got back, Juanita was gone."

I remember at that moment Ed put his arms around me from behind. Everyone knew how close we were. I adored Bill "Juanita" Wallace like a favorite uncle, and I knew that he loved me very much.

Ed said, "Do you want me to cover your shift? You don't have to work at a time like this unless you want to."

I thought about it a minute and said, "Yes, please. Cover my shift." I couldn't go through having endless people come into the bar to console me. Work was just the wrong place for that. Even worse would be telling the people who didn't know about Juanita. I didn't want to have to spend the day breaking the bad news to them. Pretty soon Chris Osborne came in, followed by Dorthy Duster. Chris had a car, so he drove the three of us to a little restaurant on Folsom Street where we met up with Terry Thompson and Blair. Over lunch, we planned Juanita's memorial gathering at the Special for the following Sunday.

Juanita was fifty-four years old when he died, but I revered him as an elder in the gay community, or to be more precise, in the gay bar community. He had moved out here from Texas in the late 1950s with a group of gay men his age that included Charlie "Fanny" Fulbright, Sam Houston, and a couple of others whose names I can't remember. I respected all of them for being a living testimony to the vibrant pre-Stonewall gay life, for their knowledge of that history, and maybe most of all for their sense of humor.

Juanita told the funniest true stories of anyone I knew. He'd worked as a waiter and a bartender in long-gone gay establishments like Jackson's, On the Levee, and Off the Levee when I was still a kid on the farm in Minnesota. People still talked about those places and, in my mind, they became legendary pieces of the city's gay past. When someone's mother came to town for a visit, I was told that the safest way for her to meet your friends was to take her to Sunday brunch at Jackson's. Juanita was known for being the slowest waiter in town in those days, so slow that when the maitre d' seated people in Juanita's section, he handed them not only a menu but a magazine to read. Still, lots of people asked for Juanita, especially those who didn't want to be rushed. Sunday brunch with lots of cocktails was more than a tradition in those days; it was almost a religious ritual.

Juanita had taken me on my one and only trip to Ginger's in the Tenderloin. After it closed, the owner opened Ginger's Too on the sleaziest block of 6th Street, just south of Market. Juanita got a job as a waiter there for a while in the mid-80s. Dick Walters, who also wrote a weekly column in the B.A.R. under the byline "Sweet Lips," was the bartender. I'm not sure if they served any food besides Sunday brunch because I was afraid to go to that part of town after dark. The only time many of my friends went to Ginger's Too was on the Sunday of Gay Pride, because it was the closest gay bar to the parade route. Ginger's Too was a good restroom stop and you could get a drink in a "to-go" cup. Once they started televising the gay parade, you could also watch it from the bar, so after a few drinks a lot of people just settled in and never made it back outside.

A couple of years later, Juanita got a bartending job in the Castro, doing weekday afternoon shifts at 4149 18th Street. That bar had been the Pipeline when it was known as a front for cocaine dealing, but someone new had bought it and done a major renovation. It was called Festus, and was now a cowboy-themed bar decorated with bales of straw around the room and country-western music on the reel-to-reel tape player. Maybe they hired Juanita for his Texas accent, because it sure wasn't for his efficiency. It didn't matter because everyone adored him anyway, but sometimes we called ahead from the Special to place our drink orders so that he would have plenty of time to make them before we arrived.

I remember the grand opening of Festus on a Saturday afternoon. It was one of those rare balmy days in San Francisco when everyone was in shorts and guys had their shirts off because of the heat and not just to show off their pecs. The gay marching band formed at the corner in front of the Twin Peaks and marched down the middle of Castro Street with policemen on motorcycles holding back the traffic. Behind the marching band, a horse-drawn carriage carried Absolute Empress I Jose Sarria, all decked out as the Widow Norton. Festus was too crowded for everyone to fit inside, but the door and windows were wide open so the band played out on the sidewalk and Jose along with other dignitaries made speeches. I have never seen a grander "grand opening" for a gay bar in my life.

I remember going back inside when the dedication was over and finding a place to sit on a bale of straw near the bathrooms in the back of the room. I took a couple of hits off a passing joint, even though I was already stoned. Then I lit a cigarette and looked around at the crowds of people drinking and smoking amid all the bales of straw, and I realized I didn't see a rear exit. I was stoned enough to be hit with a wave of paranoia and common sense at the same time. I didn't leave the party. I just maneuvered my way to a comfortable spot that was closer to the front door in case of a fire. Festus didn't last long before it turned into a lesbian bar called Francine's and then the Edge. Juanita didn't seem to last very long at any one job, either.

The day Juanita died, the rest of us sat at lunch and talked about the many places he had worked, how each of us had gotten to know and love him. We retold some of the stories that Juanita had told us a dozen times, and we laughed at them again. Juanita loved to tell about the small town in Texas where he grew up. One of the stories went that in elementary school, all the children were gathered in the auditorium for assembly when the principal announced, "Boys and girls, for a special treat today our very own Mary Lou Weatherwax will recite from memory Joyce Kilmer's lovely poem *Trees*." At that moment, a boy in the back row of the auditorium yelled, "Mary Lou Weatherwax sucks cock!" The principal, without missing a beat, said, "Be that as it may…Mary Lou Weatherwax will now recite Joyce Kilmer's lovely poem, *Trees*." The way Juanita recounted this story in his deep Texas accent, we howled every time we heard it.

Juanita's memorial "wake" was the following Sunday afternoon at the Special. Dorthy Duster came as the "Widow Wallace" in her own version of mourning clothes: full black, with lots of layers of fabric and heavy veils she had to lift in order to smoke and drink. People brought lots of food, so we covered the pool table with plywood and a tablecloth, trays of sandwiches, fresh crudités and dips and various kinds of chips and cookies. Someone found a nice picture of Juanita, looking more sober than we had ever seen him, and stuck it in a frame. I placed it on the table with candles on either side.

The daytime crowd at the Special included a lot of movie buffs who could spend hours discussing trivia about old Hollywood, the stars, the directors, and the costume designers who worked on films I had sometimes never even heard of. Dozens of arguments were settled only after Juanita would holler, "Mark, bring me The Bible!" That was what we called *Leonard Maltin's Movie Guide*. Edwina bought the new edition every year when it came out, and we kept it behind the bar alongside a small reference library that included a dictionary, a copy of the *Old Mr. Boston Bartender's Guide* and a few maps of San Francisco and guides to scenic spots in northern California for when tourists asked for directions.

The day of Juanita's farewell gathering, while the crowds of mourners arrived at the bar, Dorthy Duster remembered to ask the bartender on duty for the movie guide so that she could place "The Bible" on the pool table/altar between the candles and in front of the framed photograph. It was the only thing that had been missing that day. Besides Juanita, of course.

Chapter Thirty-One

True stories often balk at being told. Like squirrely children in front of the camera, dressed in their Sunday best, just when you think they're in perfect focus, they jerk or blink or muss their hair. One of the regulars at the Special on Castro Street was a guy named Judy. I have no recollection of our first meeting. He was always just there. I do remember very well his grand memorial service at the landmark Trinity Episcopal Church on Gough and Bush Streets in Pacific Heights, but he wouldn't want me to start with that. Part of the trouble with telling the true story of Judy is that I never knew when he was telling the truth, but he was so interesting that I didn't care.

His legal name was Braxton Hancock (II or III or IV, at least.) He claimed to be a direct descendant and heir of the John Hancock Life Insurance Company, which made him rich beyond my comprehension. Then another day he told me that he was the person who coined the phrase, "Sometimes you feel like a nut; sometimes you don't," which had earned him a fortune in royalties from the candy people. Since Judy was about the same age as me and the Mounds and Almond Joy candy bars had been around since the 1940s, I had serious doubts about that story. Whatever the truth was, I believed him to be independently wealthy and unlike many people who cling to more money than they will ever be able to spend in even a normal lifetime, Braxton Hancock was generous to a fault.

Working in a bar on an average day or night with no special events happening, you never know when business will be busy or slow. Bartenders learn to appreciate regulars, especially if they are friendly, bright, and know how to hold their liquor. Regulars who are generous tippers are even more highly valued, but my favorites had my back in any crisis situation, which was rare, and my absolute favorites were intriguing enough to keep me company at the slowest times. Judy was all of those.

He wasn't in the bar every single day as many were, but I could count on seeing Judy at least two or three times a week when he was in town. He did travel sometimes, although his lover refused to fly, so they rarely went far or Judy went alone. We had a video game on top of the ice machine at the rear end of the bar. It was programmed to play several different games, and Judy played a couple of them when I was busy and he didn't want to talk to anyone else. Winners could enter their initials for bragging rights to the top five scores, but every couple of weeks the vendor came to take out the coins and reset the scores to zero. Judy would shovel in quarters until he won the high score on each of his favorite games, and to celebrate his achievement he always bought a round of drinks for the bar.

Judy's lover didn't drink, and I think I heard that he worked at a job somewhere downtown, so I didn't meet him for a couple of years. Judy talked about him, though. I didn't know his real name either, but Judy always called him Veda, after Joan Crawford's spoiled ungrateful daughter, played by Ann Blyth in the movie *Mildred Pierce*. Judy made his lover out to be just as selfish and venomous as the fictional character, but then he would laugh, and I suspected that it was all a joke. If Veda really existed, he and Judy were very fond of each other.

One day Judy sat down at the last bar stool on the end of the bar nearest the ice machine. He didn't usually sit down at all. He had barely touched his drink, so I asked him if he needed another roll of quarters. No, that wasn't it. He seemed down, and I asked him if anything was wrong. He said, "Mark, I'm afraid I've become a complete alcoholic, and I'm wondering what I should do about it. I could well afford to go to Betty Ford or one of those places, but I'm just not sure. What do you think?"

By this time, I had known plenty of hard-core alcoholics. They were the backbone of the business. I knew that they came in all shapes and sizes and exhibited all varieties of behavior from weepy to sleepy to whiney to angry to belligerent to hostile to violent and Braxton Hancock was none of those. I said, "Judy, let's analyze your situation, okay? Let me ask you a few questions and give me your honest answers. How many T-cells do you have?"

"Seven, last time they checked. I gave them all names. Do you wanna hear 'em?"

"Maybe later…have you ever been thrown out of a bar?"

"No, of course not."

"You've never made a complete fool of yourself? Been so embarrassed by something you did that you were afraid to set foot back inside the establishment later?

"No, I don't think so. I can't think of a time I've done anything like that."

"Have you ever lost a job because of your drinking?"

"I've never had a job."

"Have you ever lost a boyfriend because of it? Have you ever fucked up a relationship and hurt someone and regretted it? Is your husband threatening to leave you or what?"

"No! Veda? Leave me? Where else would he find a meal ticket like this one? No way!"

"Well then, Judy, I don't know what you're so worried about. Look around. There's lots of way bigger drunks than you are sitting right here in this bar every day."

"Yeah, I guess you're right. Thanks, Mark. I feel a lot better now. Buy them all another drink on Judy!"

The afternoon gang at the Special loved trivia, especially movie trivia. They could spend hours playing a game they made up wherein one person named a famous movie star and the next person had to name a different movie star whose first name ended with the last letter of the last name of the first movie star. It sounds more complicated than it is. Some games would be male stars. Some would be female. Sometimes we allowed names from stage and television, depending on who started the game. They got to make the rules. Some of the regulars were old enough to remember stars I'd never heard of, so I learned about films going back to the first talkies.

We also had several two hour VHS tapes made up of nothing but clips of Broadway and Hollywood musical numbers. Some of them went way back too, but I had at least heard of most of the movies. Whoever had compiled the tape must have recorded every Tony Awards show ever broadcast. Having only been to New York a few times and seen only a handful of Broadway shows, I had never even heard of many of the performers. One day the tape came to a scene from the 1943 Busby Berkeley musical *The Gang's All Here* with Carmen Miranda singing "The Lady in the Tutti-Frutti Hat." I was familiar with the movie because we had tried to recreate this song and dance in one of our *Men Behind Bars* shows. Judy had once told me that his mother was a Busby Berkeley girl, but I'd forgotten all about it. I'd had other friends my age tell me their mothers were in the Radio City Music Hall Rockettes, so it seemed plausible.

When the big production number came on the screen, Judy stopped playing his video game and moved over to look directly up at one of the large television monitors over the bar. "There's Mom, holding a tray of bananas for the xylophone number."

"Which one is she?" someone asked.

"She just turned her back to the camera." We all tried to pick out Braxton's mother, but all of the girls looked identical, and the camera usually showed them as a group in a distant kaleidoscopic view from above or in long rows.

A few minutes later, he shouted, "Now, those are her feet, but this shot will pan back and show her face. See? She's the fourth banana from the end. Now she turned around, and she's lowering her banana on the left side of the screen."

When the scene ended, everyone had questions for Judy about growing up with a Busby Berkeley dancer for a mother and what it was like to know someone who had been in the movies back then. I got a little busy behind the bar again, so I didn't get to hear everything Judy said, but the gist of it seemed like his mother had been retired from dancing for some time before she got married and had a family. The Busby Berkeley girls really were just "girls." I was more interested in Carmen Miranda, who died in 1955 at age forty-six. Judy told us that the day Carmen Miranda died was the first time he'd ever seen his mother fall apart. He said, "Mom just collapsed on the living room floor and sobbed, telling me what a great woman the world had lost, what a dear lady and a wonderful talent."

Braxton told me another time that he had an uncle, or perhaps a great-uncle, who died in the crash of the Hindenburg on May 6, 1937. He had left specific instructions in his will about a piece of luggage that was not to be opened until fifty years after his death. Now it was the summer of 1987, and Judy got word that his uncle's attorneys had finally allowed some family members on the East Coast to open this container, and the relatives' first thought upon seeing its contents was, "Maybe Braxton out in San Francisco would like to have this stuff."

I was curious, to say the least. Had Judy's uncle committed some nefarious crimes? Had he cheated on his wife? Was he an embezzler? A jewel thief? Now the package was on its way, and we patiently awaited its arrival. I think I was as excited to see it as anyone, but then I didn't see Judy for a while. It turned out he was sick and had a stay in the hospital.

Over the years I knew Braxton Hancock, we talked about books a lot. He was a voracious reader and while I had not yet published any of my books, he knew I was a writer. We talked about how we had both developed a love for reading from the time we were children. I told him about growing up on a farm and going into town every Saturday afternoon to the public library to check out my limit of three books and how I plowed through all of the Hardy Boys mysteries in one summer. Judy was more of a Jonathan Swift fan, and we both laughingly confessed to having read all the Nancy Drew books too.

After a long absence, Judy reappeared one day at the Special with a cardboard box the size of a small suitcase. It was a gift for me—first editions of a full set (about four dozen) of the Hardy Boys mysteries from the 1930s and 1940s. At first I thought that this must have been part of his uncle's stash, but he told me that still hadn't arrived. They must have sent it the cheapest way.

Another day Judy brought me a phonograph album, a *Vogue* "Picture Record" of Phil Spitalny's Hour of Charm All-Girl Orchestra with Eleanor at the piano, performing Gershwin's "Rhapsody in Blue." I wondered if this was in his uncle's package, but this was from the 1940s, after his uncle's death. The package still hadn't arrived. Judy was just cleaning house, getting rid of things he thought his friends might enjoy. I had witnessed this pattern of behavior several times among my friends. By 1987 someone was dying of AIDS in San Francisco every seven hours.

When the package that contained the mysterious belongings of Judy's late uncle finally arrived, he didn't announce it. The first time he brought some of the contents into the bar, he didn't even tell me right away. He ordered his usual Cape Cod and stood at the end of the bar to play the video game on top of the ice machine. He waited until I wasn't very busy. A few people left and a couple of stools emptied near where he was standing, so he sat down and waited until he had my undivided attention. Then he reached inside his jacket and pulled out a small scrapbook with its cover taped on. "Is this it?" I asked him. "Is this from your uncle's stuff?"

"Part of it," he smiled. "There are dozens of these. I only brought one. They're all falling apart."

"What is it? What does it say?" I could hardly wait to hear.

"Well, it turns out my uncle lived in San Francisco when he was a young man. He didn't exactly keep a diary, but he wrote things down, notes to himself, lists and things, receipts. This one is from 1905. He lived in an apartment on Nob Hill, and you won't believe how cheap things were then!"

"What was his big secret?"

"I'll get to that in a minute, but listen to this part. He wrote that he hired a Chinese maid to cook and keep house for him for twelve dollars a month. He says he could have hired an Irish girl who spoke English for fifteen a month, but he would have had to pay for her ship's crossing to get here and give her a two-year guarantee and he wasn't sure how long he was going to stay here."

"What else?"

"Well, I found a few pictures of him. I only brought a couple. Here's one where he looks rather handsome, I think." Judy pulled out a sepia tinted photograph, about three-by-five, from the back of the notebook. It was loosely mounted in a cardboard frame with the name of the photographer's studio on Union Square embossed in gold lettering in one corner. He was handsome, dressed in a turn of the century suit and posed with one leg up on a wrought iron bench in front of a fake tree. "I'm thinking this photographer might have been a friend of his because all the pictures have the same trademark on them."

"Maybe…"

"And there's another reason I think they were friends." Judy pulled out the other picture, the same backdrop, the same paper, the same photographer, of course, but this time his uncle was grinning broadly and dressed in full drag. He was wearing high-buttoned shoes, with one silk-stockinged leg up on the bench revealing layers of petticoats, and one hand coquettishly holding a paper fan behind his head. His face was fully made up to look like a dance hall girl who might have felt right at home in any saloon on the Barbary Coast.

Over the next few weeks, Judy brought in other notebooks and shared small passages from them. His uncle wrote about how one particular bar, in one of the most elegant Nob Hill hotels, was the place to be every Thursday afternoon from four to seven p.m. because it was filled with nothing but single gentlemen. It was obviously the closest thing they had to a gay bar in 1905. He wrote about making friends easily, and how he was often invited to parties at the beautiful homes of other single men and even some male couples who managed to find a way to co-habitate, attended to by their domestic staffs, which were usually Chinese, Irish, or African-American.

One day Judy brought in a notebook that told about her uncle joining a riding club. He said it was a great way to meet new men and socialize. They held their gatherings in various homes and apartments and a few of them even owned their own horses. They stabled them in the under-developed western region of the city, although ownership of a horse was not a prerequisite for membership in the club. I howled! "It's just like the bike clubs, nowadays. Half of those guys have never ever been on a motorcycle, but they spend a fortune on leather and they love to wear the gear," I said. I wished I hadn't said that out loud because I suddenly remembered that Judy belonged to one of the gay uniform clubs.

The next time I brought up the topic of Judy's uncle, he told me that he'd finished reading all the notebooks. He told me that his uncle was awakened in the early morning hours of April 18, 1906 by the great quake. He then packed up and left the Bay Area as fast as he could, and moved back to the East Coast, never to return. That was the last we knew about Judy's uncle until he was killed in the crash of the Hindenburg. I still wonder what happened to those notebooks after Judy died.

Judy's next big project was to plan his anniversary with Veda. I think they'd been together ten years, and he wanted them to take a nice trip together. Veda had never been to New York and Judy decided they would take the train across country since Veda refused to fly. For the average person, that would mean buying a couple of tickets at the Amtrak station, and probably booking a sleeper for such a long trip. That wasn't Judy's style, though. Since the internet didn't yet exist, Judy spent the next several weeks at the library doing research into luxury North American train travel. He brought glossy brochures into the bar for everyone to peruse, and we shared his excitement.

He finally decided to rent a private Presidential car from the 1930s, refurbished to its former pristine Art Deco glory. He discovered that, for a price, Amtrak would attach a private car to the end of its regular trains. It had an outdoor viewing area where they could ride on the back and see all the sights. It might take a little longer to cross the country, and they might be stopped for a day or two along the way, but they weren't in any rush. Judy also hired a chef to travel with them to prepare all their meals.

He sent me postcards addressed to the bar every day so I could read them out loud to the rest of the regulars. They were hysterically funny. Judy wrote about being stuck for thirty-six hours on a desolate field of railroad tracks outside of Omaha. On the second day in the scorching Nebraska heat, he was deathly afraid of running out of ice for his cocktails. Another time he complained that he was nearly out of vodka and worried about which were the "dry" states. He wrote one card to describe in detail a shirtless young man sweating as he worked in the railroad yard across from where they were stuck in Chicago for a couple of hours.

After their trip to New York and back, Judy stopped in the bar a few more times, but not as often. I could tell by his face that he had lost a lot of weight. He took on the familiar characteristics of the latter stages of AIDS: the gaunt look around the eyes, the pale papery flesh. The last time I saw him, he gave me yet another book, *Breathing Lessons* by Anne Tyler. He wrote inside, "For Mark – I hope you enjoy this as much as I did. It's the best book I've ever read. Love, Judy."

One day I came to work and got the word that Judy had died the previous weekend. I wasn't surprised. I'd lost too many friends by then. I was just numb. When I got off work at seven that day I went to the office to count out my tips and when I came out, I saw a slight young man waiting outside the office door. "Excuse me, are you Mark?"

"Yes, can I help you?"

"I hope so. Braxton said he knew you would help. I'm trying

to plan a memorial, and I don't know who his friends are."

"Oh my God! You must be Veda!"

He laughed and said, "I know Braxton called me that, but not to my face. My name is Mark too."

"Hi, Mark. It's really good to meet you. Can I get you a drink?"

"No thanks. I don't drink." Of course I knew that, but I'd forgotten.

I took him into the office and we sat down to talk and plan Judy's funeral. He already had Trinity Episcopal Church lined up, as Judy had wanted. He'd spoken to the Castro Cheesery, also known as the Castro Coffee Company, up the street in the Castro Theatre building. He said that Braxton always liked those people and they would do some nice trays of cold cuts and cheese and crackers for the bar afterwards. What Braxton wanted, Mark said, was for everyone who came to his service to drink for free for the rest of the afternoon at the bar. What he needed from me was to greet people at the door of the church and give each of them a red carnation boutonnière. I got my friend Doug Shaffer to help me. Judy's was our third memorial that week. After the brief one p.m. service, we all went back to the bar. The bartenders on the noon to seven shift at the Special kept track of all the drinks they gave away to the people with red carnations. At the end of their shift, Mark paid the bill plus a hefty tip, as per Braxton's instructions.

It wasn't until a couple of weeks later that I ran across Anne Tyler's *Breathing Lessons* on my bedside table on McCoppin Street. I had the day off, so I sat down on the couch and read it from cover to cover. I couldn't put it down. It wasn't necessarily the best book I ever read, but it was a wonderful celebration of average people in mundane situations. I realized that someone like Judy, who loved telling tales about everything from Hollywood to the Hindenburg crash, might have craved a magical escape into the lives of ordinary people, especially during his final days. I never did find out where Judy's money came from. I never saw his lover

"Veda" again, but I noticed Mark's obituary in the B.A.R. about a year later.

Chapter Thirty-Two

In 1987, the word got around that Rita Rockett was pregnant, so Patrick Toner decided to give her a baby shower at his place on Buena Vista Terrace. His apartment was huge, with arched doorways, high ceilings, and beautiful inlaid hardwood floors. San Francisco is full of great old homes, some of them divided into apartments, but still rich in early twentieth century craftsmanship of mosaic fireplaces and built-in wooden cabinetry. I don't remember hearing how or when or why Rita's pregnancy came about, but she came back from a trip somewhere with the news that the father was Samoan.

A group of bartenders chipped in fifty bucks apiece for a custom-made bassinet for the baby. A gay guy named Spike built it and unveiled it that night. It was layered in so much white lace and fabric that I thought it looked like a child's coffin, but I didn't say anything. I must have had death on my mind that evening. My friends were dying faster and faster as the 1980s wore on.

Patrick's roommate in that apartment was Sharon McNight, before she went off to New York to star in the Broadway musical Starmites, receiving a Tony award nomination for best actress. Sharon arrived late to the shower, but one of Rita's sisters and Ruth Brinker, the founder of Project Open Hand, were already there. What I mostly remember is the men who attended, and I can still picture that evening as a special time and place for us to be together.

Rita's good friend Richard Locke, a well-known porn actor who starred in several early Joe Gage films, was videotaping the party. Everyone was there from Mister Marcus to politicians like Supervisor John Molinari and State Senator Milton Marks, disc jockey Otis Campbell and Jerry Vallaire, who was one of the key people involved in the first years of the Folsom Street Fair.

When the time came for Rita to open her gifts, most of the party guests migrated toward the front of the house. Rita was seated in the bay window surrounded by piles of gift-wrapped boxes. Someone had set out several rows of folding chairs facing her, and I ended up sitting beside the singer Sylvester. We were in the back row on the right, and he was in a talkative mood too. Between the two of us, we did a running commentary on Rita and her gifts. I don't know what was so funny, but I remember thinking how I had never had so much fun with Sylvester before. I'd known him for years, but most of the times we'd spent together he was about to perform at some event I was working. The night of the shower, Rita was on center stage, so Sylvester and I didn't have to do a thing.

At one point I went to the kitchen to get us both another drink. Maybe I stood up too fast, but I felt dizzy for whatever reason. I stood there in the kitchen and looked around at who was there: Terry and Blair, Ed Stark and his lover Richard, aka "Roz." Patrick Toner was mixing himself a drink at the self-service bar. Pete Pettine was waiting his turn ahead of me. David Sarathain was in front of the refrigerator popping the top off a bottle of beer. David and Pete would soon become lovers, or maybe they already were by that night.

I have a mental image of that scene as clear as a photograph. Two men had their backs to me, so I can only recall the sleeve of a plaid shirt—maybe Drew Okun (porn star Al Parker)—and the back of a dark head with thinning hair—probably Jim Cvitanich. My mind took a simple snapshot, and I said to myself, "We are all dying."

Tim Snow, the protagonist in my *Beach Reading* mystery series is a gay man from Minnesota with a beloved Aunt Ruth, but his resemblance to me ends there. Tim Snow is psychic, which is something I have never claimed nor wanted to be. But that night at Rita's shower, I felt a shiver run through my body that I have never forgotten. The mental image remains with me to this day—the refrigerator, the sink with a bag of melting ice, the table and chairs, but mostly I see those men who are all gone. The only difference between then and now is that the picture has aged with the years from color into black and white.

I had a heightened awareness in those days that any time I

spent with a friend might be the last time I would see him. For one single moment that night, I realized that most of my closest friends in San Francisco were together in one time and place. I got our drinks, and I went back to the front of the house. I was still in a festive mood and cracking jokes, maybe to overcompensate for my sense of doom. Sometimes thoughts of death have the opposite effect one might expect, which is why I've heard some of the funniest and dirtiest jokes at funeral receptions. I sat back down with Sylvester, and we laughed some more while Rita opened gifts for the brand new life growing inside her.

A few weeks later on Sunday April 26, 1987, Rita had her baby. Patrick Toner called the Eagle to let everyone know. Terry Thompson got on the microphone to announce to the beer bust crowd that Rita Rockett had a boy and shots were on the house. The place went up in cheers and everyone raised their glasses to drink to a new life and for a woman we all loved. Richard and Jerry, Otis, Pete and David, Jim and Drew, Ed and Roz, Terry and Blair, Patrick Toner and even Sylvester all died during the next few years, the darkest days of the AIDS epidemic.

Rita's baby boy is six foot three now.

Sylvester arriving at Rita's baby shower

Photo courtesy of Rita Rockett

Chapter Thirty-Three

One foggy night in 1987, I decided to go along with the Special's bowling team on gay league night to cheer them on at Park Bowl on Haight and Stanyan. I think that was the same night my friend Doug, aka "Fluffy, "bowled five strikes in a row. His streak was so exciting that by the time he nailed his fourth, the guys in the lanes on either side of us stopped bowling when his turn came so they wouldn't distract him. By the fifth, it had gotten pretty quiet all around. I would say that a hush fell over the bowling alley, but that would be an overstatement. Noisy machines are always doing noisy jobs in a bowling alley, but by Fluffy's fifth time up to bowl, the word had spread that one of the bowlers from the Special was on a hot streak and at least a dozen guys had come over to stand in the back and watch.

Since I wasn't bowling with the team anymore, I had plenty of time to check out all the hot guys bowling in the gay league, not that having to take my turn to bowl had ever stopped me. Only now I could wander off for as long as I liked, hang out at the bar, get a hot dog, flirt with people, exchange phone numbers, and maybe even make a date for later. After Fluffy's fifth successful strike, the place went nuts. Everyone clapped and cheered and people bought him drinks. The next time he threw the ball, he ended up with a seven-ten split. He picked off the seven, but not the spare.

We all went back to the Special for more drinks after the bowling alley and the boss, Ed Stark, said he wanted to give me a lift home. He sounded like he had something on his mind, so I agreed. He confirmed my suspicions when he said, "I need to talk to you and I don't want any distractions." We finished our drinks and headed out. His van was parked next door, in the lot behind the Castro Theatre.

I hadn't seen Ed in a couple of weeks, which was not unusual when things were going well at the bar. He had bought out his old partner, Jack South, some time ago and business was great. Ed made a lot of money, and he could afford to travel and dabble in other projects like some real estate in the city and at the Russian River, plus his career dancing in drag and *en pointe*. As we pulled out of the lot and onto Castro Street, I asked Ed what he had been up to lately. I assumed he'd been out of town, but as we stopped at the red light in front of the Twin Peaks he said, "I was in the hospital. I had that pneumonia, you know…that AIDS pneumonia, pneumocystis."

My jaw dropped. I put my hand on his knee and said, "Oh, I am so sorry…" That was all I could think to say at the moment. By then I had lost dozens of customers and ex-boyfriends and former co-workers from various jobs. But Ed was a dear friend, maybe the closest person that I knew at the time to join the ranks of the infected.

He said, "Don't worry. I'm fine now. I snapped out of it. I'm tough. I spring right back."

I was still reeling from the news on top of all I had drunk that night. He looked good. Aside from a constant battle with an extra fifteen pounds or so, Ed kept in shape. He was always at the gym, and he was still a dancer. I knew he was strong because I had watched him physically throw a rowdy drunk out of the bar on more than one occasion. He could do it with one arm and not break a sweat. But then he said, "You know what this means, don't you? There is no cure. I have full-blown AIDS. I'm okay now. I'm doing the AZT regimen, but it's only a matter of time, and I wanted you to know because you're my best friend."

That was almost as shocking as his diagnosis. I loved Ed as a friend, but I didn't think of any one person as my "best friend." If I had to say who my lifelong best friend was, it would have to be Carl Beck, who was an actor at the Minneapolis Children's Theatre when I was a musician there. He lives in Seattle now, but we can go years without seeing each other. When we do, we pick up right up where we left off. With Ed, a couple of weeks might go by when we didn't talk, but I always loved seeing him.

I'd never had a boss I liked to hang out with as much. Unlike most bar owners, when Ed came in on my shift, it meant good times. He could talk to anyone, entertain everyone, buy a round of drinks for the house and leave a hefty tip for me.

Ed had one of the fastest wits I've ever known. He could be sarcastic and sharp, but he could also cut someone down in a way that came off as flattering. If Ed Stark paid enough attention to you to make you the butt of a joke, he was actually paying you a compliment. That was his way of giving you a hug and showing that he cared enough about you to make you the center of attention. It was a remarkable ability of his and almost everyone loved him for it.

The night he told me of his diagnosis, I sat there in the darkness of the passenger seat and wiped away a tear as it rolled down my cheek. I didn't want Ed to see it. He told me, "I have Roz at home, of course." He was referring to his lover, Richard. "I have lots of friends—good friends like Henry and Randy, but they're a couple. I just realized a while back that you are my best friend, so I needed to tell you, to let you know what to expect. You just never know."

I could imagine the next few weeks, maybe months of decline. This would also affect the bar and eventually my job. I loved that job. I loved the way Ed treated his employees. I loved tending bar on Castro Street. I made more than enough money to pay all my bills. I got to meet lots of interesting people, and I had my evenings free to take some of them home and mornings free to sleep in after sex.

We pulled up in front of my apartment on McCoppin Street, and I gave Ed a hug and a kiss on the cheek. He said, "Don't worry about me. We have another *Men Behind Bars* show to do. This time I'm going to teach the big girls to do the ballet. It'll be great! Good-night."

Chapter Thirty-Four

In September of 1987, Pope John Paul II came to town to pay a visit. I was never Catholic, so it didn't mean much to me, but the media made it out to be the biggest happening in San Francisco since the Beatles' last concert at Candlestick Park. You could always tell for those couple of days what part of the city the Pope was in by the swarms of helicopters in the sky. Hordes of the faithful lined the sidewalks for a glimpse of his glass-topped Pope mobile. It looked to me like a giant claw machine full of toys and stuffed animals, and if you dropped a coin in one side and spun a knob, you could win a life-sized Pope-on-a-Rope bar of soap.

The Secret Service ordered everyone who lived on Geary Boulevard to keep their windows and shades closed, but after an avalanche of protests to Mayor Feinstein, they compromised on no open garage doors. The next day's *New York Times* said a hundred thousand people lined the parade route, while the police were prepared for a million. I was tending bar on Castro Street, and we were packed for Happy Hour. The local news was on without sound. I had put on a cassette tape of show-stoppers from Broadway musicals—it was that kind of gay bar—and just when the Pope appeared on the television screens, the speakers blared the chorus of "Hello Dolly!" Everyone roared because the song seemed to fit so perfectly with the grand arrival of the Pope and his gowned cronies at the Golden Gate Bridge.

The second day of the Pope's visit, he went to Mission Dolores and that night after work I went to dinner at the home of my friends up the hill on Castro Street near 16th. Terry Thompson was the manager of the Eagle and even though I didn't work there any more, he was like a big brother to me, and his partner Blair was a dear friend. During dinner we talked about the Pope's visit, and they told me about their downstairs neighbor Bob who had full-blown AIDS. Bob was one of the sixty-two people with AIDS who had been selected for a special papal blessing that afternoon at Mission Dolores. Blair told me Bob had Kaposi's sarcoma. His

KS lesions were getting worse all the time, but Bob had such a great sense of humor that they loved having him around. They'd invited him for dinner too, but he was busy baking a cake and he might stop up later if it turned out.

By 1987 I'd gone to lots of AIDS memorials, but I hadn't been diagnosed yet. I just assumed I was positive because everyone around me was, but I was in no hurry to confirm the fact. I tried to keep going and take life one day at a time. Each Thursday I read the obituaries in the *B.A.R.* and knocked on wood. Any of us could be next. I knew people who went through their photo albums to pick out a favorite picture to use with their obituary when the time came. I changed my hair so often in those days that I could only narrow it down to a handful of photographs. I hoped to have enough time on my deathbed to decide on one picture for my final appearance in the local gay press.

I'd seen the pictures of KS in the window of Star Pharmacy when people started to look for those scary spots on their skin. I'd seen a guy at the Folsom Street Fair dressed only in boots and a jock strap, sitting alone in the sunshine on the curb outside the Ramrod. He was stick thin, face gaunt, cheeks sunken in. He was probably beautiful up until a few months before that. He was connecting the dots of the lesions all over his body with a red magic marker. His face had the expression of an innocent child with a coloring book. He took his time drawing one long red line from under his arm to his nipple and then to his nose, down the side of his face to his neck to his crotch and back up to connect all the lesions that were scattered across his chest. He was taking control of his life as best he could and making his own personal statement about AIDS. I stared at him for a minute and then I had to look away.

I'd been surrounded by AIDS, but I tried to keep it at a distance by drinking every day and going out every night. I kept on doing whatever drugs were available and there were always plenty of drugs. Sex was another great escape. When you think you're about to die at twenty or thirty -something, why not get all the sex you can get on your way out? We kept on dancing and partying as hard and as fast as we could. Because we still could.

That Thursday, September 27, 1987, at Terry and Blair's apartment on Castro Street, the three of us were having after-dinner drinks in the living room, smoking cigarettes and snorting cocaine. I didn't hear their neighbor Bob arrive; he must have come up the back stairs. I just looked up and there he was holding a gorgeous three-layer chocolate cake on a silver platter. It was right out of *Better Homes and Gardens.*

Blair introduced us and I stammered, "Hello! The guys were just telling me about their friend with k...k..." I was stunned and all but speechless. His face was so covered with lesions there were hardly any spots of flesh tones left. He was a white man with a face the color of the chocolate cake he held in his hands. I finally spit out, "...their f-f-friend with the c-cake."

Bob sat down and told us about his afternoon at Mission Dolores. There was even more of Pope's visit in the next day's papers, about how one of the sixty-two sick people was a four-year-old boy named Brendon O'Rourke who had weighed less than two pounds at birth and had gotten AIDS from a blood transfusion. He was dressed in a little blue suit and carried a Toys-R-Us backpack containing an IV pump that sent the HIV drug AZT through a catheter into his chest.

When the Pope got to Brendan, he embraced the little boy, which made big news because people still thought you could catch AIDS by touching someone. The newspapers and TV reporters gushed about the Pontiff's great compassion. I thought then and still think it would be more compassionate to encourage condoms and birth control, especially in countries where children were starving. That same week, in a statement about AIDS to the *New York Times,* the Pope said something about healing and the church trying to prevent the "moral background" that causes AIDS.

Blair made coffee to go with our cake, and I asked Bob what meeting the Pope in person had been like. He said it took a while for the old guy to work his way down the line. Some of the patients were kneeling, others were in wheelchairs or on crutches, and he blessed each one in turn. When the Pope got to him and said, "Bless you, my son," Bob told us that he looked up and said, "Oh, bless you too, honey. I sure wouldn't want to be in your shoes!"

We all laughed and I asked, "Did you really call the Pope honey?"

Bob said, "Well, I felt sorry for the poor old dear. Can you imagine? All that travel and having to drag all those gowns around, keeping up a schedule like that at his age? And everywhere he goes, people staring at him, trying to get up close enough to touch him, everybody wanting something? You couldn't pay me to take that job!"

I was glad I got a chance to meet Bob, and to laugh with him for an hour or so. Too many wonderful people died before I got to know them well. A couple of weeks later, Terry and Blair came in for drinks one afternoon, like they did both days. It was a Thursday and the new *B.A.R.* had just come out. They pointed out Bob's obituary, and I looked at it long and hard. I never would have recognized that guy I met with the cake as this handsome man in the photograph, but he looked familiar. Maybe I'd even had sex with him once years ago. I always remember that night when I ride the #24-Divisadero bus up the hill from Castro and Market past Terry and Blair's old place.

Gail Wilson in the finale of Men Behind Bars IV

Photo by Robert Pruzan, courtesy of the Gay, Lesbian, Bisexual, Transgender Historical Society

Chapter Thirty-Five

Ed Stark did pretty well after his first bout with pneumocystis, as far as I knew. It would have been like him to tell people he was in the Bahamas when he was really in the hospital. He would have made sure to go to the tanning salon up the block before he showed himself in the bar. We all started getting ready for MBB IV at the Victoria Theatre on Presidents' Day weekend of 1988. In retrospect, that year's show was probably my favorite of all of them. Gail Wilson was our guest star again, singing and acting out her version of a medley of hits by Connie Francis, ending with "Where the Boys Are." I had seen her do this act with just a piano player back in the 1970's at places like Sutter's Mill. Now she was able to do it with City Swing in the orchestra pit of the Victoria Theatre.

In the second act, Gail did a big production number with the Follies Men to Jane Russell's song in *Gentlemen Prefer Blondes* called "Ain't There Anyone Here for Love?" It was the same finale we had used in our very first MBB when Val Diamond did it.

This show was especially fun because Jim superimposed a loose plot over the typical variety show format. The first act was the auditions for the "real" show, which was the second act. Jim and I spoke actual lines over the "God" mike in the back of the house, and we also appeared onstage a few times between numbers.

Jim's roommate Joe Johns had created a drag character named Joan Eva Duarte Peckerhead, who was a shorter, younger version of Lily Tomlin's classic telephone operator Ernestine, complete with the snort and a hand reaching for a handkerchief in her cleavage. Miss Peckerhead was always running the box office at our previous shows, but this year, according to Jim's plot, she decided that the box office was too small for her talents. She was determined to be the star of the show even if she had to "lie, cheat or kill Gail Wilson!"

She was aided in her efforts by her fairy godmother, the well-known singer Irene Soderberg, whose first appearance was flying in from the wings on a crescent moon. Miss Peckerhead teamed up with the character of the stage manager, a frustrated Elvis impersonator played by Pete Pettine, who also had dreams of stardom. Their attempts to sabotage the show never went quite as they hoped, but at one point, Jim and I pushed them on stage in a desperate attempt to kill time while one of the other acts got ready, and they finally got to do their duet to "Great Balls of Fire."

Another highlight of that year's show was the ballet number. Edwina Ballerina wanted to work with the "big girls" from the previous year's opera *Revenge of the Valkyries* and decided to choreograph them as his back-up ballerinas in *Les Sylphides*, which I renamed *Les Syl-feed*, because all of them looked like they loved to eat. I came up with the idea that during the curtain call at the end of their dance, they would each get a pizza instead of flowers. The pizza boxes were empty, but the gag got a good laugh.

We did seven performances of the show that year, counting the Thursday night show which was a free performance for people with AIDS and their caregivers. We called it a "dress rehearsal," but we rarely stopped the show for any reason. We also did Friday through Monday nights at eight p.m. and two p.m. matinees on Sunday and Monday, which was Presidents' Day.

The night of the final performance, I went to the men's room in the lobby right after the ballet number had finished. I had seen Ed Stark duck inside there in his tutu and wanted to tell him what a great job he had done. I found him standing at the sink splashing cold water on his face. I said, "You were fabulous tonight, as always," but when I touched his bare back and shoulders with both hands, I realized he was burning up with fever. "Are you alright?" I asked.

He splashed more cold water on his face and told me not to worry. He'd be fine. We still had the final curtain call with the entire cast on stage to do the traditional ending with the audience singing along to "San Francisco." That night, in my curtain speech I made a point of thanking "my boss, Edwina Ballerina, for giving me the time off of work to do this show." I was very glad that version of the show was chosen for the final cut of the video that year.

When we all headed out to the cast party after the show that night, I was not surprised that Ed was missing. I found out the next day that Roz, had taken him directly from the theatre to the hospital, where he was admitted immediately. I wondered whether he checked in wearing full make-up, tutu, and toe shoes.

Edwina Ballerina takes flight in Men Behind Bars

Photo by Robert Pruzan, courtesy of the Gay, Lesbian, Bisexual, Transgender Historical Society.

Richard was nicknamed Roz after Rosalind Russell, I always assumed. He was a huge movie fan. He showed old movies one night a week on his bartending shift, and I was always afraid to ask him for a drink during a tense moment in the film. The Academy Awards season was always like Christmas to him.

While Ed was in the hospital, Roz would call or come by the bar each day with news of his condition. The first few days, he was allowed no visitors. When someone's immune system was as compromised as his, exposing him to outside germs was risky. Ed was on the mend a few days later, so we all breathed a collective sigh of relief at the bar. He'd had pneumocystis again, worse than the first time. I was sure that all the exertion of *Men Behind Bars* could not have been good for him, but he wanted to do it and now he was going to be all right again.

A week or so later, we got the first copies of the VHS videotape of the show for Jim and me to approve. It captured an excellent performance of Edwina and the big girls doing their ballet. He was still in the hospital, so I called to tell him about it. He sounded great, and I offered to bring the tape and a VCR to the hospital for him to watch. I was sure we could figure out how to hook it up to the little TV set above his bed, but Ed said, "No, I want to watch it with everyone else. We'll invite all the cast and crew and all their friends and have a party at the bar in a couple of weeks. I'm getting out of here tomorrow, anyway."

"Tomorrow? That's great!"

"Yeah, they just want to do one more bronchoscopy to make sure there's nothing left in my lungs. I hate those tests, but they won't release me without it." We said good-bye, and I started looking forward to the cast reunion party at the Special.

The next day I was at work behind the bar as usual, noon to seven. I knew that Roz and a couple of friends were going to pick up Ed from the hospital, provided that his test results were good. I figured they would take him straight home, but in some tiny corner of my brain I held out hope that he would want to stop by the bar for a minute. I really wanted to see him. When the phone rang at 6:50, I was sure it must be Ed, but it was a female voice. I wasn't really listening at first, too busy chiding myself for thinking Ed would call at that moment. He knew what time the shift change happened, for crying out loud! He would have waited until after seven, when I could talk on the phone in the office where it was quieter. "What?" I asked. "I'm sorry, but it's really noisy. What did you say? Could you repeat that please?"

I realized it was Ed and Richard's dear lesbian friend Chris Carnes on the phone. She said, "Ed died. They took him to do the bronchoscopy, and he was fine. We were waiting for him to come back so we could take him home, but they told us something went wrong. We even heard the code blue on the loudspeaker and we saw all the people rushing around, but we couldn't believe it was for Ed. He's gone now...he's just gone."

"I...I...there's no one else behind the bar. My relief isn't here yet. I've got to go. People are waiting for drinks. Talk later..." Those last few minutes of my shift that day were surreal. I worked as fast as I could to catch up, and I was a very fast bartender. I could mix and ring up drinks and make change in my sleep, but for those few minutes I tried hard to concentrate only on what I had to do. I forced myself to focus on going through the same motions I had done a thousand times without thinking. I did whatever I could not to replay in my head the horrible news I'd heard. If I didn't think about it, maybe I could make it not be true.

The next few days, I saw Ed everywhere I went. He'd be ahead of me in line at the bank. Then the man would turn slightly, and I'd realize he looked nothing like Ed. I'd see him from the window of a bus. I'd see him driving his white van with the dented roof from the year he'd ridden on top all the way down Market Street *en pointe* in full ballerina drag in the Gay Pride Parade. I heard his laugh in the next aisle at the supermarket. I saw him coming out of Walgreens. He was everywhere, but none of those people turned out to be him. He really was gone.

Chapter Thirty-Six

In 1988, I was tending bar at the Special on Castro Street one weekday afternoon when a stranger walked in. I wasn't very busy and only had a few of the regulars in their usual places. One of them greeted this guy by name, and the others turned to look. They all seemed to know him too. He started at one end of the bar and worked his way to the other, bending down between each of the stools. The customers stood up and moved out of his way as he got to them. He continued all the way around the pool table in the back of the room. I was mystified.

When he was finished, he sat down and ordered a drink. He told me that he and his partner had been regulars at the Nothing Special, which was the name of the bar before it was remodeled in 1986. They had moved to Palm Springs a couple of years ago where his "better half," as he called him, died of AIDS. His late partner had left instructions to toss half his ashes off the Golden Gate Bridge and spread the other half inside this bar where they'd had so many good times.

My first thought was that Wayne—better known as "Wanda June"—the swamper would come in to sweep up when the bar closed at two a.m., so this guy's ashes would end up in the dumpster. I didn't say anything. If someone's dying wish was to be spread on the floor of a gay bar on Castro Street, who was I to disagree? Then I considered closing time wasn't for several hours, which meant that dozens more customers would come and go. Sneakers and shiny business shoes and black leather boots and maybe the high heels of a drag queen or two would shuffle through those ashes and track them right out the door. I liked the idea of his ashes being spread throughout the neighborhood a lot more than the thought of them being swept into a dustpan by Wanda June's broom.

During the worst years of the AIDS plague, those of us who worked in gay bars managed to get memorials down to a science.

Even when someone opted for a Catholic Mass or some other formal religious funeral service in a real church, the mourners always ended up at their favorite bar afterward. I went to some gatherings held in people's homes, but even then we would return to the bar eventually. For a lot of guys, the bar was their home, or at least an extension of their living rooms or bedrooms.

A couple named Mel and Dennis came into the Special nearly every day. They'd been together for years and were two of the grumpiest people I'd ever met. Nothing pleased them. When Dennis died, his funeral was at Grace Cathedral on Nob Hill. A handful of regulars went and they all came back to the bar afterward. It was the first time I ever saw Mel smiling, even laughing! He told me that the funeral director had another service that day at Beth Shalom out on Clement Street. They sent the right casket to Nob Hill, but the wrong body. Both services were delayed for some time while they corrected their mistake. Mel thought it was hysterical that the Jewish lady ended up at Grace Cathedral while Dennis went to a synagogue on the Avenues. I pictured two hearses meeting somewhere in the middle to switch bodies. I couldn't imagine why anyone wanted their friends and families to see them dead in their open caskets in the first place.

I went to several services at the Metropolitan Community Church in the Castro. The first one I remember was in 1982 for Patrick Cowley, the record producer who created the fifteen-minute dance remix of Donna Summer's "I Feel Love" which was in every DJ's arsenal. They'd put that record on when they needed to take a break, hit the toilet or do some drugs. Patrick Cowley's funeral was in the afternoon, and the church was so packed that my friends and I ended up standing at the very top of the balcony. Sylvester got up to sing at one point, but he started sobbing instead. He collapsed and people rushed up to surround him and help him out the side door while he wailed in grief.

I think more people were cremated than buried. I don't know how many times I went out on the Neptune Society's boat to sprinkle someone's ashes on the far side of Angel Island or just beyond the towers of the Golden Gate Bridge. We watched the ashes mixed with rose petals or glitter or marabou feathers as they sank into the deep salt water and drifted away.

Most of the people I knew who died in those days didn't have church funerals here in San Francisco, though their families might have held services back wherever they came from. Most of my friends weren't religious in that sense. We had our own way of honoring the fallen, and a lot of times we did that by gathering together in their favorite bar.

We usually had a slide show of the person's life in healthy and happier times. Sometimes an actual family member would come. That could be hard, especially if the relative didn't know their loved one the way we all did. Sometimes the family member wanted to make a speech and that got everyone's tears flowing. I remember one older guy who died—everyone over about forty-five was ancient to me—and his wife came to the gathering at his favorite gay bar. Who knew he was married?

When my boss Ed died, Richard asked me to officiate the gathering. That was my first time, but it would be far from the last. It was held at the beautiful landmark 1898 Columbarium off Geary Boulevard.

I tried to keep it light. I was really nervous because the place was packed, plus Ed's father was there. I knew Ed had been adopted, so I began, "Thirty-nine years ago, a tiny baby was found abandoned in a wicker basket on a doorstep in Kansas City, Kansas, wrapped in swaddling clothes, a pink tutu and tiny toe shoes, already set to leap onto the stage and across the prairies all the way to San Francisco." I talked about Edwina's ballet performances in drag at our *Men Behind Bars* shows. Ed had been the first person to use a fog machine in his act and the first to fly out on a wire, but we had never gotten around to having a bubble machine for him, so we decided to put a bubble machine in the doorway of the Columbarium. I also thought it was much more eco-friendly than releasing plastic helium-filled balloons. The mourners walked through bubbles on their way out after the service, and it made them smile.

Then we all went back to the Special to eat and drink. We set up the bubble machine again, this time just outside the doorway to the bar so that the bubbles poured out over Castro Street all evening. The bartenders had put on a mix tape of music videos, mostly MTV or VH1 sorts of hits, but about an hour later, I realized someone had added something else to the mix, a video of Ed performing the Rose Adagio from Sleeping Beauty in *Men Behind Bars* 1986. All the talking suddenly stopped. The room grew silent except for the swelling violins of the orchestral music. Edwina Ballerina was all in pink, dancing *en pointe* with four hot bare-chested bartenders he'd trained to do the most basic choreography for that year's show.

I thought there must have been a change in the wind because at that moment, the bubbles from the bubble machine outside came floating in the door. They poured inside and filled up the bar until the ballet ended as if Ed was saying one last "good-bye." And I swear there was no wind that night.

Chapter Thirty-Seven

There is a very old joke about two nellie queens who arrive in San Francisco. They get into a cab at the airport and ask the driver to take them to the Connie Francis Hotel. The driver says, "You must mean the St. Francis Hotel." The queens gasp and scream, "Oh no! She died?"

Sometime in the summer of 1988 after *Men Behind Bars* IV—the show in which Gail Wilson did her Connie Francis medley—the *real* Connie Francis came to town. Terry Thompson called me from the Eagle and told me that she wanted to take part in an AIDS benefit while she was here. We only had a matter of days to pull something together, so Terry asked me to call Jim Cvitanich and see if the two of us could come up with some ideas for the next Sunday's Eagle beer bust.

The Eagle patio was the place to be on Sunday afternoons in those days. Each Sunday a different organization ran the beer bust to raise money for a good cause. In the late 1980s, nearly every cause had something to do with AIDS whether it was for patient care or counseling or hospice or meals or to lobby for legislation. I don't remember which group served the beer that day, but they left the entertainment up to us.

We started the festivities around four-thirty with a bunch of guys who'd volunteered to dress in drag for a Connie Francis look-alike contest. We weren't fussy. Some of the guys were even sporting facial hair. Gail Wilson, who had portrayed Connie in our last MBB show, agreed to come to the Eagle in the same campy polka-dot costume that she'd worn in the show and sing "Where the Boys Are" to a tape of City Swing accompanying her. I can't remember what the drag queens did—probably lip-synched to some of Connie Francis's other hits—but Jim and I made sure that each of them was a winner by creating several categories of competition.

That day the Eagle patio was as crowded as I've ever seen it with dozens of hot, bare-chested men boozing it up and laughing at what was going on with Gail and Jim and me onstage with a half-dozen guys willing to get dressed up in something that they thought Connie might wear. Gail was announcing which contestant won the "best lip-sync" award when I noticed some commotion near the side door into the patio from 12th Street. Our guest of honor had arrived and was being escorted through the raucous crowd. Jim went ahead with the last award for the most authentic Italian Connie Francis arm hair just as the real Connie Francis climbed the steps to join us onstage. She was laughing, so we all relaxed when we realized she really was a good sport.

Gail Wilson took the microphone back from Jim to welcome our guest of honor. Then Gail explained that the three of us had recently done an AIDS benefit variety show in which she had paid tribute to Connie, which was why she was dressed in this silly outfit. Connie told Gail that she had one just like it in her closet at home, and Gail said she was sure it must look a lot better on Connie. The two of them chatted like old friends almost as if they weren't surrounded by a group of guys in dresses in front of an audience of hunky men.

Connie Francis was utterly charming, signing autographs and posing for pictures, first with those of us already on stage and later with everyone who lined up to ask. She told us that she wasn't planning to sing, but as long as we were all there to see her, she might as well. The DJ, of course, had her recording of "Where the Boys Are" cued up, so Connie Francis took the mike from Gail, and we all stepped back to listen to her sing live over her own recording.

A lot of guys must have told their housemates that they'd seen Connie Francis at the Eagle, or they went to work on Monday morning and told their co-workers about it. I imagine that some people believed this claim and others were in doubt, thinking the claimant must have seen a drag queen or had a hallucination. Still, I'm sure that most people wanted to believe in Connie Francis. It was just another magical Sunday afternoon at the Eagle, and I wasn't even stoned.

Jim, Gail, and Mark with Connie Francis at the Eagle

Photo by Robert Pruzan, courtesy of the Gay, Lesbian, Bisexual, Transgender Historical Society.

Chapter Thirty-Eight

By the time I was diagnosed HIV positive in 1988, I had lost over two hundred friends to AIDS. I stopped counting, stopped clipping the grainy black and white pictures from the obituary pages of the *B.A.R.* and comparing them to the ones I had in photo albums. I was probably HIV positive long before 1988, but I didn't care to find out. I just assumed everyone was infected by then and that we were all at death's door. It was only a matter of time, so why not order another drink, snort another line of coke, buy another pack of smokes? Just don't buy any green bananas.

Back in the 1970s, we had the clap and syphilis countless times. Rita Rockett still tells the old joke: "What do you give the girl who has everything? …Penicillin!" My friend Bob Burnside told me about a group of roommates in the 1970s who lived near the old VD Clinic on 4th Street. Like being waited on at the bakery, you went in, took a ticket, and sat down to wait until they called your number. These guys saved the tabs, brought them home and taped them up on their communal refrigerator in numerical order from 00 to 99. Within a few years, they'd collected a full set. I can imagine them laughing about it. "We've got all the high numbers, guys. We only need eight more and they're all below twenty. We've got to get there earlier next time." A few weeks later, "Hey, we only need one more! 47! How come we've got two 68s? Remember how long we waited for 69?" Everything was a game in those days.

Hepatitis B was a big one too. That took more than a shot at the clinic. It put me flat on my back for weeks in 1976. One year at the Castro Street Fair in the early 1980s, I noticed a sign on a booth that said: "Were you diagnosed with Hepatitis B in San Francisco in the 1970s? Sign up here to help us with a new study."

"They're looking for me," I thought to myself. I was always game to sign up for a study, so I staggered up to the booth. I was probably on acid. My friends and I dropped acid for the Castro Fair every year for about a decade. I could do little more than point to the sign and nod yes.

"Great!" one of the guys in the booth said. I remember thinking they were both really hot, and I'd never seen either of them before, much less slept with them. Putting sexy guys behind the booth was smart, and not so smart to put the old geezer at the chiropractic booth down the block.

I gave them my name and phone number, and the next week someone called to follow through. The sample of my Hepatitis B infected blood from my diagnosis in the 1970s had been frozen in Atlanta at the Center for Disease Control. I went to a little office off Van Ness Avenue, signed some release forms, and let them draw more blood to compare with the thawed blood and see if I had been infected with HIV back then. It turned out that I hadn't. They asked if I wanted to know the current results, and I said, "No way!"

I knew people who treated a positive diagnosis like a death sentence. I knew one guy who called his mother when he was diagnosed. She came to San Francisco on the next flight and took her dying son on a three week cruise around the world. As soon as they got back, he checked into the hospital and died a week later. If it had been me, I'd rather have taken the money. My mother is fun, but I wouldn't want to spend my last weeks on earth at sea with her. I knew others who were diagnosed and then simply shut down, quit their jobs, gave away their belongings and planned their funerals. I'm not saying they would still be alive today if they had a better attitude, but I recognize the destructive power of negative thinking. If you keep telling yourself you're going to die, you probably will.

My first serious live-in lover in San Francisco was Armando, the high-society caterer in the 1970s. We did elegant soirees from the wine country to Beverly Hills. When I was about twenty-six, he dumped me for his new lover Art and they moved to L.A. I went through dozens of boyfriends in the next few years before I saw Armando again. It was about 1986 when I ran into him at the Mint Bar on Market Street at an AIDS fundraiser of some sort. I was with my latest fling, a stunning South American named Achilles. Armando and I hugged each other as if we had never had an ugly moment in our breakup. Then he told me he had AIDS. He and Art had just moved back to San Francisco because they'd heard that this was the only place that health care providers recognized people with AIDS as human beings.

They'd been visiting Art's relatives in New Jersey when Armando got sick. He was admitted to a hospital where they ran some tests. When the results came back that he had full-blown AIDS, the hospital moved him from a regular room to the basement between the noisy elevator shaft and the furnace. He told me the people who came to take care of him were dressed in so much protective gear that they looked like astronauts. As soon as he was able to get up and walk, he and Art got the hell out of New Jersey.

In 1988 I had HMO coverage with Kaiser from my bartending job on Castro Street. I was seeing my doctor there for something else entirely when he ordered a bunch of blood work which, unbeknownst to me, included an HIV test. When I came back for the follow-up visit, he opened the door and closed it behind him, but he didn't sit down or come any closer. He said, "You tested positive for HIV. Here's a prescription for AZT." That was it. He left it on the desk and walked out. I can't say that I was surprised about the diagnosis, but still…I was stunned at his attitude. I had expected that I was positive all along, but for a doctor—especially in San Francisco—to be too frightened to come near me and so unenlightened about the means of transmission of the virus was shocking.

Nearly everyone I knew carried an off-white plastic pill box with a built-in timer and a sliding lid that concealed the little blue and white AZT capsules. If I was in the Castro Theatre for a matinee movie at four p.m., I would hear them beeping all around me in the dark. In gay restaurants at eight p.m., the waiters walked through the dining room with a tray of glasses of water so that everyone could take their pills. Every four hours around the clock, no matter where I was, the timer went off to remind me that I was dying. With my diagnosis I had finally, officially joined the ranks of my friends. And here I am, more than two decades later, alive and kicking. The time has come to tell some of the stories of those days for the sake of all my friends who were lost and only remain here in spirit.

Chapter Thirty-Nine

In 1989, Jim Cvitanich and I took a year off from doing *Men Behind Bars*. By the time we did our last show together on Presidents' Day weekend of 1990, we were barely on speaking terms. No one specific event drove us apart. We didn't have a lover's quarrel. We were never lovers, even though a lot of people thought we were. Maybe we should have been, but I only saw him naked once and that was from the back side. My jaw dropped at the sight of his gorgeous rock-hard ass cheeks, but I wouldn't admit my momentary attraction, even to myself.

Jim had a very sexy body. I'd seen him shirtless countless times. Ever since he'd won the title of Mr. San Francisco Leather 1983, his picture was in magazines, newspapers, and calendars. In those photographs, he was usually dressed in leather chaps, a chain harness and a black biker cap. He worked out relentlessly at the gym to maintain that perfect body, but he always seemed self-conscious about his rapidly thinning hair.

In the spring of 1989, Jim invited me on another trip in his old Thunderbird convertible, which he'd restored to cherry condition. This time we didn't try to do anything creative. We didn't attempt to write another *Fiasco* or anything else. We hardly ever mentioned that project any more after our previous road trip. This one was just a fun jaunt up to Yosemite National Park and back.

The first day we drove as far as Merced, ate dinner at a Denny's restaurant and checked into a cheap motel with twin beds. That was the one time I saw Jim's ass. He bent over to pull off his white jockey shorts just inches from my face before he slid naked into bed between the thin white sheets. In the morning, he was showered and dressed and ready to go before I even woke up. We found a drive-thru McDonald's for coffee and got to the park in the early morning. I had seen pictures of Yosemite all of my life, but I had no idea of the size and grandeur of that valley. Photographs cannot capture the scale of its enormity. On that spring morning, the waterfalls were not so much falling as shooting out of the canyon walls thousands of feet above us. The Merced River roared beside the road and overflowed its banks in places. We parked the car and walked awhile. Eventually we decided to pay for a guided tour and viewed the park from benches on the back of a flat-bed truck.

Jim and I both wanted to see the inside of the 1927 Ahwahnee Hotel, so we had an early lunch beneath the spectacular beamed ceiling of the dining room. Afterward we stepped outside where a park ranger explained to a group of people how you could tell the number of days each cluster of climbers had been gone by their position. The ranger also told the crowd how climbers spent the night sleeping in hammocks suspended by spikes driven into the rock. I cringed at the thought. How could anyone fall asleep so high off the ground? A sling is high enough to make me acrophobic. I never even liked sleeping on the top bunk.

Jim and I started the drive back to San Francisco by mid-afternoon. We put the top down on the Thunderbird, and he pulled out a box of cassettes he had mixed. We blasted the stereo in the open air with classics by everyone from the Andrews Sisters to the Beach Boys. We sang along at the top of our lungs, even though Jim had a pitiful singing voice and mine isn't much better. That trip was one of our last really good times together.

I remember running into him at the Castro Street Fair in the fall of that year. He was very drunk. I could count on one hand the number of times I saw Jim Cvitanich inebriated. I had worked an early shift behind the bar at the Special and got off about four p.m. After I counted out my bank and tips, I walked across the street to the Castro Station. I saw Jim sitting at the bar reeling a bit, so I ordered myself a drink and bought him a back-up. We talked for a while; we even laughed a bit. Then things took a serious turn. The gist of it was that we had another show to do in a few months, and Jim thought I was doing too much cocaine to hold up my end of the work.

Jim was right. I was doing too much cocaine in those days, but I resented him telling me that, and I especially resented him telling me when he was so drunk. I excused myself to go into a stall in the men's room where I did another line. We never argued, but from that day forward, I felt that he was always judging me. Despite his criticism, Jim admitted that he was still going to the baths and shooting up speed, but he was only doing that on occasion. Jim said my daily cocaine use made it different than his drug and sex binges. I'm sure Jim had a lot on his mind. Jim must have known he was dying too.

I snorted cocaine almost every day for at least a decade, but I never missed a day of work. In fact, that was where I bought it. I never lost a job because of cocaine or missed a bill payment. I never broke up with a boyfriend because of it, either. People laid out lines of cocaine with silver straws on fancy mirrors at all the best parties. Coke was the perfect accompaniment to champagne in the back of a limousine. It went with practically everything, and being able to afford it was a status symbol. Nearly everyone I knew was doing coke in those days.

And nearly everyone I knew was dying of AIDS. I felt suspended between the living and the dying. I couldn't take the risk of falling in love again because I was too afraid of losing another lover. Every week I got the news that two or three or four more people I knew had died. Every week I went to at least one memorial. If I wanted to blow my tips on cocaine, what was the harm? If I wanted to numb myself a bit, Jim wasn't going to discourage me. I knew I could function well enough to do my part when the time came to put on another show. I always loved Tallulah Bankhead's old line: "Cocaine isn't habit forming, dahling. I should know, I've been using it every day for years."

Chapter Forty

AIDS seemed to be killing gay men at random. We were like moving ducks in an arcade game. Some got shot and disappeared while others dodged the bullet this round, but might get it next time. It didn't matter if someone was wildly promiscuous like me or in a steady relationship. Given the incubation period of the virus, a person may have been exposed right before he met his "lifelong" monogamous partner. That one time was enough to cause their sero-conversion, sometimes years later. Ducks were falling in front of me and in back of me, but I kept moving straight ahead. I knew I could be taken out on the next go-around. Every cough could turn into pneumocystis. Every bump or bruise or rash or zit might be the beginning of Kaposi's sarcoma. I never imagined that I would live to be forty or fifty or sixty. I doubted any of us would. We were all doomed.

AIDS had been picking us off, one by one for years and then on October 17th, 1989 at 5:04 in the afternoon, the Loma Prieta earthquake struck. The quake killed sixty-three people in minutes. I was alone behind the bar at the Special on Castro Street that Tuesday afternoon. The San Francisco Giants were playing the Oakland Athletics in the World Series. Many people left work early to watch the five p.m. game. The bar was packed with regulars and "occasionals" and many more "drop-ins." I was a fast bartender, so I loved that mix. I could easily handle a crowd that was three-deep, especially if I was well prepared and in a good mood. That afternoon I was slinging drinks, popping open beer bottles and ringing up big numbers on the cash register. My tip jar was filled to overflowing.

I had my back to the customers when the earthquake hit. I put my hands on either side of the register and held onto the shelf of the back bar for the longest fifteen seconds in my life. The whole building rolled, and the sensation was like being on a small boat when it crosses the wake of a much larger one. The shaking seemed to go on forever. The rows of bottles above and around me clanked against each other and a few fell over, but none of them broke. We heard glass breaking somewhere; the storeroom window out back shattered, and a few bottles smashed in the liquor room upstairs. Then everything went silent, or maybe it only seemed like silence compared to the noise of before. After the shaking stopped, there was no music, no TV sports announcer's voice, no one ordering drinks or laughing or even talking. Within seconds, we heard sirens begin to wail outside. Their sound seemed to fill the air for the next several days.

When I turned around to face the crowd, no one was in sight. Everyone had hit the floor when the earthquake started. I was shocked at first, then I started to laugh. When the customers had ducked down under the bar, they'd taken their drinks with them!

By this time, Ed Stark had been dead nearly two years, and the bar was still holding on, business as usual, doing the best we could. Mother was still the manager, and Roz was too sick to work anymore. Business was fairly good, but the spirit of the place had waned quite a bit without Edwina Ballerina. My friend Nelson was my relief bartender at seven p.m. that day. Fortunately he had come in early because of the big baseball game. He ran next door to the hardware store and bought dozens of candles. Cliff's wasn't exactly open for business. After the quake hit, they escorted their customers out of the darkened store with flashlights. They only let Nelson inside because they knew him, and the Special had a charge account there.

After all my customers stood back up and got their bearings, I was just as busy as I had been before. Without electricity, I couldn't ring up drinks on the cash register, but I could still sell them, make change and keep track of sales on a pad of paper. I did that for a while, anyway. The management would just have to trust me and everyone always had.

Chris Osborne, one of the regulars, had a small battery-operated television set. He stood in the doorway of the Special with the antenna extended outside. Most of the local stations had temporarily gone off the air until they could get their backup generators started. They would soon send reporters out to the field, but without traffic lights navigating in the city was hard. Chris' TV set showed a huge fire in the Marina District. Newscasters made it sound as if the entire northern waterfront was engulfed in flames. I told Chris to step outside the door and look to the north. He reported back that he could see the huge clouds of smoke with his bare eyes.

More customers came in and told us that a drag queen had taken center stage down on the corner of 18th and Castro in the middle of the intersection. She was directing traffic with great flourish, as if she were conducting the symphony with the dance moves she had learned while a member of the *Folies Bergere*. She was a star who had finally found her calling, and she was truly being appreciated for her good work.

People kept pouring into the bar. Nobody wanted to go home to their dark apartments. They wanted to stay with their friends. I stayed past seven to help Nelson get caught up and to make sure he was okay. I stocked more ice and liquor for him too. I didn't want to leave him alone if the bar was going to keep getting busier, and I had no desire to rush home to my dark apartment either.

The electricity was out everywhere. We wouldn't know for a long time what happened at Candlestick Park. Friends who were there when the earthquake hit told me later that there was no panic, but a sense of camaraderie when they realized the game was called off. Their fear set in when people who'd brought portable TV sets, like the one Chris Osborne had, saw news reports about the partial collapse of the Bay Bridge. When those thousands of shaken baseball fans found their way out of the stadium, they could see clouds of smoke over San Francisco. They headed into the city as dusk fell, not knowing what they would come home to. None of us would hear until later about the people who were crushed in their cars between the decks of the fallen Cypress Freeway.

It wasn't even eight p.m. when the police told us we had

to close down. We announced "last call" and everyone booed. Sending everyone out into the dark of night didn't make any sense, but the mayor or the police chief or someone in authority decided that the bars had to close early for safety reasons and/or fire prevention. A lot of candles were burning in San Francisco bars at that moment, but I figured they were probably more concerned about drunk prevention. They didn't want mobs of people partying and the possibility of looting when the city was dark, so we closed.

One of the last of the regulars to leave was Charlie "Fannie" Fulbright, who lived on Duboce Street a couple of blocks from me. I knew he would be walking home in my direction, so I hollered at him to wait up. Neither of us had a car, so we would walk together. The electric buses wouldn't be running. Cabs would be near impossible to find, and the fares ridiculously expensive since all vehicles were stuck in the maze of traffic outside. As we locked up the front door of the Special, we could see that the bar across the street, the Castro Station was still wide open. Guys were standing in the front archway with drinks and cigarettes in hand. The police must have been working their way through the neighborhood clockwise, starting with Café San Marcos, the Twin Peaks and then us. If they continued left at 18th Street to the Village, the Men's Room, Moby Dick and the Midnight Sun, it could take them a good forty-five minutes to close the Station. Fanny and I made our way across the middle of the block. We heard updates about the earthquake damage on radio news stations blaring through the open windows of cars stuck in traffic. We had plenty of time for two more drinks inside the candle-lit Castro Station before we headed on our way.

Fanny and I hurried down the north side of Market Street, got a quick drink at the Detour and continued to the bar on the corner of Noe and Market where we sat upstairs and watched the headlights and taillights as far as we could see in the distance. We drank our vodka by candlelight until the police eventually arrived. We dashed on ahead of them for one more drink at the Mint and then another at the Eagle Creek Saloon. I was home on

McCoppin Street before ten.

I opened my apartment door and groped my way to the kitchen. I found some matches, lit a candle and had a look around. My thirty-six inch television set, which I kept on a stand at the foot of my bed, had flipped over and landed in the middle of my mattress. That would have hurt a lot if I had been sleeping there when the quake hit. Books had fallen off the shelves. Plants were tipped over and the soil had spilled onto floors and carpets.

The worst damage was to the back room, which was really just an added-on porch I used as a living room. The entire room had moved over about five inches. I could no longer open and close the back door to the stairs, and I realized for the first time that one wall of my living room was actually the outdoor siding of the building next door. I had painted that room a deep forest green with white enamel trim, but now it would need a lot more than a paint job to make it livable again. I could look up from the couch and see the sky between the buildings.

I called my parents in Minnesota where it was about midnight. I knew they'd be worried. They said they'd been trying to call me since they heard about the quake on the news. They hadn't been able to get a line into the city, but I had no trouble calling out. I told them I was fine and to go back to bed. They had nothing to worry about as far as I was concerned, and we wouldn't know the extent of the damage for some time.

After I hung up, I called Terry Thompson at the Eagle. The cops had closed them down too, even though they had their own generator already running when the police arrived. Terry was pissed off because they had a great crowd; lots of people had come to watch the ballgame on their big-screen TV and stayed after the quake to watch the national news. Even more customers had arrived later since it was about the only bar around that had electricity. Terry told me that I might as well come down and join him and the bartenders. He told me to knock hard on the side door until someone let me in.

As I headed to the Eagle that night, the streets South of

Market were pitch black. It was still an industrial neighborhood in 1989; leather bars were scattered among warehouses and printing shops and small manufacturing businesses that closed at night. A few people lived in the old, dilapidated Victorian apartment buildings like my place on McCoppin and in some of the alley streets, the ten-by-fourteen one-story earthquake cottages, built to shelter the survivors of the last big quake of 1906, still stood. There was no sign of life that night, no headlights from cars or motorcycles to light my way. I told myself that I had traveled all those streets dozens of times when I was stoned or blind drunk. I ought to be able to do it in the dark, but this was a new adventure for me. I had to run my fingertips along the sides of buildings from time to time when I couldn't see anything.

The next morning I woke up in my own bed, having apparently managed to wrestle my heavy television set to the floor when I got home drunk from the Eagle. My part of town still didn't have electricity, and power wouldn't be restored to several neighborhoods for two or three days. Castro Street had lights in the prime business blocks, so I'd be working that day. They had opened at six a.m. just like every other day, and the bar was already very crowded at noon when my shift started. Dozens of aftershocks happened that day and in the days that followed, but I'm not sure how many of them I really felt. Knowing they were happening made me jump every time I heard a loud noise or felt the rumble of a passing truck on the street outside.

Nelson rented a couple of appropriate VHS tapes at the video store. First we showed the 1939 movie *San Francisco* with Clark Gable as Blackie Norton, the Barbary Coast saloon keeper who falls hard for the virginal Jeanette MacDonald. She eventually loves him enough to sing the title song in his Paradise nightclub when the 1906 earthquake hits and starts the fire that destroys most of the city.

After the closing credits rolled on *San Francisco* we played the 1974 disaster film *Earthquake* starring Ava Gardner and Charlton

Heston, which was set in Los Angeles. I didn't put the sound on for either of the movies, except at key moments in the action. The customers wanted to tell each other about where they had been when it hit, what damage they had at home, whose friend of a friend got hurt or killed, how long would the Bay Bridge be closed, and who got lucky and had sex with whom last night by candlelight.

A favorite topic of conversation and outrage at the Special was the police department's decision to close the bars early. It might have made sense in terms of the fire hazard with so many candles burning, but not in the case of bars like the Eagle. There must have been other bars with their own generators, especially in major hotels and restaurants. Then they did it again. By mid-afternoon on Wednesday, the police notified everyone with a liquor license in San Francisco that they had to close their doors by eight p.m. People were furious to be sent home so early to apartments that were, in many cases, still dark. It was much more fun to stay out and cruise and visit.

Everyone was on edge, too. During times of natural disasters when people are under stress, they like to congregate and console one another. They value the fellowship of like-minded friends, even if they are only bar friends or casual acquaintances.

Jim Cvitanich and I might have barely been speaking, but this was a highly unusual time in our lives in San Francisco. Whatever our problems with each other, we were still friends. We just had to share our earthquake experiences, if only by telephone. Like me, Jim had been at work that afternoon with crowds piling into the Pilsner Inn on Church Street to watch the third game of the World Series. Jim told me he was just coming out of the men's' room when the shaking started. His first thought was to dive under the pool table, but two or three guys had already gotten there first. I told him about all of my customers disappearing under the lip of the bar and taking their drinks with them. We both had a good laugh over that. Though it was a horrible tragedy, the earthquake of 1989 may have been responsible for us communicating enough to work together again on *Men Behind Bars* 1990.

Chapter Forty-One

I didn't know it yet, but at the age of thirty-nine, Jim Cvitanich must have sensed that he was getting near the end of his life. For his final *Men Behind Bars* show, he wanted to pull out all the stops. No expense was too great. No idea of his was too outlandish to pull off. We moved from the five hundred-seat Victoria Theatre in the Mission District where it had always been to the thousand--seat Palace of Fine Arts Theatre in the Marina, on the opposite side of town. The Palace of Fine Arts was originally constructed for the 1915 Panama-Pacific Exposition. Its enormous stage is second in size by only a few feet to the stage of the Opera House. On the downside, it had no vertical fly-space to move sets up and down, but we had enough room backstage to store anything imaginable. It was so big that in Gail Wilson's introductory remarks to the audience, she mentioned that the entire Victoria Theatre, seats and all, would fit on the stage of the Palace of Fine Arts Theatre, "…and there would still be room leftover for Tatiana!"

Tatiana was a beloved drag queen we had used in a running gag about Sonny and Cher a couple of times. As a man, he was already well over six feet tall. We borrowed a pair of enormous boots that the San Francisco Opera used for the giants when they staged Wagner's *The Ring Cycle* and covered them with Cher's bell-bottom pants. Sonny was played by a popular Folsom Street bartender who was about five-six and appeared on stage first, lip-syncing to the opening bars of "I Got You, Babe." When Cher made her entrance, she towered over him by a good two feet, tossing back her long dark hair with her long fingernails and knocking Sonny down onto the floor. The audiences went nuts for this silly sight gag every single time.

Jim also pulled in Wayne Fleisher as a third producer/director, which was fine with me. Wayne had been an integral part of our shows from the very beginning. He was the head of the San Francisco Tap Troupe and a terrific choreographer. I liked

Wayne and I trusted him.

For the first act finale of *Men Behind Bars #5* in 1990, we tried to recreate the first act finale from our second show at the Victoria Theatre in 1985, only much bigger. The first act finale was traditionally a silly medley of pop culture characters doing lip-sync to well-known songs. Our rule of thumb was always to entertain, first and foremost, which meant that we didn't do anything too obscure or ask the audience to think very hard.

The medley started with Wayne Wanger, aka "Wanda June" the swamper from the Special, as Ethel Merman doing "There's No Business like Show Business." Wayne was still available, so he recreated the role for the Palace of Fine Arts stage. We got him a bigger wig, taller heels, a showier dress, and a line of chorus boys in tails with canes to dance behind him. This was done in front of the show curtain. When Ethel and the boys exited stage left, the Andrews Sisters entered from stage right.

In the 1985 show, we used three former San Francisco Empresses to play Patty, Maxine and Laverne: Empress VII Jonni, Empress XIX Remy Martin, and Empress XX Sissy Spaceout. In 1990, we used The Crème Sisters in that segment: Albolene, Joline, and Porcelana, who had been in the show before. They were three guys from the SF Tap Troupe who were not only terrific dancers and did perfect lip-sync, but were also incredibly funny.

Then the curtain opened to reveal Desiree, a tiny drag queen who also did all the wigs for our shows, lip-syncing as Carmen Miranda to "The Lady With the Tutti-Frutti Hat." The first time we did the number at the Victoria, Carmen had six of the Follies Men as backup dancers wielding heavy eight-foot long painted plywood bananas with holes to stick their faces through. They twirled them around and did a few dance steps in their bare feet. They were naked except for little flowered sarongs tied around their waists like towels at the baths. I had borrowed those bananas from the Gay Men's Chorus after they'd used them in one of their concerts or maybe at their annual retreat at the Russian River.

Toward the end of the song, when Carmen Miranda plays the xylophone, we had Patrick Toner and another sexy guy come in, also dressed in tiny bits of fabric, but they each had a row of plastic bananas strapped down their backs, so that when they bent over, butt-to-butt, Carmen pulled out a couple of mallets and pantomimed playing a banana xylophone across their backs.

For the 1990 show, Carmen got an even bigger fruit hat, and she had twelve dancers instead of six. This time we got six-foot inflatable bananas, a full case of twenty-four each from Dole and Chiquita, just for sending them a polite request in the mail. Whenever we mentioned "AIDS benefit" in those days, nearly everyone was eager to help, even big corporations. I'm sure it was also a tax write-off for them, plus they also wanted their brand advertised, so we alternated the bananas from one performance to the next. Somehow, I ended up in charge of choreographing the banana boys, so my holiday season that winter of 1989 leading up to the February edition of *Men Behind Bars* included banana boy rehearsals at least once a week.

We rehearsed different numbers in different places, wherever we found free space. Most of the larger numbers and all of the City Swing rehearsals were held at the Jon Sims Center on Mission Street, named for the founder of the Gay Marching Band who died of AIDS in July of 1984. The banana rehearsals were held at a bar at 2140 Market Street which had been a gay dance club with various names for years. I had gone there most often in my twenties when it was the Mind Shift and later Alfie's. I had been to parties there where Sylvester performed and spent an evening there at a Christmas party that same winter—a benefit for Rita Rockett's brunch fund at the AIDS ward at SFGH—drinking vodka with Herb Caen, the Pulitzer Prize winning *San Francisco Chronicle* columnist, and John and Louise Molinari.

What I remember best about that night was that Herb Caen told me he'd heard all about our MBB shows, but he was always in Europe that time of year. When the Molinaris were ready to leave for their next event of that holiday season, Herb Caen told them, "Go on ahead, I'll catch up with you later. Mark and I have too much to talk about." And he ordered us another round of "Vitamin V" vodka martinis.

I don't think we had a single banana rehearsal where they all showed up at the same time. I usually got ten or eleven, and the missing ones were different guys each time. It turned out great in the end, though. On the stage of the Palace of Fine Arts, the boys all looked sexy and gorgeous, barefoot and bare-chested, wrapped in their scraps of colored fabric, raising and lowering their bananas in time to the music like the Radio City Music Hall Rockettes or Busby Berkeley chorus girls.

After the banana/fruit hat number came Mister Marcus as Kate Smith. The first time we'd done this medley in 1985, we had him wearing a mechanical hat made by Alan Greenspan—hat-maker for *Beach Blanket Babylon*—with the Statue of Liberty on it. Marcus lip-synced to "God Bless America" while an enormous American flag was lowered behind him. At the end of the song, the entire hat lit up, and Lady Liberty's robes opened up to reveal a one foot miniature statue of a muscular man in black leather boots and a jock strap.

By the time we were planning the 1990 show, we had already sold the hat and Marcus's dress at an auction to make up for the losses from our High Tea party. Gilbert Baker, the man who first created the gay rainbow flag, came to the rescue. He loaned us an enormous glittering silver, red, white, and blue dress for Marcus to wear. This time, at the end of the number, the entire Gay Freedom Day Marching Band and Twirling Corps entered through the back of the house, marched onto the stage and performed a rousing rendition of "Stars and Stripes Forever" to close Act I.

One of the best numbers in that year's show and possibly the one I was most proud of was "Bosom Buddies" from the musical *Mame*. I had little to do with creating it. Wayne Love, our musical director, wrote all the arrangements for City Swing, our pit orchestra. He also put the stars through their paces and taught them the duet. We did a brief slide show to introduce two of the best known drag queens in San Francisco's long and illustrious gay history.

Michelle had been a legendary performer since before I arrived here. His real name is Maurice "Mike" Gerry, and he lives in upstate New York today. Whether in or out of drag, he can entertain for hours just by telling stories—more commonly referred to as "holding court"—at the bar. As Michelle, he played the lead in the all-gay version of *Hello Dolly* at the enormous Kabuki Theatre in Japantown before they chopped it up into a bunch of little movie rooms.

In *Men Behind Bars*, Michelle sang the Vera Charles part and Auntie Mame's lines went to Jose, the Widow Norton, Absolute Empress I. That was the plan, anyway. Jose and Michelle were both such seasoned entertainers that they made the roles their own, ad-libbing a ton of business so that each night was different, and all of their performances were hysterical. When Michelle asked Jose how old she looked, Jose doubled over in laughter and played it for all it was worth, while Michelle harrumphed, put her back erect and firmly planted both hands on her hips. The audiences loved it every time.

Michelle, Mark, and Miss Peckerhead onstage in the finale of Men Behind Bars V at the Palace Theater

Photo by Robert Pruzan, courtesy of the Gay, Lesbian, Bisexual, Transgender Historical Society

Jim spent a couple of thousand dollars on each of their costumes and hats and had everything meticulously hand-made to fit them. They looked amazing, Michelle all in white with black trim and Jose in black with white trim. I still have a photograph of the two of them standing in the sun beside the fountain in the pond outside the Palace of Fine Arts, elegantly attired in their show costumes, almost like a wedding picture. The tourists didn't know quite what to make of them.

It was even more fun to see the tourists' reaction to the Follies Men. I told all of them at the end of Saturday night's performance that we'd have an outdoor photo shoot before the Sunday matinee, so if they wanted to be part of it, they should come an hour early and wear their flesh-colored dance belts. I also invited three prominent photographers, who all showed up. We took the boys outside, posed them around the ancient statuary and lined them up on some of the staircases with their asses facing the camera. They really did look like they were naked. The tourists took as many pictures as our photographers did, covering their children's eyes at the same time.

Follies Men pose at the Palace of Fine Arts

Photo by Robert Pruzan, courtesy of the Gay, Lesbian, Bisexual, Transgender Historical Society

I only appeared on stage twice in that year's show, to introduce the "big girls" and to make a brief thank you speech at the curtain call. With Edwina Ballerina gone, we decided that the Greater Ukiah Opera and Ballet Company would expand their dance repertoire to include the cancan. We rustled up a few more bears until we had a dozen overweight drag queens to kick up their heels, pick up their knees, and lift up their multi-layered petticoats.

We set the scene in a French sidewalk café and picked a dozen of the Follies Men to play half-naked waiters carrying cocktail trays to dance between the girls at times and escort them around the stage. At one point in the dance, each of the big girls was behind one of the guys and pulled off their breakaway pants to reveal them in G-strings. On opening night, one of the girls grabbed the waistline of dancer Terry Mahaffey in the wrong place and pulled off his G-string too. Our shows had always been rife with titillating beefcake, but this was the first time we gave the audience a few seconds of full-frontal nudity. Terry was a real cutie and a seasoned pro. He quickly covered his crotch with his tray, grabbed his G-string and dashed into the wings to Velcro it back in place before joining the dance again seconds later. I only wished we had videotaped that night's performance.

Terry Mahaffey (center) loses his G-string in the Cancan from
Men Behind Bars V

Photo by Robert Pruzan, courtesy of the Gay, Lesbian, Bisexual, Transgender Historical Society

When we were casting the boys for the waiter parts, it occurred to us that we could put a couple of impostors among the big girls in the cancan number. I asked if any of the Follies Men would consider getting padded and dressed in drag to make it look like some of the big girls could not only shake the hems of their skirts, but also do some acrobatics as part of the dance. We had already picked out the taped music and the number was long, with lots of choreography to fill. Nearly all of the Follies Men were eager to show off their athleticism, so they got in line and one after another showed us their leaps and twirls and cartwheels and handstands across the floor of our rehearsal space. I wondered if they had even heard the part of my question about getting dressed in drag.

The best gymnast of all of them was a guy named Mark Cliser. He was able to do complete flips in the air from a standing position without touching his hands to the floor, both frontwards and backwards. Mark had been in the show the previous year, and

I always found him somewhat intimidating. He always showed up at rehearsals on his motorcycle with a big helmet in his hands. He was obviously talented and very smart, a quick study no matter what we asked him to do. He was quiet, always prompt, and totally reliable. When I asked if he would consider doing drag for the show, he said, "Sure!"

A couple of years later when I was watching CSPAN's coverage of the 1993 March on Washington for Lesbian, Gay, and Bi Equal Rights and Liberation, I saw a group of performers on an outdoor stage doing a song called "French Bitch." The emcee said that the lead singer was called Pussy Tourette. I was familiar with the name from VH1 or MTV videos, and I liked the performance a lot. When I mentioned it to Gail Wilson, she told me that Pussy Tourette was Mark Cliser. She couldn't believe that I didn't already know that.

Also for the show that year, Tim Garner returned as Dianne Feinstein. The real Mayor Feinstein had finally succeeded in closing down all the gay bath houses. Now she was in the news for her campaign to get the battleship Missouri based in San Francisco. For the finale of our show, we had Tim dressed as Dianne perched like the figurehead on the prow of the ship as if the battleship Missouri had crashed through the back wall of the theatre to the lip of the stage.

Then as she stepped off the ship, the prow opened down the middle and disappeared into the wings to reveal a couple dozen bare-chested sailors—the Follies Men—on the deck of the ship with cannons and masts and flags behind them. We borrowed another song from *Best Little Whorehouse in Texas*, and I rewrote the lyrics for Tim, as the mayor, to sing, "It's Just a Lil' Ole Bitty Pissant Battleship." Then the entire cast, including the gay marching band, came onstage for bows. We said our thanks to the audience and ended, as always, with the traditional "San Francisco."

That last *Men Behind Bars* show that Jim and I did together cost over a hundred grand to produce. When all was said and done, we turned over ten thousand dollars to charity. It was the same amount that we netted on the first show we did six years earlier, and that one had only cost a thousand dollars to produce. For this one, Jim had pulled out all the stops, indeed. I said to him, "And you wonder why I do drugs!"

Our final performance was a matinee on Monday, Presidents' Day, February 19, 1990 at four p.m., followed by the final cast party. We spent all day Tuesday striking the sets and clearing all of our belongings out of the theatre. I had a hangover that no amount of cocaine could help. The next day, Wednesday, February 21, 1990, Terry Thompson and I flew to New Orleans to get a head start on Mardi Gras.

Chapter Forty-Two

Terry Thompson, the manager of the Eagle and my good friend, had long ago made plans with his lover, Stephen Blair, who was simply known as "Blair," to go to Mardi Gras in 1990, but Blair died before they could go to New Orleans. Terry invited me to use the extra plane ticket, and we somehow managed to scrounge up another room in the same hotel where he was staying in the heart of the French Quarter. We both insisted on having separate rooms because I was determined to have as many sexual escapades as I could possibly fit into that week, and Terry and I never had sex with each other.

I don't remember the date that Blair died, but I remember the day pretty well. He'd been bed-ridden for quite a while, so it was not unexpected. I was home alone that afternoon and had finally gotten around to renting and watching the Bette Midler and Barbara Hershey tearjerker *Beaches*. The movie ended, and the credits were still rolling on the screen when my phone rang. It was David Stoll, aka "Stella," who had long been Terry's assistant manager at the Eagle and one of the most popular bartenders in the city. Stella was calling on Terry's behalf to relay the news to me that Blair had just died.

I held the phone a few inches from my face, stared at it a moment and then looked up at the ceiling and yelled, "Nice timing, Blair! What did you think, that I wouldn't cry over you? You waited until I finished watching *Beaches*? I was already crying, damnit!" Stella heard me and started to laugh, which got me laughing too.

A week or so later, Terry held a memorial service for Blair in a beautiful little church in the Duboce Triangle. He asked Gail Wilson to sing, and she asked me to go with her for moral support. The church was packed. The balcony was packed. I heard later that the crowds spilled out onto the sidewalks and into the street. Gail and I sat in the second pew on the left outer aisle so that she could easily get out and up to the front when the time came for her to sing. I remember her telling me, "I know I can get through this as long as I don't look at anybody." She stood beside the pianist, facing the wall on the opposite side of the church so that she was in profile to the mourners and sang, at Terry's request, the old Carole King/James Taylor hit, "You've Got a Friend."

After she sang, Gail sat down in the pew beside me again and placed one hand on my thigh. Her perfectly manicured fingernails squeezed through my slacks so hard that I was sure she would draw blood, but she made it through the song and had done a beautiful job. I heard sniffling all around me and looked across the aisle at Terry to see his shoulders moving up and down in silent sobs. After the service, we all went back to the Eagle and got very drunk.

When Terry and I flew to New Orleans that Wednesday, two days after Presidents' Day, our flight stopped in both Phoenix and Dallas. We sat in the second to the last row on the plane so that we could smoke. We knew this would be the last time we'd ever be allowed to smoke on a plane. The regulations were scheduled to change the week we were in New Orleans. Flying back, we made sure to get seats near the front so that we could get off in both Dallas and Phoenix with enough time to have a cigarette inside the airports.

Mardi Gras was great fun, what I remember of it. I was looking good, still in my thirties and wearing a full beard that season. I felt good too. The show was over. My job on Castro Street still seemed as secure as bartending jobs ever are. I had saved up some money, and I was ready to have a good time. Terry and I checked into our hotel, threw our bags down in our rooms and walked directly to Bourbon Street, just a couple of blocks away. I hadn't even finished my first drink at Café Lafittes in Exile when I met someone tall and handsome, horny and hung. On the way back to my hotel, he told me he was the conductor of the gay band in whatever Midwestern city he came from. I laughed to remember the orchestra conductor I had sex with in Chicago at

IML in 1984 and wondered if there was a pattern. "That's nice," I told him. I wasn't there to talk about John Phillip Sousa marches. I was there to get laid!

We didn't even get undressed. He must have peeled off his shirt because I remember that he had a great body. It was a farmer's body, corn-fed and muscled from hard work, hairy chested with wide smooth nipples and eraser centers. We undid our belts and flies, and he bent me over the side of the bed for one amazing vanilla fuck, complete with condom. I only know he used a condom because I found it later in the trash can. It was still full of his come. I thought about saving it as a souvenir of the trip, but I knew there would be others.

Terry and I made a point of meeting for breakfast every day at ten a.m. We both agreed that it was a good idea to put some solid food on our stomachs to balance out all the drugs and alcohol we were consuming the rest of the time. We were never in the mood for anything fancy, so we weren't looking for Breakfast at Brennan's or Dinner at Antoine's, even if we could have gotten seated with such crowds. Whenever I'm in New Orleans I always like to eat at the Clover Grill on Bourbon Street. It reminds me of Orphan Andy's in the Castro; both are open twenty-four hours and must go through a ton of eggs every day. As the tourist crowds grew each day, the Clover Grill developed a line outside the door and by the weekend, we noticed they had switched from their regular menu to a simpler, more limited one with higher prices.

One afternoon I discovered a little corner store a couple of blocks from our hotel. It looked as if they mostly sold cigarettes and liquor because the shelves were full of dusty cans of food and sundries. In the back was a big chalkboard listing all sorts of Southern food and a pair of old glass display coolers, cracked and duct-taped together. Inside them were fabulous pies and cakes and salads and side dishes under plastic wrap and pots with lids that held who-knew-what delectable treasures. Even better than the food was the woman who worked behind the counter. She looked just like Bonnie Raitt but with a thick Southern accent.

I went there three or four times that week, and each time I ordered something different, a main course of chicken or ribs or hot links and side orders of biscuits or potato salad, greens with ham hocks or sweet, hot bubbling baked beans that would still be warm when I got back to my hotel room. I always bought some pie or cake or pudding for dessert in case I got hungry at some point later in the night. One day I said to the woman, "Do you know you look just like Bonnie Raitt?"

She said, "Child, I get that all the time! I wish I was her. I wouldn't be back here scoopin' up this grub. I can't carry a tune in a bucket, but anyway…hey, we got chitlins today, honey!"

I always took a big sack of Styrofoam containers back to my hotel room and woke up a few hours later with a chicken bone in my armpit or a barbecued rib on the pillow, jambalaya in my hair and a pristine slice of pecan pie on the bedside table for later. Then I'd look at the clock and realize that a quarter to twelve didn't mean I had slept all morning. It meant it was nearly midnight and the perfect time to shower, do another line of coke and hit the bars. I usually knew where I could find Terry within an hour or so and I'd ask him, "Have you eaten since breakfast?"

He'd tell me he'd gotten a burger and fries at the Clover Grill and ask about me. I'd tell him, "I had dinner off my pillowcase again," and we'd both laugh.

The streets and bars of the French Quarter were already busy the day we arrived and each day the crowds seemed to double as more tourists flew in and Mardi Gras grew nearer. Terry and I went to lots of different bars and sort of fell into a routine. At around four each afternoon, we went to Good Friends to meet up with the gang from Portland. I already knew the fabulous drag queen known as Mame, from her many appearances in San Francisco over the years. She introduced us to all of her friends who came to Mardi Gras together every year. We had a favorite bartender who worked the upstairs bar wearing nothing but boots and beads and a fanny pack in front. Whenever he had time, he was happy to unzip the fanny back and show off his enormous penis, nestled inside with a string of white beads that looked like pearls.

Another favorite bar was a total dive located just across the street from the French Market, about a block or so up from Café du Monde. I don't remember the name of the place, but I remember that it had a picture of a ship painted directly onto the wall opposite the bar. We were told that the painting was hundreds of years old, so in order to preserve it, the place was never painted again. New Orleans was founded in 1718, so the story might have been true. By 1990, when we were there, the ship was covered with a thick film of nicotine from decades of cigarette smoke. The place reminded me of an old South of Market leather bar, maybe a cross between the Ambush, the No Name and Febe's. In their day, most of those San Francisco dives had a back room where men could step into the darkness for quick anonymous sex.

In those days, some places didn't need back rooms because the guys carried on openly in the main part of the bar. I remember when I was in my twenties, John Preston took me to a place where they covered the pool table with black plastic and put a full can of Crisco in each of the six pockets. That was back in the pre-AIDS 1970s. Still, in 1990, some of the bars in New Orleans were nearly that decadent, and they never closed. Someone just came in with a garden hose before sunrise and flushed the place out. I'd seen it happen. Everyone just got out of the way. If you were sitting on a bar stool, you lifted your legs. Terry and I spent so much time in that bar across from the French Market that we were on a first name basis with all of the bartenders on all of the shifts.

One morning I met Terry there as usual. We always had at least a couple of screwdrivers or Bloody Marys before we went to breakfast. That particular morning, I couldn't remember leaving last night. The bartender served us our drinks and told us there was a problem. He understood that Terry and I had "befriended" a young man the night before, taken all his clothes away from him and fisted him right on the bar.

Terry didn't remember any of this happening either, but the boy's face started to register in my addled brain. I remembered that under his blue jeans he wore a leopard print Speedo which I peeled off his (by then) bare legs, twirled around on the tip of my index finger until it was spinning fast and then let it fly over the heads of the crowd. I could still picture the arc of that tiny piece of fabric across the room. It hit the wall behind the cigarette machine and then fell out of sight. Those little puss-print underpants were probably still there if the hose had missed them, or they might have landed on a beer case and never hit the floor. At the time I wondered if they might still have the scent of that boy's sweet crotch. I was tempted to get up and go look for them, but I sat still and told the bartender I didn't remember anything either.

The bartender said, "Even though it's Mardi Gras time and people get a little crazy, there are some things where we just have to draw the line."

Terry and I both apologized for not remembering what occurred and promised to behave ourselves in the future. The bartender bought us our first round of drinks and said he thought we must have been mistaken for some other guys from San Francisco and well…it was Mardi Gras, after all.

I don't remember the names of any of the men I played with on that trip to New Orleans. I remember some of their faces, some of their arms and hands and the clothes they wore when I first laid eyes on them. I remember them better out of their clothes. They were mostly a blur, blended together in varying combinations of genitals and pectorals, an armpit here, an ankle there, buns of steel or sweet pink rosebuds surrounded by beefy flesh and soft brown hair. One guy from L.A. came to my room at least three times. He was working that week as a stripper in one of the bars. His shift ended at four a.m., so I would meet him after he got off work. One night I watched his earlier performance around midnight and told him I was tired, so he should just come by my room when he was done.

I slept for a couple of hours and woke up when he knocked on my door around 4:15. The first thing he wanted was a long hot shower, during which I got the bright idea to get my camera ready. As soon as he came out of the bathroom, I started snapping pictures of him, but he got very shy all of a sudden, pulling pillows and blankets and sheets up in front of him. I thought it was funny, since he'd been making tips all night by taking off all of his clothes in front of crowds of strange men in the back of some sleazy French Quarter gay bar. Still, he wouldn't let me touch him until I put the camera away, so I never got any good naked pictures of him. He was beautiful. I discovered later that he was an artist and had done a famous self-portrait in a black leather biker's cap. It was shot from the rear, like he'd done it in a mirror or from a photograph. It showed his face in profile and his gorgeous ass full on. It looked like it might have been done in pencil—black and white—and for years the drawing was on a poster that advertised The Gauntlet, one of the leather bars in Silverlake.

Another man I saw more than once that week was a hippie-type from Santa Cruz. I've always loved long hair on some men, and his was very sexy. He told me that his job was matting and framing pictures in an art shop near the beach in Santa Cruz. I also got to know his best friend and traveling companion who later moved to San Francisco and got in touch with me. They even came up for my birthday the following year. I have no way of knowing whether either of them survived AIDS, but I do remember that the picture framer had some excellent drugs.

I must have gotten some sleep after he left on Monday night because I woke up on Fat Tuesday morning to find a note from my Santa Cruz framer. It simply said, "Happy Mardi Gras! Here's something to get your day going – ENJOY!" Beside the note, on a separate sheet of hotel stationery, I found a nice little pile of pinkish powder. I went across the hall to knock on Terry's door and asked him to come over and have a look. He wasn't sure what it was either, but he had a taste and we decided we should share it, since there was quite a lot. I grabbed my trusty straight-edge razor and chopped up two fat lines across the dresser. We each snorted one and headed out for our final day of debauchery before Ash Wednesday when the city quiets down for most people.

Time has little meaning when you do so many drugs. I remember events from so long ago out of order sometimes. A friend told me later he went to New Orleans for Mardi Gras one year, and the only hotel room they could get was clear out by the airport. They never made it to any of the bars, didn't see any of the parades, didn't take any pictures. They had brought enough drugs along, though, that they just stayed in their hotel for four or five days and had a wonderful time. Terry and I never left the French Quarter, but we did see a few of the parades. I heard that the floats were used over and over again, since there were so many parades in the weeks leading up to Mardi Gras. Each group restocked them with fresh beads and doubloons to throw to the masses of people crowding the streets. Terry and I bought our own beads, nicer ones than the floats gave out, and constantly traded them with people we met, especially sexy guys who were willing to "earn" them.

We walked to North Rampart for a parade one afternoon— or did we just happen upon it? I don't know. I do remember that we watched most of it from inside the doorway of a bar because I had such a hard time getting used to the legality of taking drinks outside. One evening we walked to Canal Street to see a nighttime parade. The tawdry floats looked better in the multicolored electric lights than they had in the daytime, but the crowd was louder and the area more congested. As stoned as I was, I kept focusing on the trees overhead. Their branches were filled with strings of beads that had been thrown too hard, too high, or too far and gotten caught in them.

Too high was also a good description for Terry and me. Looking back, I don't think he had nearly as good a time as I did. After all, he'd planned to be there with Blair. I could only keep him company, do drugs with him, and share my stoned observations, make him laugh sometimes and be a reliable breakfast companion. One night we were walking through the

French Quarter together, maybe heading to our hotel to take a break from the madness. The noisiest mobs on Bourbon Street were behind us, but we could still hear the music pouring out of the bars. Drunks in far worse shape than us kept howling at the moon and stumbling down the blocks of closed up shops, little boutiques and ancient small hotels.

I had no idea what Terry was feeling until he raised his fist into the air, shook it toward the old wrought iron balcony railings above us and yelled, "Goddamnit, Blair! You know I'll always love you, but would you mind so much if I got LAID one of these days?!"

I gave him a hug, and we both laughed. That was about the best I could do.

Chapter Forty-Three

There's an old nightclub on Columbus Avenue in San Francisco's North Beach neighborhood—technically on the edge of Russian Hill—called Bimbo's 365 Club. The place has been there since 1931 and has always reminded me of a time before I was born, or at least what I imagined that bygone era to be. My main concept of those glamorous days and decadent nights was from watching old movies on television. I envied that generation. Growing up on a farm in Minnesota, I imagined what it must have been like: cocktails poured out of silver shakers, cigarettes lit by the person on the next barstool or across a candlelit table while ordering a rich Italian dinner and watching a floor show. Bimbo's always seemed a place where handsome mustachioed men in tuxedos would be dancing with women in gowns. That was the trouble. The downside of my fantasies about Bimbo's and old Hollywood nightclubs was that they were strictly heterosexual, and I didn't emigrate all the way from the Midwest to San Francisco in order to experience any more "straight"-ness than was absolutely necessary.

Bimbo's was so straight, it was known for the world-famous "girl in a fishbowl" named Dolphina. It was only an illusion, of course. In the recesses beneath the club, a live woman reclined naked and dry on a rotating platform. Her only instructions were to keep her knees together and pretend to be swimming, slowly. A periscope with angled mirrors projected her image up into a fishbowl behind the bar, where it looked like a tiny mermaid, six inches long, was writhing in an underwater grotto. For a while, the role of Dolphina was played by the legendary burlesque dancer, Tempest Storm. Years later for his fortieth birthday, the singer Chris Isaak appeared in the fishbowl dressed in boxer shorts. Unfortunately I missed that party.

I'm not sure when Bimbo's starting hosting gay events, but I've been there for several of them over the years. The place can only hold two or three hundred people seated for dinner, maybe twice that many if the chairs are in rows facing the stage. The first time I remember being inside the main room was in 1977 when my lover Armando took me to a show billed as *An Intimate Evening with Bette*. We dropped acid when we left the house, and the drug was starting to kick in as we found our second row center seats. The Harlettes came out first—Sharon Redd, whom I would later get to know during her disco career, Charlotte Crossley, and Ula Hedwig. They had just released an album on Columbia Records called *Formerly of the Harelettes*, and they must have sung half the songs on their LP that night. They were amazingly good or I was just ridiculously stoned, but I could have listened to them all night. Suddenly an unseen voice announced, "Ladies and gentlemen, Bimbo's is proud to present...Bette Midler!" I couldn't believe it! She was there too? I'd completely forgotten who we had come to see. It was a fabulous evening, and it's a pity I don't remember more of it.

I went to my first specifically "gay function" at Bimbo's sometime in the late 1980s. By then I had discovered that I usually had more fun creating and hosting an event like a show or a dance or a birthday party than attending one. There seems to be something to go to nearly every night of the year in the gay community. My Texas friends wouldn't ask, "Where are you going tonight?" but "What's the function at the junction?" I don't remember the name of that first gay event I attended at Bimbo's, but it was full of drag queens. I don't think it was a coronation, but maybe an investiture of royalty like Grand Duke and Duchess.

I don't remember who I went with either, but we sat at a round table for ten not far from the stage, where a very formal ritual was taking place. Half the people were kneeling, and I saw a lot of crowns, even on some of the men in suits. Gays can do high holy rituals that rival the Masons, the Elks and the Catholic Church combined. I wasn't much interested in any of that. My main focus upon sitting down was to figure out which cocktail waitress was ours.

This sort of function goes for hours. Nobody goes for the

show as much as to see and be seen. These kinds of events were always a good excuse to get dressed to the nines and buy some really good cocaine and/or hashish to do in the back of the limo. They're a good place to show off a new boyfriend or a new piece of jewelry or a new tan or a new facelift. Your table serves as home base, but you end up spending most of the evening on your feet, coming and going from your table to the bar, or from your table to the restroom to "powder your nose" with more coke.

I saw Cher arrive and sit down at our table directly across from me. It wasn't the real Cher, of course, but I was stoned enough to almost believe it for a moment. This drag queen looked exactly like her, and she had all Cher's mannerisms down pat. She was spell-binding! Since most of the people at our table were mingling or wandering around the room, I got up and moved over to sit next to Cher and introduce myself.

His name was Joel Herzog, and we became friends right away. He turned out to be really good-looking as a guy, too, but he already had a lover, so I was never tempted to go there. Joel was funny and warm and incredibly talented, not only as an entertainer, but as an artist. Like my friend Kirk Ramsey, Joel had also worked for Bob Mackie. Joel designed and sewed all of his own costumes as well as those of several other drag performers.

Joel told me that he was in San Francisco because he was appearing as Cher in a new show called *An Evening at La Cage*. He also told me that Kenny Sacha, my old pal from the International Mr. Leather contest in Chicago, was emceeing the show as Bette Midler. I decided right then and there that I had to go see it.

La Cage Aux Folles was a terrific French film with English subtitles that came out in 1978. Based on a 1973 French-Italian play by Jean Poiret, the film spawned a sequel and also a 1983 Broadway musical written by Jerry Herman. The musical was so successful, a revised and revamped version of the film called *The Birdcage* was made for U.S. audiences with Robin Williams and Nathan Lane, but that was much later in 1996.

The original French film was one of the first movies I ever

saw with openly gay characters who didn't end up miserable and lonely, if not dead, in the final reel. I suspect that the Broadway stage helped the story to reach a wider audience than those willing to read subtitles. Someone got the idea to capitalize on the success of *La Cage* by doing a live drag show like the one in the 1978 movie. The San Francisco version of *La Cage* was on Broadway Avenue in North Beach, near Montgomery, practically across the street from the world-famous Finocchios, which might have already been dying by then.

An Evening at La Cage must have hoped to draw the same package tour crowds as Finocchios, the straight couples visiting from Omaha or Akron. Tourism is the lifeblood of San Francisco. People who aren't quite daring enough for Vegas come to San Francisco instead. They want to experience something they don't see every day on Main Street, so they take a cable car ride, eat clam chowder out of a bowl made of sourdough bread and order drinks before dinner like it's New Year's Eve. In the 1960s, they took a tour bus down Haight Street where they could snap photographs of "real live hippies" through the tinted bus windows.

We knew a gay guy who drove a tour bus in the 1980s. He would hang out drinking in the Castro bars after work and on his days off, usually mid-week. All of the bartenders knew him and liked him. My friend Danny "Mitzi" Marsh tended bar in several of the Castro bars over the years. One day our friend the bus driver had a load of Japanese tourists. When he turned down Castro Street, he saw Danny Marsh waiting to cross in front of the Twin Peaks. He announced over the loud speaker, "This is Castro Street, known as the center of the city's gay or homosexual population…and there's one now!" He opened his window and yelled out, "Hey, Mitzi," who waved back while all the tourists excitedly waved at their first sighting of a real live homosexual and snapped his picture.

The night I went to see *An Evening at La Cage* must have been on the opening weekend. I think I went with Jim Cvitanich, my *Men Behind Bars* co-producer. Joel Herzog did not only Cher, but also Julie Andrews in the second act. Kenny stuck with Bette

Midler and the other performers did stars like Liza and Diana and Tina and Judy, the divas with one name recognition. I think the only star with two names was portrayed by a woman who cross-dressed as Michael Jackson. After the show, we went backstage and met everyone. Kenny and I made plans to catch up over lunch the following week and of course we told Joel how *fabulous* his performance was.

Joel—out of drag—soon became something of a fixture at the Special on Castro Street. He had his days free, and I was working afternoon shifts. I liked having him around, and he became friends with many of the regulars. That Halloween he came to the Special dressed in his Cher drag and literally stopped traffic. In later years, the Castro would become dangerous on Halloween when tens of thousands of people poured into the neighborhood. In 2006, seven people were wounded when someone with a gun opened fire. The city forced the Castro to close down the next few years to avoid any more violence. In the 1980s, Halloween on Castro Street was crowded, but it was almost all gay. The police closed off 18th and Castro and one block in each direction, but not the entire neighborhood. Everyone was in costume and the bars were packed, but so were the streets and sidewalks. We weren't worried about getting shot back then.

Joel and I were standing in the doorway of the Special, and people were lined up to take his picture or to have their picture taken with "Cher." Joel said, "Wait a minute! This could be a good thing. Go get the penny jar, and I'll make a sign for it."

Every gay bar and business had a penny jar where people could donate to the AIDS Emergency Fund. People brought in huge containers that had been gathering dust for years at home. Nearly everyone had a bunch of pennies they would never get around to using, so why not put them to good use? Joel grabbed a pen and a trick pad and wrote: "$1.00 Take a pic w/Cher for AIDS!" and he stuck the sign inside the glass. I held the jar and people posed for pictures with Joel all evening as singles and fives and tens filled the penny jar.

Joel Herzog as Cher

Kenny Sacha stopped by the bar a few times to see me at work when he was in the Castro, but he wasn't in San Francisco for very long. He had explained to me over our lunch that first week that the producers of *An Evening at La Cage* had only sent him here to get the show off the ground. He was the only big name drag queen, since he'd been in movies, on TV shows, and on stage with Cher and Bette Midler. Once the show was up and running smoothly, they could replace him as emcee, and he could open another show in another city.

I never saw Kenny Sacha again before he died in August of 1992 at the age of thirty-nine. I'll always remember him as doing a very funny Barbra Streisand and a pretty good Bette Midler, but more fondly as the sweet lost boy I met in Chicago who seemed so out of place in his pastel preppy clothes the night I took him out on the town amid a sea of black leather. He seemed much more at ease emceeing a drag show in San Francisco than emceeing the International Mr. Leather Contest.

October 17, 1990 was the one year anniversary of the Loma Prieta earthquake. My friend Nelson and I were bartending at the Special that day, so we decided to throw a party. The week before the anniversary someone—probably Joel—drew a map of the bar. We taped it up on the wall and asked everyone who had been at the Special when the quake hit to write his name on the map on the exact spot where they were at 5:04 p.m. the year before. We made Red Cross arm bands for each of the "survivors" to wear, which gave them free drinks for an hour. Joel hadn't been there on the day of the earthquake, but he volunteered to help us decorate. He made amazing scale replicas of the broken Bay Bridge and the Ferry Building with its tower bent from the quake. I don't remember all the other silly things we did, but I remember getting a huge box of day-old donuts for next to nothing from the twenty-four hour donut shop that used to be on Castro Street. We decorated the donut box with yet another Red Cross and set it out on the pool table with paper cocktail napkins and Styrofoam cups like the ones that might be used to serve coffee to disaster victims, but nobody was drinking coffee that day.

An Evening at La Cage didn't last too long in San Francisco. Joel moved away when the show did, and I lost touch with him. So many close friends here in San Francisco were getting sick and dying that my focus narrowed to my immediate surroundings. I didn't hear his name until at least a year later. I was bartending one afternoon in 1991 or 1992 when Joan Rivers had a daytime talk show. I'd seen a teaser advertising that her guests that day would be from the cast of *An Evening at La Cage* in Las Vegas. I made a point to watch and turn the sound on, hoping to see Kenny or Joel or both, but I didn't recognize any of the drag queens in the current show. They were portraying the usual one-named divas. I suppose they each did a lip-sync number and Joan interviewed them between songs. The part of the show I do remember was when Joan Rivers asked one of the drag queens who had designed her dress. It was a sparkling construction of sequins and bright bangles over a padded form and very realistic looking cleavage. The drag queen said, "Our good friend Joel Herzog made this. He was in the show too, and he did most of our gowns. He died yesterday."

By then I had heard the news of so many deaths of so many friends, but this was the first time it came to me by way of Joan Rivers on a daytime talk show. I think Joel would love to have known that was how I found out about his passing.

Chapter Forty-Four

Rita Rockett and I have been celebrating our birthday together for at least twenty years, maybe closer to thirty. Patrick Toner must have been the one who figured out we had the same birthday. The first time we made it official was before her boys were born, when she was working weekends as a cocktail waitress at the Castro Station, and I was tending bar across the street at the Special. We were both off that night, so we kept going back and forth, maybe spending a half hour in each place. We had cake in one bar and then went across the street for cards and cocktails and back again to drink champagne.

Our birthday is June 25, the same date as *Rosemary's Baby*, which is half way between Christmas and Christmas, so I've always said that gives my loved ones six full months to shop for presents for me. It always falls on or near San Francisco's Gay Pride weekend, the anniversary of New York's Stonewall Riots, which means a big parade and parties and dances and a huge influx of tourists from around the world.

During the years that Rita lived in San Francisco and served her Sunday brunches at the AIDS ward at San Francisco General Hospital, we threw our birthday parties to raise money for the brunch fund. In more recent years, when she's been able to come back to town on our birthday, we sometimes have a party to raise funds for another AIDS organization.

Drew Okun, also known as the porn star Al Parker, moved up from Los Angeles to San Francisco in the late 1980s. I discovered that he was also born on June 25, the same year as me—Rita is three years younger—so I got his phone number from Mister Marcus and called to ask if he would like to join us. I had never seen him in any of his films as Al Parker, but when I told him about Rita and the brunches and our fundraising, he said he would be glad to and the three of us became friends.

Rita and I have held our parties at the Pilsner Inn, the SF

Eagle, the Special, Castro Station, the Transfer, Trax and the Edge, usually wherever I was working as a bartender (or patronizing regularly) at the time. The first couple of years that Al Parker joined us, we held them at the Eagle. Nearly every time I saw Drew, we smoked hash in the back of his white van, unless it was for breakfast at Orphan Andy's or running into him at Cliff's Hardware. The interior of that van reeked of hashish smoke so badly he was lucky he was never stopped by the police.

Another good friend of mine was Donald Montwill, a regular at the Special, who was one of the managers of the Valencia Rose and later Josie's Cabaret and Juice Joint. I also knew Donald through Jane Dornacker. They were both friends with Whoopi Goldberg, who had developed a lot of her early material at the Rose and done a two-woman show with Jane at the Victoria Theatre a few years before we started *Men Behind Bars* there. Each year when our birthday was coming up I would ask Donald if he had any new talent who would like to perform at our party in exchange for some good exposure. He always found us someone.

One year Donald got us Dexter Madison, a recent winner of the San Francisco Stand-Up Comedy Competition, which had previously been won by such comic legends as Dana Carvey, Will Durst and Sinbad (who beat out Ellen DeGeneres that year.) In hindsight, Dexter's high-brow tuxedoed comedy act might have been a little too sophisticated for the Eagle crowd, but I thought he was hilarious with lines like, "I'm seeing someone new and I'm very excited. I just bought the binoculars last week."

Another year Donald got us the guy who claimed to have built the puppets for Wayland Flowers, the ventriloquist who, along with his outrageous puppet Madame, built his bawdy barroom act into a syndicated television series. Flowers died in 1988. This new guy brought Madame to our birthday party at the Eagle and had her tell a few jokes on stage. He was fine and he tried hard, but Madame wasn't quite as funny without Wayland.

One of the years that Rita, Drew, and I had our birthday fundraiser at the Eagle, Donald told me he had a young Korean comic who was just starting out. He thought she was a lesbian, but Donald (or maybe the comedienne) still wasn't sure. He said she'd heard about our legendary birthday parties and wanted to perform for us. This was only a couple of days before the event, and I was overwhelmed with party plans. I told Donald I was sorry, but that I had too much lined up for that year's birthday party already. My feeling was that you cannot demand a bar audience's undivided attention for too long a stretch without giving them time to drink and socialize between the events on stage. I said, "Please tell your Korean maybe-lesbian comic thanks and maybe we can use her next year."

Donald said, "Sure, okay…if she's still around next year. I can see her really going places. Her name is Margaret Cho, and I'll bet we'll be hearing a lot from her in years to come."

Drew and I talked privately and agreed that we each wanted to surprise Rita by contributing something to the auction. For my part, I contacted my friend Robert Pruzan, the photographer for the *B.A.R.*, and asked him to enlarge one of the photographs he took of the naked-looking Follies Men at the Palace of Fine Arts. I had it carefully packaged and mailed it to my Mardi Gras sex partner, the picture framer from Santa Cruz, who was happy to give it a beautiful matting and framing job and deliver it personally in exchange for a place to stay over Pride weekend in San Francisco that year, not to mention getting to meet Al Parker and Rita Rockett as well as some more good sex from me.

Drew's contribution was his own plastic recreation of an approximately three foot by four foot rendering of a brick wall. On the corner of 11th and Folsom Streets, there is an old brick building with a tall archway on the Folsom Street side that opens into an open-air alley through the center of the building. The back end abuts a different brick building on 11th Street that houses Boz Scagg's nightclub, Slim's. On the outer wall of the older building, a plaque explains that it was the home of the Jackson Brewery, built in 1912, and operated for seven years before Prohibition. I remember seeing still photos in gay porn magazines that were shot in that alleyway. Drew even included some graffiti and part of a sign on his plastic recreation of that wall. As I remember, the bidding went high, probably because people wanted to own something that was hand made by Al Parker.

Our other fundraisers for the brunch fund were the margarita booths at the annual leather street fairs - Up Your Alley and the Folsom Street Fair a few weeks later. Drew came down to 10th and Folsom to help out at the Folsom Fair that year, but it didn't work out. He was fast enough and had no problem adding, subtracting, or making change. The problem with having Drew tend bar was that word spread through the crowd that Al Parker was working the margarita booth. We suddenly had a huge line at his corner, but nobody wanted drinks from anyone else. They also wanted autographs and pictures taken with him. I told Drew to stand out in front of the booth instead of serving drinks. He still attracted the crowds and the other volunteers could go back to making money.

Al Parker, Rita, Jerry Vallaire and Patrick Toner setting up our margarita booth at the Folsom Fair

The following year he called me the week before the Folsom Street Fair and asked how much it cost for all the tequila and mix, the paper cups, the rental of blenders, the booth cost, the works. I added it up and early on the morning of the fair he came to meet us at 10th and Folsom with a check for that amount. Every dollar we made that year went to Rita's brunch fund.

As 1990 drew to a close, I had no inkling this would be the last winter I lived in that McCoppin Street apartment. We had no *Men Behind Bars* rehearsals over the holidays that year, no show to plan for Presidents' Day weekend of 1991. Jim Cvitanich was too sick to tend bar at the Pilsner Inn anymore. I didn't see him, but occasionally a mutual friend would give me a report. He'd lost a ton of weight, I'd hear. Emaciated now, that beautiful body he'd always taken such pride in was gone. On one of his best days, a close friend could talk him into going out to lunch and maybe a movie matinee if they drove. I was no longer a close friend, unfortunately, and Jim's only remaining project was to plan his own memorial service, which would be much sooner than I had even imagined.

In February of 1991, Terry Thompson and I went back to New Orleans for our second Mardi Gras in a row. It was probably just too soon for me. Maybe my expectations were too high, but I didn't have nearly as much fun as I did the first time. My second Mardi Gras was another one of those instances when the return trip was not as much fun as the first time.

It reminded me of when I was in my early twenties and new to California. My first serious live-in boyfriend Armando decided to show me Disneyland. I had never been to Southern California, and he'd grown up in L.A. We got up early Tuesday morning, flew to LAX—you didn't even need to buy a ticket in those days; flights left every hour, and they took cash at the gate, $18 each way—rented a car and dropped acid on the drive to Anaheim. Space Mountain had just opened that week, so we went on it twice, plus all the other rides. We ate all the junk food we wanted, and it was a magical day to be young and in love.

That weekend, back in San Francisco, we took our friend Sarah Hilton out for a good-bye dinner in the Castro before she moved to New York. We loved to eat at the Neon Chicken on 18th Street because even if it was full, you could leave your name at the door and wait at the Corner Grocery bar on the corner of 18th and Hartford, where Moby Dick has now stood for decades. It was just an old grocery store converted into a bar to cash in on the gay renaissance of the old Irish neighborhood. The glass display cases became the bar top, and they added a few stools, chairs and funky round oak tables. The walls were covered with autographed opera posters and the jukebox played nothing but opera. The raised area in the back of the room was a stage where aspiring opera singers would sometimes perform. The place was a haze of cigarette smoke mixed with the smell of cheap cologne.

I was never a big opera fan, but the place was so different from any gay bar I was used to that I thought it was fun. The drinks were cheap and good, and the Neon Chicken would call them on the phone when our table was ready.

Over dinner that night, Armando and I told Sarah about our adventure in Disneyland. Sarah confessed that she had never been to Disneyland and she also mentioned that she was going to visit an old friend in L.A. before she moved. Armando and I insisted that she see Disneyland and we offered to meet her there, show her all the sights, go on all the rides, and experience the "magic" with her.

We set the alarm to get up early Tuesday morning to fly to L.A. We rented a car and drove to Anaheim to meet Sarah by the star in the center of the sidewalk "…right in front of Sleeping Beauty's Castle. You can't miss us! Ten o'clock this Tuesday morning. We'll be there!"

On our second Tuesday morning at Disneyland, one week after the first trip, the acid was coming on strong by ten-thirty, and still no sign of Sarah. Armando and I glared at each other angrily for what seemed like long stretches of time, but maybe we were just stoned. We scanned the crowds, hoping to catch a glimpse of her. She was tall and blonde, and she would stand out in a crowd. When eleven o'clock had passed, we finally had to admit that she wasn't coming. She hadn't thought we really meant it. She couldn't believe we were serious about a thing like that. We were so serious that we'd already bought her a mouse hat and had **SARAH** embroidered across the front. We couldn't wait to give it to her the minute she arrived so that we could welcome her to Disneyland!

Now it was just the two of us on acid, and we might as well make the best of it. We took Sarah's hat all over Disneyland. We took pictures of it with Space Mountain in the background. We took a picture of Sarah's hat on an empty seat on the tea cup ride. We took pictures of it sticking out of Disneyland trash cans. We decided to send her the pictures when we got home, just to prove what we had done, but the acid that had made everything sparkle a week ago just made it look tawdry that day. The LSD exposed the coarse and ugly inner workings of this evil place and laid its secrets bare. It made the seams show and revealed the nuts and bolts and machinery behind the brightly painted sets. I didn't go back to Disneyland for years.

My second trip to Mardi Gras with Terry reminded me of that second trip to Disneyland. On my return trip to Mardi Gras, the floats showed their wear, and the shiny plastic beads that were so much fun a year earlier seemed simply cheap. The energy of the party that I'd enjoyed the first time was a nuisance now. The crowds made it hard to get up to the bar for drinks, and I felt like I was always being shoved and elbowed.

I've been back to New Orleans since then, when it was *not* Mardi gras, and fallen in love with the city all over again. I've even said that if San Francisco fell away into the sea in a huge earthquake, the only other place I think I could live would be New Orleans. But that Mardi Gras trip was kind of a drag. I didn't feel well. Maybe that was it. I lacked the perfect combination of drugs and alcohol in my body. Terry seemed to be having a good time, though, so I didn't complain. I didn't see any sense in bringing him down.

On Fat Tuesday night, I met a guy on the street outside the Bourbon Pub and invited him back to my hotel room. It was the same hotel as last year, but I didn't get my old room this time, and I had some very fond memories of that room. This time I was upstairs and all the way in the back overlooking the courtyard.

I don't even remember whether we had sex. I woke up at some point in the middle of the night to use the toilet and I noticed that my suitcase was even messier than I'd left it. All my pants pockets were turned inside out. All my cash was gone, credit cards and worst of all, he took all of my cocaine. On the floor beside the toilet, he'd forgotten a Zip-loc plastic baggie full of hypodermic needles that I hadn't even seen before. I hoped he would really miss those later, since I knew he'd never dare to come back for them after ripping me off.

At least my journal, my driver's license, and my plane ticket were still there. I could get home alright. Later that morning I borrowed enough money from Terry to tide me over until I was back in San Francisco. I went right back to work on Castro Street, paid Terry back from my tips what I'd borrowed in New Orleans, bought some more cocaine and checked the *B.A.R.* obituaries to see how many people I knew had died while I was out of town for a week. I was back in my old routine until about ten days later when something strange began to happen. I fell in love.

Chapter Forty-Five

Kelly was a bartender at the Pendulum on 18th and Collingwood, across the street from the Edge, just around the corner from where my job at the Special at 469 Castro Street. The Pendulum was a "black" bar, meaning that its primary clientele was African-American. I had been there dozens of times over the years for special events and parties, just as I'd been in almost every gay bar in San Francisco by that time, but the Pendulum wasn't one of my regular hangouts.

Kelly and I met late one night on the popular South of Market cruising ground that my favorite coke-dealer, Jim Bayer and I referred to as Green Acres. It was cold and drizzling after the bars closed, and I was too buzzed to go home to bed alone. Kelly must have been in a similar mood that night. I stopped to light a cigarette at the corner of Pink and Pearl, two tiny alley streets just south of Market near the central freeway. Kelly was standing across the narrow alley from me, a tall slender dark-skinned man—Italian or Spanish or South American, I thought—and very handsome.

He asked if he could "borrow" a cigarette. I've always hated that line because I've never known anyone to give one back, but I walked the few steps in the dark across the empty alley to get a closer look at him and pulled out my pack. He told me he didn't smoke. That was just his way of breaking the ice. I invited him to get out of the cold by coming back to my place on McCoppin Street where I had vodka, ice, mixers in the kitchen, and a mirror beside my bed with a razor blade, a straw and a fresh bindle of cocaine. I'd run into Jim Bayer on Green Acres that night too.

The sex was phenomenal, but we also talked for hours that night. As the sun came up, I started to drift off. Kelly gave me a good morning kiss and left me alone in my bed.

We hadn't exchanged phone numbers or anything, but we each knew where the other one worked and now he knew where

I lived. I found out later that he lived near the U.S. Mint on Hermann Street, not too far from me at all. Best of all, though, was that when I finally woke up that Sunday afternoon, I found a silver ring on the edge of the bathroom sink. I've learned in gay life that it's always a good sign that you'll see someone again if they leave jewelry behind, especially cock rings. This was a finger ring with three square stones in it, two black and one turquoise, and it fit me perfectly.

It was Sunday afternoon by the time I found Kelly's ring, and I knew that Terry Thompson would be holding court at the Eagle by now. The patio would be packed for the Sunday beer bust, and Terry would be sitting at the back end of the main bar, directly outside his office door, so that if anyone wanted to offer him a line, they could duck inside. The day was sunny, at least for the moment, and I needed a drink, so I headed down to the Eagle see my good friend Terry.

After his lover, Blair died, Terry was known to have a thing for black guys. He hung out at the Pendulum sometimes. When I arrived at his end of the bar, a stool opened up next to him, so I tossed my jacket over it, sat down and ordered a drink. I flashed my hand with the silver ring on my finger in his face.

"What's that?" Terry asked. "It's not stuck, is it?"

"No!" We both laughed. A few weeks earlier I'd put on a ring that a trick had left at my apartment, but it was too small for me. By the time I got to Castro Street, my finger was swollen to almost twice its normal size. I tried sticking my finger in a glass of ice water, but nothing worked. Someone told me to go next door to Cliff's Hardware. I told the cashier I had a ring stuck, and he paged someone on the microphone who appeared momentarily and told me to follow him to the back room. I held up my finger and said, "See, it's so swollen I can't move it at all."

He stopped and said, "Oh, it's on your finger! We can take care of that out here." He told me that they sawed off so many stuck cock rings at Cliff's that the Emergency Room at Davies Hospital up the street sent patients to them if it was during store hours.

I told Terry, "No, it's just something my trick left, but I thought you'd be interested to know that I pulled a Terry Thompson last night."

"You what?"

"I slept with a black guy. You might even know him. His name is Kelly. He's a bartender at the Pendulum."

"Sure, I know Kelly. He's a real stud!"

"Have you had him?"

"No."

I don't suppose it should have mattered. Kelly was only two years younger than I was. He'd moved out here from New York, where he had worked as a fashion model. He was no virgin, but I was glad that Terry said he hadn't *had* Kelly. From the very beginning, I sensed that Kelly was unique and if I was going to dive into anything serious with him, I wanted it to be special. After all, it had been a long time since I'd even dated anyone.

Kelly and I were both HIV positive. We talked about that the first night, right before we had sex. Otherwise, we would have used condoms and rubber gloves. Maybe even face masks— people were getting crazy paranoid in those days. Our mutual HIV status was another reason Kelly felt right. We couldn't infect each other. We'd both lost many of our friends. We were both living on borrowed time, so we reasoned that we might as well enjoy whatever time we had left.

Kelly and I both had lots of blood relatives who lived back east, which we always indicated with a tilt of the head towards the east instead of saying the words. Mine were in Minnesota for the most part, and his were spread out between New York, North Carolina, and Florida. It turned out he was half black, a quarter Cherokee and a quarter Irish. Kelly was actually his last name, but that's what everyone called him. He explained his surname on one of our first nights together. "Obviously, someone on my father's side of the family fucked one of his slaves."

Whatever blood relations we had back east and whatever families of friends we had in San Francisco, Kelly and I became a family of two. We made it three when we adopted a lovable mutt we named Charlie, because Kelly said that he'd always wanted a dog named Charlie. The best guess the people at the pound could make regarding his breed was that he was a cross between Norwegian Elkhound and Cairn Terrier. Not as much of a mixed breed as Kelly, but just as adorable.

I wore that silver ring he'd left on my bathroom sink until the following Christmas when we got new matching ones and made a solemn commitment to each other, all by ourselves, in our own new apartment on Castre Street, with only Charlie and the Christmas tree as our witnesses.

Kelly

Chapter Forty-Six

A week or two after I met Kelly, I got the news about Jim Cvitanich. I was at work on Castro Street when Kirk Ramsey came into the bar that afternoon. I knew Kirk because he was an old friend of Gail Wilson. Kirk had worked for Bob Mackie in L.A. for years and designed most of Gail's performance costumes. Jim and I both liked Kirk a lot, but I don't think I'd ever seen him inside the Special in the daytime.

"What's up, Kirk?" I asked. It could have been that he was on Castro Street to pick up a prescription from Walgreens or something from Cliff's next door, but I sensed from his demeanor that he hadn't just stopped in to say hi.

"I take it you haven't heard about Jim."

No, I hadn't heard, but it didn't come as a shock. My former business partner, friend, and co-creator Jim Cvitanich was dead. We'd had so many fun times together, and I had such colorful memories of him. Jim had joined the ranks of our friends who had already left us. I couldn't be surprised.

I couldn't even be saddened. I had been made numb by the news of countless deaths for a long time. I also knew that Jim had been miserable for months and now the suffering and the slow inevitable end to his dynamic life had come to end. If I was sad about anything, it was the fact that we hadn't spoken to each other in months. I couldn't even remember all the reasons we were so estranged, but neither one of us could apologize now. None of that mattered anymore.

I'd heard lots of guys I knew talk in hushed tones about a book called *Final Exit*. They said it was the definitive manual on how to end your own life once it had reached a point of unbearable suffering. Gay guys with AIDS had been buying copies, passing them around and handing them down to the next friend who might want to at least know their options for "self-deliverance" when the time came.

A lot of gay men create extended families that I like to call tribes. In the worst of the AIDS years, some of those tribes grew closer while others dwindled and died out entirely. Jim and I had lost a lot of mutual friends and in the course of it all, the two of us had drifted apart, but I knew somewhere along the line that he had read that book.

Master planner that he always was, Jim had taken control of everything. Jim sent his roommate Michael out on a long errand, put on his favorite opera album and turned up the volume in his bedroom. He took whatever pills he needed to do the job. I like to imagine that he rose from his frail body on the wings of an aria. I heard later that his death was one year to the day after his beloved mother died.

Jim also took control of the events that would happen afterward. He designed his own panel for the AIDS Memorial Quilt and had our friend Charles Batte sew it for him. He wrote his own obituaries, one each for the *B.A.R.*, the *Examiner* and the *San Francisco Chronicle*. For his memorial service, he booked the Victoria Theatre where we'd had some of our most rousing theatrical successes, a place where we had sold out every show we produced.

The memorial was on Sunday March 10, 1991 at two p.m.. I asked Kelly to come with me to Jim's service, but he had to work that afternoon. Kelly and I had been getting more serious every day and/or night. Our bartending schedules were such that we got together for sex whenever we could and spent a lot of time talking over the bar at the Special or the Pendulum, depending on who was working and who was visiting. I had always warned my friends to never date a bartender...unless you are one.

I don't remember much about Jim's service, but I know that I met up with a bunch of friends at the Special so we could go together. My friend Doug "Fluffy" drove his car and it was pouring rain, and I remember that he got a ticket afterward for parking in a red zone in the driveway of the parking lot behind the Castro Theatre.

Most of the people who came to the memorial were involved with the shows in some way or were Jim's old customers at the Pilsner Inn or his friends from the gym. I remember how uncomfortable I felt, even debating beforehand whether I should go at all. I worried about how I would feel to be there, since Jim and I weren't even on speaking terms. Then I considered that my absence might be more conspicuous than my presence. In the end, I was only there, like everyone else, to pay my respects. It was not about me.

I ended up sitting in the left rear side of the orchestra section between my coke dealer, Jim Bayer, and the wonderful comic Marga Gomez who had performed in some of our shows. Jim's AIDS quilt panel was unveiled to the public for the first time on that stage that day. It had his leather vest sewn into it with silver studs that spelled out "Mr. SF Leather 1982." Jim's brother spoke, as did Wayne Fleisher, who was our third co-producer on the final show and choreographer for all our productions. Gail Wilson spoke. She didn't sing. I don't think anyone sang. I didn't like the fact that Jim's service had no joy. I can't remember a single drag queen there. Jim's old roommate, Joe Johns, came in boy clothes instead of dressing as the star of the MBB box office, Joan Eva Duarte Peckerhead. None of the many drag queens who had been in our shows came in drag. Some of them came in suits and ties that made them look like dreary old men.

The obituaries in the papers specified that mourners should make donations to the charity of their choice in Jim's name in lieu of flowers. I've often wondered how many people actually did that. I never did. If I would have donated money at every request, I would have gone broke by 1987! Only one person ignored Jim's wishes and sent flowers. A huge bouquet in a lovely vase arrived that morning from none other than former Mayor (not yet U.S. Senator) Dianne Feinstein. I laughed so hard when I saw her name on the card. I could almost hear Jim laughing with me that good old Dianne had broken the rules and sent flowers anyway, maybe to get even for all the times we had made fun of her in our shows.

Chapter Forty-Seven

In 1985, while planning a candlelight march to honor Harvey Milk and George Moscone, Cleve Jones got the idea to create a quilt. AIDS deaths weren't always formally memorialized, especially when they were coming so fast and when so much stigma was attached to the virus. Some gay people were already ostracized from their blood families, which was why they had moved to more accepting cities like San Francisco in the first place.

The AIDS quilt is comprised of six by three panels of fabric, each the size of a grave, sewn together in blocks of eight to make the twelve by twelve squares. Materials found on the panels consist of everything from denim and leather to sequins and lace, to jock straps, jewelry, feathers and even cremation ashes. I have never taken part in the making of a quilt panel. I walked by the Names Project headquarters at 2362 Market Street countless times. It always looked open and welcoming, as if anyone could just walk in and volunteer to sit down at a sewing machine and set to work. I was too overwhelmed to go inside, but I always saw people in there sewing. That space was also the home of Harvey Milk's first camera shop before he moved to Castro Street. Cleve was also a good friend of Harvey's.

Someone told me that my friend James' mother had made his quilt panel. She included all the prizes he had won in high school and college, blue ribbons from the county fair, his old basketball jersey, straight "A" report cards, and some of the bright red satin from a dress he wore the first Halloween he ever went in drag. She must have been a very understanding mother.

When I heard that the quilt was going to be displayed at the Moscone Center in December of 1987, I decided to go have a look at it and find James' panel. It was a weekday afternoon when I was off work, so I took the bus downtown and walked the few blocks south on 3rd Street to Howard. I rode down the escalators to see thousands of multi-colored panels spread out on the floor and people slowly walking between them, kneeling beside them. It felt like being in a church or a cathedral, a huge space wrapped in silence broken only the occasional sounds of escaping gasps of grief.

Boxes of Kleenex were everywhere.

Someone handed me a piece of paper—a booklet, a program? It turned out to be an alphabetical list of names and numbers of rows and blocks and pathways. I found James' name, and his panel was somewhere in the middle of the room, something like 14-L. I was in no hurry. I took my time and looked around at the enormity of this project. I thought about the hours of work that people had done, much of it probably blinded by tears.

I took a deep breath and headed toward row "L" but realized long before I got there that I recognized someone's name in nearly every block of panels on my way to James'—old boyfriends, customers I'd served drinks to, other bartenders and waiters who had served me, a bank teller I used to flirt with, my old neighbor from when I lived on Bush Street for a while, the guy who used to cut my hair a few years ago, a guy who used to date an old roommate of mine. By the time I got to James' panel, I was nearly wrung out.

Two men I didn't know at the time, also strangers to each other, went to see the display of the quilt that December in San Francisco. Each of them went to see the panel of his lover who had died that year. Those two panels had been sewed side by side in the same block, so those two young men met each other that day while mourning their lovers, shoulder to shoulder on their knees. I didn't know that was how they met until several years later, but they've been together ever since. I've always been happy for them and knowing their story gives the quilt even more importance in the hopelessly romantic and all too rarely visited corner of my mind. I didn't meet anyone there that day or any of the other times I have viewed the quilt. I only saw more and more names of people I knew. The quilt has grown to the size of dozens of football fields, too large to be displayed all at once anywhere now except maybe on the moon.

Chapter Forty-Eight

The Cable Car Awards used to be one of San Francisco's gayest, most gala events of the year. It was always fun to get dressed up and schmooze, enjoy the top-notch entertainment and check out the movers and shakers in the gay community. The first time I attended the annual soiree, it was being held in the old Kabuki Theater in Japantown. At the time, the venue was still a working theater with dressing rooms and a fly loft and one of the biggest stages in San Francisco. The stage even featured a turntable in the center for smooth set changes. The local gays held many big events there prior to the building's renovation in the early 1980s, when it was divided into eight smaller movie houses.

I was still living at the Russian River when I first experienced the awards show, but seeing the excitement of that crowd, the celebrity presenters and the ecstatic winners made me even more eager to move back to the city. All sorts of new parties and events and organizations had sprung up since I'd left in 1981. The second year I went to the Kabuki for the Cable Car Awards, I had just moved back to the city. I spotted Sharon McNight at a ringside table and went over to say hello. I knew her from her performances at the Woods Resort north of Guerneville. She gestured, subtly pointed and whispered to me, "That's Johnnie Ray at our table. Ask him for his autograph. He doesn't think anyone remembers him."

I didn't remember him, really, but of course I did what Sharon told me to do. He seemed pleased and flattered as he signed my program. Later that night, they introduced him and he got on stage and sang. Still later, I did a little research and realized that in the 1950s Johnnie Ray was a household name with a number of hit records. He co-starred in the 1954 movie musical *There's No Business like Show Business* with Ethel Merman, Donald O'Connor and Marilyn Monroe. In 1969, he was Judy Garland's opening act at her concerts in Sweden and Denmark and served as best man at her London wedding to her fifth and final husband

Mickey Deans.

Besides his accolades as a performer, I discovered that Johnnie Ray was arrested twice for soliciting men for sex in the restroom of the Stone Theater, a burlesque house in Detroit, before I was even born. I have always loved knowing people like me have been around forever, even though I felt sorry for what they must have had to endure. I was happy that Sharon had pointed him out and that I had the chance to meet him. Johnnie Ray died a few years later in 1990 at the age of fifty-seven from cirrhosis of the liver.

Another year at the Cable Car Awards, I met the Tony Award winning actor Robert Morse. He was there as a presenter while he was in town starring as Truman Capote in the one-man play *Tru*, which I'd just seen at the Curran Theater. The awards show had moved to the Gift Center Pavilion by that time. I also bumped into Phyllis Diller in one of the Pavilion's glass-walled elevators that night. She was there to present an award later that evening, and I had just won one. She looked at me and said, "Let me see that thing!" So I handed it to her. She looked it over, handed it back and said, "Nice. Congratulations!" Then she stepped off when we got to her floor, and I continued on to mine. I had adored Phyllis Diller since seeing her on TV when I was a little kid on the farm in Minnesota. I've always regretted that I didn't get to say anything more to her than "thanks."

Jim Cvitanich and I were nominated and won the Cable Car Award for Outstanding AIDS Fundraiser three years in a row, 1984-1986, and then we were retired to the Hall of Fame in order to give someone else a chance, but even that fourth year, we each got a plaque and a chance to make another appearance in our tuxedoes.

A few years later in 1991, I was nominated for another Cable Car Award for the birthday party for Rita Rockett, Al Parker, and Mark Abramson at the Eagle. Drew and Rita and I met in the Castro that night to ride together in his van to the Gift Center. Drew and I found seats in an empty upper balcony and watched Rita present an award. The stage was so far below that Rita was just a dot of red and blonde. Drew and I were wasted on some hash that we'd smoked in his van on the way over there, but when weren't we stoned on something in those days? I was telling him about my new lover Kelly, and I asked him if he'd ever been with a black man.

"Sure, I've been with black guys, why?"

I told him about meeting Kelly and how race had never meant much to me, but this was the first time I had felt myself falling in love with a black man. Then I realized that I was so stoned I was talking to him like a therapist, forgetting that he was also Al Parker, porn star. I confessed that I had never seen any of his movies. I said, "I hope you're not insulted. It's just that I think of you as Drew, as a friend that Rita and I share a birthday with and how cool it is that we can help raise money for her brunches at the AIDS ward."

"I know. Isn't she amazing? Look at her down there, such good energy!"

"Yeah," I agreed. "Amazing, but if I saw your movies, I think I'd have a hard time talking to you like this. It was the same way with Coral Browne."

"Who's that? Was she in porn?"

"Oh no," I had to laugh. "I knew her as Vincent Price's wife. She played Vera Charles in *Auntie Mame* with Rosalind Russell, but I didn't know that until later. I hadn't seen the movie yet, but if I had, I probably would have thought of her differently and we wouldn't have been able to talk the same way, like friends...not because of her, but because of me...does that make sense? I am so stoned."

"Yeah, that was some good stuff, wasn't it? I think I know what you mean, though. I was just back east visiting my dad a while ago and when I got home to San Francisco I was really horny, so I went out and ended up meeting this really hot guy at the Badlands. I was sure he didn't recognize me, so I went home with him. Everything was great until he turned on the VCR in his bedroom with one of my movies already in it!"

"What did you do?"

"I got dressed and went home! What a bummer! I just couldn't deal with it."

"Bummer," I agreed. "Something similar happened to me a while back."

"Oh, yeah?"

"Yeah, but the guy turned on one of his movies, and I didn't recognize him. I think he was insulted. He was hotter in the movie than in person, even in the dark. It must have been a pretty old movie."

Drew laughed, but he stopped as the rest of the story unfolded. I had sex with the guy a few more times after the night he showed me his own porn film. He lived on a tiny alley called Elgin Park in the midst of Green Acres. His apartment was on the second floor, and I sometimes saw him standing naked in the window late at night, masturbating with just the light from the television screen. If he beckoned and I walked up to his gate, he would buzz me in. Then I didn't see him in the window any more for a long time.

One night a couple of weeks before my second trip to Mardi Gras, before I met Kelly, I walked across Castro Street after my shift at the Special ended and had a couple of drinks at the Castro Station. I met a very sexy guy I'd seen around and he ended up inviting me home. He lived on Elgin Park. When we got to his building I realized it was the same place that other guy lived, the one who I used to trick with late at night.

Drew asked, "Did you run into him again?" but I said it was even weirder than that. When we climbed the stairs to the second floor, I noticed signs in the hallway about oxygen being used there and warnings about smoking and fire hazards and such. The guy I met at the Castro Station told me his neighbor across the hall had been really sick lately. Then his door opened, and these two guys came out carrying a black bag. They were removing his body. He'd just died that night.

"Wow, what did you do?"

"Well, I sure didn't say anything. I didn't let on that I knew the guy. I didn't really. I mean...I didn't know his name. We'd just fucked a few times, and he never played his own porn tape again. The guy I'd just met at Castro Station didn't seem too surprised or upset about his neighbor dying, so we just went inside his apartment and fucked, like we'd planned all along. What else was there to do, right?"

"I guess."

"Sorry to bring up a downer."

"No, that's all right, Mark. And I think it's cool that you've never seen any of my movies. It's kind of refreshing. What does Kelly do?"

"He's a bartender at the Pendulum. He used to be a model in New York. We just met a few weeks ago, but it's going great! He's at work tonight. Hey, I can't believe I missed you on the *Merv Griffin Show* and now your foreskin surgery is all over Herb Caen's column. What's up with that? He's been writing about you every other week. "

"Only three or four times."

"Still, it's interesting. Where did the extra skin come from? Did it hurt a lot?"

"It didn't hurt at the time, not until later when it was healing and the first time I got hard, whoa-ho!"

"Ooooh, ouch! I don't really want to know."

"They bring the skin up from the base. The surgeon had never done anything like it, but he was cool. I had it done at Children's Hospital. They sort of loosen the skin so it can slide further down the shaft, and it looks like I was never circumcised at all."

"Ee-ew! I said I didn't want to know! I'm sorry I asked!"

"I can't wait to make another movie with it. You know, I never really celebrated my birthday before I met you and Rita. I'm glad you got me into it for a good cause and all."

"Me, too. You've always been a good sport about it. So, how did Herb Caen find out all about your foreskin surgery?"

"Mostly over the phone, but he didn't print everything I told him, like how much it cost. I told him that was a lot of money to pay for cheese."

We both cracked up, and I said, "That must be the most expensive cheese in town."

"I know. That's exactly what I told Herb Caen, but he wouldn't print that part!"

We saw Rita coming toward us from the elevator. "Come on, you guys. I've been looking all over for you two. It's almost time for our award. We've got to hurry downstairs. We're going to win, you know. It's a public vote in our category, and those two drag queen events will cancel each other out. You guys are stoned! What's so funny?"

"Cheese!" we both said at the same time, and I was still laughing about smegma as the two of them pulled me toward the elevator.

Afterward, Drew and I smoked another bowl of hash in the van as he drove us back to the Castro. Rita said we should stop for a beer somewhere and show off our new Cable Car award. Drew suggested going to the Pendulum since Kelly was working. He'd worn a black fur jacket over a skin-tight white t-shirt and even tighter Levis. When we got out of the van, he said, "Wait! I'm not dressed right!" and he turned his reversible jacket inside out to reveal basic black leather. Whenever he was worried about what to wear, I reminded him that no one who recognized him would have seen him before with his clothes on anyway!

The Pendulum was packed to the rafters that night, but we

worked our way to Kelly's station in the back, and I introduced him to my friends. Kelly shook hands with them and got our beers before he leaned across the bar to kiss me and we made plans for him to come over to McCoppin Street after he got off work. I'm sure the hashish had nothing to do with it, but all in all, it was one of the most perfect nights in San Francisco that I can almost remember.

Chapter Forty-Nine

Robert Pruzan and Robert Gothie were both friends of mine. I have no reason to believe they even knew each other, but I think of them together because they were roommates in Davies Hospital for a few days in early 1992. With so many people sick and dying, I was bound to visit friends in the hospital and find them in the same room. Outside the hospital, they each lived alone.

Bob Gothie was a regular customer at the Special. He was a big fan of the San Francisco 49ers and during football season, he wrote the initials "BG" on the illegal football pools that all the gay bars ran in those days. Rita Rockett and I started calling him "BeeGee" and the nickname stuck, although it reminded me of the singing brothers Gibb, the Bee Gees from Australia. He owned a house on Castro Street about a block from the bar on the north side of Market. I don't ever remember being inside his house while he was alive, but I spent some time there going through his things after he died. That was when we discovered some fascinating mementos that revealed the life he led before we knew him. He never talked about his past.

The house was at the bottom of the hill where States Street runs into Castro. BG always said that if anyone who lost their brakes coming down that hill would smash right into his house. That was one of the reasons he lived on the second floor. It was a duplex, but he never rented out the lower level even though the income would have been sizable for a nice two-bedroom apartment in that location. He said he liked having it quiet, didn't want to be bothered with tenants living downstairs, and he didn't need the money. At one point he talked about leaving the house to Rita in his will, but that wasn't the way it worked out.

BG was a generous man. One day at the Special, he heard us talking about the bubble machine we always placed on top of our margarita booths at the Folsom Street and Up Your Alley fairs.

It drew a lot of attention and made our booth easy to find since people could just look up and follow the bubbles. Four times each summer, I had to drive out to the industrial part of town on the far side of Potrero Hill to Holzmueller Productions, the theatrical supply house, to pick up and return a rented bubble machine. It wasn't the cheap kind you can get for children's birthday parties. It cost several hundred dollars, but when Bob Gothie heard about it, he just wrote a check and said, "Go buy our own bubble machine."

BG was nearly twice my age but still really handsome with a strong masculine air of sophistication that I admired. He was wickedly clever, too, and it was always satisfying to make him laugh. We would talk about the events of the day across the bar, and he would sometimes write down something I'd said. Sometimes he sent my remarks to Herb Caen, who might use them in his Pulitzer Prize winning column in the *San Francisco Chronicle*. When I sent items directly to Herb Caen, he always sent back a pleasant hand-signed thank you note in the mail. Sometimes his assistant Carole Vernier even called me to follow up or to clarify a fact, but Herb never used anything I sent him unless it went through BG.

The other Robert, Robert Pruzan, was a fabulous photographer who seemed to have always been a part of the Haight/Ashbury neighborhood where he lived. He was actually born in Seattle and, according to his obituary in the *Bay Area Reporter*, he was once a serious and respected mime who studied with Etienne Decroux in Paris in the 1960s and later taught mime to Bill Irwin, Leonard Pitt, Geoff Hoyle, and Bert Houle. He was also a friend of Robert Mapplethorpe and his equal as a photographer, at least in my eyes.

I first met Robert Pruzan when I was at the Russian River producing one of the big male beauty pageants at the Woods Resort. I asked Mister Marcus, who was going to be the emcee, who I should invite to be judges. He suggested Robert Pruzan,

Jim Cvitanich and Alan Selby, founder and owner of Mr. S Leather. Marcus often referred to Robert in his B.A.R. column as Pruzan Pruzannadanna after Gilda Radner's character Roseanne Roseannadanna on *Saturday Night Live*. I usually called him Pruzan. He lived in a ground floor apartment on Ashbury Street a few doors north of Haight. It looked like he'd been there since 1967, the "Summer of Love," because it was filled with crystals and bonsai and fish tanks. In my memory of visits there, often with our mutual friend Jane Dornacker, I envision beaded curtains, peacock feathers and beaded lamp shades, but it would be more factual to state that the walls were covered with photographs, some of them famous ones he had sold to magazines. Others were funny or sexy. Some were downright obscene.

Pruzan and I developed a ritual over the decade or so before he died. Every year at the Gay Pride Parade, he gave me magic mushrooms. We hadn't planned to do this, at least not at first. We just happened to run into each other, and he offered. I always said yes. I'd been in the habit of dropping acid for Pride starting in the 1970s. I was probably still doing acid when I knew Pruzan, but now I took mushrooms too. It might seem unlikely that we would just run into each other year after year amid hundreds of thousands of people when the parade was several blocks (and hours) long, but for some of those years, I was on the Eagle float or with the leather contingent or representing whatever bar I worked at that year. Even when I wasn't officially in the parade, Pruzan was out there on Market Street photographing everything, so I could always spot him from behind the barricades.

Sometimes we didn't even try to speak over the noise of the crowds. He would notice me, smile and come over to where I was. I would open my mouth and he would tuck something inside. They tasted nasty, but I knew enough to chew them a little. Someone older and wiser had once told me that they took a lot longer to digest if you swallowed them whole. The best way to consume them was in tea, but we didn't have time for that in the middle of a parade.

I never asked Pruzan where he got them, but knowing him

as I did, I would not have been surprised to hear that he just walked over to Buena Vista Park after it rained and knew which mushrooms were poison and which ones were psilocybin.

Pruzan was invited to every gay event. Whenever we did a *Men Behind Bars* production, we gave him full access to the entire theater, to anywhere in the house, backstage, upstairs and down. If you wanted free advertising in the papers, you wanted Pruzan to be there. The community had other gay "event" photographers like Crawford Barton, who always tried to hit on me, or Rink, who is still going strong, as is Harvey Milk's good friend Danny Nicoletta, but Pruzan was my good friend, and the one I knew best.

He always carried at least three cameras around his neck. I always assumed one was for color film and one for black and white, but I didn't know about the third one for some time. Whenever he came across a drunk, screaming, "Take my picture!" he picked up the third camera. It had a flash, but it was empty. Pruzan wasn't wasting any film on them, and he didn't have to be rude by refusing to take their picture. Even if they remembered the evening later and asked about their photograph, Robert could tell them that it didn't turn out.

The day I saw both Roberts—Gothie and Pruzan—in the same room in the hospital was not the last time I saw either of them. Sometimes AIDS took a long time to kill. For every young man who died quickly after his diagnosis, several others struggled and held on as long as they could. The word was always that new drugs were coming soon. That was our hope, our mantra, so a bout with pneumocystis pneumonia didn't necessarily mean you wouldn't come back from the hospital. We always had hope for another spurt of strength and another chance to go home for a while, at least, before the next time. You might be one of the lucky ones who was still around when a miracle drug was discovered.

Robert Pruzan even moved out of that dark little low-ceilinged apartment on Ashbury Street before he died. One afternoon he invited Gail Wilson and me to come to see his new place. He was having people in small groups over to go through files of photographs and order what they wanted him to print. He had brought out all the pictures he'd taken of Gail performing in *Men Behind Bars*, but hundreds of others were spread all over the place. And what a place it was! Robert Pruzan was living alone in the penthouse of 555 Buena Vista West.

The building looks like it belongs on Central Park in New York City. The facade is covered in molded gargoyles and cherubs, seals, pedestals, and crests. You can see it from a ways off, a startlingly white and extremely ornate forty-unit Neo-Churrigueresque apartment building from the 1920s. For those unfamiliar with architectural styles, the best way to describe it might be to say that the grand entrance looks like it was designed by a crazed wedding cake baker on some serious recreational drugs.

His views from the penthouse were spectacular, facing north and west to include the Golden Gate Bridge, the Marin County Headlands and the Pacific Ocean. Beneath the huge windows lining the living room were his tanks of precious tropical fish. The interior white walls and a few big potted plants made the place feel enormous. I asked him why he moved up here to this gorgeous sunny place after living down in the valley for so many years. Pruzan looked around with a sweep of his arm and told us, "I wanted a nice place to die." It seemed to me a harsh way of putting it, a stern look at reality, but I knew what he meant. It was a beautiful place to live, too, for what little time he had left.

That was the last time I saw my friend Robert Pruzan alive. Some of my most valued memories in photographs albums are pictures that he took at events that I organized or at parties and celebrations I attended. He was soon admitted back into Davies Hospital on Castro Street, where he died on May 29, 1992 at age forty-six.

Bob Gothie told us at the Special that if his newspapers started to pile up, someone should come in and check on him. He subscribed to several magazines that sometimes didn't all fit inside the mailbox and he had the *SF Chronicle* delivered every day. He assured us that if he was going out of town, he would always put a hold on the paper.

Sure enough, that was exactly what happened. I think it was my friend Doug "Fluffy" who first noticed the papers. Doug was living on States Street at the time, so he could see BG's front door when he came down the hill to the Castro. He didn't notice right away that the papers were piling up, and then he didn't want to go in there alone, so he came down to the bar to fortify himself and find a couple of guys to go with him. I know that one of them was Chris Osborne and another might have been his lover, Kenny.

They discovered a way to get in through the back of the house and found BG upstairs on the floor, barely alive. They called an ambulance that took him away, first to the hospital and then to a hospice. They figured he had gotten up to use the bathroom but ran out of strength before he could get back to bed. Judging by the dates on the accumulated newspapers, he could have been lying on the floor for four or five days.

A couple of weeks later, Rita Rockett, Charlie "Fannie" Fulbright and I went to visit him in the Zen Hospice on Page Street. I'd been to Coming Home Hospice in the Castro for a reception before it was open and in use. I'd taken part in a lot of fundraising efforts to turn the old Catholic Convent on Diamond Street into a comfortable place for people to spend their final days. This was my first trip to a working hospice though, and my first time seeing a friend who was that close to death. I foolishly assumed that I would find him sitting up in a chair reading the newspaper or writing a letter to the editor of some sophisticated periodical. I thought about what he might like me to bring him from the outside world and stopped at Safeway to pick up the current issue of *TV Guide* and a big bag of Reese's Peanut Butter Cups, BG's favorite.

The people who worked at Zen Hospice were as kind and pleasant as could be, almost too pleasant. I was already nervous, their behavior made me feel guilty for not being as chipper and cheerful as they obviously were. I set my little gifts on the dresser and looked down at my friend. He was just a skinny little pile of bones beneath a layer of papery, pale skin. I stood there for a moment and watched him, just to make sure he was breathing. We spoke to him, but his eyes didn't open, and I doubted whether he heard us. I could see the outline of his feet sticking up under the blankets, so I gently touched his big toe with the palm of my hand and he winced! That was the only reaction I could get, and I didn't want to torture him, so I quickly pulled my hand away.

We said goodbye to him and thanked the attendants. I wanted to run all the way home, just to remind myself that I was still alive. I left the candy and the *TV Guide* in his room, even though he would never enjoy them. Lots of things must get left behind at a place like that. He died there on June 18, 1993 at sixty-three years old.

When we went to clean up his house a couple of weeks later, I sat down at his desk and found hundreds of newspaper clippings. His name had been in Herb Caen's column dozens of times. He'd saved every one, along with all the little notes that Herb had written back to him. I saw other correspondence too, with people I had never heard him talk about. He'd written letters that were printed in lots of magazines. He'd sent comments and suggestions to many celebrities regarding their TV shows and movies and he'd gotten letters back.

Then we found his photographs. Our friend had been a Hollywood actor, and he had been absolutely stunning to look at. We found his eight by ten glossies and black and white screen shots going back to the 1950s. He'd appeared in dozens of popular television series, including *Sea Hunt* and *Zane Grey Theater* as a very hot looking cowboy, a sexy cop, a scary gangster and several other handsome characters. He was also a character actor in a few movies, including *Palm Springs Weekend* in 1963, starring Troy Donahue and Connie Stevens. Bob Gothie. None of us knew anything about those years of his life, but it dawned on me that some of the famous people he corresponded with might have been his friends too.

BG ended up leaving his house to the AIDS Emergency Fund, and they sold it for one dollar to another AIDS service organization called Family Link. Rita's and my good friend Gary "The Queen" Rahlf, who served on the board of directors for many years, was instrumental in transitioning that prime piece of real estate at 317 Castro Street from Bob Gothie's home to a place of comfort and solace since 1985. Family Link provides temporary low-cost accommodations and counseling to families who are visiting their children with AIDS and other life-threatening illnesses in San Francisco. I'm sure that BG would have been happy to see his house go to such a worthy cause.

Chapter Fifty

My old friend Roger, whom I had stayed with for a while on Seward Street, eventually got too sick to work and moved back to live with his parents in Seattle. He had AIDS, but it couldn't have been too hard for the disease to kill him. Anyone who starts his day with gin and grapefruit juice and a Valium before work and chain smokes menthol cigarettes can't really expect a long and healthy life. Roger was funny, though, and he had a huge cock. It was too bad he never liked to use it… a total bottom.

Roger must have been a few years older than me. He knew all the old guard gay "royalty" and was friends with lots of bar owners in San Francisco too. He was probably one of their best customers. One day when I got off work at the Special, I jaywalked across Castro Street to the Castro Station. I ordered a drink and noticed an older man who looked familiar sitting next to me at the bar. He looked at me with a sense of recognition too, so we smiled and nodded. Then I realized he was Reba Robertson, aka Empress IV Reba or, in Roger's words, "Reba the rattlesnake. Watch out—she bites!" I'd met him through Roger a couple of times at formal gay functions, but I'd never seen him out of drag. I didn't know him well, but we visited and laughed a while, bought each other a drink and talked about who had died that week and what was happening around town. We discussed some of the people we knew in common, other old-time drag queens who were still around like Mame in Portland or Goldblatt and Gladys Bumps in San Francisco. Finally, Roger's name came up. I said, "I haven't heard a word from him since he went back to Seattle, have you?"

Reba smiled softly and shook his head, looking more like a sheep than a rattlesnake. "Roger's gone now too." We raised our glasses and drank to Roger. It seemed appropriate.

After Roger left town and Jonathan's house on Fell Street was sold, Bob moved into Roger's old apartment on Seward Street.

This was the Bob with the floor refinishing business where I had worked for a while. Once I started bartending full time, I didn't need the extra work so I didn't see Bob nearly as often. He settled down and got "married" to a much younger, incredibly handsome Hispanic man named Miguel or Manuel. They invited me over to Seward Street for drinks and hors d'oeuvres once they were all settled in. It was strange not to see all of Roger's heavy furniture, ornate lamps and bulky wood-framed art on the walls. Instead the place was furnished with Bob's uncomfortable 1950s modern hard plastic chairs, pink and turquoise tables and magazine racks, Melmac dishes, and overflowing ashtrays. We listened to those damned old Yma Sumac records of his again and ate microwaved cocktail wieners on toothpicks with a wheel of brie and crackers. Copious cocktails were consumed, of course. I was just jealous that Bob had found such a beautiful lover. He died a year or two later.

The strangest thing about Bob, which I didn't find out until I had known him for years, was that he didn't exist on paper. I don't think he even had a driver's license. He must have been very lucky not to get stopped, especially when he'd been drinking. I discovered his secret around election time one year. We were talking politics, and we agreed on all the major candidates, meaning that we liked the ones who were the least hostile to gays, who just happened to all be Democrats. Some things never change. But I was confused about one of the local propositions on the ballot, so I asked Bob how he planned to vote on that one.

He said, "I can't vote. I'm not registered to vote, but if I were I'd vote no on that one." As the conversation continued, I found out more. He had never paid taxes. He had no credit cards and no bank accounts. I remembered when I worked for him, he always paid me in cash, and I thought nothing was odd about that. But he also paid his rent and utility bills in cash. Then I remembered driving around with him to different banks so that he could cash his clients' checks. He couldn't simply deposit them without a bank account of his own. He also never flew. I never asked why. I guess I just didn't think it was any of my business. I was sure that

I saw his obituary in the B.A.R. but when I searched their online listings later, I couldn't find his name. Maybe he found some way to erase his existence there too, but I will always remember Bob with great affection.

Chapter Fifty-One

Kelly wanted us to move in together almost from the very beginning of our relationship, but I insisted that we wait a year. I liked the arrangement we had. Kelly lived nearby on Hermann Street, we had keys to each other's apartments, and we spent nearly every night together. Besides, I had once given up an amazing apartment in the Castro to move in with a lover after six months and to this day I still gaze longingly at the windows of that place whenever I walk by. It had views from the Bay Bridge to the top of Twin Peaks and all of Eureka Valley in between. To top it all off, the rent was only a hundred and sixty-five dollars a month! My apartment on McCoppin was nowhere near as nice or as cheap as that, but I like think I learn something from my mistakes.

About six weeks after we met, Kelly and I were having sex in my bedroom at about four a.m. My roommate Derek was also up having sex in the other bedroom with some trick he'd brought home after his Saturday night bartending shift at the Eagle. As Kelly and I took a break to chop a couple more lines of coke on the mirror, the smoke detector went off.

Derek and Kelly both pulled on their pants and raced to the kitchen in the back of the apartment. The door at the end of the hallway was closed, but we could see thick, black smoke scarring the walls and ceiling as it crept over and around the door. Smoke even came through the keyhole. Derek opened the door and within seconds the smoke enveloped the ceiling fixture in so much soot that the hallway was dark again. The only light came from beyond the living room. In the kitchen, bright red flames leapt from the floor to the ceiling.

Kelly and Derek grabbed towels from the bathroom and tried to smother the flames, but the fire had spread too much for them to contain it. The only telephone in the apartment was on a table in the corner of the living room. I tried to find it to call the fire department, but I couldn't see it. I was coughing. The smoke was just too intense. I yelled at Kelly and Derek to get the hell out of there as I ran to the front and pounded on the next door neighbors' door, begging them to wake up and call 9-1-1.

I ran back inside my bedroom to get some clothes on and shut the door behind me. I realized that if we kept both bedroom doors closed, we might be able to limit the smoke damage to our personal belongings, provided that the fire didn't consume the entire apartment. I quickly got dressed and grabbed the rest of Kelly's clothes and ran back outside, yelling once more to my roommate and my lover that they had to get the hell out of there. I was starting to worry that they'd choked to death. All I could hear was the deafening screech of the smoke detector on the ceiling between the bedroom doors.

Derek and Kelly finally appeared, and the three of us ran down the steps from the landing to the sidewalk where all the neighbors from the other five flats in the building stood around in various stages of undress. We heard the fire trucks' sirens approaching, and at last they pulled up out front. Kelly and Derek, who was a redhead with the palest flesh I think I have ever seen on a human being, were both completely covered in thick black soot. I told them they could be twins, and I started to laugh. Neither of them thought it was funny. The firemen raced past us down the hallway with all their tools and hoses and equipment and put out the fire in minutes, but the soot would take hours to settle into every crease and crack and crevice of that apartment beyond the bedrooms. Even the clothes in our bedrooms had to be washed in order to get rid of the nasty smell.

Kelly pulled me close and gave me a deep, wet sooty kiss. We breathed a sigh of relief and he asked, "Are you ready to rethink your one-year rule now?"

Derek went to stay with some of his friends from work. I don't know what happened to his trick. Maybe he got picked up by one of those sexy firemen. Kelly and I walked back to his place on Hermann Street. I had no place else to go.

Kelly and I returned the next day to assess the damage. It was a sunny Sunday afternoon, but we couldn't see anything in the rear of the apartment because the windows were so caked with soot. Turning on the light switches would be futile until the blackened light bulbs were replaced with clean ones.

The fire had been electrical, apparently starting in the six-pronged outlet on the back wall of the kitchen. Six electrical cords had been plugged in there. Now they were all melted, as were the attached appliances, with only the metal parts of the toaster, the blender, and the can opener remaining. The microwave was an empty box, and the Cuisinart was no more than a blackened shape on the counter. The refrigerator was completely black, and its cord was melted too. The smell of burnt plastic was sickening.

The door to the pantry had been left standing open, so everything that was in boxes burned up along with the labels on all the tin cans. All I could rescue from the kitchen were some dishes and pots and pans.

Chapter Fifty-Two

Settling into married life with Kelly forced me to live in the present. Despite the fact that so many of my friends—now oftentimes our friends—were disappearing one by one, at least Kelly and I could lean on each other. Sex was great, but it was so much better knowing when the sex was over and we finally fell asleep, that we genuinely loved each other. With such hugely different backgrounds, Kelly and I had so much to learn about each other, from favorite foods to basic housekeeping. He was always neater than I am. However, the trust was there from the beginning.

Now my old friends were not only dying, some were leaving San Francisco. Eureka Valley, the Castro district where I had spent my gay twenties in a crazy dream of fast, fun times, and young healthy flesh that seemed immortal began to look more like a nightmare. The city I had grown to love so much in the stoned 1970s was turning into a ghost town. I assumed that some of my friends could no longer bear to live in a place so overwhelmed with grief, but more often they could no longer afford it. Many returned to their home towns if they had a loving family there to care for them. Even though many organizations had sprung up to help people coping with AIDS, they weren't always enough. Many lingered near death, still clinging to life but far too sick to work anymore.

I don't remember why Patrick Toner left town. First I heard that he had moved back to his hometown of Birmingham, Alabama. Then I heard that he had found his dream job in Clearwater, Florida and fallen in love. I couldn't imagine myself living anywhere else but San Francisco, no matter what happened, but I had to file situations like Patrick's under good news.

I'm not sure exactly when he left either. He performed in all the *Men Behind Bars* shows except the last one Jim and I produced with Wayne Fleisher at the Palace of Fine Arts Theatre in 1990, so it must have been before then. I always missed friends when they moved away, but we were all growing used to that. At least if they left for a job or a relationship, we could be happy for them.

Patrick came back to San Francisco for his thirtieth birthday in 1992 and stayed through leather week, when he would have had his choice of all-night dance parties to attend if he wanted to. I know he was at the International Mr. Drummer finals because I read it in the papers. I remember that he came to the Folsom Street Fair. When he showed up at the margarita booth, I asked him if he'd come all the way back to town just to help us sling drinks again. I was kidding, but I knew he would have if we'd needed him. He looked terrific. This was probably the first year he hadn't worked behind the booth with Rita and me and so many other volunteers. I have photo albums full of pictures of him in previous years looking handsome as ever.

We didn't have time to talk much that day. He introduced everyone to his partner Derek, and they seemed enormously happy together. Seeing Patrick that day was great, just as it was great to see so many other people. Half the fun of going to those huge annual events is running into people you don't get to see every day. I had no reason to think that I wouldn't see Patrick again.

Rita kept in touch with him more closely than I did because he was the godfather to both her boys. She even named her second son Michael Patrick after him. Rita told me that Patrick and Derek went to Mexico on vacation that winter, and Patrick got sick while they were down there. I assumed it was food poisoning. I knew dozens of people who went to Puerto Vallarta on vacation every year. Some had even bought property down there, and each of them had come back at some point with stories about getting sick. It became a running joke to warn travelers about Montezuma's revenge, not to eat the hot dogs from the sidewalk vendors late at night, no matter how drunk you were. When one friend complained about being constipated on vacation, I remarked, "You were in Mexico! Drink the water. That'll take care of that."

Then someone called me at work one day and told me that Patrick had died. It was January 26, 1993. I was in shock. How many hot dogs had he eaten? How much of the water did he drink? It never occurred to me that our beautiful, healthy, handsome loving young friend could have died of AIDS. He was only thirty years old.

The obituary in the *B.A.R.* said he died of AIDS-related bacterial pneumonia and listed among his survivors "domestic partner" Derek Townsend of Atlanta. A huge funeral was held in Birmingham, Alabama. According to the local press, three hundred people celebrated mass and a mile-long procession followed the casket to the burial site.

A full month passed for us here in San Francisco before we organized our "official" good-bye to Patrick Toner. By then it felt like a bit too little and too late. I had come to terms with his death a long time ago. I knew he was gone, but he'd moved away a while ago. I preferred to think of him that way, as if he might be back any time, popping up with his bright smile and an offer to lend a hand to whomever was in need.

The San Francisco version of the "celebration of life" for Patrick Toner was held on February 28 at Chez Mollet, a SOMA restaurant and bar at 527 Bryant Street. I remember little about it except that my friend Doug and I took his car to North Beach to pick up several sheets of focaccia bread from Danilo's Italian Bakery. It was a gathering of all the remaining leather-glitterati, a good time to have a look around, do a head count and wonder how many might still be alive to come to our funerals when we died. Or had we already waited too long to get a decent turn out?

I preferred to remember Patrick with me naked in the rain an hour and a half north of the city, running through the dark under the trees on a winter night in search of dry firewood. That was only a few weeks after his twenty-first birthday. Could it be true that it had been less than ten years since we met? Could he really be gone for good? No. He was more than a lifelong friend. He started the Up Your Alley street fair. Patrick will always be with us.

Chapter Fifty-Three

Kelly and I didn't talk very much about our health during our first year or so together. We both had HMO coverage with Kaiser through our bartending jobs, his at the Pendulum and mine at the Special. We both took our AZT every four hours around the clock and continued to drink as much as everyone else we knew, especially our bartender friends. We also went to a lot of funerals. I had lived in San Francisco several years longer and knew more people, so I'm sure I went to more than he did. Sometimes I dragged him along for moral support when it was the death of someone close to me or if it was my third or fourth service that week.

There were a few times when I told myself, "That's it. No more! I cannot go to one more fucking funeral! I refuse!" As soon as I made that decision, the next person to die was always someone really close, like my boss Ed Stark, or an old roommate or a former serious boyfriend like Kap, and I had to go. Those deaths forced me to break my own rule, and I vowed not to make that rule again until the next time…and the time after.

After the fire on McCoppin Street, Kelly and I lived in his little studio apartment on Hermann Street for a few weeks. It was definitely our honeymoon period, and I remember those times as some of the happiest we spent together. I didn't care much where we lived because I had grown to realize that being with Kelly meant being *home* to me, but his little place was just too small for the both of us. The bedroom and kitchen were each about the same size as the walk-in closet and the main room held only his bed in the bay window, a lamp, and some photographic equipment. We started to spend more of our free time searching for a bigger place where we could make a home together.

When Kelly retired from modeling and moved from New York to San Francisco, he took up photography, and he was good at it. He did a lot of male nudes that he sold to the gay flesh and fetish magazines like Mandate, Honcho, and Inches. I told him that I would miss the view from his bed the most so he took three pictures for me: one in the morning facing east toward downtown, one at mid-day facing south toward Mission Dolores, and one at night facing west toward Twin Peaks. He had all three blown up and framed to hang on the south wall above our new bed, wherever that might be.

On May 1, 1991, we moved into a flat on Castro Street, a two-bedroom railroad apartment with six identical units on three floors, a gate down in front, and our own little deck in the back off the big sunny kitchen. We were now a quick block and a half from the bars where we worked. No more daily MUNI bus or streetcar rides to the Castro, no more late night problems trying to hail a cab when the bars closed. Now we lived in the thick of it. We could walk anywhere we needed to go, not only to work, but to buy groceries, liquor, clothes, to mail a letter, and as I often said, if we got too loaded we could "crawl home on our lips" afterward.

A group of friends and customers threw a housewarming party for us at the bars where we worked. They replaced all the kitchen things that had melted in the fire on McCoppin Street, so we had a new blender, toaster, mixer, microwave, and Cuisinart, but much, much more. Fluffy bought us a new rainbow flag to fly from the front bay window over Castro Street every June. Terry and Nelson chipped in and bought us a fancy gas barbecue grill for the deck. Kelly started planning a party at our new apartment from the minute we signed the lease. Rita Rockett, Al Parker and I had our annual birthday fundraiser at the Eagle on the Friday night a week before Pride weekend in June, but Kelly insisted on having another, more private birthday party at home. He thought that having a house party on Saturday afternoon would be a good way to repay everyone's kindness and generosity in helping us furnish the new place. It also gave all our friends a chance to hang out with Rita and Drew and me in a more relaxed setting than at our big fundraiser. At home, the three of us didn't have to worry about being on stage.

I have an album full of photos from that day, and I remember it as a wonderful party. Kelly made tons of great food, baked a coconut layer cake, and spent a fortune on booze and mixes. I also remember that one of the first guests to arrive, Ken Smith, who co-owned Trax Bar on Haight Street, brought the news that Maury Miller had died of AIDS that morning. Maury had been a bartender at Trax and an old boyfriend of mine. I was standing in the middle of our new kitchen when I got the news, and all I could do was take a deep breath, picture Maury in my mind and hear his loud and boisterous laugh. He was a huge sports fan, too much of a jock for me, but I loved him in small doses. I'd known Maury for years but hadn't seen him in ages. I hadn't really thought about him since I had met Kelly.

Maury and I probably met on the dance floor at the I-Beam at a Sunday T-Dance or maybe I'd met him across the bar. He was a wonderful bartender. I remembered his great big grin and his long arms and legs wrapped around me in the hot tub at his condo in Diamond Heights. We were both Midwestern boys, born only a few months apart, him from Iowa, where they grew tall corn and tall boys with big Iowa cocks. One day we bought live lobsters at Safeway and brought them back to McCoppin Street. They squealed when they went into the boiling water, and we squealed even louder. We feasted on them, cross-legged and naked on the kitchen floor, newspapers spread out to cover the linoleum.

One more good man was now gone, but I had only a moment to grieve for him that day. It was party time. Kelly was out on the deck at the barbecue grill. The doorbell was ringing. More guests were arriving. The show must go on. Dozens of our dearest friends came by to see our new apartment that day. Looking back at the photo album, hardly anyone is still alive aside from that day besides Rita and me.

To my doctor's dismay, I still smoked cigarettes in those days. Kelly didn't. We both still drank and smoked pot as much as always, but I gradually gave up cocaine. It wasn't as if I made some kind of deal with myself. It wasn't a rational or economic decision, like "If I stopped doing cocaine for a month, I could put that money in a savings account and buy us plane tickets to somewhere fun." Part of being married meant that I no longer stayed out every night looking for sex. I had all the sex I wanted at home.

If Kelly brought home some cocaine, I still did it with him, especially if we both had the next day off. We had some wild sex on cocaine! Sex was always good with Kelly anyway because he was hot, I was in love with him, and I trusted him completely. It was damn good! When we had sex on cocaine we were even less inhibited, if that was possible, but I would sometimes get so high that I might as well have been having sex with a stranger...or a sex machine...or on a cloud somewhere. It didn't matter.

I stopped buying drugs at work, for the most part. If I looked like I was dragging behind the bar during my shift and a customer offered me a quick toot in the bathroom, I wasn't about to say no.

Kelly and I loved to travel. We went to New York City together for a long weekend, and I got to experience the city through the eyes of someone who had grown up there. Kelly took me places I never would have seen on my own, especially in Harlem. I always wished I could have taken him to Minnesota, but he probably would have hated all those wide open spaces and all the fresh air.

We traveled to the Russian River with the Eagle's annual employee retreat, even though I hadn't worked there in years. Terry Thompson and Blair had been two of my closest friends. Although Blair was gone now, Terry adored Kelly and welcomed him heartily into our family of friends. I sometimes accused my oldest friends in San Francisco of liking Kelly better than me, but I like to think that they were happy for both of us. In some ways he was a nicer person than I was, more even-keeled and comfortable.

Wherever we traveled, Kelly had a rule that we each had to buy a new pair of shoes to bring home. I don't know why, but we always settled on the same shoes. We both wore the same size, and I can't remember afterward that we ever purposely went out together wearing matching shoes. We might have chosen different styles and doubled the options in our commingled shoe wardrobe, but we never did. It's hard to imagine where we found a shoe store in the tiny town of Guerneville when we went to the Russian River. Maybe we bought matching flip-flops at Kings Sporting Goods or at the Guerneville Five and Dime. That trip had come at the hottest part of the summer, so we wore little else. On our first full day at the Triple R Resort, I remember we dropped acid and I got terribly sunburned. The rest of the weekend I had to sit in the shade. Kelly didn't care. He was happy to join me playing cards, listening to music, and drinking fruity cocktails with paper umbrellas.

One Christmas I did save enough money to buy us two round-trip tickets to Seattle. Kelly had mentioned that we needed a new stock pot, so I bought him one at Cliff's Hardware and gift wrapped it with the plane tickets inside.

Another time we flew to Reno for a couple of nights, went to the show at the old MGM Grand where a Boeing 747 landed on the stage with show girls dancing on the wings. Our gambling luck was lousy and we barely had enough money left to get home from the airport at SFO.

Kelly was fine on trips, but I didn't always fare as well. Flying could easily mess with my sinuses or my stomach. I'd spent our entire time in New York running a fever from bronchitis. I always bounced back when we got home, though - like a typical Cancer. At the beginning ill health didn't bother us, but finances did, even without spending much on cocaine anymore.

We both worked the Castro Street Fair that fall. I had my regular shift from noon to seven and made about three times what I did on a typical Sunday. I worked the front station, and my friend Nelson worked the back. Between us that day, we broke all records for sales in the history of the bar. I loved working at such a fast pace and thought it was fun.

Kelly worked around the corner at the Pendulum, but he had a ten-hour shift from ten a.m. to 8 p.m. with two half-hour breaks, during which he could come home if he wanted to. He probably bought some coke that day and some more that night when he finally got off work. When I got off work at seven, it took me a good half hour to count out my tips and chill out with Nelson in the office. Then I went to see Kelly at the Pendulum, where it was still crowded too, even though the booths on the streets had been taken down by then and automobile traffic had resumed in the neighborhood. I asked him if he wanted something for dinner when he got off work, but instead of dinner, we celebrated our massive earnings in tips by buying some more coke to have at home. This was definitely a time to celebrate.

A couple of weeks later, things started to fall apart. Kelly and I agreed to meet one evening after we both got off work in order to go to an AIDS fundraiser at Most Holy Redeemer Catholic Church on Diamond Street in the Castro. Maybe it was the Sisters of Perpetual Indulgence holding a bingo game in the basement. That part of the evening is fuzzy. I can remember Kelly waiting for me on the corner of 18th and Collingwood outside the Pendulum. I rattled on about my day at the Special as we walked to the church. I was in such a good mood and so wound up that I was talking a mile a minute. We were almost there when I realized that Kelly had hardly said a word to me. I shut up for a minute and looked at him. "Is something wrong, babe?" He had tears in his eyes.

"I just got fired from my job."

"What? Why? Who fired you? Was it the owner, Rod?"

"No, the new manager."

"Why?"

"Because my bank was short about fifty bucks on the day of the Castro Street Fair."

"Fifty bucks?! You must have taken in hundreds…thousands! Didn't you tell me that you took breaks where other people relieved you for a half hour? Did you ring out your till each time? Did they have their own banks?"

"No, we all worked out of the same register."

"So how can they pin the blame on you? Does Rod even know that this jerk fired you?"

"I don't know."

"Well, you've got to go talk to him. He's the owner. This isn't fair."

"No."

I felt like Kelly was disagreeing with me. "No what?"

"I'm not gonna talk to anybody. I don't want to work in a place that treats me like that."

That made sense, I had to admit, but I was still really angry. A few months later, that manager was fired too. I told Kelly he was probably the one who stole the fifty bucks from his register on the day of the Castro Fair, but by then Kelly had already moved on. I always loved that about him, but I never managed to learn it from him. I always hated changes in my life, especially big ones, and I tended to hold on to things long past their time—jobs, lovers, fickle friendships, even clothes. Kelly always knew when it was time to let go and move on. He made it look effortless, and I envied him that.

The Special went through big changes that year too. When Ed Stark died, his lover Roz inherited the bar and when Roz died, it went to his two straight brothers who lived back east somewhere. They weren't interested in running a gay bar on Castro Street in 1992, so they put it on the market. Who could blame them? Ed Stark had died unexpectedly. Otherwise I'm sure he would have made plans for the bar to stay the way it was. He probably thought he had at least several more weeks or months to make sure that his wishes would be carried out. At least he would have wanted the place to continue to serve the clientele he had built up over the years, to keep giving back to the community that had made him wealthy, continue to hire good people to work there, and to continue to treat them right.

Instead, the bar was sold to a guy named Larry from Washington D.C. He wanted to remake the bar, so he ripped out all the mirrors and wallpaper, tore down the lighting sconces and uncovered the raw wood of the old meat racks. He renamed the bar "Headquarters" and decorated the entrance with sand bags.

I told Kelly I might have to cut my hair for job security. My hair had been pretty long when we met. It wasn't quite shoulder length, but it was thick and wavy and Kelly loved it. He never wanted me to get a haircut. I was only half-joking, but when he didn't react, I figured it must not mean that much to him anymore, so I got it cut really short. He didn't tell me until afterward how much he missed my long hair and hated the fact that I had to cut it off for a stupid bartending job. He didn't say anything earlier because he figured I was gonna do what I was gonna do.

Larry didn't care about the old regular crowd of heavy drinkers that paid the bills. As soon as the after-work crowd started coming in each day, Larry instructed the barback to start removing the barstools. He wanted a younger crowd, a butcher crowd, a sexier crowd. Customers who had been sitting there drinking all afternoon could get up to use the bathroom and come back to find they had no place to sit down. Larry wanted a standing crowd. I just wanted to keep my job, but my haircut didn't help. Larry fired the morning bartenders, so each of the rest of us took one morning shift per week to keep the place open for the early crowd.

Mine happened to fall on Christmas Day that year. Kelly and I had an early Christmas Eve, and I opened the doors at six a.m. like always. People trickled in and out all morning, but I never had more than a handful of customers at a time. Someone had a VHS tape he was going to return to the video rental store up the street. I asked him what it was and he told me, *Silence of the Lambs* so I stuck it in the machine and we watched it, even though everyone had already seen it before. It was a very Clarice and Chianti kind of Christmas that year. Kelly came down to keep me company for the last hour or so of my shift, and then we went home to cook Christmas dinner.

The next day, I was back on my noon to seven shift. I got to the bar a half hour early, and Larry took me aside to tell me that I didn't fit the image he was looking for and he was letting me go. I wanted to scream, "I cut my hair off for this? I fucking dragged my ass out of bed to work on Christmas morning for this?" I was furious inside, but I knew I'd been fighting a losing battle ever since he took over. Instead of speaking my mind, instead of saying anything, I just handed over my keys and went home... got undressed and crawled back into bed with Kelly. He asked me what happened and then held me while we both went back to sleep.

Chapter Fifty-Four

Philip Turner and Richard Speicher, his lover of many years, were regular customers at the Special. They ran a business that took care of people who had been transferred overseas for their jobs. I remember riding in Philip's Thunderbird along the Embarcadero one day when he pointed to a ship on the bay and told me that some of those containers were packed with furniture, dishes, art, clothing, and other personal belongings. He explained to me that their business was packing up a person's entire life and shipping it across the sea to plop down in another country far away.

Philip must have sold the business after Richard died. He had started bartending at the Headquarters by the time I was canned. Larry had Philip lined up that morning to take over my afternoon shift. Philip told me later how terrible he felt about all that, but I didn't blame him. Larry also fired Philip a few months later. Philip bought a bar across the street at 440 Castro called The Bear and changed its name to Daddy's. He ran Daddy's the way Ed had run the Special, and the way Terry ran the Eagle. His bar was the site of countless fundraisers, and he proved himself to be a fair boss to his employees as well as a good friend.

Across the street, the Headquarters didn't seem to be working out so Larry changed the name of the bar once again to the Night Shift and moved the opening time to later in the day. The Night Shift was reputedly part bar and part sex club, but I never went inside to find out. Daddy's grew more and more popular, and Larry finally closed the doors of the Night Shift. When it went out of business, I felt that both Philip and I had been vindicated.

The building at 469 Castro Street had been the site of so many wonderful events, home of one of the best jobs I ever had, and was filled with memories of so many good times and the wonderful people I had already lost. I hated to see it change. The building never became another gay bar again. Ever since Larry closed the doors on the Night Shift, it has been some kind of restaurant. No matter how fondly we remember certain times and places, they can never go back to the way they were.

When I lost my job on Castro Street, I was only out of work for six days. My friend Nelson, who had become Larry's manager at Headquarters, found me my next job. He put in a call to Ken Smith at Trax on Haight Street. Kenny said they were about to let one of their bartenders go and he would fit me into the schedule.

Kelly and I took the #33 Ashbury bus over the hill to Trax a couple of days before I was scheduled to start. It was early afternoon, and the bar was fairly quiet. We each ordered a screwdriver and pretended we were tourists. I just wanted to get a feel for the place without letting on that I would soon be coming to work there. The bartender on duty was a stranger to me and, for all I knew, he might be the person I was replacing. If so, I felt sorry for him. I knew all too well how it felt to get canned from a job.

I hadn't been inside Trax in years, but it had been a gay bar for as long as I could remember. I rarely went to the Haight, especially since I lived in the Castro where so many bars were within easy walking distance. In the 1970s, Trax was a gay bar called the Question Mark. It was one of many gay places on that side of the hill which included Gus' Pub, the Deluxe, the Theater Club, the I Beam, Bones, Bradley's corner, and Maud's. Maud's was also where Jim Cvitanich and I had gone to hear the Pussies sing for the first time. We had asked them right away to be in our next *Men Behind Bars* show. Knowing so many lesbian bartenders was great. They were always nice to me and poured good drinks at Maud's and also at Amelia's on Valencia Street, which was another bar owned by Rikki Streicher. On the other hand, men couldn't get served at all at Francine's, which was the only lesbian bar in the Castro.

I already knew Ken Smith, co-owner of Trax, also known as "Kenneth Anne" from his performances as one of the "big girls" in a couple of the *Men Behind Bars* shows. His business partner,

Bob Douglas, became a good friend of mine too. He was great fun to go drinking with, and I soon discovered that Bob, like Kenny, loved to throw on a dress, a wig, and a pair of high heels now and then. Kenny and Bob were retired from banking by the time they bought Trax. Running the bar was something for them to do in their elder years.

I liked working at Trax, even though most days the money wasn't as good as on Castro Street. The crowd was a lot more mixed, too, but I enjoyed most of the regulars and discovered that I could make friends with straight men and women just as easily as gay ones, as long as they knew they were in a gay bar. Tourists sometimes got a little freaked out when they noticed two men kissing. I remember one guy asked me, "Are we in the wrong bar?" I answered by telling him everyone was welcome at Trax, unless being around gay people bothered him. I said if that was the case, he and his girlfriend weren't in the wrong bar, they were in the wrong city.

Kenny loved to decorate and throw parties at the bar for holidays as well as events like the Super Bowl, the Oscars and any other excuse to have a bash. Trax held its share of funerals, too, or as people usually called them, "Celebrations of Life." My first year working at Trax, we moved my birthday party with Rita Rockett and Al Parker from the Eagle to Haight Street. It was a beautiful sunny Sunday afternoon in June of 1992, and it would turn out to be Drew's last birthday. I remember that day well. Gail performed with the Fabulous Velcros and the place was mobbed with people.

Trax had a back door behind the office that led outside to a spectacular garden. The owner of the building had it beautifully landscaped, complete with decking and a koi pond. He was a gay guy who lived upstairs. His deceased parents had owned the bar when it was called the Question Mark. At one point in the party that afternoon, I realized I hadn't seen Kelly in a while. The crowd was thick, and people near the stage were drunkenly trying to dance. It took me a while to make my way to the back and then out to the garden, and there I found Kelly smoking a pipe with Drew. They offered me a hit, but I knew better. I'd spent many nights out with Drew, and I knew how strong his hash was. I thought I'd better remain coherent, especially since I felt responsible for the party.

Drew had a redheaded friend with him that day, another porn star, but not one whose name I remember. He was handsome, even with his clothes on. He pulled me aside and said, "Drew is getting really tired. He's pretty sick, you know. How long do you need him to stay here?"

"Until we have Gail sing 'Happy Birthday' and cut and serve the cake. Drew always serves the cake."

"Well, can you move that up?"

I told him I thought we could, but first I went looking for Drew. I had lost track of him again. This time I found him standing out in front of the bar signing autographs on Haight Street, but not for any of the people who had come to our birthday party. These were just a bunch of gay tourists who happened to be walking by on a Sunday afternoon and recognized Al Parker. I asked Drew how he was feeling and told him what the redhead had told me. Drew laughed and said he was fine. "Don't change anything on my account. He's just bored and wants to leave because he doesn't know anyone. He can leave. I'm staying."

I might have moved the cake cutting up a bit, but not much. I was probably tired too, but we were raising lots of money for Rita's brunches at the AIDS ward.

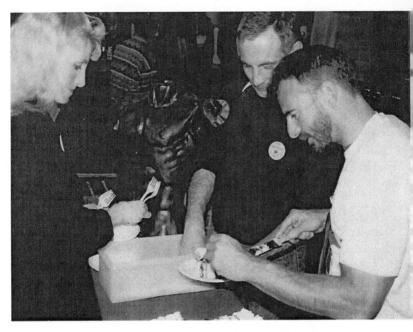

Rita, Mark and Al Parker cutting our birthday cake

Chapter Fifty-Five

On August 17, a couple of months after our birthday party at Trax, I got a phone call one afternoon while I was working. It was Doug Shaffer telling me that Drew had died that morning. I just sighed and shook my head. He was the only other person I knew at the time who was born on the same day and year as me. My bosses, Bob and Kenny, seemed devastated. I guess Al Parker had charmed the pants off of them too.

Rita and I didn't go to the memorial gathering that Drew's last partner Keith Reiter had for him in their purple house in Noe Valley. It was a Sunday, so Rita was busy serving brunch at the hospital, and I barely knew Keith or any of the other people he'd invited, so I made up some excuse. I went to the Eagle that afternoon instead and raised a glass to both my friend Drew and the legendary Al Parker. I felt closer to his presence there on the patio where we'd had so many good times celebrating our birthdays and raising money for Rita's brunch fund. Every year when our birthday comes around, I still miss Drew. Rita Rockett lives in Ohio now, but most years she manages a trip to San Francisco in late June so that we can see each other on or near our birthday and make a toast to Al Parker too.

I got to know Keith Reiter very well in later years. We became friends and spent long hours talking politics and reminiscing about Drew and those happy times. We talked about Drew and Kelly hanging out in the afterlife now, sharing a hash pipe and maybe comparing dick sizes. Keith told me about his childhood in New York. His mother was a prostitute. At eight years old, Keith had discovered his father in the laundry room of their apartment building, hanging from the overhead beams. Keith moved to the West Coast and made a fortune with his company called Pump Works, with he and Drew personally demonstrating how the vacuum devices worked to enlarge their own penises anywhere they could make a sale. Keith told me about his dreams and his nightmares, too. He never got over the loss of Drew.

Keith's background was so different than mine that I found him fascinating. We spent hours at a time exchanging stories until the last day I saw him, one warm sunny day in December. I found out a week later that Keith had hanged himself from a tree in Buena Vista Park just a couple of hours after our last, seemingly normal, conversation there.

Lots of people took their own lives in the AIDS years, but I don't know that Keith had anything physically wrong with him except that he didn't like growing older. Sometimes nightmares come in the daylight—dark, horrifying stories all jumbled in the brain, not necessarily in chronological order, but all of them true. I remember friends who were diagnosed with AIDS, but appeared to be holding up well until their vision started to go one day and within a week they were blind. Even worse was when it entered the brain.

Our friend Pat disappeared one day. He just didn't show up anyplace he was expected. His truck was gone, as well as his keys and his wallet, but no suitcase, no backpack. We didn't even know if he had taken a change of clothes. Several days later, the "authorities" called from Florida. Pat had driven across the South and been stopped a half a dozen times for driving erratically, but released each time. They couldn't arrest him on a DUI because he passed every sobriety test. Another friend had to fly to Miami and drive the truck back. Pat died a couple of weeks later, not knowing who or where he was.

Our friend Peter disappeared from his apartment in the Castro a couple of months after his lover died. Days later, someone found him asleep on a bench in Washington Square Park in North Beach. He had no wallet, no identification, and no idea who he was or how he had gotten there, but his dog was beside him, watching over him when help came. The dog had its license tags, so they were able to trace it to Peter's name. His car was found parked on a nearby street with a stack of parking tickets under the windshield wiper.

Chapter Fifty-Six

John Preston was one of my oldest friends in the world, so I remember very well the last day we spent together. He was back in San Francisco for a writers' conference, and we met for Sunday brunch at a place called Lety's Grill on Market Street at the corner of Sanchez. Lety's had a full bar, so we drank several Bloody Marys just like in the old days when we haunted the Castro together in the 1970s. We both ordered steak and eggs, the steak rare and the eggs over easy, so the yolks and the blood ran together on our plates, and we sopped up the juices with whole wheat toast slathered in butter and strawberry jam.

John hadn't put out a book of his own in some time, but he had compiled and edited *Hot Living: Erotic Stories about Safer Sex*, and he'd asked me to submit an essay for another anthology he'd done called *Personal Dispatches: Writers Confront AIDS* (1989). He was starting work on a new project called *Hometowns: Gay Men Write About Where They Belong* and again, he was after me to contribute an essay. He said I could write about growing up on the farm in Minnesota or the years we had both lived in Minneapolis. He said my options were wide open and John was convinced that I probably had something already written in my journals that, with some polishing, would be perfect for the book.

I am sure that I gave it some thought afterward, but I just didn't feel like much of a writer in those days. I barely kept up with my diary, and I hadn't submitted anything to a magazine in ages. Maybe it was the heavy aura of death all around me or maybe my muse had come down with AIDS like almost everyone else I knew. Whatever the reason, I didn't have the energy to commit to anything creative in the midst of the plague. John and I had a lot of catching up to do that day, so each time he started to encourage me to write again, I changed the subject.

I told him about Kelly, who must have been busy that day or pretended that he was, so that I could spend time alone with my old friend. I told John all about the success of the *Men Behind Bars* shows and Jim Cvitanich's death and the deaths of so many others. John and I had dozens of mutual friends from our lives together in Minneapolis. I was only nineteen when we first met at "Gay House," a safe haven that he and a lesbian friend had created for gay youth in South Minneapolis. After Gay House, we had both lived in a gay "commune" south of Lake Street on Portland Avenue for a while. The six of us considered ourselves hippies, I suppose. It wasn't the sort of commune where members shared organic vegetarian meals. We were more apt to share a delivery of pharmaceutical speed—white crosses or black beauties—from one of our drug dealers.

After the commune broke up, John Preston and I lived in the same apartment building near the original Guthrie Theater. We had hitchhiked from Minneapolis to Kansas City and back one summer when Patsy Cline seemed to be blasting from the car radio of every ride we got. We'd taken wonderful winter train trips to Chicago together. When I eventually followed him to San Francisco, I stayed in John's apartment on Potrero Hill during my first several weeks here. He was the editor of the *Advocate* by then. He proudly introduced me to the South of Market scene and so much more. We continued to travel together—first class (at his insistence) to Miami and Ft. Lauderdale, to New York City for New Year's Eve. He scored us tickets to Colt Studios' new calendar launch party at the Man's Country Baths where I got to meet the amazingly beautiful model and porn star Bruno. John took me to New York's notorious Anvil and the Mine Shaft that same week.

Still later, we'd been neighbors in the Castro, meeting for lunch at the Badlands every week. We had dinner out at least once a month and drank in nearly every gay bar in San Francisco. We had so many adventures to reminisce about and old friends to discuss that day over brunch, but we were hard pressed to come up with the names of even a few mutual friends who were still alive. We talked about them anyway, and caught up on each other's health status, which was always a major topic when meeting an old friend you hadn't seen in a while.

I had been diagnosed HIV positive in 1988, but I hadn't gone on any medication or developed any symptoms yet. John told me over brunch that his doctor in Maine had started him on a massive regimen of AZT that nearly killed him. That's not surprising now; knowing its toxicity, but the newer life-saving AIDS drugs hadn't been developed yet. John had stopped taking the AZT before this trip to California and was feeling much better. He looked good, for John, but he had always been too thin and taken lousy care of himself. I can still see him sitting there over brunch, putting down his knife and fork to take a break and light up a Tareyton. I could be smug because I smoked low-tar Merits, but our conversations had always been held in a haze of cigarette or pot smoke. Alcohol was a given as well, usually beer in the afternoon and as the evening wore on we typically switched to something stronger, John to scotch and me to vodka.

John told me that his friend, the author Anne Rice, had bought him a puppy that he named Vlad. The puppy chewed up everything in the house, including his favorite penny loafers, but he was still crazy about that dog. I laugh now to look back at my friend who was an icon to leather men around the world and remember that he was always most comfortable not in boots, but in penny loafers.

Years later I emailed Anne Rice, and she confirmed to me that the puppy was a purebred Viszla. His friend Robert was planning to buy the dog for John for his December birthday or for Christmas, but knowing he had AIDS, Anne said, "Why wait?" She bought the puppy and wrote me that John loved taking the dog on walks. Only in his last days, when John became bed-bound did the dog need someone else to care for it.

That Sunday morning, John and I reminisced a lot about my first few weeks in San Francisco. He used to take me to a place called the No-Name Bar at 1347 Folsom Street on the corner of Dore Alley when his favorite bartender, Warren, was working. Warren was also one of John's regular playmates. The establishments at that location have had many names, but it has been a gay leather bar for decades. In those days, the lighted sign outside had nothing written on it—just a pair of boots thrown over it—so everyone called it the No-Name.

On one of my first trips there with John, I had a few beers and headed to the toilet. As my eyes slowly adjusted to the darkness, an enormous man sidled up next to me. I wondered how many cows had been slaughtered to cover him in head to toe black leather. I moved over to make room for him and tried to keep my eyes on the ceiling. Even if the gay bars in Minneapolis had trough urinals, they didn't have mirrors over them. I heard my piss hitting porcelain, but then the sound stopped and I knew I hadn't finished. I looked into the mirror and then down. He was holding his beer bottle to catch my piss. As I buttoned my Levis and made my way around him, he raised the bottle to his lips, guzzled it all down, burped and threw his head back to let out the most maniacal laughter I had ever heard. Back at the bar, I told John what just happened, and he laughed too.

Almost every weeknight, John and I told ourselves we simply had to be at the Ramrod at 1225 Folsom Street by eleven p.m.. That was the time when the black and white TV sets around the room flickered on to watch *Mary Hartman, Mary Hartman*. Everyone laughed for the half hour the show, but at 11:30 sharp, the smiles disappeared and the crowd turned back into hard-core leather men. In my naïveté, I asked John what it all meant. How could people be so open and full of laughter one minute and then turn to stone the next? He told me not to worry about it. I learned from John at an early age never to take myself too seriously. By the time I spent my last day with John, I had certainly learned the value of that advice.

Even before he moved away from San Francisco, John had started hustling. I loved hearing stories from that part of his life, about the wealthy men who could afford to fly him wherever they wanted him to play the part of the serious leather top. After his book *Mister Benson* came out, he was even more in demand. I didn't care as much about the specifics of what he did with his clients as I liked hearing about where he went and who he met. John didn't usually name names, but I liked hearing him describe a certain "highly successful fashion designer" or a well-known married politician "you would never suspect."

John told me that one of his clients invited him to lunch the next day with the playwright and memoirist Lillian Hellman. He knew I was a big fan of hers. He explained to me that most of his clients didn't even want sex. They wanted role play, perhaps, or they wanted to spend time with the image of him that they had created in their own minds, through his writing and reputation. John and I had mutual friends who were professional actors. I told him it sounded like he had been more successful at "acting" than most of them, at least financially speaking, and we both laughed.

That afternoon after brunch at Lety's Grill, we went to the Eagle patio for their Sunday beer bust. John introduced me to his friend Victoria, who was a professional dominatrix. She was also in town for the writers' conference and John told me she wrote for *Penthouse* magazine. I noticed that she was leading around a couple of collared leather boys on leashes. I liked Victoria. She was charming. I just didn't understand why these boys were with her at the Eagle. Were they gay? It would have made more sense to me if John was holding their leashes, but he seemed to be almost retired from his heavy-leather, high-priced hustler days. Still, I knew John well enough that there was little he or any of his friends could do to shock me.

I talked to John Preston on the telephone several times after our Sunday together. We still wrote letters to each other in those days and mailed them off in paper envelopes with postage stamps in the upper right-hand corner, but the letters grew more infrequent and the phone calls became further apart as John's health failed.

Chapter Fifty-Seven

Even though Terry Thompson was one of my closest friends, I can't remember the day he died. I remember bits and pieces from the day of his funeral, but not the phone call. I can't even figure out who would have been the closest, most logical person to have told me that Terry had passed on. So many others were already gone by then. It usually worked that way. Someone close to the deceased called most of his best friends right away, before word spread through the bars and the newspapers. It wasn't necessarily the lover, who would probably be too distraught, but maybe his best friend since high school or college days, someone who had become like a brother to both of them. Sometimes the call came from a close family member who had come to stay at the house during his final days.

Terry's lover Blair had already been dead a few years by then, and I don't remember if he had any local relatives. It seemed like Terry and I had known each other forever, but in fact it had only been about a dozen years since he shoved the hit of MDA up my ass when I was working at the Russian River. His older sister Nina (pronounced "Nynah") came to visit now and then, so all the San Francisco family knew her. Terry was born in southern Minnesota, not far from where I grew up, but we never exchanged stories of farm life, sex with the livestock or neighboring farm boys. He was proud of having supported himself from an early age, still in his teens. I think he told me once that he ran away from home, which suggested a childhood background far less bucolic than mine. We always had plenty to talk about in the present. Something was always going on in our lives, especially in the early years of our friendship: another leather contest, another birthday, another anniversary party, or another Mardi Gras trip to plan.

Terry had a dear old friend in L.A. named Beverly Redding, a woman singer who epitomized the term "chanteuse." She came up to San Francisco now and then and was always treated like part of the extended South of Market family. Someone told me that her real claim to fame was that her voice had been used on some of the recorded bird calls and singing flowers in the Enchanted Tiki Room at Disneyland. I don't know if that was true, but I heard it more than once. I thought asking her would have been tacky. She had a rich sweet soprano and a style more suited to a Manhattan nightclub than a San Francisco leather bar. Still, Terry asked me to arrange for her to perform at the Eagle once with Val Diamond's backup trio, the Crosswinds.

Beverly Redding also sang at Terry's funeral. Gail Wilson had sung at Blair's, and I think she was relieved not to be asked this time. Gail came over to Kelly's and my apartment and Rita Rockett joined us there to walk over to the church together. Kelly wasn't feeling well that day, but he insisted on both of us putting on our best suits with freshly-ironed dress shirts, shined shoes, and crisp neckties. I almost never got dressed up. That was a major attraction about bartending all those years. I could wear whatever I wanted and sometimes the less I wore, the better the tips.

The service was at Most Holy Redeemer Catholic Church on Eureka Street in the Castro. Gail and Rita and Kelly and I might have looked almost like two straight couples in our Sunday best, except for Gail's magenta hair and fans of both Gail and Rita calling out to them. They were two of the best known straight women among San Francisco's gay community in those days.

I don't know why Terry's funeral was held in a Catholic Church. I don't think Terry was Catholic. I never heard him mention any church-going in his past. Maybe someone at the Eagle had an in with someone who went there...or a key to the front door. Maybe it was the only church in the neighborhood that was big enough to hold so many people. Terry was highly respected and under his management, the Eagle had long ago surpassed the million dollar mark in fundraising for AIDS. I'm sure local politicians were there that day, other bar owners and managers, customers, employees and many friends. I looked around at all the people in the rows of pews and noticed not so much who was present as the fact that so many people who should have been there were already gone. Terry, like most of us, was going to join a much bigger crowd than he was leaving behind.

Kelly grew progressively sicker during Terry's service. He wanted me to stay until the end while he went home alone, insisting that he would be fine. I don't remember much about the rest of that day. I was too worried about Kelly. Beverly Redding sang from the choir loft upstairs in the rear of the church. The crowd was too big to get to her afterward, or I would have said hello. Most everyone went from the church to the Eagle for drinks on the patio, raising their glasses to the memory of Terry Thompson. I went home instead. Terry was a good friend, but Kelly needed me more that day.

Chapter Fifty-Eight

One day I got a big heavy package in the mail. The return address was from John Preston in Portland, Maine. He had sent me autographed copies of every book he had written and published. There was *Mister Benson* and the other tomes of sadomasochism and pornography, his wonderful *Franny, the Queen of Provincetown*, which had been made into an off-Broadway play, a copy of *The Big Gay Book: A Man's Survival Guide for the Nineties* and each of the anthologies I'd been too lazy or busy or distracted to submit my writing to. He had also included *Hustling: A Gentleman's Guide to the Fine Art of Homosexual Prostitution* and all of the Alex Kane adventure series.

Kelly's health was failing fast, and I realized I could only keep my sanity if I controlled my thoughts and emotions. I could only allow myself a certain amount of dread. Knowing friends all over the country who had AIDS, I subconsciously created a system of emotional triage. The people who were physically closest to me had to come first. I had friends in San Francisco who were dying every week, but Kelly and I shared a home. He had to be my primary concern. It would do no one any good for me to worry about what I could do for John Preston, but Kelly I could physically care for.

Kelly wasn't home when the mail arrived. I spread out all the books on our bed and smiled as I read each of John's inscriptions to me. Then I put the books back in the box and carried it downstairs. I took them to a used book store on Castro Street in one of the storefronts across from the Sausage Factory. I don't remember how much they gave me for the books, but it was far below their cover price. Maybe they paid a little bit more because they were autographed, but what I got was enough to keep the gas and electricity turned on for another month. I never told Kelly about the books or the PG&E bill. I wrote a letter to John to thank him for the books. It was my last letter to him.

Kelly grew weaker day by day in our apartment on Castro Street. One morning I picked up *The Chronicle* on my way to work and saw John Preston's obituary. By this time, I had become so numbed by death that I paid only slightly more attention to the news of John's passing than I did to the weather forecast on a different page of the paper. I just sighed and got on the bus to go to work and moved on with my day, my life.

When I think of my old friend, I think of those who only want to remember John Preston as some kind of leather icon. I wonder what he would think of that. They must not realize, like the stone-faced men at the old Ramrod who only laughed when *Mary Hartman, Mary Hartman* came on the TV screens, how many sides of him there were. How silly even John Preston could be.

I still have an old Rolodex from the 1980s. I use it now to record passwords and user IDs for bank accounts and websites and memberships to places that I rarely explore. During the worst of the AIDS years, I could never bring myself to throw someone's card away when they died. I would turn them over and write a new friend's name, address and phone number on the other side. John Preston's index card is still right where it always was. I never even turned it over. Every time I flip past it, I think about picking up the phone. Then I wonder how late it is in Portland, Maine and I wonder if the people who live there would be asleep by now.

Chapter Fifty-Nine

We walked in a daze through the dying years, trying our best to keep up our daily routines. I appreciated the value of an average day with no tragic phone calls, no new lab results. I reveled in the ordinary and thrilled to our humdrum patterns—coming home from work to find dinner on the table.

Kelly downplayed his cooking skills while I had always been proud of mine. I loved to experiment, read a dozen recipes for a dish I'd never tried to make, then put them all away and go at it. Kelly kept a little gold box full of recipe secrets that had been handed down from generations of Southern black women. While I always just tossed in a dab or this or a pinch of that and threw some cheese on top, Kelly approached the kitchen like a scientist heading to the lab, but he had a feel for it too. Fish and seafood? My attempts at anything more complicated than a canned tuna sandwich were pathetic, while Kelly could sense how high the heat should be, how many minutes on each side. As he grew too sick to do much else, most days he could still plan and carry out a meal, and I was grateful for all of them.

The security of our daily routines extended to watching the same channel every night for the ten o'clock news with Kelly. I was so superstitious about our habits that I resented the usual weatherman taking a night off. How dare he? Maybe Kelly didn't mind. I was the crazy one in our relationship. I could barely stay awake through the news, anyway. Kelly might stay awake half the night if he was feeling good and working on a project in his sewing/crafts/photography room.

My bartending job at Trax had its patterns too. The regulars weren't as set in their ways as those on Castro Street had been. There were fewer of them too by the early 1990s. Trax had lost a lot of customers as well as several bartenders to the plague. I only worked the afternoon shifts, but the guys who worked evenings and closed the bar each night told lots of scary stories about the ghosts that haunted the place after two a.m. A couple of the night bartenders talked about sitting down at the last two stools at the back end of the bar to count out their banks and tips. They looked up and saw a bartender at the front register wearing a plaid shirt, bushy mustache, tight Levi 501's, and boots—the typical Castro clone look was just as big on Haight Street in its day. Then more young men appeared and filled the stools around the front corner of the bar. They all ordered beers and drinks, served by the phantom bartender. They silently drank and smoked cigarettes and rolled dice and laughed at unheard jokes before gradually fading from sight.

This was not a onetime occurrence. Another bartender saw empty boxes moving on their own in the liquor room, lifted high off the floor in a neat stack and toppling over in a jumble. Some of them talked about seeing a huge billowing cloud of black smoke that swirled over the pool table, a vortex that blocked the light. Everyone who closed the place had stories like these. The more I heard about the late night spooks, the more I was determined to stick to my daytime shifts.

On weekday afternoons, the local PBS television station showed reruns of the British sitcom *Are You Being Served?* about a quirky cast of characters who worked at London's Grace Brothers department store. I usually only had a handful of customers during that half-hour, so I got into the habit of turning up the sound so that we could all watch and laugh together.

One season the station announced that Mollie Sugden, the actress who played Mrs. Slocombe—full name Mary Elizabeth Jennifer Rachel Abergavenny Slocombe (nee Yiddel), the senior saleslady in the Ladies' Department—was coming to San Francisco to appear at the studio for a live *Are You Being Served?* look-alike contest. Mrs. Slocombe was the most distinctive character because she wore her hair a different color for each show, so Kelly decided that I simply had to go as her.

I told Kelly I would love to meet her, but I was never big on playing dress-up. I could count on one hand the number of times in my life that I'd had to do drag in order to work on Halloween and I'd have fingers left over. I didn't want to do it again. I didn't want to shave, either, but Kelly insisted that if I was going to do it, I had to do it right. I was secretly terrified, but he was so excited about this project that I couldn't let him down. I made up my mind to rise to the challenge, and I finally let him talk me into it.

On Friday afternoon before the Sunday of the big event down at Channel 9's studio, I was working at Trax, and we watched *Are You Being Served?* as usual. At two-thirty, the program ended, and I turned the music back on just as a big truck pulled up and its shadow covered the front door. It was a liquor delivery, so I grabbed my keys to let the driver through the office to the storeroom. He looked up at the TV set in the nearest corner and asked me the time.

When I told him it was just past two-thirty he said, "No! Damn, I must have just missed it. Don't you watch that show here, the one about the department store in England?

"Yes, it just ended."

"I wanted to see it, but the traffic held me up. I'm just crazy about that lady with her pussy."

"Mrs. Slocombe? Me too," I said. "You know she's coming to town and I'm going to meet her on Sunday."

"Really? I'd love to meet her in person! Well, would you please give her my regards?"

"I will."

On Sunday, I shaved off my mustache and Kelly tucked me into this outfit he had made for me—a simple brown skirt and vest, brown flats with two or three pairs of opaque pantyhose layered so that the hair on my legs didn't show through. I wasn't about to shave them! He took a white dress shirt of mine and made layers of ruffles to cover the cleavage, but the best part was a curly blonde wig that he died blue.

In a city like San Francisco, I was sure a dozen men would be done up in fabulous versions of Mrs. Slocombe drag, but I was the only one! Several women came as her. Several women came as Captain Peacock too, but that didn't require much creativity. We each had to sign in, and then we were directed to a waiting room where a large table was covered in snacks and soft drinks and urns of coffee. I'd smuggled in several one ounce airline bottles of vodka in my purse, hidden under my "pussy," a stuffed cat Kelly had found somewhere. He insisted that Mrs. Slocombe's pussy was an important part of her character, even though we rarely saw it on the show. She only referred to it with lots of double entendres.

A half hour before the show started, we were ushered into another room to meet Mollie Sugden, who was accompanied by her husband, the British actor Bill Moore. We took seats in rows facing her, and that this was our time to ask any questions we might have. Once the show was underway, we would all be too busy answering phones and taking pledges from the callers at home, and she would be too busy being interviewed on camera.

I sat in the back row, still looking around to see if I was the only gay person there. I poured a couple of little bottles of my contraband vodka into my paper cup of orange juice and decided to make the best of things. When it came time for anyone in the back row who had a question, I stood up and said, "I don't have a question, exactly, but I have a message for Mollie Sugden. I work in a bar, you see. It's on Haight Street and every afternoon at two p.m., we watch *Are You Being Served?* On Friday a big truck pulled up out front at two-thirty and the driver rushed in, terribly disappointed that he had been tied up in traffic and missed the show because he said he just loved that Mrs. Slocombe and her pussy. I told him I did too and that I'd be seeing you on Sunday, so he asked me to give you his warmest regards, and I wondered if I could also have my picture taken with you now too, please."

Whoever was in charge at the studio announced that we had about fifteen minutes until the show started, so we should take pictures now and then find our places in the next room where we would get our instructions about how to work the phones.

I worked my way over to Mollie Sugden and handed my camera to some Mr. Humphries wanna-be, a young woman, to take a few shots of the two of us. I towered over her as she took my hands and said, "My goodness, you look more like Mrs. Slocombe than I do!"

We smiled into my camera and were soon hustled off into the next room, but she grabbed my arm and pulled me back. "Don't hurry off, now. I want to hear more about that truck driver. Was he terribly big and handsome?"

"Oh yes!"

"How big were his arms?"

"Oh, they were enormous! As big as footballs!" I held my hands out around one of her tiny arms to show her the size of an enormous bicep, and she giggled and swooned like a naughty little girl.

Before I could find a seat, a couple of the guys who were working on the technical crew came over to ask me which bar I worked at on Haight Street, so I wasn't the only gay person there that night, after all.

Mark and Mollie Sugden

During each of the breaks, I called home to talk to Kelly who was watching everything on TV in our bedroom. He had something to say to me each time. "Find a mirror. Your lipstick is smudged." Or, "Straighten out your ruffles." Or, "Keep your face up. When you look down to write, the camera only sees the top of your wig."

The phones and chairs were on risers and each time we sat back down, we were told to find a different place to sit, so that the studio would appear on TV to be bigger than it was. One time I called Kelly and he said, "Next time don't sit with your left side to the camera. Your left side is your better side. You ought to remember that."

I said, "Left side, right side, who cares? I'm not Barbra Streisand, you know."

I talked to Mollie Sugden a couple more times that evening. She introduced me to her husband, and I had my picture taken with both of them, some with all three of us and a few of some of the other contestants. I managed to use up a roll of film with twenty-four pictures on it. When all was said and done, I caught a cab home. I could hardly wait to get out of that wig and costume and make-up and take a hot shower. Kelly used something to gently remove the make-up without scouring my face. I looked in the mirror and missed my mustache, but knew it would grow back soon enough. I think Kelly was a little bit turned on by getting me all dressed up like that. When I came out of the bathroom he was already naked in bed waiting for me to join him out of drag, man to man.

About a year later, I heard that Mollie Sugden was back in San Francisco to appear in a speaking role when *Daughter of the Regiment* was staged with the San Francisco Opera. The part was originally performed by Hermione Gingold. I got her local address and sent her a letter with a few of the photographs enclosed. I told her once again that she had many gay fans in San Francisco. I mentioned that I was involved in lots of fundraising to help fight AIDS and wondered if she would consider doing an AIDS benefit here sometime. A few days later I got a handwritten note from her:

Dear Mark,

Thank you for the letter and photographs. What fun that competition was. What a lot of good work you have done to help combat AIDS. If I do ever return to San Francisco, please contact me again, and I will most certainly try to make time to join in the fundraising. Good luck for your continued efforts.

Yours Sincerely,

Mollie Sugden

Opera Plaza.
30th September.

Dear Mark,
    Thank you for
your letter and photographs.
What fun that Competition
was.
    What a lot of good
work you have done to
help Combat AIDS.
    If I do ever return to
San Francisco, please Contact
me again, and I will most
certainly try to make time
to join in the fund raising.
    Good Luck for your
continued Efforts,
        Yours Sincerely
        Mollie Sugden

When I recently looked up Mollie Sugden's obituary, I found out that she died July 1, 2009 in Royal Surrey Hospital, a widow, with her twin sons by her side. It mentioned that the character of Mrs. Slocombe also had a pet canary named Winston and that she referred to her pussy named Tiddles as a male, even though it gave birth to kittens in at least two episodes. It also said that Mollie Sugden was a close friend of the singer Bjork, and that she enjoyed cooking, gardening and driving fast cars.

Chapter Sixty

My friend Chris Osborne knew a couple named Todd and Roy. I only knew them in passing. They traveled in very different circles from me. For many years, their lives revolved around shopping for the perfect clothes to wear to all the best parties and knowing all the right people. I imagined they must talk about nothing but decadent weekends in Palm Springs, fabulous gay cruises, or their awesome summer place on the Russian River.

Now they'd both had AIDS for a while, and Chris got a call from Todd asking him to come by for a drink. "Roy wants to say his goodbyes, you know. He's very sick. It won't be long now. I'm trying to have people over in shifts, so would Sunday afternoon be all right?"

A couple of weeks later, Chris told me he had arrived at the condo in Diamond Heights around six p.m. on Sunday. Two other guys were running out the door giggling, which Chris thought a bit odd, but he soon forgot about it. He'd brought flowers and a bottle of chilled vodka. Todd thanked him for coming and welcomed him in while yelling toward the bedroom, "Roy, Chris Osborne is here to see you." Then he whispered to Chris, "Get yourself a drink while I clean him up a little and change his shirt. He spilled something on it and you know how vain he is."

Chris went to the kitchen and found a vase for his flowers. He poured a drink for himself and snorted a couple of lines of coke off the mirror next to the bar. He'd been here often enough to know the routine. He could barely hear someone talking in the bedroom about what to wear and then finally Todd announced that Roy was ready for another visitor. "Come on in, Chris. Bring your drink. Roy decided on one of his favorite shirts, the one you bought him for his birthday last year, remember?"

Chris told me the bedroom was filled with flowers, and white candles burned in silver candlesticks on every flat surface. Roy was upright, eyes wide open, one hand sticking straight out, holding a cocktail glass. He had obviously been dead for some time. In the corner was a hamper full of shirts that had all been cut up the back. Chris realized that Todd had been changing Roy's shirt for each visitor as if he were dressing a life-sized doll, and he'd kept on talking to him as if he were alive.

Chris told him it was time to call someone. "How long has this been going on? Who's your doctor? How long has Roy been... you know...how long has it been since he's answered you back?"

"Ahhh...I don't know...Thursday, maybe? I'm not sure. He gets real quiet sometimes. You know how he is."

Chris found the phone and called for help. They came and took Roy's body away, all the while Todd argued that he still had several more nice shirts he hadn't worn in ages. The paramedics gave Todd something to calm him down and took him along to the hospital.

Chris stayed behind to blow out the candles and lock up the place, but first he had another stiff drink and a couple more lines of coke in the kitchen. Todd died too, a few days later.

When Kelly was dying, I wondered if I would turn out like Todd, unable to let go. I could see myself re-enacting a scene like that. Kelly had enough clothes, that's for sure. From the time we met and even while we were moving in together, we knew we wouldn't have much time. We were both dying, so we figured we might as well make the best of whatever time we had left and take care of each other.

It was warm that August 9th of 1995, the day when Jerry Garcia, the front man of the Grateful Dead, died. At Trax during the next few days, the neighborhood seemed to jump back thirty years in a twisted time warp. Hundreds of old hippies reappeared in their rusty flower-power vans to light candles at the corner of Haight and Ashbury Streets. They weren't great tippers, but every hundred quarters meant twenty-five bucks that I wouldn't have made otherwise. Kelly had been too sick to work ever since the past Halloween, so money was tight.

He was always so happy to see me come home. Sometimes I'd get him out of bed, get him dressed and help him out to the kitchen, or we'd sit on the back deck for a while when summer daylight lasted into evening. Some days I could get him to eat a little and talk some and laugh at my stories about the crazy old hippies who descended on Haight/Ashbury, just over the hill from where we lived on Castro Street.

We wondered how so many Deadheads could afford to buy tickets to their concerts from just panhandling all day. In one of the store windows on Haight Street a big sign read: "Jerry Garcia's last words to his fans: GET A JOB!" Kelly loved that one.

He decided to go visit his family in North Carolina in September. I didn't want him to go because I knew I would miss him so much, and two weeks seemed like an eternity for him to be away. I tried to convince him to cut it back to a week or ten days, but he said it would be the last time he would see his family, so I gave in.

As Kelly's health began to fade, things that would normally seem unimportant took on more meaning. For example, I'd gone to Costco and bought, among other things, a six-pack of Jockey shorts and a big bundle of socks for both of us, but Kelly insisted that I not open them. He wanted to save them for his trip.

Sometimes we talked about the coming Christmas, which he was convinced would be our last together. Kelly loved Christmas, so we argued about what kind of tree to buy and where we would put it this year and which decorations we'd use and then we laughed at ourselves because it was only August. The red geraniums I'd bought at the farmers' market in the spring were bursting out of their redwood box on the deck. Alongside them, the pink petunias were like lovable old showgirls, loud and leggy and well past their prime. That time of year in San Francisco is glorious, when the fog leaves and the residents can enjoy some summer heat.

This was the only way we knew to spend those last golden evenings together. We sat on our back deck on Castro Street and argued about Christmas, laughing and waiting for a cool breeze to nudge us back inside to the warmth of the kitchen. I knew I would be alone here one day, but I never imagined it would be so soon.

Kelly seemed to sleep almost around the clock, though not very well. One night I rolled over in bed and thought he'd been tossing and turning because our bodies were in an odd position. I had my right arm partially wrapped around him. As I slid my hand back, my fingers closed around something hard. How sweet, I thought. He has a hard-on. I hadn't seen that old friend in a long time. Kelly and I hadn't had sex in weeks, maybe months. I'd simply told myself he was too sick to have sex, so I had blocked sex from my mind for the longest time in my life since puberty. Sex had to take a back seat to taking care of this man I loved. Now it was right here in my hand again—the stiff, lovely flesh of this man whose body was fading from our world while giving way to this dreaded disease.

I pulled up on Kelly's cock to tug the uncut flesh toward the head. As I awoke, I opened my fingers and realized that instead of his cock, I was holding Kelly's upper arm in my hand. He was that thin now.

Kelly told me one day that if he grew to be too much for me to take care of, I could ship him back to his parents in North Carolina. They would have to take care of him. Kelly was the middle child of seven, and I knew that one of his younger brothers was gay and had settled down with a man. Another time Kelly suggested living out his final days with his Aunt Claire in New York City. He had lived with her through high school when his parents were going through a trial separation. He was sure Claire would take care of him again.

I insisted I wasn't shipping him off to anyone. I had met his Aunt Claire when Kelly and I had gone to New York together. She was a former stage and film actress and had been the lover of the great jazz singer Carmen McRae. I loved Claire too, but she was already elderly and somewhat infirm and would likely soon need someone to take care of her.

I had met Kelly's mother, too. She came to San Francisco and spent one Easter weekend with us when we were both healthy and strong. We took her to Glide Memorial Methodist Church for Easter services. The music and the singing was all too wild for her, I thought. She was much too proper for the raucous Tenderloin crowd. I suppose she would have taken care of him, but by then he was beyond being healed by prayer. He needed the comfort of home—our home, not his mother's. I wasn't ready to let him go. He needed to be held, very gently through the night, or truthfully, maybe I was the one who needed to be held.

Kelly's forty-first birthday was coming up on Tuesday, August 29, and he wanted to have a party on the previous Sunday. I was glad he had something to keep his mind occupied, designing the invitations and planning the menu, even though I would end up doing most of the work. Kelly's old friend Ed Scruggs could help with shopping, and I started baking cookies a couple of weeks in advance. Kelly wanted lots of sweets, and the chest freezer we'd found at a yard sale for seventy-five bucks was deep enough to store all his favorites—chocolate chip oatmeal cookies, lemon bars, and brownies.

He had his good days and his bad days. One morning before I left for work, Kelly asked me about Coming Home Hospice on Diamond Street in the Castro. "Didn't you raise a bunch of money for them once? Didn't you say there was a plaque on the wall from Men Behind Bars?"

"I don't remember. I suppose that hospice might have been a beneficiary of one of our shows one year." I know I had organized a benefit for them at Café LuPann, a restaurant across 18th Street from the Midnight Sun owned by my friends Curtis and Tom. That benefit had sold out. Tom Ammiano did his comedy shtick to open for Gail Wilson who was accompanied by Bill Delisle on the piano. Gail did her old cabaret act, complete with a Karen Carpenter medley. She was great! All the wine, the talent and most of the food had been donated, so we raised several thousand dollars that night for the hospice. I asked Kelly why he was asking about it.

"I was thinking maybe you could pull some strings to get me in there. You could come and visit me any time you wanted."

I wouldn't hear of it. As long as I was healthy, Kelly would stay home. Ed Scruggs was only a couple of blocks away on 17th and Castro. He didn't work, and he had a car, so he took Kelly to all his doctor appointments. Ed could be here in a matter of minutes if we called him. He was already in the habit of coming by most days when I was at work. On good days, he took Kelly out for a drive or a bite to eat, just for a change of pace. I don't know what we would have done without Ed. The three of us fell into a routine. On the days when I worked the noon to seven shift at Trax on Haight Street, I would take care of Kelly in the mornings and again at night. Ed would come by in the afternoons. By August, taking care of Kelly meant changing his diaper first thing in the morning. His butt was so skinny, and he weighed so little that lifting him and cleaning him up wasn't hard. I was always afraid of hurting him. He grimaced a lot, but rarely cried out in pain.

I took each dirty diaper out the back door and down the stairs to the garbage can. I told Kelly something about not wanting to leave it in the trash can to stink up the kitchen, but the real reason was so that I could throw up downstairs without him hearing me. In front of him I had to remain as cheerful as I could, for his sake. Some days he would say, "Mark, I'm dying."

I couldn't argue the fact, so I would kiss him and smile. The best I could say was, "Well, you're not dying today, so can I get you anything before I leave for work? Are you comfortable?"

Ed also drove Kelly to his endless appointments at the University of the Pacific Dental School. They had pulled all but his front teeth on the top and most of the bottom ones. They said they would take the rest as soon as soon his full set of dentures was ready.

Some days I helped Kelly out to the living room where he could lie on the couch and watch TV. At that stage, being in the living room was at least a change in scenery. One day he asked Ed and me to move our California king-sized bed several inches closer to the bay window for a better view of Corona Heights. He would lie there staring out at that rocky red outcropping above the Castro for hours, and he told me he wanted most of his ashes scattered there when the time came. The Native Americans considered it holy ground, and Kelly reminded me that he was a quarter Cherokee. Kelly always slept on the window side of the bed, even though my side was closer to the bathroom. It really didn't matter since he'd started using the diapers. He had a plastic hospital urinal on his side of the bed as well, which I emptied whenever I thought of it. I don't know much about science and had never seen what the AIDS virus looked like under a microscope, but when Kelly's urine was nearly black I knew that he must be very sick on the inside.

I'm sure Ed changed his share of Kelly's diapers too. One morning I had to change it three times before I left for work. And I went down the back stairs to vomit all three times. I got Kelly moved to the living room, and he seemed weaker than he'd ever been. We even talked about contacting his doctor. I said, "I will call him if you want me to. Do you think there's anything specific that they can do? Can I do it for you here at home?" I knew how much Kelly hated hospitals.

"No, there's nothing they can do. Ed will come by. You'd better get to work. You'll be late." I bent down and kissed him three times on the lips and said, "I love you" between each kiss and Kelly said "I love you" back. That was a parting ritual we'd started a long time ago, and we stuck to it very closely the sicker he became.

That afternoon at work I got a call from Ed about five p.m. He said he'd had to leave Kelly alone for a while to go home and let the plumber in. When he got back, he found Kelly on the floor in the hallway trying to get to the bathroom, but he was still lying there, and Ed couldn't get him on his feet.

"What did you do, Ed? Where is he now? Was he conscious?"

"He wasn't really awake. I had to call an ambulance. He was so weak."

"This is where it starts," I said to myself. From this day on, Kelly will spend most of his time in the hospital, and I will become a visitor. I'd known lots of men who'd gone through the same thing, mostly customers at the bar. They would come in after visiting their lovers and tell me how they were doing while I listened and served them their drinks as they briefly tried to forget the hellish helplessness they felt. I could almost smell the hospital on those poor guys, and I felt so sorry for them. Now it was going to be my turn. Somehow I had always pictured that Kelly would be the one taking care of me at the end.

Ed told me over the phone that he would come to get me in a half hour and take me to see Kelly in the hospital. I just had to get someone to cover the rest of my shift. Ed pulled up in front of Trax in his VW bug, and we drove from the Haight through the Castro and across the Mission District through a maze of back alleys and one-way streets to General Hospital. Ed handed me Kelly's hospital ID card to bring inside, which he thought might facilitate them finding his chart or something. I don't know what we were thinking. All I knew was that I had to get in there and see Kelly as soon as they would let me. I could help. I could talk to him. I could hold his hand very gently and somehow pull him through this crisis. I knew there would be more crises to come and some would be worse, but I couldn't tell Kelly that. Knowing that they would get progressively worse would give me the strength to pull him through this first one. I was sure of that much.

I shoved the hospital card at the chubby male nurse behind the desk. "Hi, I'm looking for Robert Neal Kelly. Here…here's his ID. He was brought in by ambulance this afternoon. Can I see him now?"

He looked down at the card and asked, "Was that the call on Castro Street? The guy they found on the floor in the hallway in his own…?"

"Castro Street, yes."

He handed back the plastic card and looked up at me. "Oh, he's not here. They called in, but I told them if he was in that shape, they'd better take him to Davies. That's the closest hospital. He's not here. He's at Davies...good luck."

Ed and I drove back through the Mission. He knew all the alley shortcuts in the opposite direction too. I rolled down the passenger side window and smoked another cigarette, which was at least my fourth since I'd left Trax. I don't think Ed "allowed" people to smoke in his car, but under the circumstances he didn't say anything.

The Emergency entrance at Davies Hospital is down a steep ramp from Castro Street on the basement level. I ran up to the window with Kelly's card again. "I know this isn't General, but here's this card, if it helps any. Kelly was brought in here by ambulance a while ago. We went to General first because that's where his doctor is, but they told us he was here instead."

The woman behind the glass looked down at the card and up at me again. "Hold on a minute." She turned to another woman behind her, who disappeared through a door. Then a third woman emerged from another door, took my arm and said, "Come, let's sit down over here."

I realized that no one else was in the waiting room. The one at General was crowded and filled with the noises that crazed junkies make, the air clouded with street smells, the stench of filthy clothes and dirty bodies, and a constant sense of rage and panic. This place was luxurious by comparison, so quiet and civilized. If this was to be the beginning of my becoming a visitor, maybe Kelly could get a room in this hospital. I wouldn't even need to take the bus here. I could walk. I hoped they wouldn't get him stabilized only to send him back across town to General.

"Your friend...?" the lady said.

"My lover...Kelly," I corrected her.

She put one hand on my shoulder and the other on my knee. "I am so sorry to have to tell you that Kelly didn't make it. We did everything we could, since we had no directive not to, but he didn't make it. He wasn't able to speak when he was brought in, but I want you to know he wasn't in any pain. I gave him a big shot of morphine and…"

How could she know about his pain, I thought, but what I said was, "Kelly died? Oh, no! I thought this was going to be the beginning. You mean this is it? I thought we had months yet. He's hardly been in the hospital at all. He hates hospitals. I can't believe it!"

Just then, Ed arrived from parking his car. I looked up at him and said, "Kelly was worse than we thought, Ed. He didn't make it. He's gone." Ed spun around and ran outside. I didn't see him again until Kelly's memorial gathering a few days later.

I was numb, but I knew I had to do something. I turned back to the woman sitting beside me. "Can I see him? Please! I've got to see him. I need to say good-bye."

She told me they needed a few minutes to clean him up, but then I could see him. I sat there alone for an eternity. I told myself I just wanted to hold him one more time, but I lied. I just wanted to take him home. I wanted all of this to be a big misunderstanding, the wrong patient, the wrong name, the wrong ID card. I wanted Kelly to be back there right now, sitting up on the edge of his hospital bed eating dinner, complaining about the lousy food, waiting for me to bring him a magazine to read.

"You can see him now." She was back. "Come with me." She led me through a doorway, down a hall, and another doorway that led to a large cold room. She stood in front of me a minute and said, "I'm sorry, but we can't remove the breathing tube until after the coroner comes and signs the death certificate. It will have to stay in the corner of his mouth."

"That's okay…and I promise I won't be long."

Kelly was across the room on a tall platform draped with a sheet with only his head sticking out. I touched his feet through the fabric, then his hands, his shoulders, his neck and finally his face, that sweet handsome face. The tube sticking out of the corner of his mouth was yellow and looked like the stub of a corncob pipe that Kelly might have been smoking. Was it yellow or was it pink? It didn't matter. I knew this was the last time I would see him, so I'd better make it good.

I took a deep breath and gently kissed his lips, avoiding the tube as best I could. "I love you." I kissed each cheek and the tip of his nose and said, "I love you," three more times. Then I said, "And thank you, Kelly. Thank you for letting me know how it felt to love someone this way. Thank you for everything."

Chapter Sixty-One

After I said my last goodbye to Kelly's physical existence I walked south on Castro Street in a daze. Davies Hospital, now known as California Pacific Medical Center—Davies Campus, is at the corner of Castro and Duboce Streets. North of that intersection, the street takes a left curve, becomes Divisadero and goes downhill to Haight Street. South of the hospital, it runs due south up and down over a couple of small hills until about States Street, where the view becomes a picture postcard. The Castro Theatre looms on the left, with two blocks of shops and bars and restaurants, mostly housed in old Victorian buildings with apartments upstairs.

I came to a pay phone and found some change in my pocket to call Gail Wilson. "Gail, it's Mark. Kelly just died."

"What? Where are you?"

"I don't know. I'm so out of it. I'm walking down Castro Street from Davies. He died in the emergency room. At least it wasn't General. Davies is so much more civilized."

"Go straight home. I'll get a cab and meet you there in a couple of minutes."

I hung up the pay phone and realized I was carrying a small brown paper bag in one hand. Where did that come from? I looked inside and pulled out a sheet of paper, but I couldn't make my eyes focus on it. Then I remembered one of the three kind women at the hospital had asked me to sign something, tore off my copy, folded it and placed it inside the bag. In the bottom of the bag was Kelly's silver ring that matched mine. He had bought them for us on our first Christmas together. I put it on my finger next to mine. The only other thing in the bag was Kelly's wallet, thin pale brown eel skin. Inside were a couple of dollars, some business cards for his photography studio—our spare room— and his driver's license. I must have left his hospital card behind because I never saw it again.

I crossed Market and Castro Streets, stopped at Rossi's Deli and bought myself two packs of cigarettes. Heading south again, I literally bumped into Philip Turner who was coming out the front door of his bar, Daddy's. We turned our awkward shuffle into a hug and I said, "Kelly died."

"What? When?"

"Just now. I'm coming from Davies. Gail Wilson is on her way over to my house. I knew he was really sick, but I thought we'd have months yet."

"I'm so sorry, Mark. You go straight home and meet Gail. I'll come by later."

Gail was climbing out of a cab as I stuck my key in the downstairs gate. She stayed the night, sat beside me and held me while I called Kelly's mother, his Aunt Claire and, finally, my parents. They had loved Kelly too.

I never officially came out to my parents. It didn't seem necessary, and I always thought the very existence of people like me was so foreign to the life on the farm where I grew up that I didn't know how to explain my feelings to myself, much less my family. I knew that they loved me. By the time I reached my early twenties, they just stopped asking questions about girlfriends and getting married. I had started bringing boyfriends home from college for weekends on the farm anyway.

I always kept in touch with my parents by writing letters. My mother wrote most of their letters, and my dad would add a line or two at the end. They would call me a few times a year, especially on holidays or my birthday. After Kelly died, they called me every single day for weeks, until they knew I was going to survive. Then it became once a week and now that my dad is gone, my mother still calls every Sunday morning when she gets home from church.

The night Kelly died, my doorbell never stopped ringing.

Philip Turner must have called everyone that Kelly and I had known. I remember Doug "Fluffy" and Curtis and Gary "The Queen" Rahlf, but I know several others showed up. Everyone brought something, mostly vodka and mixes and ice, and we all got terribly drunk. That was Wednesday, and most of the following days and through the weekend are a blur. My sister and her husband drove down from Oregon. I was never alone for a minute.

Fluffy drove me to Costco to buy buns and cold cuts and potato and pasta salads. All the cookies and bars I had baked for Kelly's birthday party came out of the freezer to thaw. Kelly had just gotten a big bag of pot the week before, so I asked my best lesbian friend Corrine to roll it all into joints. We put them in short clear glasses like cigarettes at an old-fashioned cocktail party and set them around the apartment for people to help themselves. Kelly had told me once that when he died, he didn't want any bar where he had worked to make money off him, but that it would be okay if I had some friends over to the apartment. So on Sunday afternoon, instead of celebrating his birthday, we gathered to remember him. On Monday, Corrine and Bridget took me over to their house in the Haight where I did all of Kelly's and my laundry.

Someone stayed with me every night after than Wednesday. On Tuesday morning, I went back to work. My favorite customer at Trax was Bill, a retired Coast Guard man who knew a wealth of gay history from long before I arrived in San Francisco. He was a kind and gentle soul whom I had grown to love, not only because he was such good company but also because he was a generous tipper. Every day, he left a twenty dollar bill for my tip and in the last year he was alive—a few years after Kelly died—he gave me tips for Christmas and birthday of ten thousand dollars each. Somewhere in the mid-afternoon of my first day back at work when the bar was filled with regulars, I mentioned to Bill that it was Kelly's birthday. He told me to set up the house, which I did, and we all drank a toast to Kelly together. That was it. I was suddenly too busy to think.

I took the #33 Ashbury bus home after work, like always, up over the hill toward Twin Peaks and down the other side into Eureka Valley, off at 18th and Castro, and a one block walk to our apartment. I opened the door and realized that I was alone for the first time since Kelly died. I threw myself down across Kelly's side of the bed and fell apart. If I had thought I was numb to death by this time, I was mistaken. Knowing Kelly was never coming back, I sobbed like I hadn't since I was a little kid. I bawled until I soaked the pillowcases. My life would never be the same again, and now I had no one to take care of but myself.

Chapter Sixty-Two

I realized after Kelly died that I couldn't always focus on my sadness, as much as I tried. Perhaps no human brain is wired to concentrate on anything forever. Maybe mystics, monks, and geniuses have the discipline to exclude all external thoughts and static from their minds. I didn't have that skill. In my case, I was relieved when I recognized that I experienced breaks in my pain and that I could still eat and brush my teeth and get ready for work.

I already had an appointment with my doctor scheduled for the following week after Kelly's memorial gathering at our apartment. I had just sat down in his office when he said, "I'm sorry if I'm distracted today, but my wife and I just decided to get a divorce."

As if I felt the need to engage in a childish game of one upsmanship, I said, "I'm sorry. My lover just died last week." He reached for the phone on his desk and got hold of a woman who happened to be in the same building and free at that moment. I don't know what kind of therapy she practiced, but she was the most comforting person I had talked to so far. Maybe I could express myself more freely to a stranger. She was the perfect listener, and she said something to me that I have never forgotten: "Grief is healing. Hold onto your grief for as long as you need to. Think of it almost as a friend. Don't let go of it until you are good and ready."

On the bus ride home that day, I thought about how a wound heals. The scab may be ugly, but it protects you. I thought about Kelly as hard as I could and wondered what he would say to me. If our loved ones really watched over us from the "other side," this would have been a perfect time to hear from him. Instead, all the guidance I had to go on was what he had said in the past.

He'd told me to be sure that his youngest brother got his best camera. He'd said that he wanted most of his ashes spread on Corona Heights. He'd mentioned all sorts of things in the past few weeks and months that came back to me slowly over the following days, things I hadn't wanted to hear at the time because he knew he was dying when he'd said them. I always wanted to change the subject, but he also knew that I would do whatever he asked.

It occurred to me that now that Kelly would always remain the same age as he was when he died. That pissed me off. Anger felt better than sadness. Kelly's student dentist at the dental school called one day and asked to speak to him. I didn't know who she was at first, so I just told her he couldn't come to the phone. She had a snotty tone in her voice when she said, "Well, tell him his dentures are ready, and he didn't show up for his last appointment to have the rest of his teeth pulled and get his dentures fitted. If he misses two appointments in a row, he'll be dropped from the program."

I said, "I'm sorry. I'm afraid you're too late. He's already dropped out of the program all by himself. He died last week. Maybe if it didn't take so long for you to get anything done around there he wouldn't have starved to death!" I hung up the phone, and she never called back.

One afternoon I was watering plants when someone rang my doorbell. I wasn't expecting anyone. It was early September, about a week after Kelly died. My first thought was that it must be someone from the funeral home delivering Kelly's ashes. They had said it would take a few days. I buzzed the gate open, and a deliveryman came up the stairs with a beautiful arrangement of all white flowers. I was impressed that the funeral home had made such a lovely gesture as to send flowers along with the cremains. I took the clear glass vase from the man—whom I'd seen around in the Castro for years, but had never met—and looked down at his empty hands. I was sure he must be carrying an urn or a box or something else. Then I had the disturbing thought that Kelly's ashes were dissolved in the water in the vase, but I knew that couldn't be. Bones and teeth don't dissolve in water, even though Kelly didn't have many teeth left.

I looked at the vase of white lilies and roses and baby's breath and asked the deliveryman, "That's it? Where did these come from?"

"I don't know. There's a card."

I thanked him and took the arrangement inside, set the vase in the middle of the kitchen table and sat down to open the envelope. The flowers were from the Edge, a bar where I had never worked, but one that Kelly and I had certainly patronized. The note was handwritten by Eric Weinman, the manager at the time. I don't remember his exact words, but they were an extension of his condolences and a welcome to come down to the bar any time with a reminder that I could be among friends there as soon as I was ready.

Then I called the funeral home. Whoever answered the phone told me they'd already had Kelly's ashes for a couple of days and wanted to know when I was coming to pick them up. I considered the fact that they had a whole fleet of limousines and hearses, but they didn't deliver ashes, only cadavers. Bitches! My friend Doug drove me over there and waited in the car while I paid the bill and took custody of Kelly's cremains.

A guy named Bernard, whom Kelly and I had known as a customer in the bars for years, was working that day. I knew he worked for a mortician, but not which one, so I was surprised to see him. He told me he'd been on duty the night Kelly died and how surprised he was to unzip the body bag and find his favorite bartender inside. The body bag was more than I wanted to visualize at the moment. I just wanted to take Kelly's ashes home and be far away from this place. Bernard also told me that the charred piece of metal on the string that held the ashes shut was the "toe tag" and that it went through the fire with the body. It had a number on it so that the ashes could be easily identified by matching a name to that number. "TMI!" I wanted to scream. Too much information!

It didn't matter. This wasn't really Kelly anymore. I thought about when I was a little boy going salmon fishing off the coast of

Seattle. We were visiting relatives in Tacoma. I grew up fishing in Minnesota lakes and streams. I probably learned to hold a cane pole before I learned to walk, but this trip was the first time I had ever seen the ocean, much less gone out in a boat on it. My dad and Uncle Dick and I each caught our legal limits of salmon that day, and I was ecstatic! When we arrived back at the pier we took all our fish, save for one that we barbecued on the grill that night in Tacoma, to the nearby cannery. They weighed them and charged us by the pound for canned salmon that we could take unrefrigerated in the car all the way back home to Minnesota.

I knew the salmon in the cans wasn't the same fish we caught, because they hadn't had enough time to prepare and can them. I suspected that the crematorium might operate on the same principle as the cannery. I wasn't convinced that these were really Kelly's ashes. They might only be an illusion that I was just supposed to go along with like it was all part of a mediocre magic act. It's not polite to point out the smoke and mirrors.

I moved the flowers aside and dumped some of "Kelly's" ashes out onto the kitchen table to spread them around with my fingertips. I wanted him back so desperately that I even tasted them, from my fingertip to the tip of my tongue, but I couldn't sense anything of Kelly there. I pulled myself together and put the ashes back inside the bag. I went to the drawer where Kelly saved empty little brown bottles—one size that poppers came in and even smaller ones from when we used to sometimes buy a gram of cocaine at a time. I filled the bottles with ashes and also placed some inside a small envelope to send with a card to his beloved Aunt Claire in New York. Kelly had told me to ask her to take them to the Apollo Theatre and sprinkle them in the doorway during a concert so that when the audience left, they would track Kelly's dust all over Harlem.

I found a little brass heart-shaped box that Kelly had used to store filters for his pot pipe. I filled that with ashes and taped that batch shut with masking tape to send to his mother. He wanted her to spread some of them at the entrance of the church that his late grandfather had built in Florida. The heart-shaped box went inside a larger box with Kelly's best camera for his little brother. I packed up his long wool winter coats. They were a little too small in the shoulders for me and hardly anyone wears long coats in San Francisco. When I went through Kelly's jewelry, I found all sorts of sparkling shiny things I had never seen before. Kelly was never one to wear bracelets, but I found several watches. One had tiny diamond chips to mark each hour. I had never owned a diamond in my life and saw no need to start.

I packed up everything of value—monetary or sentimental— that his family might want and shipped it to them. I felt no obligation to send back anything that we'd acquired together or gifts I'd bought for him. Another time, when Kelly had an especially good day, Ed took him out shopping. One day a couple of weeks before Kelly died, I had come home from work to discover a dozen pair of brand new shoes on our bedroom floor. Ed had taken him out shopping, and Kelly had charged them on his credit card. I said I felt like I was married to Imelda Marcos, but he didn't laugh. We had the same size feet and he told me he was sick of seeing me going around in old beat-up shoes and that all of these new ones would be mine soon enough. So I kept all the shoes he'd wanted me to have. I kept his everyday watch, which I still wear sometimes, and of course the "wedding" rings that Kelly bought us for our first Christmas together. I let our old friends pick through what remained and let each of them choose a piece of Kelly's jewelry to remember him by.

Several friends invited me out to dinner. I've always liked fine dining in good restaurants, especially when someone else was paying, but when my friends were couples, we'd be seated at a table for four. It was impossible not to stare at the empty chair. When I perused the menu, I'd think of what Kelly would have ordered from it. When I got home, I wondered what Kelly would have said about the evening. Something clever, no doubt; he could be so funny without even trying, sometimes with only a comment, a single word or just a facial expression.

I found going out with single friends was easier than with couples. My friend Doug and I started going out to lunch on

Mondays and then to a bargain matinee movie. Then Bob Douglas, one of the owners of Trax, started to join us. Some Mondays we would have four or five people, depending on who had the day off and wanted to see the movie we'd decided on that week. The next time the Academy Awards came around was the first year I had seen all the nominees in nearly every category.

Kelly died on a Wednesday, and I counted each Wednesday that passed as another milestone, another week I had survived. I had once been so sure that I would go first or at least go with him. When his scent on the pillowcase faded, I stripped the bed and did laundry, another step toward admitting that I had to continue. I gasped and held back tears at times like seeing his hair in a comb or his handwriting on cards and little love notes that he'd left for me to find during our first weeks together. I had long talks into the night on the telephone with his beloved Aunt Claire. She loved Kelly too and we comforted each other, but her health was failing much faster than mine.

I also took comfort in the strangest things. One evening at home, I turned on the television and after an endless series of commercials, Betty White came on. She wasn't acting, but being interviewed. It might have been Larry King Live on CNN, but I paid no attention to the interviewer, which probably meant he was doing his job well. Betty White was captivating. Having lived in Minneapolis when the Mary Tyler Moore Show originally aired, I had been a fan of Betty White's since she had played Sue Ann Nivens. As long as I've been going to gay bars in San Francisco some of them have shown TV shows, but nothing was ever more popular in the bars than The Golden Girls.

The interviewer asked Betty White about her late husband Allen Ludden. She said that when he died, George Burns called and suggested that she move to the other side of the bed. That's what he did when Gracie Allen died. I was blown away to hear this, because I had instinctively moved to Kelly's side of the bed ever since the first night I'd slept without him. No one told me to, but I figured that I wouldn't be reaching out for him that way. Hearing Betty White say this made me feel incredibly smart and somehow connected to all the mourners in the world. Silly little things can have a profound effect when their timing is just right. Betty White reminded me that lots of people out there, especially in a city as rife with AIDS as San Francisco was at the time, had survived the same sort of grief that I was going through and many more would in the near and endless future. I would miss Kelly for the rest of my life, however short or long that might turn out to be, but I would simply have to go on.

Chapter Sixty-Three

I bumped into Philip Turner one morning outside Walgreens on the corner of 18th and Castro. He was carrying a cardboard box with a pink feather boa wrapped around it like a ribbon and tied in a bow on top. I asked him if it was a gift, and he said, "No, it's Dorthy Duster. I just picked up her ashes, and I thought she needed a gayer touch than plain old cardboard. I think she would approve, don't you?"

"Absolutely!"

I remembered that Dorthy had one leg amputated a while back and been in a wheelchair ever since. I said to Philip, "I hope the crematorium gave you a discount, since she only had one leg," and we both laughed. We'd already used all the obvious jokes like, "She already has one foot in the grave" to her face when Dorthy was still alive. It was such a relief to be able to laugh at death in those days.

I thought back to a sunny day on the bay with Dorthy on the Neptune Society's boat to spread the ashes of another friend beyond Angel Island. Philip was probably there too. We had so many friends in common from the Special that I can't remember which one had died that time, only that it was a perfect day with no wind or fog, and we watched the ashes fall from the urn over the side of the boat. They were mixed with red rose petals that floated on the surface of the deep blue waters as the ashes slowly sank and disappeared.

On the way back to shore, we speculated which of us would be next and someone remarked that Dorthy had a good start with one leg missing already. Someone else suggested—maybe it was Dorthy—that we could save some money and another boat trip if we just dumped her off now. Several of us lit our cigarette lighters and surrounded her with them as if to set her on fire. Dorthy loved being the center of attention, and we laughed all the way back to Fisherman's Wharf. Then we drove in a caravan of cars back to the Special on Castro Street for the larger, more public gathering where everyone got roaring drunk.

When Philip Turner died in 2001, he'd left a request for Gail Wilson to sing at his funeral. She asked me to go with her for moral support, as I had when she sang at Blair's service, and I agreed. Philip was "Daddy" of Daddy's Bar at 440 Castro Street, across from the old Special, so his memorial was sure to be huge, involving all the bar people and the entire leather community, not only from San Francisco but far and wide. The morning of the service Gail called me to say that she was sick and couldn't sing. She was running a fever and could barely talk. I hardly recognized her voice on the phone. I decided not to go either. As much as I loved Philip, I knew that I could pay my respects at the gathering at his bar afterward. I also knew that I would sense his sprit there more fully than I would inside any church.

I walked into Daddy's just as the crowds were starting to arrive. One of the first people I ran into was my friend Joe Mac who told me how nice the service was, "and your buddy Gail did a fabulous job!"

"What? She could barely talk a couple of hours ago."

Joe Mac was sitting so far back, he couldn't see the singer, but Gail's name was in the program, so he thought it was her. They had gotten another woman who was also beloved in the gay community, Jo-Carol, formerly of the Patrick Cowley Singers, to take Gail's place at the last minute. I'd known Jo-Carol since my days at the Russian River, and I was happy to see her again that day. It was a shock when she died a couple of years later on June 4, 2003 of a cerebral aneurysm.

Chapter Sixty-Four

In 1996, only a few months after Kelly died, my doctor told me that I was a prime candidate for a new HIV drug. It hadn't yet been approved by the FDA, so this was only a study, but it would cost me nothing and it showed great promise. I don't mind being a guinea pig for science. The way I figured, even if it did me no good, the research might help someone else down the road. I had been with the same trusted HIV specialist, Dr. James Kahn, for years, and I've always been the sort of patient who tends to agree to all my doctors' suggestions, especially after they are fully explained to me.

I have a lot of silly superstitions. I have trouble falling asleep unless I've left one light on in the kitchen. I have to fold all of my t-shirts a certain way when they come out of the dryer. On an airplane, I have to eat everything they serve me, or I did, when they served food on domestic flights, in order to make sure that the plane landed safely. With medicine, if I ever denied a recommended treatment, I was absolutely certain that I would later find out that it would be the one that would have cured me.

This new study required frequent trips to the main hospital at San Francisco General, to Ward 4-C where they weighed me, took my vital signs, drew my blood and dispensed my precious pills every couple of weeks. My HIV viral load quickly dropped to undetectable levels and my T-cells soared. We still didn't know what side effects might come from this treatment in the short or long term, but instead of preparing to follow my fallen comrades into death, I was suddenly faced with the unbelievable prospect of living a "normal" life. It was terrifying. I wasn't prepared for this news when most of my friends didn't make it. I had survived a war only to return and discover that hardly anyone is left to join in the celebration, and the other survivors are still too shell-shocked to celebrate.

I felt as if I had been shoved into the last space on a lifeboat after the ship had already gone down with most of my friends on it. I was more prepared to go with them than to go on without them. Why me? What had I done to deserve to live? What entitled me to this opportunity when so many smarter, nicer, sexier and far more creative people had their lives cut short? Even though I had never physically left, I suddenly felt like San Francisco had changed. My home town Main Street—Castro Street—was still there, but it was somehow different. The same MUNI buses ran every few minutes, but the passengers were getting younger, healthier-looking and seemed to be more full of life. If I was going to survive, I would have to keep my head up and move forward, if only for the sake of all my friends who didn't have that opportunity.

New people still arrive every day. The tourists still come and some decide to stay here, just like in the years before AIDS. They take pictures of the grand marquee of the Castro Theatre, standing proudly in the middle of the first block, like a great cathedral looming over our village. People flock to see where Harvey Milk's camera shop stood, especially since the movie Milk. The filmmakers shot most of it right there and recreated the entire block to look like it did in the late 1970s, when I was in my twenties.

I see gay men in their twenties now who remind me of my friends when we were their age. I see them out having fun, exploring the bars, meeting new people and having lots of sex. We did the same things, but we didn't know the sex could be deadly. I see personality types that match the people who are long gone from my life. My friends' ghosts still walk through the neighborhood whenever I see a face or hear a voice that reminds me of someone from back then. These young people remind me that we are all members of the same tribe. I look at them and wish them the best. I want to tell them to enjoy every minute of their youth, try not to worry too much, take care of each other and believe in a bright future. We did too, before AIDS came along.

Knowing I had a chance to live, I was forced to reckon with where I stood in my life. I still had a rent-controlled apartment on Castro Street. I still had a few "family" friends near and far. I still had my blood family, mostly back in Minnesota but spread all across the country by now. I still had my job on Haight Street and a "family" of customers there. Most of all, I still had San Francisco.

Rita Rockett always said, "If you love San Francisco, it will love you back." I doubt that the line originated with her. It might have come from the late columnist Herb Caen, or it could go all the way back to Emperor Norton, but no matter the source, it's true. It was time to make new friends, some younger and some older than me. The generation before me wasn't wiped out so much by AIDS as by age, but some of them still had their stories and their wisdom to pass on. It was time for me to look forward to things again. And it was time for me to rediscover the fun of sex.

When I moved to San Francisco, a couple of weeks after my twenty-third birthday, I spent nearly every day off work at the beach if the weather was good. If the sky was dark, I might bundle up and head outdoors to one of the parks or go for a quiet walk in the rain. Having grown up on a farm, I relate best to living, growing things. I am used to the color green in nature, so I gravitate toward the smells of eucalyptus leaves and jasmine in the fresh air. I listen to the caws of crows in the trees and the foghorns along the waterfront. I crave the taste of sourdough bread and fresh cracked Dungeness crab. From the first day I set foot in San Francisco, I realized that my generation had all the freedom in the world. None of us had a clue that death and devastation were waiting just around the corner.

I meet other guys like me sometimes. Survivors. We can recognize each other in an instant. I think it's something in the eyes, some mix of loss and laughter, pain and wisdom, a little bit of residual fear and anger and usually a lot of love.

I read an article by Dave Ford in the San Francisco Chronicle a few years back in which he tried to explain surviving AIDS. He suggested trying to imagine a big party with all of your friends there. Everyone is having a wonderful time until you notice that they are all starting to disappear, one by one, and you never get to see them again.

I couldn't write about those dark times while they were still too raw to bring into focus. We try to forget the pain of wars and tragedies and natural disasters. It's the same with epidemics. Now, only after many years have passed, I am able to look back and realize how many good times are blended into my memories of those dying years. We found ways to entertain ourselves between the funerals and memorial gatherings. We had to keep going: one more sunrise, one more drink, one more laugh, one salty tear after another. Far too many good people were lost who deserve to be remembered. Maybe part of the reason why I am still here is to tell a little bit of their story. I only got to know a few of them.

Afterword

I have sometimes tried to make sense of life by writing things down: grocery lists, chores, the names of the dead. I started keeping a journal on my eighteenth birthday when I left the farm where I grew up in southwestern Minnesota to tour Europe with my saxophone and a hundred other virginal, wide-eyed all-American kids. In later years, I made a list of the people I had known who died before me. I can't tell you everything I knew about each of them. Some I hardly knew except to serve them a drink when I was a bartender at the Russian River or in gay bars in San Francisco. A few of them, like Liberace, I never met in person, but I would still have to say that they touched my life in some way.

Some were co-workers, neighbors, or guys I ran into on the streets in the Castro every day. I had sex with lots of them and I fell in love with some. Many were friends. Enough years have passed now that I could look back and record some of the fun times as well as the heartbreak and even the beauty of those dying years.

Not everyone on my list fell to the plague. Some died in accidents or overdoses, some took their own lives—"self-deliverance," they called it. Some were even murdered, but most of them died from AIDS. I think it's important to remember what we did in those days besides going to funerals, the ways that my gay brothers and I kept on going while we waited our turn to die. Maybe that's why I'm still here, to write some of it down. Although this is mostly my story, I tried to do justice to the memories of some of the fine people who didn't live long enough to tell their own.

1982

January
- Reverend Ray Broshears

November
- Patrick Cowley - Record producer

1983

June
- Mark Feldman - Gay activist
- Emperor Jim Ostlund
- Jim Sullivan - Pianist

November
- Lawrence "La-La" Beach - Co-owner of the Balcony, an outrageous bar

1984

February
- John Ponyman
- Donald McLean aka Lori Shannon aka Beverly LaSalle, who was Archie Bunker's favorite female impersonator on All in the Family

March
- Gary Walsh

April
- Dennis Yount- Bartender at the Eagle
- Michael Shiell
- Tom Rogers

May
- Allan Estes - Founder of Theatre Rhinoceros

July

- Robert Hagopian - Pianist
- Jim Sell - Pool player
- Jon Sims -- Founder of the Gay Marching Band
- Tom Wilker

August
- Bobbi Campbell aka Sister Florence Nightmare

September
- Jonathan Berdell - Boyfriend
- Donald Baker - Owner of the Wild Goose Saloon

- October
- Frank Lobraico - Lighting and set designer
- Jim Murphy
- Michael Maletta - Legendary party producer
- David Caravalho - Was refused a flight and embalming because of AIDS

November
- Mark Hughes

December
- Jimmy Simmons
- Dick "Zelda" Zautke

1985
January
- Robert L. Wasson aka Fat Fairy

February
- Dutch Garcia aka Sister CPR
- Joe Schmall - Produced the Castro Street Dog Show

March
- Ramon Vidali
- Arthur Blake - Noted female impressionist

April
- Dale Edward - Co-owner of Canary Island
- David Venn - Bartender

May
- Michael Avedon - Men Behind Bars

June
- Tony Gerken
- John "Flo" Good
- David Goodstein - Gay activist, owner of The Advocate
- Paul Castro - AIDS activist

July
- Steve Hasemeier
- Paul Diamond
- Richard Roesener - Baton twirler

August
- Michael Frawley - Pendulum co-owner
- Ron Garner

September
- Milton White
- Fred Hibberd
- Tommy Zalewski - Owner of Tommy's Plants on Castro Street

October
- Rock Hudson - Actor
- Paul Harmon
- Tom Doyle
- David Tibbits

November
- John Fletcher

December
- Billy Gaylord - Renowned designer
- Billy Price - Bartender
- Jim Slick - Bartender

1986

January
- Kap Pischel - Boyfriend
- Bill Kraus - Gay political leader
- Chuck Morris - Publisher The Sentinel

February
- Everett Hedrick - Owner of The Village - murdered
- Russ Glenn - Owner of the White Swallow
- Chuck Bennett
- Michael Gomez - Singer

March
- Jim Tuttle - Model
- Dan Sharp

April
- "Little Hank" Magdaleno - Bartender The Village
- Earl "Animal" Belk - Men Behind Bars

May
- Bill Pope
- Ray M. Frost - Febe's bar manager
- Herman George - Costumer

June
- Robert Uyvari- Artist
- Steve Loignon - Eagle bartender
- Edwin Bean
- Jim Silva - Bartender

July
- Gary Erwin - Mr. Febe
- Les Spurlock - Russian River bartender

August
- Robert Haskell - Disc jockey
- Vern "Verna Mae" Arvin - The Pendulum
- Way Bandy - Make-up artist
- Chaz Watson - Drum major
- Dean Halsey - Singer
- Roy Ourso
- Mark Sigers - Sued Delta Airlines for AIDS discrimination when they threw him off a flight

September
- Joe Curley - City Swing
- Robert Valencia, Jr. - Bartender at Castro Station
- Lesesne VanAntwerp - Conductor

October
- Jane Dornacker - Trafficologist
- Gary McDonald - Manager of Fife's Resort
- Jay Baughman - Manager of the Bakery Cafe
- Robert Magan - Bartender The Arena
- David Moldovan - Sound technician

November
- David Summers - Singer, actor, activist

December
- Chuck Solomon
- Bill Coates - Bartender at Boot Camp, Ramrod, Arena, Eagle
- George Dutra
- Larry Hoyt - Teacher
- Hugo Niehaus- Set designer

1987

January

- Charles Gilman - Owner of the Walt Whitman bookshop
- Dennis Ickes
- John Price - Lighting designer
- Karl Stewart - Bay Area Reporter columnist
- Dr. Donald Baker
- Gary Lamoureux - Creative Power Foundation
- Francisco Hernandez
- Mike Wooldridge - Chaps bartender
- Herb Finger - Super-chef
- Douglas Figley - Waiter at Mommy Fortuna's
- Mark Hermes - Bartender Molly Brown's - Guerneville
- Jay Brewster
- Tom Reynolds
- Bob Patterson

February

- Larry Harrison
- Michael Lamberta
- Liberace - Celebrity pianist
- Bob Koenig - Bartender
- John Hanson
- Dennis Mitchell
- Matt Harmon
- Jerry Rothman
- Gene Peterson - Playwright
- Gordon Utter
- Bobby Hilton

March

- Scott Ladiser
- Michael Abling - Square dancer
- Robert Flaherty - Co-owner Hayes Street Grill
- Dennis "Toby" Tyler - Waiter/bartender P.S., Rendezvous, Chez Mollet, End-Up

- Lain Foos - Bartender Eagle, Pendulum, Church Street Station
- Brian Keith
- Peter Hogg - Fellow bartender at The Woods
- David Jackson - Bartender Fife's, the Rusty Nail
- David Pasko - Filmmaker/ bartender Moby Dick

April
- David Lynch - Composer
- Robert Hill
- Matt Newman - Men Behind Bars, The Fourskins
- Mike McKinnon - Castro mailman/ singer with Vocal Minority
- Greg Guerin - Waiter at Without Reservations
- Richard Hennigh - First runner-up IML 1985
- Jimmy Coney- Bartender, stained glass artist
- Bobby Reynolds - AIDS activist

May
- Ricky Eastman
- Gary Seeger
- Lee Joseph
- Colin Groom
- Jim Peters

June
- Jerry DeGracia - Music critic
- Mark Hanson
- Marc "Mavis" Sterling - Beloved bartender on Polk Street
- Dennis Lauriano
- Albert Jones - Member of Barbary Coast Cloggers

July
- Buster Zoutte - Men Behind Bars belly dancer
- Timmy Green - Badlands bartender
- Ron Carey - Created the x-rated Cake Gallery in SOMA
- Dr. Tom Waddell - Founder of the Gay Games
- Billy Lowenthal - Owned the Magic Garden on Haight Street

August
- Tom Hunt - Polk Street bartender
- Michael Hale
- David Hummel - Gay activist
- Casey Donovan - Porn star
- Peter Jacklin - Alan Selby's lover
- Richard Truelove - City Swing
- Jon Wright - Castro Lions' president
- John Trowbridge - Entertainer
- Ralph DuPont
- Warren LaFollette, Jr. aka Connie Cadaver

September
- Ron Rosendo - Performer
- George Cano
- Gene Kopek
- Martyn Loveday - Boot Camp/ Ambush

October
- Richard Loughran
- Wayne Quinn - Artist and friend
- Zohn Artman - Philanthropist, Tom Waddell's lover and Bill Graham's publicist
- Bob Hunter
- Robert Ward - Terry and Blair's neighbor who got to meet the Pope at Mission Dolores
- Jack Latham - Writer, founder of Gay Fathers
- Fred Cohen
- Rob Kimbel - Disc jockey
- David Lee Williams - Pianist

November
- Timo Butters - Actor with the Gay Men's Theatre Collective
- Eddie Reyes - Cook at Hamburger Mary's
- Glen Mercier - Castro bartender and disc jockey
- Mike Lowson - Founded Animals' Friends Clinic on Castro

Street
- Bobby Caldera
- Jack Kavulish- Bartender at the Ambush
- Dr. Alan Rockway - Fought Anita Bryant's bigotry
- Ken Shutwell - Painter/ gymnast

December
- Daryl Glied
- Perry Watson - Bartender at the New Bell Saloon
- Peter Zimmerman

- also died in 1987 -
- Gene Zuchelli
- Bill Wallace aka Juanita

1988
January
- Jim Hornsby - City Swing

February
- Glen Palmer - World-class ballet dancer
- Guy Masson - Men Behind Bars dancer with Winchester
- Tim Lee
- Perry George - Columnist, activist, singer
- Ron Dykstra - Mr. Russian River

March
- Chuck Arnett - Artist who created the famous mural at the Tool Box
- Ted Aldrich - Poet
- Ed Stark aka Edwina Ballerina - Boss, dear friend
- Ken Leetzow - Bartender at Trax
- Gordon Merrick - Novelist

April
- Jimmy Stoker - Bartender at the Midnight Sun
- Nick Gell - Castro Station bartender

- Fred Johnson - Model
- Jeff Sciera - Bartender at the Balcony
- Dean Davis - Bartender
- Andre Watson

May
- Fred Beckmann
- James Mock - SF Band Foundation president
- Lew Baxter - Bartender at Twin Peaks and Pilsner Inn
- Tommy Gene Brown aka Empress III Shirley

June
- Richard Ruggiero
- Michael Nameth aka Empress XII Jane Doe
- Andrew Meltzer - Conductor and friend
- Larry Phelps - Member of the Barbary Coast Cloggers
- Leonard Matlovich - Owner of Stumptown Annie's pizza parlor
- Danny White - My friend who had the unfortunate same name as Harvey Milk's assassin
- D.W. Wachsnicht - Bartender
- Henry Von Dieckoff aka Baroness Eugenia Von Dieckoff

July
- Robert Baranyi
- Tim Levens - Starred in the Cockette's film "Elevator Girls in Bondage"
- Kent B. Brown- Boyfriend and bartender at the Elephant Walk
- Larry Hough aka Deidre - Men Behind Bars
- William Ferguson
- Robert Ferro - Novelist
- John Friberg
- Michael Bower
- Peter Grote - Set designer

August
- Tommy Pace - Performer with Angels of Light
- Chuck Waltz - Singer/actor
- John Hyer - Chef and bartender
- Gary Bell
- Jack Essex - Producer of the annual Cabaret Gold Awards
- Michael Lewis- Disc jockey at the Detour
- Steve Harris - Creator of the Castro Country Club
- Rick Ordonez - Theatrical producer
- Nicholas Cortland - Film actor, tryst

September
- Dick Roberts - Bartender, Rainbow Cattle Company, Guerneville
- Arthur Toth
- Doug Trantham - Entertainer
- Joe Kleinow - Co-owner of Folsom Prison Bar
- Dennis May
- Chris Munkers - Waiter at Trinity Place

October
- Nikos Kafkalis - Stage manager for Nunsense with Sharon McNight
- Gary Giza - Bartender at Trinity Place and the I Beam
- Wayland Flowers - Puppeteer
- Phillip LaKose- Manager of LeSalon Bookstore on Polk Street
- Kenny M - Morning shift coke dealer at the Special on Castro Street

November
- Dennis Beenken
- Joe Curry
- Jack Mance - artist
- Marvin Nolan aka Mr. Dolly
- Wayne Spangler aka Empress XXI Sable Clown
- Bobby Trujillo

December
- Robert Hunter
- Rey Richardson
- Sylvester - Disco star
- Michael Stanzione, Jr. - Co-owner of the Galleon
- Duke Armstrong - Community leader, nice guy, but a gay Republican

---

1989

January
- Richard "Roz" Howe - Ed Stark's lover
- Jim Phillips
- Bill Teeter
- Bill Walker
- Bill Ward - Pianist

February
- Pat Campano - Costume designer for the Supremes, Charles Pierce, Gloria Swanson...
- Peter Keane - Graphic artist
- Thomas Cooper - Square dancer
- Skip Daniel
- Sammy Flake - Twirler with the SF Flag Corps
- Randy Johnson - B.A.R. columnist, Mae West in Men Behind Bars III
- Barry Littleton - Musician, City Swing

March
- Brent Jensen - Cockette/ Yellow Cab Driver
- Dr. Dick Hamilton - The first openly gay doctor I ever went to
- Jeff Brown
- Jack Caster - Co-founder of the Names Project AIDS quilt
- Michael Chandler - Fellow Minnesotan
- Tom Edinger - Artist in pencil and oils, jazz record producer
- Joe Fraser - Actor
- John Hobbie

- Jeff Kriger - Photographer
- Fred Lee
- Robert Mapplethorpe - Photographer
- David Morris - A sweet man
- Pauline - Headliner at Finocchios
- Terry Peterson - Pianist
- Richard Speicher - Philip Turner's lover and business partner before he bought Daddy's

April
- Joseph Cappetta - Actor/ director
- David Chastain
- Gordon "Tiger" Stacey - Powerhouse bartender
- Terry Sutton - Founding member of ACT UP
- Richard Valentino - Textile designer for Janis Joplin, T-Shirt king for the gays
- Leland "Butch" Walsh aka Ida Nevasayneva
- Larry Whitlock - Valiant swimmer, singer, computer expert
- George Whitmore - Novelist

May
- Andrew Hammond aka Andy Barron
- Bill Paul - Gay rights activist
- Jim White
- Donn Wheatley
- Jack McCarty - Manager of the Elephant Walk

June
- Gary Poole - Dance champion with his sister as "Gary and Gloria Poole"
- Will Tucker aka "Binky" in Men Behind Bars
- Rick Albright
- Jim Boyd - The sexiest bartender at the original Midnight Sun on Castro Street
- Bob Damron - Creator of the famous address book
- Jim Lansdowne - Community leader and activist
- Tom Lindsey

- Roger Madison - Worked at Andy's Donuts, Without Reservations and Orphan Andys
- Geoff Mains - Author of Urban Aboriginals
- Schonn Michaels
- Mike Twinn - The Catacombs

July
- Stephen Darrow - Bodybuilder, model, and bartender at Studio 54 in NYC
- Mark Friese - Performed in MBB as "Pineapple Princess" and Oliver Douglas from "Green Acres" with Mister Marcus in Eva Gabor's role
- Brian Lee aka Johnny Dawes
- Will Shepardson
- Fred Heramb - Catacombs owner

August
- Mark Bovee - Bartender
- Jack Campbell - Original member of the Gay Men's Chorus
- Ted Knipe - San Francisco Flag Corps
- Lee Uhlenhake

September
- Stephen Blair - Terry Thompson's lover
- Doug Kimball - Badlands bartender/ musician/ singer
- "Big John" Strother - Bartender
- Jim Kahl - Mr. No. Cal Drummer 1988
- Kenny Lackey - Drummer Magazine
- Warren Thomas - Bartender at the Rusty Nail/ Russian River
- A.B. Tucker

October
- "Fast Eddie" Brener
- David Cafferty - Bartender at Moby Dick
- Braxton Hancock aka the Divine Judy
- Jeff Carillon
- Dr. Don Dragoni

- Robert McQueen - Editor of The Advocate (after John Preston)
- John Muir - Bartender at the Pilsner, direct descendant of the John Muir
- Donald Shadle
- Tony Wormus - Bartender at Polk Gulch

November
- David Filler - Moby Dick and needlepoint aficionado
- Henry "Jun" Hill
- David Mease
- Joey Mickelsen
- Tristano Palermino - AIDS activist
- Michael Rubin - Writer
- Rusty Vega
- Richard Zidell
- Tyrone Benjamin

December
- Bill Brown
- Paul Casto - Skier, hang-glider
- Hank Cook - Co-founder of the SF AIDS Emergency Fund
- Royal Liner - Pendulum bartender

1990

January
- Mark Ryan - Disc jockey at the I-Beam
- Tim McKenna - Sylvester's manager
- George Ash - Muscle System "sisters" Gym co-owner
- Chuck Brigance - Eagle bartender
- Gary Lee Brown - Eagle bartender
- Gary D'Alois
- Tim Elliott - Swimmer
- Reggie Jones - Playwright, singer
- Scott Goldschmidt - Manager of Moby Dick
- Preston King
- Dennis O'Neil - Singer, bartender

- Larry Purl - Bartender Pilsner Inn
- Greg Sutton - Fan dancer
- Peter "Puffer" Switzer - Bartender at Sutter's Mill
- Bruce Trondson - Sound engineer
- Emperor Ken Wright

February
- Russell Silva - Chef
- Bud Alley
- John Belskus - Co-founder of the AIDS vigil outside the federal building
- Joel Daily
- Keith Haring - Artist
- Obie Howell - Imperial Czar of the Golden Stage
- Rick Oldham

March
- David Waggoner - Founder of the SF Gay and Lesbian Film Festival
- Bill Bishop - Twirler with the gay marching band
- Ron Brateman
- Bruce Davidson - Manager of the Watering Hole
- Halston - Designer
- Ray Hosgood

April
- Ryan White - Thirteen-year-old spokesman for people with AIDS
- Armando Arroyo - My first lover in San Francisco
- Michael Cole Becker - Boyfriend
- Bob Bellville
- Brian Bliss - Conductor/arranger for Men Behind Bars I
- Jon Clendenin
- Bill Granfors
- Hector Romo - Owner, Cafe San Marcos
- Hal Slate - Opened the Cauldron
- Paul Titus

May
- Ed Siegel
- Robert Allen
- Dane Baker - Disc jockey/ doorman on Castro Street
- Michael Bourgoin
- Richard Christopher
- Peter Cyr - Bartender at Alfie's and Bob Cramer's lover
- Randy Osier - Eagle bartender
- Rome Pardy
- Edward Siegel
- Joe Tippy

June
- Ernie Viola - Eagle bartender
- Dan Turner - Playwright
- Robert Pitman - Theatrical producer
- Jim Baroni - Castro Station manager
- Will Bolger
- George Burgess - Activist/ humanitarian
- Larry Glover - Men Behind Bars
- Dennis Hicks
- Hadley Johnson - Bartender at the SF Eagle
- Doug Reutter - Swimmer, musician

July
- Adam Hunt
- Michael Pietri aka Tony Bravo
- Denny Whitworth

August
- Jim Belk - Nikole Dushay's lover
- Robert Bennett Jr
- Fred Bugay
- Ethyl Eichelberger
- Jim Markey - Deena Jones' lover
- Terry Martin
- Gary "Grandma" Mosley - Men Behind Bars

- Bill Schade - Classic car lover, owner of "Shades of the Past"
- Tim Spangler

September
- Joel Coleman
- Tony Haar
- Jim Heady - Owner of Male Image Leathers and Barbers
- TJ Jaworski
- Ken Johnson
- Jim Phelan
- James Shaw - Friend from the 70s, model for Macy's
- Les Stephens - Bartender at Buzzby's on Polk Street
- Worth Young

October
- Nicky Tilsen - Chef/fellow Minnesota transplant
- Randy Braswell
- Kim Ditzel
- Jim Foster - Gay activist
- Gary McDonough - Cafe Flore/Caracole
- Richard Wright - Co-producer of M.E.N. Productions, videographers of MBB III, IV and V

November
- Ron Thill - Old boyfriend/manager of All American Boy
- Norman Baizley - Ambush bartender
- Donald Catalano
- Keith Coppin
- Bob Duncan
- Ed Drucker - Founder of Elysian Fields Booksellers
- Bill Henderson - Performer
- Lyle Madsen
- David Monroe - Manager of the Tool Box, one of the first leather bars in SF
- Peter Pender - Owner of Fife's Resort in Guerneville
- Angelo Rosardo-Marquez
- Randy Tyler

- Tom Youngblood - Self-appointed local critic

December
- Reinaldo Arenas - gay Cuban exile and writer
- Walter Black - Waiter at the Metro
- Mark Case aka Veda
- Robert Chesley - Playwright
- Emperor III (after Norton) Bob Cramer - Founder of the Cable Car Awards
- Brian Jackson aka Trudy Yoors
- Paulie Walliker - Bartender at Twin Peaks
- Ray Woods - Leatherman

1991
January
- Michael Weber - Fellow bartender at The Woods
- Ron Silva
- Mikie Winnings - Bartender at the Twin Peaks

February
- Jim Cvitanich - My partner in Men Behind Bars
- Peter Austin - Mr. San Francisco Leather 1989
- Gordon Curtis - Gentleman and friend since the 70s
- David Duran - Bartender at Fife's, the Woods, Moby Dick
- Dannie Fallin
- Michael Silber

March
- Richard Wellner aka Empress XXIII Lily Street
- Darryl Heard - Men Behind Bars "Maybe"
- Brett Brown - Men Behind Bars as Gail Wilson's fireman

April
- Joe Altman - Photographer, Drummer Magazine
- Alan Bing
- Richard Burt - Art director for the B.A.R.
- Dwayne Crowell

- John Hartis
- Mike Hippler - Bay Area Reporter columnist
- Linn Kieffer - President, California Moto Club (CMC)
- Christopher Rage - Filmmaker
- Roger Ramses aka Frank Vickers
- Larry Bush - Porn star/bartender at Fife's Resort, Guerneville

May
- Gregory Hahn - Model
- Rick Mullinax - Bartender, stand-up comic
- Luc Pelletier - Owner of Le Domino restaurant
- Pete Pettine aka Vito in Men Behind Bars

June
- Anthony Bruno - Friend and playwright
- Maury Miller - Boyfriend and fellow bartender
- Thomas Copeland - Bartender at the Balcony
- Emperor Chuck Demmon
- Philip Mills aka Doris Fish
- Steven Grossman - Singer, song writer, recording artist
- Don Levine - Producer, fundraiser
- Zach Long - Gay rights activist, fundraiser, Leather Daddy V
- Larry Wilkes - Bartender

July
- Frank Benoit - Secretary of the Society for Individual Rights (SIR)
- Mal Bonardi
- Dennis Conklin - Bartender at the Phone Booth
- Steve Perkins - Poet, master of high colonics, fixture on the corner of 18th/ Castro
- Robert Pyron aka Lee Ryder

August
- Tippi - Performer known as "The Oldest Living Child Star in Captivity"
- Lou Lusietto - Believed that he started the White Night Riot

- Steven Allen Cates aka Joanzi Blackfish (who crashed Men Behind Bars)

September
- Chuck Dupuy - Tap Dancer/Men Behind Bars
- Carter Stevens - Singer/dancer in Men Behind Bars
- Jerry Berg - Activist and philanthropist
- Marty Blecman - Major record producer, DJ, stand-up comic
- David Cobb - Bartender at the Men's Room
- Dom "Etienne" Orejudos - Artist

October
- Billy Achorn - Bartender at the Stallion, My Place
- Jacob Albright - Member of the SF Tap Troupe
- Harold Gates - Model
- Ken Harrison - Star of the 1977 erotic film Bijou
- Geoffrey Hay - Owner of Paradise Cove Resort, Guerneville
- Al Ognibene
- Jim Steininger

November
- Rich Demarest - Biker
- Tuoko Laaksonan aka Tom of Finland - Artist
- Jim Livingood - Founder of Vocal Minority
- Freddy Mercury - Singer
- Henry Soares - Co-owner of the Fickle Fox
- Eric Staal - Defined his own vision of muscle-drag
- Gabriel Starr - Fellow bartender at the Woods

December
- Jim French - City Swing
- Phil Tuggle - Community arts advocate
- Pat Bond - Performer and great dyke activist
- Bob Cramer - Founder of the Cable Car Awards
- Art White - Bartender at the Pendulum
- Cirby Kirk - Erotic artist, model, bartender at the original Midnight Sun on Castro Street

- Celso Martinez, Jr. - Men Behind Bars
- Don Penniman - Chief fundraiser for Coming Home Hospice
- Phil Tuggle - Producer, active with the Jon Sims Center for Performing Arts

---

1992
January
- Don Crawford aka Jayne Savage
- Jonathan Kinnett - Artist
- Bill Kroeger
- Peter Lowry - Performer with class and camp
- Gary Magnusson - Bartender
- James McGinnis aka Hazel Maud McGinnis
- Mark Nathan - Band manager of the SF Lesbian/Gay Freedom Band
- Clint Royce - Bartender at the Twin Peaks
- Fred Stone

February
- Aquiles Zapata - Boyfriend
- Officer David Lee Anderson
- Rob Fairchild
- Bob Page aka Patti
- Jeffrey Roach aka Anna Conda

March
- Jack Tarr White, Jr. - Men Behind Bars tap dancer
- Tom Gschwind - Performer
- Bryce Fleming - Bartender
- Patrick Perry aka Patty Party
- John Canalli - Videographer
- John Hillerns aka Lurch
- Tony Trevizo - Founder of the Godfather Service Fund
- Ron Umile - Bartender

April
- Michael Ferrell
- Normy Mason - Disc jockey

May
- Odis Campbell - Disc jockey
- Robert Pruzan- Photographer
- Carl Andry - Manager of the Badlands and the Phoenix
- Randy Fontana - Designer
- Dan Kahen
- Mark Perry
- Ambi Sextrous - Performer
- Empress XXII Tina Tanner - Murdered outside the Victoria Theatre

June
- Bern Boyle - Co-founder of Giovanni's Room in NY, organized first SF Gay Film Festival
- Allen Hemming
- Robert Massotti aka Mother, manager of The Special
- Jim Merron - Drove Rita Rockett at Pier Pressure

July
- Bobbie Callicoate - Renowned female impersonator
- John Calori - Designer who wrapped City Hall rotunda in red to salute the Russian Ballet
- Tom Esway
- Gary Hogue
- Alvino Lopez aka Lopez - I never knew he had a first name
- George Lowy - Set designer, choreographer, Sutter's Mill bartender
- Dr. Larry Petko
- Wayne Starns

August
- Pierre Nadeau- Men Behind Bars
- George Dalton aka George Buchanan

- Bill Graham - Founding member of the Sisters of Perpetual Indulgence
- Fred Hilliard aka Empress IX Frieda
- Drew Okun aka Al Parker - Porn star, birthday-mate and friend
- Dennis Parker - Musician, producer

September
- Robert Caviano - Leading light in the world of pop and dance music
- Coulter Thomas - International Mister Leather V
- Randy West - Ran West Graphics greeting cards
- Tony Lindsey - General manager of the Bay Area Reporter

October
- Don Collins
- Steven Good - Writer, teacher, clown
- Don Hansen
- Dr. John Walsh aka Jacquot

November
- David Diebold - Recording artist, writer
- Jim Dutra - One of the first male go-go dancers at the 524 Club in the 1960s
- Jimmy Ferguson
- Big Ed McMillan - Men Behind Bars
- Dan Westergard - Square dancer, manager of the Neon Chicken

December
- Mark Ferrari - Men Behind Bars
- Steve Abbott - Poet and friend
- Paul Bentley aka Luscious Lorelei
- Jerry Downing - Manager of the Bear at 440 Castro Street
- Tommy Gossett - Men Behind Bars with the Barbary Coast Cloggers
- Lonnie Hamm - Bartender

- Erik Nielsen - Record producer
- George Stambolian - Editor
- Ignacio Baldor - Bartender at the Midnight Sun on Castro Street
- Dennis Graff - Leather Daddy '89
- Lee Trevino

Also died in 1992, although I don't know the date:
- Bob Gothie aka BG
- Joel Herzog - Cher impersonator

1993

January
- Patrick Toner- IML VII
- Jerry Vallaire - Men Behind Bars
- Frank Banks - Piano bar legend
- Bill Clendenen - Bodybuilder, model, novelist
- David Fernandez - Disc jockey
- Wayne Flynn - Clothing designer
- Ken Hemingway - Planted the flower beds outside the conservatory in Golden Gate Park
- Bob Mack
- Rudolph Nureyev - Ballet dancer I knew from the Ritch Street Baths

February
- Patrick McGonigle - Emperor XV
- Randy Owen
- David Sarathain - CMC president and Minnesota friend

March
- Ron Arvin - Men Behind Bars
- Mark Dopuch - International fashion model, bartender at Pier Pressure
- Edward Doty
- Dick Ferris - Model for the High Tea poster - killed in a hang gliding accident

- Zoltan Gray
- Dick Petroff - Bartender
- George Thomson - Boyfriend, gymnast

April
- Gene Arnaiz, Jr. - Co-owner of the Woods Russian River Resort
- Sando Counts - Actor, writer, critic
- Rick Redewill - Owner of the Lone Star Saloon
- Evan Zapata - Founding member of the Golden State Police Officers Association

May
- Hilary Ayers
- Michael Gorman
- Scott Shipe - Bartender
- Steve Lowell - Co-founder of Paperback Traffic bookstore

June
- Crawford Barton - Photographer
- Tom Frazier
- Joe McDonald - Member of the Barbary Coast Cloggers
- Victor Villella

July
- Wayne Lee
- Harold Sherman- Bar owner - the Wooden Horse and Molly Brown's

August
- Greg Cowden - Boyfriend
- Steve Endean - Fellow Minnesotan and gay rights pioneer
- Alvin Nadolski
- Erwin Neff

September
- Gene Bates aka Marina Safeway

- Chuck Cyberski - Partner in M.E.N. - Male Entertainment Network
- Chris Fitzgerald aka Big Bird - Bartender
- Mike Gallagher

October
- Bob Burger
- Nicky Guinta - Fan dancer extraordinaire
- Marc Herberg - Bartender at the Castro Station
- Martin King - My first San Francisco boyfriend
- Billy Ray Parker - Mr. Cowboy '81
- Wade Southwick
- Jay Stanquilla - Bartender at Leticia's Restaurant

November
- John Burciaga - The cute Mexican cashier at the Castro Walgreens
- Bill Camillo - Party promoter/ producer
- Jerry Faber - Boyfriend, fellow bartender
- Charlie Lare
- Martin Worman - Cockette
- Joey Stefano - Porn star

December
- Wayne Buidens - Co-founder of the Artfull Circle Theatre
- Mario Simon - Co-publisher of Drummer Magazine
- John Rowberry - Writer, editor of Drummer, Fourskin Quarterly, Macho, Inches, Uncut
- Dan Sweeney - Bartender
- Kevin Tippy - Pharmacist
- Michael Callen - Writer, performer, AIDS activist
- Joe Ellis - Co-owner Trinity Place

1994

January
- Tony Arroyo - Armando's younger brother
- Bert Lacquement - Artist, poet, performer, writer

- Jean-Yves Lefebvre - A beautiful man
- Mike Rogers - Bartender at the Badlands

February
- Randy Shilts - Author and drinking buddy
- Terry "Tess" Scott - Bartender and cohort of Rita Rockett
- George Mendenhall - Political activist, writer
- Tomm Ruud - Dancer - San Francisco Ballet
- Michael Schoch - Bartender at the original Toad Hall on Castro Street

March
- Steven Colvin - Lunchtime host at the Badlands restaurant
- Paul Hernandez - Singer
- William Parker aka Mama Billy
- Stephen Sutton - Photographer for Drummer Magazine
- Billy Wright

April
- John Preston - Author, roommate, one of my first big brothers
- John Rothermel - A Cockette I knew from Minneapolis
- Kevin Kane
- Kurt Oxley
- Marlon Riggs - Videographer of Tongues Untied

May
- Jimmy Coker - AIDS activist, educator
- Keith Blanton aka Pristine Condition - One of the Cockettes
- Chuck Forbes
- Carl Matchett, Jr. - Bartender at the Edge
- James Sherman
- Law Wilson - SFPD attorney
- Chuck Zinn - Theatrical director

June
- Jeffrey Abraham
- David Arnold - Bowler

- Brad Forrest - Chef
- Don Manning - Bartender at the Edge
- Bill Moore aka Tammy Lynn
- Darrell Yee - President of the AIDS Emergency Fund

July
- Ed Guest
- Jim Beale - Owner of Mainline Gifts
- Bob Sandner - Piano bar entertainer
- Al Martino - Biker
- Derek Rainer
- Tom Relihan
- Tom Vetrano - Bartender

August
- Aryae Levy
- Patrick Saatzer - Fundraiser for the Deaf AIDS Center

September
- Mark Bathke
- Carl Berry - Set designer, make-up artist
- Jay Manning - Art director for Vector Magazine

October
- Bobby Ehrenthal - Waiter at Gordon's, Jackson's, the Galleon
- Peter Goddard - Bartender at Bear Hollow, 440 Castro Street
- Jack Gordon
- Brandy Moore - Gay, AIDS, and African-American activist
- Gus Swenson - Of Haight/Ashbury's Gus' Pub
- Chris Whipp - Receptionist at Drummer Magazine

November
- Christian Andrew - Men Behind Bars
- John Angeles
- Jim Sweet
- Peter Caldwell - Worked at the Folsom Street Barracks and Cliff's

- Tim Curbo - Teacher, life-mate of Tom Ammiano
- Billy Forman

December
- Brian Bluteau
- Tony Gagna
- Dennis Green aka Erica, Queen of South Shore
- Tom Keightley - Model for Colt Studios
- Michael "Rusty" Dickens - Biker

Also in 1994:
- Kirk Ramsey - Costume designer

1995
January
- Michael Chase - Fundraiser/ bartender
- Johnie Garcia
- Marc Sato
- Joe Hollinger - AIDS fundraiser, Sentinel columnist, Mr. Eagle Leather
- Michael Valerio - Creator of the Folsom Street Fair
- Sparky Kauffman - Bartender at the Rainbow Cattle Company, Guerneville
- Tim Napier - Political activist

February
- James Lee Bransetter - The baton man of Haight Street
- Jay Smith - Leather Daddy VII
- David Flores
- Scott Smith - Harvey Milk's lover and archivist
- Keith Gockel
- Stephen Kuttner aka Jason Steele
- Paul Monette - Writer

March
- Garrett Dorsey - Manager of the Castro Country Club
- Danny Denning - Carpenter, pool player

- Larry Glasser - Bartender at Fife's Resort
- Marc Madary

April
- Michael Canfield
- Robert Casetta - Drummer magazine
- Chuck Shivly
- Ram Wagman
- John Dowdy - Guerneville realtor
- Steve Whitney - Builder
- Bill Henderson
- Steven Lindsay aka Empress XX Sissy Spaceout
- Alan Thrall

May
- Red Bentzinger - Manager of Mr S Leather, created the leather teddy bear
- Glenn Burke - Pro baseball player
- Bill Kruse
- John Miles - Bartender at the SF Eagle
- Greg Stevenson - Baker
- Mason Curtis
- Warren Sonbert - Film critic
- Denis Deeth
- Jim Kerley - Artist, activist
- Chris Osborne - Dear friend to many

June
- Brett Averill - Journalist
- Officer Ray Benson SFPD who helped me get the Pier Pressure money to the bank
- Randy Fowler
- Steve Silver - Creator of Beach Blanket Babylon
- Buddy Montgomery - Men Behind Bars

July
- Wayne Love - Conductor/ arranger for City Swing
- Skip Blaikie - Trumpet player
- David Dodson
- David Detrick - Police Commissioner
- Stephan Guintard

August
- David Rich
- Gary France
- Gary Garrison
- Robert Neal Kelly aka Kelly - My lover - August 23, 1995

Many friends have died since then, but this memoir ends soon after Kelly's death, so this is a good place to stop counting.

THE END

Trademark Acknowledgement

The author acknowledges the trademark status and trademark owners of the following places and items mentioned in this memoir:

Speedo – Speedo Holdings, B.V.

Levi's – Levi Strauss & Co.

Pendleton – Pendleton Woolen Mills, Inc.

Calvin Klein - The Trustees of the Calvin Klein Trademark Trust Delaware

Southern Comfort - Southern Comfort Properties, Inc.

Toni Home Permanent – Gilette Co.

Amtrak - National Railroad Passenger Corporation

Absolut - The Absolut Company

Stoli/Stolichnaya - Spirits International B.V.

Boy Scouts of America - The National Boy Scouts of America Foundation

Safeway – Safeway, Inc.

Jose Cuervo Gold - Tequila Cuervo La Rojena, S.A. de C.V.

Ben Davis – Ben Davis Co.

Blue Angels – Office of Naval Research

Sno-Balls – Hostess Brands, Inc.

Twinkies – Hostess Brands, Inc.

Honda - Honda Motor Co., Ltd.

Walgreens - Walgreen Co.

King Kong - Universal City Studios LLC

Coke - The Coca-Cola Company

Hamburger Mary's – Hamburger Mary's International, LLC

Sizzler - Sizzler USA Franchise, Inc.

Bank of America - Bank of America Corporation

Budweiser – Anheuser-Busch, LLC

Bombay Sapphire - Bombay Spirits Company Limited

Jell-O - Kraft Foods Holdings, Inc.

Yellow Cab - City Cab Company of Orlando, Inc.

Heineken - Heineken Brouwerijen B.V.

Tiparillos – General Cigar Co., Ltd.

Datsun - Nissan Motor Co., Ltd.

Burger King - Burger King Corporation

Whopper - Burger King Corporation

Tony Awards - American Theatre Wing, Inc.

San Francisco Opera – San Francisco Opera Assn.

Porta Potti – Thetford Corp.

Crisco – Procter & Gamble Co.

Zippo - ZippMark, Inc.

Pepe LePew – Warner Entertainment Co.

Cruella DeVil - Disney Enterprises, Inc.

Tanqueray - Diageo Brands B.V.

John Hancock Life Insurance - John Hancock Life Insurance Company

All My Children – American Broadcasting Companies

Mounds - Cadbury Ireland Limited

Almond Joy - Cadbury Ireland Limited

Better Homes & Gardens - Meredith Corporation

Toys R Us - Geoffrey, Inc.

Denny's - DFO, Inc.

Dole - Dole Packaged Foods, LLC

Chiquita - Chiquita Brands L.L.C.

Radio City Music Hall Rockettes - Radio City Trademarks, LLC

C-SPAN - National Cable Satellite Corporation

VH1 – Viacom International, Inc.

MTV – Viacom International, Inc.

Brennan's – Ella, Adelaide, Dick & John Brennan Restaurants, LTD

Antoine's - Antoine's Name and Recipes, LLC

Styrofoam – Dow Chemical Corp.

Disneyland - Disney Enterprises, Inc.

Space Mountain - Disney Enterprises, Inc.

Sleeping Beauty's Castle - Disney Enterprises, Inc.

Ziploc - S. C. Johnson & Son, Inc.

Kleenex – Kimberly-Clark Worldwide, Inc.

San Francisco 49ers - San Francisco Forty Niners, Ltd.

Saturday Night Live - NBC Universal, Inc.

TV Guide - TV Guide Entertainment Group, LLC

Reese's Peanut Butter Cups - Hershey Chocolate & Confectionery Corporation

Valium – Hoffman-LaRoche, Inc.

Inches – Mavety Media Group

Cuisinart - Conair Corporation

Boeing 747 - The Boeing Company

Thunderbird - Ford Motor Company

Super Bowl - National Football League

Oscars - Academy of Motion Picture Arts and Sciences Corp.

The Advocate – Liberation Publication Corp.

Colt Studios - Prowest Media Corporation

Tareyton - Brown & Williamson Tobacco Corporation

Merit – Philip Morris USA

Penthouse - General Media Communications, Inc.

Enchanted Tiki Room – Disney Enterprises, Inc.

PBS - Public Broadcasting Service

Jockey - Jockey International, Inc.

CNN – Cable News Network, Inc.

San Francisco Chronicle -- Chronicle Publishing Co.

Bay Area Reporter -- BAR Media, Inc.

Beach Blanket Babylon -- Steve Silver Productions, Inc.

Dodge -- Chrysler Group, LLC

MGM Grand - MGM Resorts International

West Side Story - The Leonard Bernstein Office, Inc.

Green Acres - Orion Pictures Corporation

101 Dalmations -- Disney Enterprises, Inc.

Project Open Hand - Project Open Hand

Betty Ford Institute - The Betty Ford Center at Eisenhower

The Hardy Boys - Simon & Schuster, Inc.

Nancy Drew -- Simon & Schuster, Inc.

Vogue - Advance Magazine Publishers Inc.

McDonald's -- McDonald's Corporation

An Evening at La Cage - Aleman, Norbert A.

Melmac -- Cytec Technology Corp.

Mark Abramson

Besides the Beach Reading mystery series, Mark Abramson is known as a producer of Men Behind Bars and mega-dance parties Pier Pressure and High Tea. For My Brothers is his first major work of non-fiction but he hopes to publish more stories of his life in San Francisco before and after AIDS.

Also By Mark Abramson

Beach Reading

Cold Serial Murder

Russian River Rat

Snowman

Wedding Season

California Dreamers

Love Rules

CPSIA information can be obtained at www.ICGtesting.com
Printed in the USA
LVOW07s1525140615

442432LV00001B/4/P